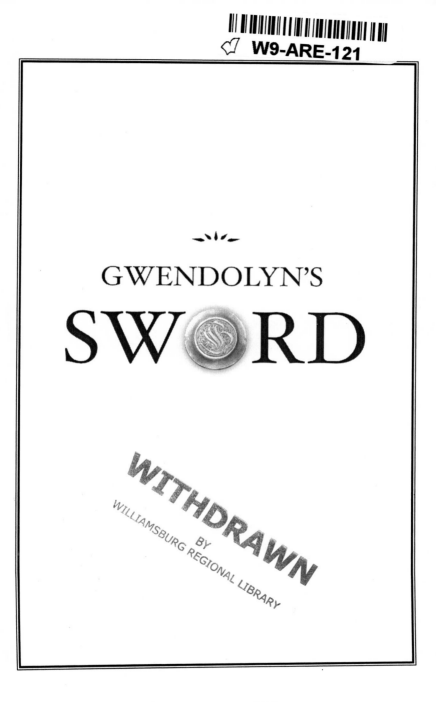

GWENDOLYN'S
SW🜨RD

E.A. HALTOM

GWENDOLYN'S

SW RD

GWENDOLYN'S SWORD

Cover and Interior design by Ted Ruybal

Manufactured in the United States of America

For more information, please contact:

Wisdom House Books

www.wisdomhousebooks.com

Paperback ISBN 13: 978-0-9963073-0-7

LCCN: 2015907121

FICTION / Historical / Fantasy

1 2 3 4 5 6 7 8 9 10

www.smittenbythewords.blogspot.com

TABLE OF CONTENTS

DEDICATION

For my family.

ACKNOWLEDGEMENTS

As this is my debut novel, I asked for and gratefully received the free commentary, proofreading and feedback of several among my friends and family. Put bluntly, this story would not have happened without their constant support and encouragement. For their kindness and their reassurance that the story was worth the effort to see it through, I am entirely in their debt. I would also like to thank my excellent editor, Ashley Davis, and also Ted Ruybal of Wisdom House Books for a fantastic book cover design, and for generous advice and guidance in layout and formatting. Having said that, all errors that may still be found in this book are my own.

I would especially like to acknowledge the Writers' League of Texas, for providing such excellent resources, classes, and networking for new authors. The annual agents' conference was an eye-opener for me, and the opportunity to submit my manuscript for consideration in the historical fiction category (and win!) was another irreplaceable source of encouragement and information that I desperately needed.

Lastly I would like to thank all of the independent authors out there in the interwebs for all of your advice, informative blogs, tweets of encouragement, and general camaraderie. I hope over time I can give back what I've received.

I

THE END OF SOLITUDE

Cornwall, England
August, The Fourth Year of King Richard's Reign

A broadsword was a difficult thing to hide in a dress. Gwendolyn wore a long cloak to conceal her weapon where it hung against her hip. She was as accustomed to the weight of it as she was to her own skin. But she had donned the cloak to conceal more than her sword. Years of training with the manor guard had added lines of muscle and scars across her forearms. Hers was a body formed for combat, her temperament more inclined to exercising command. These traits, she had learned, were not generally praised in women, and until her marriage she had tried to cloak them, as well, with mixed results. Here in the forest where she sought a few moments of solitude, she dressed herself in the ordinary garb of a lady of the manor, the wife of a landed knight who had taken up the cross and traveled to Outremer to join the king's crusade. Standing tall, with shoulders as broad as those of any of the men in Penhallam's manor guard, her bearing drew enough attention as it was. But walking through the woods without her weapon was unthinkable; outlaws took refuge here.

Beneath the leaves and ferns and fallen trees, a welcoming coolness persisted in the forest floor throughout all of the seasons. Long branches arched gracefully over her like a cathedral vault and shivered with a gentle breeze as she passed beneath them. She granted herself these moments of calm, accompanied only by two of her maids, as her sole respite from the constant work of managing a growing estate. She paused in the still air and turned to mark the progress of Anne and Martha behind her, the two friends happily absorbed in their conversation. Her constable had warned her sternly about the dangers she flirted with by taking these walks, and she conceded that he had a point. *But so have I*, she thought to herself, her hand resting casually against the hilt of her blade beneath her cloak.

From daybreak to nightfall, Gwendolyn occupied herself with the business of the manor and its lands. Some nights she sat at the trestle table in the hall, scratching out the manor's accounts on the wooden surface with charcoal while the rest of the house's residents slept in the straw around her. Her men sometimes woke to find her there in the morning, fast asleep, a night's worth of calculations spread across the table around her. The coming winter would mark four years since Robert had taken up the cross. She had been a new wife of sixteen when he left; since then she had managed the estate alone. She had succeeded in earning the respect of her trade partners, sometimes exploiting her decidedly unfeminine demeanor toward that end—dressing as a man, sporting cuts and bruises from training with the manor garrison, and keeping up with her men-at-arms cup for cup when the ale flowed.

Gwendolyn paused for a moment to study the canopy above her, full and green. By its lush shade, she estimated that the harvest of the grain was at least a month away still, maybe more. She smiled to herself, thinking of the days and nights of hard work that lie ahead, and the months of relative leisure that would follow through the winter.

She had grown up in Restormel Castle, the jewel of the de Cardinham family's holdings, as an orphaned ward. The baron's wife had passed soon after Gwendolyn arrived, and with no other daughters, the household had lacked any feminine influence. To Gwendolyn's great pleasure, no one had attempted to instruct her in needlepoint or song or any other of the finer skills expected of well-heeled ladies. Left to her own devices, Gwendolyn had helped herself to the library of books and manuscripts accumulated by the intellectual baron over decades of travel and war. As soon as a large compilation of the works of Plato was available in Latin translation, a copy had arrived at Restormel. Gwendolyn had wept the first time that she read the text, with its clear logic and methodical application of reason in all things. War, she had concluded, was the worst of all evils; nothing brought more waste and destruction than its capricious appetite. She had decided at a young age that she would put her size and strength to good use and learn to fight so that war, when it came, would find its match and slink away like the cur that it was.

When the baron discovered the breadth of her learning, he had accused her, scarlet-faced and shouting, of deliberately rendering herself unmarriageable. But then his own son Robert had surprised him by asking for her hand, and the baron had shrugged and given his consent. The baron's title and the grand estate of Bodardel, including Restormel Castle, had gone to Robert's older brother, Walter. Robert was allowed the smaller estate of Penhallam, at that time a dilapidated timber house used for seasonal hunts. Shortly after her wedding, the baron, a man who had spent most of his life with a sword in his hand, had died quietly in his sleep. With Gwendolyn's promise to keep Penhallam safe until he returned, Robert had departed for Outremer as soon as he received his knight's belt. He had fulfilled her request for a sword and ordered his constable to see to her instruction in its use. Gwendolyn and the constable had both kept their promises, and she had the tough, scarred hands of a soldier to show for it.

Twilight approached, but Gwendolyn allowed herself the indulgence of lingering to inspect a growth of mushrooms. She stooped, loosened the cluster from the earth, and cradled it under her nose, inhaling the musky scent. As she tucked the mushrooms into the pouch at her waist, a flash of movement through the branches above caught her eye. The screech of a peregrine falcon on the hunt sounded high over the treetops, momentarily silencing the forest birds that had been merrily singing above her. For a moment death's chill breath seemed to brush her cheek, then pass by. Whatever troubles weighed on her mind, these walks reminded her that all things passed, and that change—birth, death, and rebirth—was the natural order of things. She stretched and relaxed the muscles in her neck and breathed the sweet forest air deeply, feeling the tranquility around her finally ease her mood. Her left shoulder still ached from a well-placed blow she had received during training that morning, and she rubbed the joint to loosen some of the stiffness.

Gwendolyn narrowed her eyes and gazed down the road, keeping watch over Anne and Martha as they idled far behind her. Like her cloak, Gwendolyn had brought the young maids with her for appearances only, to satisfy the village gossips who she knew might otherwise suspect she had stolen away alone for a secretive romance. During her husband's absence, Gwendolyn was well aware that such rumors could do as much damage to her as a blade. And the girls, both in their sixteenth year, were friends; they looked forward to these walks, to talk freely beyond the manor house and its complete lack of privacy.

A faint hum of deep voices approaching ahead brought Gwendolyn to attention. She stepped quickly off the road behind a large tree and steadied her breath, listening for the sound of rushing hooves or footsteps charging toward her. Hearing nothing but steady conversation, she craned her head to peer around the tree. Four men approached on foot, carrying small packs and fully engaged in what sounded like an argument.

She had a few moments to look them over. Two were older than the others and carried their packs across their backs; the other two, younger and slighter of build, each carried a smaller sack slung across the shoulder. One of the larger men wore his long hair tied back; the other's was trimmed close to his skull. Dust from the road clung to their mantles that they wore draped around their shoulders. Even from the distance she could see that their clothing was rough and worn, showing patches and faded colors. Although the group appeared strong and well fed, their clothing suggested poverty, and the incongruity immediately caught her attention. The men were within a few paces of her hiding place, and she smoothed her skirts and stepped out to confront them directly.

Gwendolyn stood her ground as the men paused their squabbling and took notice of her. She watched their eyes register her long cloak that reached to the ground around her feet, its length marking her as a woman of some measure of wealth. Her red hair hung in a single, thick braid down her back, and she wore no adornment in the braid or on her cloak. She stared back at them steadily with green eyes.

The tallest among them, the man with his long hair pulled back, shifted his pack to the ground and bowed deeply before her with a courtly flourish of his hand. He wore a wooden cross strung on rough wooden beads that swung forward as he bowed. The roughness of the beads struck her as odd; it was the habit of pilgrims to work the beads one by one through their fingertips in never-ending cycles of prayer, leaving the beads polished to a dark sheen. These beads had been left alone, ignored. Strands of the man's hair fell forward, framing intelligent brown eyes. One of his smaller companions elbowed the man beside him, looking uneasy.

"Good evening, my lady," the taller man said with a faint smile.

She curtsied slightly in the courtly manner, inclining her head to steal a sideways glance. Anne and Martha had observed the men's approach and walked casually up the road toward her.

"A fair hour for a stroll," the man observed, looking around them at the towering, ancient woods. "I see you and your maids walk unescorted."

Gwendolyn answered lightly, "What need do ladies have of an escort in the company of godly men?"

The man smiled softly. "You take us for pilgrims, then, my lady?"

"I take you for men of the cross. If you are on pilgrimage, what brings you to Cornwall?"

"We travel to the abbey of St. Michael's Mount, my lady, to give glory to God."

Gwendolyn's mouth went dry and she felt her chest tighten, but she forced her breath to remain steady and she returned the man's faint smile while her mind raced. St. Michael's Mount stood on a rocky point off of Cornwall's farthest coast, two days' ride away. Henry de la Pomerai, a supporter of Prince John, had sailed a group of fighting men to the mount and violently overrun it. He had then sent messengers to John's supporters in London asking for supplies and men. Those headed there now would be mercenaries, blood-thirsty men ready for war, travelling under cover and ready to kill to keep their secret. But perhaps these men really were pilgrims, unaware of the attack; word had only reached Penhallam a week ago.

"I am in charge of these lands and this road in the name of my husband, Robert de Cardinham, who has taken up the cross with King Richard. If you have any trouble while you pass through here, you may rely on the protection of my men."

Her tone was perfunctory and impersonal, calculated to evoke a reaction or a comment, anything to give her a clue about the men's intentions. She understood the danger clearly. If they suspected she saw through their ruse, they would kill her and her maids. Here, alone and unobserved in the forest, she had provided them the perfect cover for murder. And their mantles, she realized, were long enough to conceal weapons. If she drew her sword now, with all four ready to react, she might die where she stood.

"England's men returned from Palestine a year ago, my lady," the larger man said, and she thought she detected a hint of malice in his voice.

Gwendolyn paused to measure her breath, check that her tone remained casual. "My husband continues to serve the king in his captivity until he is returned to England."

The man pressed his point. "Unless, as Prince John claims, the king is already dead."

Beneath her cloak Gwendolyn's hand gripped the hilt of her sword, and she felt her face flush in spite of her full effort to appear calm.

"What you suggest is treason, sir." Her voice was low and steady. "The queen mother has sworn that her son lives."

A moment of tense silence followed. Martha and Anne stood within ten paces, oblivious to the threat of violence unfolding ahead of them. The girls continued talking in low voices, stepping aside to make way for the group to pass them, and their light murmurs and laughter hung strangely in the air. Gwendolyn held the man's gaze, her expression inscrutable. The second of the larger men touched his companion on the arm, gestured down the darkening path. The day was coming to an end; they had lingered long enough. Gwendolyn hoped the men were convinced that their pretense had worked, that she suspected nothing, and she made mental note of their size and number. She would send the manor guard after them as soon as she returned to Penhallam. Riding on horseback, her men would easily catch up with them.

"Of course, my lady," the man agreed smoothly. With another deep bow, he shifted his pack up onto his arm and nodded to his companions. Together, they turned to continue on the path through the woods, the larger men leading. Gwendolyn exhaled and flexed the clenched muscles of her hand.

The girls stood facing each other, Anne's back to the road, as the men walked past. Suddenly the man nearest to Anne, the large man who had spoken with Gwendolyn, swept his arm out and scooped Anne up off her feet, bracing her tightly against his chest.

Anne was tiny and light as a bird. She screamed and struggled to twist and kick in his grasp, but he easily pinned her with one meaty forearm while he wrestled both of her wrists into his other hand. In that instant Gwendolyn's years of training crystallized. Her mind measured the distance between herself and the men, the speed with which the man who held Anne would be able to snap her neck.

Her cloak muffled the sound of her sword against its scabbard as she drew it. She lunged, running her sword through the man's waist from one side to the other. The blade entered his body with surprising ease, and she felt the slight shudder against her palm as her steel ground across the bone at the front of the man's spine. Martha screamed, and one of the younger men lunged at Gwendolyn, pulling a dagger from his belt as she freed her sword from the man in front of her, now collapsed onto his knees in the path. She pivoted, swung her sword, and cut off the arm with the knife still clasped in its hand. Blood surged from the man's exposed elbow, splattering red across Gwendolyn's pale blue dress.

Gwendolyn swung around to face the two remaining men, sword raised in battle stance, eyes unblinking. Less than a heartbeat had passed, and yet as she stood frozen in the path, her eyes locked on the men in front of her, the moments seemed to have stretched, slowing down all movement around her. She was sharply aware from the smell that the man beside her had emptied his bowels as he stooped to pick up the stump of his severed arm from the ground, looked at it blankly for a moment, and then fell face-down by her feet. Martha and Anne's screams sounded far away over the rushing of her blood through her veins.

The younger of the two remaining men approached the kneeling form in the path and touched his shoulder with a trembling hand, then realized he had stepped into the damp, warm pool that surrounded the man's body and withdrew with a shudder.

"He's dead." The young man looked up at her, horrified. "He's dead!" He backed away slowly.

"Who are these men? What are their names?" Gwendolyn's sharp voice snapped the younger man out of his stupor. He was perhaps younger than her and plainly unaccustomed to the sight of blood.

"You are John's men," she said evenly when he failed to answer her, and she lowered her sword slightly. "Rebels against the king. You will come with me now to Penhallam."

The younger man's features blanched as he realized how much she knew, and he took another tentative step back toward his companion. The sky above shone a rosy color, and Gwendolyn raised her sword again and took a step toward the men. The larger man, who had been staring at her in shock, suddenly came to his senses and they both turned abruptly and dashed into the woods, quickly disappearing into the shadows.

"The outlaws may do worse with them than William will when he finds them," she said to herself, listening to the sounds of their steps growing fainter. She looked down at her sword, bloody for the first time since the smith forged it for her. She had to wipe and dry it or the blade would begin to rust. She looked around her, as if a clean rag might materialize for her there in the forest. Finally she gathered up a handful of her skirt and carefully wiped down the blade. The dress was already ruined, after all. As she sheathed her weapon, Gwendolyn felt a wave, unstoppable, roll up from the pit of her belly. She turned, bent over, and heaved the full contents of her stomach into the brush beside the path.

When the gagging finally passed and she could stand upright again, she spat and wiped her mouth with her sleeve and turned on trembling legs to face her maids.

Tears streaked Anne's cheeks, and the girl frowned hard to stifle her sobs. Her fists clutched a rip at the neck of her gown.

"Are you hurt?" Gwendolyn asked.

Anne shook her head, her eyes fixed on the ground. Gwendolyn considered moving the men's bodies to the side of the road, but decided she would send her men for them. Her priority was to get Martha and Anne safely back to Penhallam.

"Come on," Gwendolyn said, pulling her cloak across her shoulders again and concealing the dark spatters on her dress. She drew her sword again, in case the remaining two men had stayed near for another attack. Together, they started the walk back, Martha's arm protectively circling Anne's shoulders.

The taste of bile still sour in her mouth, Gwendolyn realized her days of stealing these moments of solitude in the woods had ended. The intrigues of the royal court had finally reached into the far west of England, all the way to Penhallam. She had been foolish to ignore the plain fact that John's plots for the throne had divided loyalties and brought England to the brink of war with itself. When Henry de la Pomerai took over St. Michael's Mount, he had killed most of the monks and the abbot himself. She had known all of these things, had been warned by her constable, and yet she had refused to believe that the danger was real. You've been such a fool, she admonished herself, trying not to think of what could have happened if she had been without her sword. Then again, she realized, she had just intercepted rebels against the king. If she had not been walking the forest that evening, they might have safely reached their destination.

"There will be no more walks in the forest," Gwendolyn announced.

"Yes, my lady," Martha answered. "It's for the best. William will be glad to hear of it."

As Penhallam's constable, William Rufus commanded her men and had provided her no quarter in her training on account of her sex or her status. For this she respected him. But he held no authority over her, and this was a frequent source of aggravation for them both.

The road emerged from the woods and Gwendolyn paused to take in the view of Penhallam's estate. Two swift-flowing streams cut the ancient valley before them; where these streams joined, a Cornish warlord had built a timber stronghold long before the Normans came to England. The low valley provided shelter from the terrible sea gales that raked the land every winter, and the streams gave a ready supply of fresh water and fish. To improve defenses, a low moat had been dug out, the excavated dirt and stone used to build a ring-work to fortify the inner banks. In the year before their marriage, Robert had persuaded his father to dismantle the clay and timber house and build in its place a stone stronghold, complete with a large hall for the manor household and a private chamber for himself and his young bride.

Beyond the moated area, the manor's outbuildings stood in a cluster surrounded by a high timber palisade. The rest of the household's eighteen residents lived and worked in these buildings brewing ale, baking bread, rendering tallow, and tending the horses. Penhallam's men-at-arms kept a rotating guard living in both the outbuildings and the manor. Her constable, however, had not slept anywhere but the manor hall during Robert's absence. Gwendolyn was, after all, the only member of the de Cardinham family in residence at Penhallam, and William considered her protection to be his first and personal duty. Along with the household, Penhallam was supported by—and in turn aided and protected—a dozen or more small hamlets and farmsteads that dotted the valley and neighboring lowlands.

The largest of these villages lay between the forest and the manor house, directly ahead of Gwendolyn and her maids. Its buildings huddled in a cluster of cottages, shared longhouses, small gardens, and shops, all of it encircled by a collection of small yards for livestock. The manor house stood shrouded in evening shadows just beyond the village, its dark walls pierced by the glow of the hearth visible through narrow window slits. The village church stood to the north, the sole stone building other than the manor house. The mill and the blacksmith's hut, its fires glowing, stood alone beside the stream north of the manor. On their left a low hill swelled, marked by the rubble outline of an ancient fortress. A large cesspit lay at the bottom of that rise, downwind from the village and the manor house. To their right, strips of cultivated ground, some set aside for individual families and some shared, crossed the hillside. Rows of grain, legumes, and vegetables gently waved in the evening breeze, cooler now with the setting sun. The last harvest of the season would be upon them soon, and the hard work of reaping, storing, pickling, and salting would keep the full village occupied. It was an exhausting but joyous time, and Gwendolyn looked forward to the shared meals in the fresh air and the songs and stories of the traders that would come through afterward offering trinkets, pretty ribbons, amusements, and news from the larger towns. Old rivalries were set aside, if only for the harvest, and many courtships took root in the side-by-side labor that put young men and women in the fields together for days on end.

Gwendolyn and her maids covered the last bit of road quickly, threading their way between the low stone walls marking fields and pastures and into the muddy lanes of the village. Around them, men and their older sons returned from the fields, sweaty and tired, and their whistles and calls and the barking of working dogs greeted them. Women called to their families, announcing the evening supper, and the smoke of cooking fires curled into the dimming sky. The usually welcome smells of evening stews and breads caused her stomach to lurch with a new wave of nausea. She said nothing to the familiar faces that she passed, keeping her eyes downcast and hoping that no one stopped her for a word.

Gwendolyn stopped where a small footpath led to a timber and thatch cottage beneath the outstretched arms of an oak. She gently touched Anne's arm and gestured for her to return to her own home tonight. Anne held Gwendolyn's gaze for a moment before turning down the path, and Gwendolyn saw reflected back a new hardness that replaced some of the innocence they both had lost that afternoon. Anne said goodnight and walked briskly toward her family's cottage, her hands in tiny fists at her sides.

Gwendolyn and Martha crossed the wooden bridge and passed through the timber gatehouse into the manor yard, where her hounds loped out to meet them, baying excitedly around their skirts. A rack of fish hung over a smoking fire, out of the dogs' reach. Osbert, Penhallam's cook and steward, stepped out from the undercroft as Martha ducked in on her way up to the hall. He wiped flour from his hands onto a leather apron and greeted Gwendolyn with a tip of his chin. Gwendolyn dodged Osbert's curious look and wordlessly tossed him the pouch of mushrooms she carried from the woods. She ducked through the low doorway into the kitchen, a small building attached to the side of the house, leaving Martha to climb the stairs to the hall without her.

Osbert had set out a supper of bread and stew, ready to be carried up to the hall. Gwendolyn placed her hands flat on the worn, wooden table, fingers spread, and willed her body to become steady. She only had a few moments by herself, and she refused to allow her men to see her so unsettled. After all, this was what she had trained for; she had known this day would eventually come. Stacks of bread trenchers filled shelves lining the walls next to pots of butter and honey. Jars of dried fruits and berries had been shifted to make room for the smoked fish that would be stored there. Clusters of potherbs from the manor garden hung from the rafters above her. The tenants of Penhallam were well provided for, she reminded herself, and the thought helped to calm her. She stepped outside and entered the undercroft through the same low opening Martha had taken.

The space beneath the hall was as crowded as the kitchen, storing barrels of salted meats and fish, wheels of cheese, and jars of lard. Sacks of grain stacked as high as the timbers leaned against the row of thick oak pillars that ran the length of the undercroft. The pillars supported a long, massive beam, the backbone that braced the manor hall above. A narrow, spiral stairway, built of stone and standing in an enclosure attached to the side of the building, provided the only access up. The turn of the stairs, upward to the right, would force any would-be attacker to shift his weapon to the weaker left hand, giving right-handed defenders above the advantage. The same style of construction could be found in the royal castles around Cornwall and the rest of England, but it was unusual in a humble manor house. William had insisted on the design, however, and the baron had grudgingly agreed to the expense. Tonight she found new appreciation for William's foresight.

She started up the stairs, steadying her feet on the narrow ledges, but suddenly found her way blocked by William, moving quickly on his way down. He stopped abruptly two steps above her, so that her eyes were level with his chest. William had a thin build, but in the narrow stairwell his height and broad shoulders still gave the impression of towering bulk that reminded her of the oaks that supported the house.

"Are you hurt?"

Martha had been up to the hall already; she would have given details of the attack to the men-at-arms gathering for the evening meal. Gwendolyn took a deep breath and looked up as she shook her head, her jaw set. She studied William's face, pale blue eyes glowing in the dim torchlight, but she was unable to discern his thoughts from the taut lines of his expression. She paused with a hand on the stone wall beside her, felt its soothing cool beneath her palm, and lowered her eyes to receive the reproach that she knew she deserved. She had refused to heed his warnings; as a result she had placed herself and her maids into the path of mercenaries.

"Martha's white as a sheet."

"Yes, I am aware, thank you," she replied, eyes cast downward. Her voice was clipped and full of guilt. When she looked back up at him, his face had softened.

"This wasn't your fault."

"Of course it was. You warned me, and you were right. I was incredibly foolish." Her mind vividly recalled the blood, the grating of the sword against bone.

Her cloak had fallen open, and she waited while William's gaze took in the pattern of blood on her dress, the straight lines across her skirt where she had wiped her blade. "You discovered rebels against the king and you stopped them. The two that are left will be easy to find." He put a hand on her shoulder. "You did well, Gwendolyn."

With all of her work in the kitchen to calm herself nearly ruined by this unexpected kindness, she looked up at him again. "I feel like my heart is breaking. How do men live with this?"

William looked straight ahead for a moment, his eyes focused on the inner images of his memories.

"Not easily. You should go get something to eat, if you can," he finally said.

Gwendolyn blinked and took a moment to regain her composure, but then remembered the ordeal was not yet over.

"There were four men travelling on foot to St. Michael's Mount, disguised as pilgrims. Of the two that are left, one has certainly never held a sword. He was close to losing his wits. The other one is big. Not as tall as you, but heavier. He'll fight you."

"Any weapons?"

"I didn't see any. The way they took off running, they were travelling light."

"And pilgrims carrying swords would have brought more attention than they would have wanted."

"Take Gerald with you," she added. Gerald was Penhallam's youngest knight, eager to please William and hungry for experience.

William nodded and moved past her, making an effort to press himself against the wall of the narrow passage to avoid brushing against her. William's sense of propriety around her had always been flawless, although somehow it only reminded her that she was different, still only a woman despite the sword she carried.

2

WILLIAM'S CURSE

Penhallam's hall smelled of smoke, straw, dog excrement, and the sweat of men. Fresh straw laced with fragrant herbs was laid down across the timber floor every Sunday, and by the end of the week the manor's residents picked a careful path through the hall. Tom Butler, Gerald's uncle and the oldest of Penhallam's household knights, crossed the floor to her with a large cup of ale in his hand.

"You'll be wanting this, my lady," he said gravely, handing the wooden cup to her.

She thanked him and took her usual seat on the stool at the end of the trestle table, across from the hearth. Without tasting the ale, she set the cup down on the table, bent her face into her hands, and rubbed her eyes. She felt as if she had aged ten years since that morning.

Martha set bread and ale out on the table, her usual chattiness gone. Death seemed to have followed them back from the woods, and the hall was quiet and somber in its presence. Gwendolyn picked up a crust of bread, felt her stomach turn, and put the crust back down onto the plate. She stared into the hearth, wishing she could enjoy its warmth without being reminded of the night when her parents had died. She had been five years old, but she remembered the heat of the fire clearly, the look on her mother's face when the flames reached her skirts while Gwendolyn's father lay unconscious beneath a collapsed timber. A man had rushed in and grabbed Gwendolyn beneath her arms, swept her out of the cottage, and then left. She had watched the roof of the house collapse, sending a burst of orange sparks up into the night. She remembered her shock that something so terrible and cruel could be so beautiful at the same time. When others arrived from the village, they had found her safe beside a tree, quiet and alone. The man who had rescued her was never found. As young as she was, she had known that night that her life had been altered in an irrevocable way, that joy and laughter were gone from her future.

Foolish or not, the woods had been her only sanctuary. Now that was gone, too.

Osbert stepped into the hall, carrying the heavy black pot of stew in front of him, followed by the stooped figure of Gamel, William's father and a spicer. Gamel's knowledge of the healing uses of herbs and salves had served Penhallam and nearby villages and abbeys since before Gwendolyn was born. Gamel had instructed William as his apprentice until William's fourteenth year, when Gwendolyn's parents died and she left to live with the baron and his family at Restormel. She had wondered later if Gamel resented his son's decision to take up arms, to pursue a life of breaking men's bodies instead of healing them. But after she returned to Penhallam years later as Robert's bride, on many nights she had found William conferring with his father quietly in a corner of the hall, receiving the old man's instruction in the method of setting a broken bone or gathering a specific wort to contain the plant's essence, listening intently even while polishing the blade of his sword.

"Got into a bit of a scuffle, did you," Gamel remarked. The old man crossed the hall to the hearth and helped Osbert hang the heavy stew pot by its handle from an iron arm set deep into the masonry. Gwendolyn greeted the old man and shifted in her seat to make room for him at the table.

"Have you tended to Anne? She got the worst of it."

"Aye, she's in good hands with her mother. I'm here for you now, my lady," he said.

Gwendolyn took a deep breath, trying to loosen the tightness in her chest. "I'm fine, Gamel. Just a bit stiff."

"You killed two men, Gwendolyn. Your body may be fine, but being so close to death can shatter a man on the inside." He turned to face her and reached his hands toward her face, and she complied by leaning toward him. With steady hands he tilted her chin gently down and looked into her eyes. He said nothing and lay his hand gently across the inside of her wrist and closed his eyes, breathing softly, reading some unknown message in the throb of her pulse. Finally he opened his eyes and inspected the inside of her palm, turning it in the firelight to better see the fine lines etched into it.

"Pitched your stomach, I see," he said, reaching into the worn sack that was permanently hung from his side.

Gwendolyn nodded. By now she was accustomed to the old man's skill.

"It's all in the humors, child. There is a balance for each of us, and you have too much bile," he said, selecting certain small packets from the handful of glass vials and tiny pouches that he had pulled out onto the table. He began measuring and combining powders into a cup.

"Did you know that I treated Gwyn, your father, when he first came here?" he asked, pausing to raise his eyes to her. He had told her the story many times, but she still enjoyed hearing him retell it, part of her hoping he might recall some new detail he had not told her before.

She shook her head, and he continued.

"When your father arrived at Penhallam with the baron, he was on death's doorstep. He was lucky, though. None of his organs were pierced, and the baron's surgeon had done his work well with the bone and muscle. But it was the sickness in the wound that almost took him."

She had only a few memories of her father, a Welshman, and by all accounts a force to be reckoned with. The baron had told her of the time that he met her father while on a campaign into the Welsh Marches with King Henry. The king had led a substantial force of mercenaries up the Ceiriog Valley to attack the Welsh fortresses in the Berwyn Mountains, to end their resistance once and for all. Instead, the Welsh princes had sent small bands of skirmishers to pick off the marching English from cover of the surrounding forest. The Welsh attackers had painted their faces and bodies with paint and dressed themselves with the skins and bones of animals. They had screeched and howled from the dark shadows of the woods and called upon Welsh gods and demons with descriptions of such violence that even some of the battle-numbed mercenaries had fled their posts. The king had finally ordered the woods cleared with axes, but too late. The reduced English armies were met by the full onslaught of the Welsh attack on the valley floor. Days of rain had left the ground slippery even before the first blood was spilled, and the baron lost his footing in the heated battle and fell face-down into the muck. In that moment he had awaited death, but instead he felt the hands of his attacker lift him upright to face him again. The baron had stared at the flaxen-haired mountain of a youth who had righted him, trying to fathom the display of chivalry, and in that moment a spear had pierced the youth's shoulder, sending him sprawling backward. The baron had stood over the youth, protecting his life only to see him become one of twenty-three Welsh prisoners kept by Henry upon the English king's humiliating retreat. Baron Robert Fitz William had fought with Henry on many campaigns, and he knew the king's reputation for cruelty was in fact milder than the reality. That night, at the risk of his own life, the baron had quietly rounded up his surgeon and his men, and they kidnapped the youth from the king's camp, fleeing north to a ship and finally to safety in Cornwall. Furious at the insult of losing one of his prisoners, King Henry had mutilated the remaining twenty-two

Welsh prisoners the following morning. Hatred for all Normans had solidified among the Welsh when the captured men returned to their villages, their tongues, noses, and hands cut off.

Gwendolyn watched Gamel finally empty the mixture of powders into her cup.

"You will sleep tonight, without dreams. But the memories," he added, as if he read her thoughts, "are yours to keep."

—

William reined in his courser, slowing the stallion to a walk. Gerald pulled up beside him, his black mare blowing hard. From Gwendolyn's description, William guessed they were getting close to where the bodies of the two men lay in the road. He motioned to Gerald to cover the right side of the road while William kept his eyes on the left.

The forest was cast in blackness, and a chill breeze had swept away the afternoon warmth. The woods lay quiet and still, and William felt as though every sound they made could be heard miles away. Moonlight shone through in shafts slicing down through the canopy, casting eerie forms when a breeze shook and stirred the branches above. William shivered in spite of the heavy mail tunic he wore and the layers of quilted padding and under-shirt beneath. He had been visited by nightmares since he was a boy. Some nights he saw glimpses of phantoms and demons, the unnatural monsters of darkness, hunting in the night for a victim. His father had tried different remedies, but none had worked.

"This has naught to do with the humors," Gamel had told him. "You have been touched by the finger of God. You have the gift of sight, William, but you are only a mortal vessel to carry it."

What his father had called a gift, William considered a curse. He had convinced his father to send him south to the priory at Launceston, and the monks there had helped him. The visions still came, his own private Hell, but now they played out for him as a reflection on water, distant and set apart. It was the best that could be done, they said. Like dogs, cats, and birds of prey, he sensed things unseen yet very real. The prior had told him that his mind was an open doorway to all things forbidden and condemned by the Church, and because all things had a purpose, William would discover his, in time. For now, William knew too well that not all of the shadows dancing in the forest around them now were mere tricks of the moonlight.

"Be on your guard," he said in a low voice to Gerald, but as he said the words Gerald's horse reared and twisted on its hind legs, pawing the air and trying to turn back while Gerald struggled to keep his seat. The young knight cursed and flung himself forward over the horse's neck, standing in his stirrups and using his weight to force the panicked horse back down onto all four legs. William's horse skittered sideways beneath him in agitation and tossed its head, the whites of its eyes flashing. A dark lump lay on the ground between them, and another in front. William recognized the rusty smell of spilled blood, the stench of guts pierced and emptied.

William steadied his horse and swung down, holding the reins while he crouched beside the body of one of the dead men. A stump of bone from the severed arm glistened in the moonlight, and he knew before he removed his glove and touched the man's cheek that he would find it cold and hard. The man's eyes were open, his mouth frozen in an unspoken question. Gerald swung down beside William and walked over to the other figure in the road with his hand covering his nose against the smell. William decided not to bring the bodies back to Penhallam. Whoever these dead men were, they were not from Cornwall. Despite King Richard's bequest of the title of Earl of Cornwall to his younger brother, there was no love for the prince here. The people of Cornwall prized valor, honor, loyalty. John had none of these. All that mattered now was to find the two who had fled and prevent them from reaching St. Michael's Mount.

"Get the bodies off the road, out of sight. Let the crows bury them."

"Yes, sir," Gerald answered, then coughed slightly as William picked up the severed limb from the ground and wrapped it in a cloth that he pulled from his saddle.

William watched Gerald tie a rag tightly around the lower half of his face to cover his mouth and nose. He turned to William, his eyes smiling.

"Gwendolyn did this?"

William nodded, taking in the scene and imagining the fight.

Gerald clicked his tongue and whistled quietly. "I knew she had it in her."

So did I, William thought grimly. As he continued to scan the area, he noticed the packs abandoned by the mercenaries when they had fled. Going over to one, he loosened the ties and found inside a mason's hammer, a bulky tool with a flat, heavy head. He fixed the hammer under his belt and stood up.

"I'm going on foot. With any luck, they're still nearby."

William loosened a couple of leather ties from his saddle to take with him. He chose his dagger, a lighter weapon for an ambush, and left his sword hanging from the saddle. As he moved noiselessly through the dark brush that covered the forest floor, he was grateful to be free of its awkward weight and the creaking leather of the scabbard. These men would not be the sort to run far. Their bodies were trained for battle, like a bull's, not for speed. Or for stealth, he realized as he spied the faint glow of a campfire in the distance, perhaps a quarter of a mile away.

William approached slowly, checking the direction of the wind first. The men had no horses or dogs to alert them of his approach, but he was not one to take chances needlessly. The men might have reasoned that no one would follow them until sunrise—a fair assumption. Few people cared to venture out of their houses after sunset, much less into the wild woods. Even without William's vision, many swore they saw the souls of the restless dead or their demon tormentors walking at night.

As he approached downwind, he realized the reason for the fire. Their appetites had gotten the better of them. Three small birds, cleaned and plucked, hung over the fire on a sapling stick held by one of the men. William could smell the meat roasting and wondered whether wolves would also be drawn by the scent. They talked with each other in low, hissing voices, and William crept closer, holding the stump of arm bundled at his side as he placed his dagger into his belt and pulled out the hammer with his free hand.

"Where will we go now?" the younger man said, sounding like a frightened child.

"Shut up," said the second man, who held the stick with the skewered birds on it over the fire. "We're free now. Don't you understand?"

"But you heard what she said. The people here have been warned. We'll be discovered by someone else!" The first man hunched down further where he sat, pulling the edges of his mantle up to his eyes.

The second man clenched his jaw and spat into the fire. "Just eat and we'll start moving again. We're exposed here. We need to get past this place before the sun rises."

The younger man lowered his head, as if he could conceal himself entirely from the strange noises of the forest that seemed to circle beyond the pool of light cast by the fire. William realized that Gwendolyn had judged the men correctly; only the larger man would offer any resistance. The other only needed a little encouragement to give up altogether.

William unbundled the severed limb and stood up, feeling its weight in his right hand and gauging the distance. He stepped back, took aim, and tossed it over the men's heads so that it landed at the edge of the fire, right in front of them. The arm made a solid thud, the whoosh of air causing sparks to fly up from the fire.

The effect was exactly as William had hoped. The two men stared for a moment. As recognition dawned, the first man shrieked and scooted himself on the ground away from the fire and the arm, kicking his legs out as if the arm were still alive. The second man, however, dropped the birds into the fire and jumped to his feet, wheeling to face the darkness behind him, his dagger drawn. But he was looking for an attack at eye level, and William, dagger in his left hand and hammer in his right, lunged out of the darkness, swinging the hammer low to slam into the man's knee and knock him off his feet. The man screamed in pain and fell to his side. Before he could brace his hands against the ground to right himself, William swung again, this time smashing the man's hand that held the dagger. William glanced to see where the first man had gone, and in that moment the man on the ground swung his good leg in a low sweep, knocking William off his feet. The heavier man flung himself at William, using his weight and bulk to pin William down onto his back. But bulk alone could not hold William, and as the man sharply thrust his head to break William's nose with his skull, William twisted and rolled, positioning himself to straddle the man's back.

The man found himself flat his stomach with William's arm locked around his neck and the edge of William's dagger at his throat.

"Be still!"

William tied the man's arms behind his back with one of the leather ties that he had brought with him, then stood up and hauled the man up to his feet unsteadily.

"It's not broken," William said, watching the man test his weight on the injured leg. "Answer my questions and it will stay that way."

William heard approaching hooves and looked up as Gerald arrived at a walk leading his horse, holding the reins to William's horse beside him. William squinted and saw a figure sitting in Gerald's saddle, eyes downcast, difficult to make out in the darkness. Gerald grinned broadly, led his horse a few steps closer, and the form of the younger man emerged into the firelight, his wrists tightly bound in front of him. His hands, fine and small, rested on the pommel. The younger man still had the look of a boy about him, or maybe it was his expression that reminded William of a pouting child.

"This was too easy, William," Gerald said with mock disappointment. "He's a she!"

"*What?*" The man beside William erupted into a string of muttered curses. William stared at the woman, who raised her eyes to glare at him.

3

A PROPHECY

"Wake up, my lady! Wake up!"

Gwendolyn stirred and answered Anne with a sick-sounding groan. Gamel's herbs had been effective. Her body felt weighted down, and with a great deal of effort, she opened her eyes halfway, aware that the room was lit with the glow of midday. Anne stood before her looking unreasonably firm in her conviction that Gwendolyn ought to be out of bed.

"My lady, you must get up. Roslyn is here!"

Her sister-in-law's name registered in Gwendolyn's mind like a jolt, and she pulled herself up to a sitting position and swung her legs over the side of her bed. Her private quarters, originally shared with her husband, were separated from the manor hall by a narrow passageway. Robert had added a heavy door prior to their wedding, and she was grateful for the privacy as she muttered a few choice remarks at the news of Roslyn's unannounced visit. Walter's wife never came to Penhallam except to deliver some tidbit of nastiness.

Bracing herself, Gwendolyn leaned uncertainly onto her feet, frustrated by the persistent fog in her mind. The church bells rang the hour of Nones, and Gwendolyn realized in a panic that she had slept for the greater part of the day.

"How long has Roslyn been waiting?" Gwendolyn asked while Anne lifted her sleeping gown over her head and reached for an undershirt.

"She arrived for the midday meal, my lady. She and her men have kept Osbert busy filling their stomachs."

Gwendolyn sighed loudly. "I suppose the wait hasn't improved her mood any."

"No, ma'am, I'm afraid not," Anne agreed, reaching for one of the light tunics Gwendolyn wore when making her rounds through the fields and training with the manor's garrison. "Your dress…isn't ready to be worn yet," she said, discreetly omitting mention of the bloodstains that may have permanently marred the garment, Gwendolyn's only concession to feminine attire. Gwendolyn stepped into her leggings and sat down on the edge of the bed to braid her hair while Anne laced up her boots.

Her sword, polished and gleaming again, leaned against the wall across from her, and she stared at it, all trace of the previous day's bloodshed erased.

"Tom's squire took care of that for you, my lady," Anne said quietly, reaching for Gwendolyn's sword belt, but Gwendolyn shook her head.

"Roslyn will see it as offense enough that I present myself to her dressed like this," she said. "And my sword is no use against Roslyn's tongue." Anne flashed a small smile at Gwendolyn's remark, and Gwendolyn was relieved to see it. She splashed some water on her face and dried it with a towel, allowed Anne to tidy the strands of her hair that had already come loose again, and stepped into the hall.

Roslyn sat in Gwendolyn's seat at the table, flanked on either side by a rangy knight. Greasy plates, wooden cups, and crusts of bread littered the table. Roslyn's knights slouched in their seats and appeared in need of a nap. Anne cleared the dishes, brushed the scraps into the straw for the dogs, and exited the hall quickly. Roslyn looked Gwendolyn over with unmasked disapproval.

"I suppose I should have sent word to advise you of my visit, sister," Roslyn said icily. "It did not occur to me that you would still be sleeping past midday."

"I have been ill," Gwendolyn said simply.

"Oh, I am sorry to hear that." Roslyn put special emphasis on the word "am," an unconscious habit that Gwendolyn had learned indicated that every word that followed it was a lie.

"Thank you, sister. I am sure your concern is equal to your kindness."

Roslyn considered this for a momentary pause, her eyes narrowed and her mouth slightly askew. She decided to treat the remark as a compliment and smiled indulgently.

"Will you and your men be our guests tonight? I will ask Martha to prepare my chamber for you. You are welcome to rest here after your journey."

Roslyn scoffed through her nose.

"That won't be necessary. We have rooms in Stratton and will return there shortly."

"As you wish," Gwendolyn said, bowing her head slightly to her sister-in-law. "Then what can I do for you? What business brings you so far from the comfort of Restormel?" Restormel Castle, Roslyn was pleased to remind Gwendolyn frequently, had been occupied by the de Cardinham family since the reign of Henry I—nearly one hundred years.

"I might as well get straight to the point, Gwendolyn," she said, straightening up to her full height and tilting her chin upward imperiously. "Robert has not returned from crusade in almost four years. And while your steadfast faith in his safety is commendable, I feel that it is time that you admit you are a widow and consider your options. You cannot continue to live like this forever."

Gwendolyn—and the queen mother herself for that matter—was certain of her husband's whereabouts and safety, as Queen Eleanor's trusted advisors returning from Germany had reported Robert's popularity in the young German emperor's court. Gwendolyn could have patiently explained this and the evidence for it to Roslyn. But she was out of patience, and Roslyn's condescension and the facile manner with which she had discussed Robert's mortality had inflamed her. She saw an opportunity to insult Roslyn and she took it.

"I can continue like this for a very long time," she answered, calmly crossing her arms. "Penhallam is thriving. We have no debts, our grain stores are full, and even after the scutage for the king's ransom our treasury is not empty, which is more than you can say for Restormel." Gwendolyn regretted the words as soon as she uttered them. Her face remained hard, but she knew she had crossed a line. She might as well have declared open war against Roslyn. William stepped into the hall in time to hear her blunder.

"Why . . . you . . ." Roslyn blustered, her chin straining against the silk wimple that she wore wrapped tightly around her head. Her lips twisted with fury. "Walter has struck at every opportunity he could find. Even now he is in London seeking new buyers for the wool. In case you haven't noticed, our dear king's mother has stripped the country dry to pay his ransom!" Roslyn stopped herself and pursed her lips tightly together, regaining her composure. Gwendolyn took note of how quickly Roslyn had become defensive; things must have grown worse at Restormel than rumored. William had positioned himself beside the hearth, behind Roslyn, so that Gwendolyn could see his face without Roslyn or her men detecting a shift in her glance.

"You know well what my opinion of Walter is," Gwendolyn said quietly.

"Robert is dead and Penhallam is ours," Roslyn said with such force that both of her knights stirred to attention. "If you will not go voluntarily, on his return from London, Walter will come with his men, and they will carry you out of here with only the clothes on your back."

Gwendolyn's eyes bored into Roslyn, and for a moment the older woman looked to her knights uneasily, in case she might have need of their defense. "Roslyn, do you not realize that we are on the verge of war here in Cornwall? Only yesterday—" she began, then abruptly stopped when William subtly shook his head at her.

"Only yesterday what?" Roslyn demanded.

Gwendolyn shifted her gaze to the narrow window, thought of something plausible, then continued. "Only yesterday, I was wondering who would be foolish enough to go against Eleanor and the regents and side instead with a man who has failed in every single battle or siege that he has ever undertaken."

Roslyn shifted forward in her seat, looking confident again. The reference to Prince John's treachery had been plain, and her sister-in-law excelled in veiled innuendo.

"Yes, what fools indeed," Roslyn answered calmly, recovered from her outburst. "Gwendolyn, I will not tolerate your selfishness any longer. I will apply to the Chancery to have Robert de Cardinham's death formally recognized. You have been warned."

With these last words, Roslyn rose from the table and gestured to her men that they were leaving. Her sweeping stride across the hall would have been more impressive if not for the lumbering figures that trailed behind her. Gwendolyn watched through the window slit as Simon, Penhallam's groom, led the party's horses out to meet them at the bridge and then assisted Roslyn into the sideways-facing saddle atop her elegant palfrey.

~'~

Walter de Cardinham was older than Gwendolyn by ten years, and his favorite sport during her childhood at Restormel had been to torment her. One particularly bad afternoon he had locked her in a chest and loaded the chest onto a cart, threatening to kill her if she cried out. She was only nine years old, and so skinny that the nineteen-year-old Walter could lift her over his head with one hand. Whistling cheerfully, he had driven the cart deep into the woods and unloaded the box far from the road, sitting beside it while she cried and pleaded with him to let her out. After she had finally fallen asleep from exhaustion Walter returned alone to the castle. She was found by poachers a day later, terrified, soiled, and dying of thirst. Fortunately they guessed by her fine dress that they might earn a reward for her safe return. Instead, when the poachers showed up with her at Restormel, Walter accused them of kidnapping his dear young sister in a plot for money. The baron tried and hung the men that day. Gwendolyn had pleaded with the baron for the men's lives but he dismissed her; she had realized that day that he would never take her word over his own son's.

From that day forward, everyone in the baron's household was charged with keeping a close watch over Gwendolyn. Walter's attacks were reduced to verbal reminders that she was not in fact the baron's daughter, that she had no noble blood. Her real father had been a landless knight, he had told her—a Welsh savage who had died before his time. Walter promised her that her own life would come to a similar end.

There was a time when Restormel's wealth had dwarfed the modest income of Penhallam, but that time had passed. Walter had taken over the largest of the baron's estates at an early age when the baron's health began to decline. Walter had seized as much in payment and fines from his villeins and tenants as he and his men-at-arms could extract. Despite his son's reputation for brutality, the baron had arranged a favorable match for Walter, and things had settled down after the marriage, but only for as long as it had taken Walter to use up Roslyn's dowry. Gwendolyn had been eleven years old when Walter married, and he and Roslyn spent most of their time away from Bodardel, travelling extravagantly and following King Henry's court around England and across the sea to Rouen, Poitou, Le Mans, and Chinon. After eight years of Walter's mismanagement and tyranny, those who were free to leave Restormel had done so and had taken their livelihoods—and payments to Walter—with them. Since Robert's departure, Gwendolyn had begun to harbor a reasonable fear that her kinsman might one day decide to take Penhallam for himself. Now it appeared Roslyn would take care of the matter on her own.

William approached Gwendolyn and laid his hand on her arm.

"My lady, we captured the two mercenaries last night. But things were not as they appeared. Gerald is guarding one of them now, in the stables."

Gwendolyn rubbed her temples and took a deep breath, trying to shake off the unpleasantness that always hung in the air after Roslyn's departure.

"What of the other?"

"The one who you said would not fight was no mercenary. That was a woman."

Gwendolyn stared at William while this news sunk in. "A woman? Why was she travelling with those men?"

"The one you killed was her uncle. She had only met him a week before when her mother died. She had been working on the cathedral in Exeter as a mason, dressed as a man."

Gwendolyn smiled slightly. "It's not just me."

"Her uncle was taking her to St. Michael's Mount to work on the defensive fortifications there, or so that's what he told her.

Her father has never claimed her, and she would have been the only woman on an island of mercenaries."

"He was bringing her for their use," Gwendolyn said, staring flatly at the stone wall in front of her. "Where is she now?"

"Martha has offered her a place with her family, but she refused. She slept in the stables. This morning she walked into the forest to retrieve her tools. She has spent the day helping Simon."

Gwendolyn nodded. "And the man?"

"He says he's from London, that he was sold to the man you killed to settle a debt. From the looks of him, he's been fighting most of his life."

"Does he know if more men are coming?"

"Very likely, but that's not all," William replied, shifting beside her and taking a slow, thoughtful breath. "Walter is not in London, as Roslyn has said. He left his man there to conclude negotiations with the merchants while he traveled to France to join Prince John at the French court. John is hiding there to spin his plots with the help of King Phillip. When Walter returned, he gathered men from London, supporters of John, and marched on Glastonbury Abbey. This man and the two you killed were with him, but Walter has not been seen since Glastonbury."

Gwendolyn looked at William with wide eyes.

"If Walter is discovered, if he openly professes his allegiance to John's rebellion, the king's regents could declare Walter a traitor to the crown." She stared at William with disbelief. "They could strip him of his lands and his title. Roslyn would lose everything."

William nodded. "From what we just saw, I don't think Roslyn has any idea of the peril she's in. Walter and Roslyn are hardly seen in the same room anymore, and Roslyn's family has ties to Eleanor reaching back to her time as the queen consort of France. Roslyn would not have gone along willingly with a plan to pit Eleanor's sons against each other."

"Walter may be on his way back to Cornwall. We have no proof of his treachery other than the word of a captured mercenary, and I'm not convinced of it myself." She paused to try to put herself into her sister-in-law's frame of mind, to try to guess how someone whose first thought was always self-preservation would react to the news of her husband's terrible gamble. "If any of this is true and Roslyn finds out, she may decide to make good on her threats and seat herself at Penhallam as a means to distance herself from Walter while she can. I'll ride to Exeter and seek an audience with the bishop to stop this nonsense now. Roslyn cannot simply run me out of Penhallam just because Robert is delayed in Germany with the king."

William shook his head at her.

"Gwendolyn, there is no bishop in Exeter. Until the pope has recognized Hubert Walter as Archbishop of Canterbury, the see of Exeter will remain vacant. There is no other authority here for you to appeal to. Penhallam must stand by itself."

"As it always has," she said quietly.

Gwendolyn absently bit on a nail, a habit left over from childhood, as she ran through all of the information she had received. She paused with another question.

"Why would Walter attack Glastonbury Abbey? It makes no sense."

William looked at her for a long while.

"He was looking for something."

"That is what the man in the stables told you?"

"Walter ordered the men to bar the passage while he went down into the abbey's crypt alone. He returned empty-handed and in a rage."

Gwendolyn wondered how much persuasion William and Gerald had applied to extract the information. "Well, we can't keep that man here. The nearest gaol is at Launceston. Gerald and Simon can leave with the prisoner tomorrow."

"We must leave now," William said, looking her in the eye. "You and I must travel to Launceston as well, to St. Stephen's Priory."

Gwendolyn frowned at him. "Gerald and Simon can manage this errand without us. I am needed here, William. Harvest is coming, mercenaries are crossing through our woods, and now Roslyn's threatening to have me removed. You may accompany Gerald and Simon, if you wish, provided you return immediately."

"No, my lady, you misunderstand me." William squared his shoulders and faced her. "This is about you. The prior at St. Stephen's knew your father. It's time for you to learn who you are."

Gwendolyn eyed William closely, Walter's childhood insults to her obscure ancestry still living in her memory. "I assure you, I know very well who I am."

"No, you don't. Trust me that you need to hear this."

She tried to read his expression but found nothing there except his usual unflappable demeanor. "Can't you tell me whatever this startling piece of news is yourself?"

"You'll have questions that I can't answer." His expression was fixed, his jaw set. She had not forgotten her contrition yesterday at her failure to heed his warnings. She sighed and agreed to go with him.

"And wear your armor," he called to her over his shoulder as he headed out of the hall. "You may have need of it."

When Gwendolyn met William in front of the manor house, she had donned her mail hauberk and a surcoat bearing the de Cardinham family colors. She stepped into the stables to retrieve her horse and found the woman they had brought back the night before, shoveling manure out of the empty stalls while the horses were turned out to pasture. The woman paused from her work long enough to answer Gwendolyn's questions whether she had eaten and did she have any injuries with her eyes cast to the ground throughout. It was an uncomfortable conversation for both of them, and Gwendolyn ended it, telling the woman she would return the following morning and to remain as Penhallam's guest until then. Her name, Gwendolyn discovered at last, was Isabel.

Back outside, Gwendolyn reached a foot into the stirrup, gripped the saddle, and hoisted herself up onto Bedwyr, a dappled Barb with keen ears and stamina to outlast any English courser. Robert had presented the mare to her, along with her armor, as his parting gift. Gwendolyn wore her sword belt, the same as those presented to knights, wrapped around the surcoat, and her sword hung down along her left leg, plainly visible this time.

Tom and Osbert had followed her out of the manor house, and William called out orders to Tom to keep men posted to watch the woods for any more of Henry de la Pomerai's men. Gerald tested the ropes that bound the ankles and wrists of the prisoner sitting in the back of the cart, while Osbert handed up a bag of rolls and sausages to Gwendolyn. She passed their provisions to William and tied a small purse of coins to her belt. The priory was only a few hours' ride away; they would be back in a day.

She looked down at the bound man in the cart and winced at his purple, misshapen hand. He stared ahead, stone-faced. His dark hair was shaved close to the skull, and the pale lines of scars crisscrossing the stubble described a lifetime of battle and violence.

"Why were you travelling so far north, away from the main roads?" she asked.

"Well, now, that's a question that answers itself, isn't it," the man said, still staring straight ahead. Gwendolyn reflected for a moment before she understood the man's meaning.

"To avoid discovery."

"That was the idea."

"This far north, pilgrims are rare. There's little lodging, few manors to provide food and protection."

The man shrugged, looked at his hands in his lap. "I'll keep that in mind next time." The middle finger of the injured hand was bent to the side at an irregular angle. The man raised his bound wrists toward his face and clenched the wayward finger firmly in his teeth. He gave a sudden, hard yank with his arm and his eyes opened wide with pain as the finger's broken bones audibly shifted back into place.

Gwendolyn found she could not help but be impressed by the

man. *What turns of fortune's wheel could leave such a man on the side of a fool like Prince John?* she wondered to herself.

She found herself hesitating, unsure how to explain the decision that had just unexpectedly formed in her mind. "I don't know for certain that you would have killed us, as your companions would have. This will be my witness to the castellan at Launceston. I cannot support your execution."

William looked up at her sharply, and she avoided his eyes while the man turned his head to regard her with a cynical sneer.

"That's all very well, madam, but last I checked, unless you're a lord with pockets full of money, they hang rebels against the king. Your mercy on your own account, however, is touching, and for that I thank you."

"You never made it to Saint Michael's Mount. Your rebellious intentions were never proven in action."

The man laughed loudly and shifted to face her. "Are you my lawyer now, my lady? Because I surely cannot afford you!"

"If you survive, you will be in my debt, then. Tell me your name," she said, pulling back on Bedwyr's reins as the mare pranced restlessly beneath her.

"Nigel Fitz Richard, my lady. And I never forget a debt," he added, looking directly at William.

"I look forward to it," William answered with a smile, then turned to Gwendolyn. "My lady, we are prepared to leave."

⁓

They headed south on the road to the monastery at a gentle amble, riding one behind the other, William leading the group with Gwendolyn riding directly behind him. The dray cart moved slowly behind them, pulled by an old plough horse. Simon drove the cart while Gerald, wearing full mail and the colors of the de Cardinham family on his surcoat, sat in the back with the mercenary. Gerald kept his sword lying at the ready across his knees and stared at the mercenary with a baleful look, but every now and then Gwendolyn thought she saw a flicker of esteem in the young knight's eyes.

The summer evening seemed to come more quickly than the previous night, and the party crested a hill as the sun disappeared below the horizon. Spread out before them, a cluster of glowing dots marked the town of Launceston, with Launceston Castle, its tower keep outlined by blazing torches, rising on a high hill across the river beyond it. William pulled his warhorse to a stop, and Gwendolyn paused beside him on her mare while they waited for the cart to join them.

"The priory lies in a clearing within those woods," he said, pointing to the dim glow of candlelit walls in the middle of the patch of darkness between themselves and Launceston town. "It's under the control of the Abbey of St. Augustine, in Bristol. We will be safe here. No man may break *Pax Dei* and bring violence to this place."

"Forgiveness from sin can be bought," Gwendolyn replied dryly. Without waiting for William she leaned forward in her saddle and gave Bedwyr the rein, swinging the mare's hindquarters around and galloping down the slope for the woods. William reacted immediately, shouting to Simon behind him to continue to Launceston, and took off after her. But Gwendolyn had gained a large lead already and William's horse was tired. He cursed and leaned forward, determined not to lose sight of her.

The path through the woods grew narrow and twisted, and Gwendolyn drank in the cool night air that rushed over her cheeks and drew tears from her eyes. A day ago men had threatened her life and the lives of her maids, and she had killed them for it. Recklessness felt good. She strained to keep her blurred vision on the path, still visible in the twilight. Bedwyr was sure-footed enough to steer out of the way of anything or anyone that suddenly appeared in front of them as they swept around blind curves. A pale glow of moonlight through the branches ahead signaled that they approached a clearing, and Gwendolyn bent her head close to the mare's straining neck. Responding to her rider, Bedwyr extended her stride and flattened herself closer to the ground. Horse and rider burst from the cover of the trees into a meadow, scattering a small herd of sheep and sending a flurry of birds out of the nearby branches where they had roosted for the night.

Gwendolyn pulled back on the reins and brought Bedwyr to an agitated stop. The priory stood in the middle of the meadow, next to a stream that seemed to neatly divide the meadow into halves. She could just make out the circular edge of the top of a large wooden wheel that was visible over the top of the monastery wall and realized the monastery had its own mill. Self-sufficiency was critical for all priories, which were customarily dependent on the thin generosity of the families who sent their second- and third-born sons there. The walls that encircled the monastery were smooth along the top edge, showing no battlements. *Pax Dei* had been the rule for over a hundred years; the church lands that had grown under its protection were built without war defenses. Feeling her shoulders relax, Gwendolyn allowed Bedwyr to walk again, cooling the mare down. William caught up to her before she was halfway across the meadow to the priory.

"Christ on the cross, girl! Is there some reason you refuse my company any time you enter a wood?" His blasphemy was loud enough to draw a politely cleared throat from the priory's monks that walked within earshot, returning from the fields for evening prayers. She watched his features rearrange, as the realization that he had entered the hallowed grounds of the priory settled over him and he sat straight in his saddle again, the soldierly model of discipline and reverence. She was aware that she was about to enter a world that few women ever saw.

A boy's fair head popped up over the wall for a moment, spotted them, and disappeared again. They were close enough to hear him call for the prior within the monastery walls.

Moments later a short, spry man with white hair clipped in the customary tonsure stepped out of the monastery gate. The man looked them over keenly, and as his eyes fell on William he relaxed and smiled openly. Gwendolyn knew that William had lived with the monks as a novice until he turned seventeen, when the prior had tactfully suggested to the baron that William's skills might be put to better service at arms rather than at prayer.

"I am Prior Thomas, child," he said, walking lightly to her and reaching up to hold one of her hands in both of his, rough and warm. Her father had also been fond of the monks here, and she remembered him referring to Prior Thomas as "the old scholar of the black robe." That was nearly fifteen years ago, and she wondered how many summers the lively, sharp-eyed man before her had seen. The prior beamed at her with a genuine smile, but she was more drawn by the dark shadows beneath his eyes that reminded her of the monks' rigorous schedule of prayer. He stood facing her and paused for a moment longer than necessary while his gaze took in her stature and features.

"You have your mother's eyes, but I see Gwyn in the rest of you," he said with a note of excitement in his voice. She felt her cheeks warm at his observation and thanked him; whatever reason William had for bringing her here, she was already glad for the chance to finally meet this man who had known both of her parents.

While they settled their horses for the night, the prior and William chatted lightly about the late baron and the changes at the priory in the eleven years since William had left. When their saddles and bridles had been stowed and the horses were munching hay contentedly in their stalls, the prior escorted them to the monks' dining hall, a small room lined with narrow tables and benches. William had given their provisions of food to Simon, and her stomach grumbled at the lingering smells from the monks' supper. The prior seemed to have noticed and he told them to have a seat and left them for a moment. When he returned he carried a round loaf of bread, a chunk of sheep's milk cheese, and two cups of watery wine.

They were alone, and after they had eaten a few bites the prior leaned across the table toward them and folded his hands into a point, drumming his fingers together expectantly, his eyes on William. Between mouthfuls, William told the prior in a low voice about the mercenaries in the forest and their deaths at

Gwendolyn's hand—the first time for her to draw her sword in combat, he added, and the prior nodded, apparently unmoved by the discovery that she was capable of such violence. But when William told the prior what they had learned from the captured mercenary, that Walter de Cardinham had joined Prince John's rebellion and ransacked the crypt at Glastonbury Abbey, the prior sat up straight and took in a sharp breath, then exhaled it slowly. The old monk appeared to be sorting out some larger puzzle in his head.

"Yes, you were right to bring her, William. It's time." The prior pivoted on his stool to face Gwendolyn and stared at her intently.

"Gwendolyn," he began softly, "There is much to tell you, and I'm afraid you aren't going to like most of it." The prior cleared his throat and frowned in concentration. He appeared to be sorting his thoughts for the right words, and yet she had the feeling he had anticipated this conversation for years. "You have heard the legends, some call them prophesy, told by the Welsh of King Arthur's return?"

Thomas paused, and she nodded impatiently; she had more immediate concerns than Welsh lore. "Yes, their bards still sing that Arthur and his men will march from Avalon and expel the Normans and the English from Britain. My father told me these tales to entertain me and put me to sleep. It's one of the few memories I have of him."

"And I suppose you also heard the stories a few years ago of the discovery of the tomb of Arthur and Guinevere at Glastonbury Abbey?"

"Yes, of course. It was just after my wedding. King Richard ordered a shrine built there, declared the songs of Arthur's return proven false, and Glastonbury now enjoys a regular stream of pilgrims and their coins. What of it?" She realized she was sounding combative and tried to soften her voice. "I'm sorry, Prior Thomas, but other than being Welsh, I don't see what these tales have to do with me or Penhallam."

Thomas said the next words so quietly that she had to strain to hear him.

"It has everything to do with you and your family, child. Your father, and therefore also you, are the direct descendants of Arthur."

4

GWYN'S LETTER

G wendolyn held the prior's gaze and leaned back slowly from the table. She knew that she had heard the prior correctly, but he could have told her she had two heads and could soar with the birds for as much sense as his words had made to her. She folded her arms across her chest and bit her lip with the effort of suppressing her laughter.

"You can't be serious," she said.

The prior regarded her steadily, his sympathetic expression suggesting that it was she, rather than himself, who suffered under delusion. She felt the humor drain from her face as she registered how completely serious the man in front of her actually was. So many questions and arguments raced through her head at once that she could hardly pick which one to utter first. And granting the prior's proposition even a hint of plausibility by entertaining further discussion over it seemed the wrong way to steer the conversation back onto solid ground. Instead, Gwendolyn noticed that William had not reacted at all, and she swung around to face him.

"You knew of this?" she asked accusingly.

William had been staring at the ground, but he raised his eyes at her words and said nothing. She stared back in shock, feeling her gut suddenly become very light and empty inside her. She stood up and took a few steps back, shifting her gaze from one man to the other and distancing herself from both of them. It was one thing for an old monk to find truth in the legends sung during the long winter nights; it was quite another thing altogether that her constable seemed to believe them as well.

"How can you believe this, William? What evidence have you seen?"

William gave her a wry laugh. "You would not believe half of what I've seen if I told you." She silenced him with a warning flash of her eyes. William had tried to tell her once about the other-worldly demons and spirits he claimed to have seen, and she had ended the conversation abruptly. She had no desire to revisit the topic now.

"There was no point in telling you until tonight," Thomas explained, speaking rapidly, as if he tried to hold her in place with his words. "What would you have done with the knowledge of your ancestry when you were too young to act on it? And without Caliburn, you are vulnerable."

"Exactly," Gwendolyn cut in, latching onto an argument. "If I am Arthur's heir, then where is my sword? I'm sorry, Prior, but this is rubbish." She turned back to William, the last man she would have expected to lead her astray on such far-fetched nonsense. "How long have you believed this to be true? Is this what they taught you, after your father brought you here?" She fired her questions at him like bolts from a crossbow.

William stood up and faced her squarely, looking much the same as he did when facing off with Penhallam's knights during training in the yard. "My father brought me here at my request. The night that your parents died, I was the one who carried you from the flames. I had a vision that night of the fire. I snuck away to see that you were safe, but as soon as I got close . . ." William grimaced slightly with the memory. "There was barely time to get you out."

Gwendolyn stood stunned, struggling to grasp what William had just told her. She felt emotion rise in her chest, threatening to overwhelm the anger that was her key to maintaining control in the midst of this ludicrous conversation. After so many years, her rescuer had come forward. And with this knowledge came a new, uncomfortable realization: she owed her constable her life. And she had practically had to beat the information out of him.

"Why did you never tell me?" she snapped.

"At first I told no one because I couldn't explain how I had known of the danger. I was afraid I would be blamed for the fire, and for your parents' deaths. After I returned to Penhallam to serve in the garrison, I knew that if I told you the truth, you would feel indebted to me. I didn't want that."

Gwendolyn exhaled slowly and gazed out the high window to the stars twinkling in the clear night. Pieces of her memories and those behaviors of William's that she had written off as mere peculiarities were coming together, falling into place to form a larger picture whose meaning she was just beginning to understand. No wonder he slept outside her door in the manor hall and took such an interest in her safety. But how could he have known to come for her that night?

"Are you a magician, William? A wizard?" The words felt ridiculous in her mouth when she said them.

"My vision is a curse to me, unpredictable and useless. That's all. Saving your life was the only time it served a purpose."

"Perhaps you should sit down," Prior Thomas suggested in the awkward silence that hung between them after William's answer, but she shook her head and turned her attention back to the old monk.

"Guinevere bore no children from Arthur," she argued flatly, returning to the recorded legend. "Mordred was the king's only heir, and his sons were executed after Arthur's death."

"It's true that Guinevere bore no child. But the king had mistresses, three in fact. History doesn't follow the stories of women as closely as it does the men, which has been fortunate for us, really."

"Then he must have dozens of descendants, hundreds, all over England and Wales. Why tell this to me?"

"This isn't an inheritance, child. Just because one is descended from Arthur is not enough to make a king. Or queen," he corrected himself. "That is only part of it, and really, it's the most insignificant part. After so many generations, whatever part of Arthur is in you is barely a trace, not discernible at all. No, there's much more to it than that.

"From what you have said, I can assume that you have read Geoffrey of Monmouth and Chretien de Troyes. That's good; there is important information for you in there. But also many lies. Queen Eleanor and her family have used the Welsh legends to their own ends, and their scholars and bards have altered the tales to suit the royal family's wishes. It is a reflection of the Plantagenets' deep fear that the tales of Arthur's return are true.

"You have been seen, Gwendolyn, in a vision, with Caliburn in your hand. You are a descendant of a great warrior king, the chief of all warriors. But more than that, your heart is bound by the ancient laws of the land to shelter the weak, punish the unjust, and show mercy to those who ask it. This was the code of Arthur that he required of each of his men. And it is the code by which you have lived your life, even when everything was taken from you."

Gwendolyn turned on the prior. She had reached her limit. "No one has seen me with Caliburn. I don't even know where the sword is, if it exists. Which it doesn't."

"My child, there is no boundary between real and not real, between magical and natural. The world we live on lies flat between Hell and the heavens, and our home is a battleground overrun by forces we cannot see. But one law rules all of the realms, and that is the divine law of cause and effect." The prior clapped his hands together in demonstration of his point, and the sound echoed around the empty room and caused a bird that had been watching from the window sill to take flight into the night.

"When you drew your sword yesterday, you risked your life for another's. You could have run. You could have saved yourself. But you stood and fought to protect the innocent." Gwendolyn blinked and realized it had never occurred to her to run. She could have saved herself, as the prior said. She could have easily outrun those men. But the idea of abandoning her maids never entered her mind.

"Cause and effect. You acted selflessly, with courage and

honor. Caliburn was already reaching for you, and yesterday you reached back. The bond is formed. Caliburn will come to you. It is only a matter of time."

Gwendolyn scoffed under her breath and turned toward William, ready to leave.

"You may not believe any of this, but Prince John does," the prior added. At the mention of the king's rebellious younger brother, Gwendolyn paused; the prior sensed an opportunity and drove forward. "He is a weak man, only able to inspire loyalty with his purse and promises, and he is using the disaster of his brother's captivity to seize the throne, by any means possible. He has sent men across England to find Caliburn—including Walter de Cardinham, it would appear—and he will continue to spill innocent blood and raise rebellion against his brother as long as he believes he has a chance of obtaining it."

"Glastonbury . . ." Gwendolyn said quietly, thinking of the monks killed over such folly.

"Yes, Walter sought the sword for John. But the sword will only come to its rightful heir. John is not aware of you. Only the people in this room and one other know who you really are: the heir of Caliburn—and your champion," he added, indicating with his gaze toward William.

William had been pacing the floor behind them, and the steady rhythm of his steps ceased at the far end of the room.

"My what?" she asked in a low voice.

"The heir of Caliburn was described as a great warrior and leader of men, true to the sword's legacy, but with one weakness. He—" the prior shook his head and corrected himself. "She does not believe. So a champion was called, a warrior in his own right, who would protect her from those things she would not see. William understood from an early age that he lived to guard your life. When he confessed to us that he had pulled you from the fire, how he had been compelled that night to go to you and ran into a burning house to save you, we told him about the prophecy. That day he abandoned his novitiate's vows and asked to take up arms." The prior stood before her, watching her reaction. "In a way, Gwendolyn, it is your refusal to believe that brings the sword to you. You have no hunger for power, no ambition to rule. You will use the sword to defend and protect or not at all."

She sat down, staring at the swirling patterns in the wood on the table's surface. She was beginning to understand that she stood at the center of a plot set into motion by the lore and cupidity of distant men, some long dead, and some with the power to bring an entire nation to the brink of war.

"Does the dowager queen also believe these prophecies?"

"Well," the prior admitted, looking away, "Eleanor is a practical woman, with more immediate concerns, I'm sure."

Gwendolyn snorted, pleased to find another reason to like her sovereign's famous mother.

"You said I was seen holding Caliburn. By whom?"

"By a seer, a man who is the keeper of the story of the Britons, past and future." The prior spoke in hushed tones, as if he were sharing a mysterious secret with her. "He is the only other person who knows you are the heir."

Gwendolyn stared at the prior for a moment, amazed that he still expected her to take anything he was saying to her seriously. Out of the corner of her eye, William appeared to cringe slightly at the prior's dramatic air. She gave up the pretense of polite forbearance.

"Who are you, Prior Thomas? What kind of monastery is this?" Her tone was level with authority, and the prior took note.

"Outwardly, in our dress and our practice, we are like any other Augustinian canons. But we are also brothers to the ancient ones. The Romans called them Druids. They were powerful once, counselors to kings who stepped unarmed into the midst of battles to forge a truce. The Romans hunted them down because they feared the Druids' authority and political power. Now only a few live among us, cloaked in anonymity."

"Why do they still hide? Why don't they show themselves?"

"Now the Church would destroy them for their heresies. These ancient ones see all religions as different aspects of the same truth. For them, it is as if we are all on the edge of a wheel, seeking a way back to the center: our origin and the singular moving force that put our world and all worlds into motion. Every religion is merely one spoke of the wheel. Most will lead to the same place, but from each spoke only a small part of the center can be seen. The priest and the imam both believe their idea of God is the end of all religions, and they cannot spill each other's blood fast enough. In such a world as this, the Druids must remain hidden if their wisdom is not to be lost forever. When they have asked us, we have provided them shelter. They have lived here among the brothers, following our customs—once while William lived with us."

William had crossed the room to lean against the near wall, arms crossed, listening closely. "Far as I could tell, they still stick pretty well to the old ways," he said.

Prior Thomas blushed, but he made no argument with William.

"Why do you help them, if they are heretics?" Gwendolyn asked.

"As a Christian I am bound to offer shelter to those who need it, to live with kindness and humility, not to judge or condemn. When events began to unfold as the ancient ones had described them, beginning with William saving your life . . ." The prior spread his hands in a gesture of submission toward the heavens. "I cannot fathom what God's plan is. I can only pray that my every action serves His will."

Gwendolyn narrowed her eyes, feeling the prior's words stir up her usual distaste for all things religious. For her, the Church was on a level with the royal court, an interfering and dangerous collection of profligates who ultimately backed their dubious claims of authority by the sword. If the prior was sincere, and she believed that he was, his words would mark him as a heretic as well.

"And these Druids have told you that the Welsh prophecies are true, and that I will carry Caliburn?"

"Those Welsh songs were first spoken centuries ago as a Druid prophecy. The one who carries all of the Britons' stories and prophecies today visited us for the first time twenty years ago when you were in your mother's womb. His name is Mogh, and he saw you as a woman, holding Caliburn. He told your father that he would have a daughter, and that Caliburn would return to us from Avalon, to be carried by you."

"And he predicted the fire and William's rescue? Could he not have warned my parents?"

The prior's face dropped with true sadness. "Nothing is revealed in its entirety, not even to a seer like Mogh."

Gwendolyn rose and turned away from the monk, stifling a curse under her breath.

"Why would Caliburn come for me now? What am I supposed to do with it?"

"Every time Caliburn has returned, it comes to end tyranny. When its task is complete, it vanishes again from our world."

Gwendolyn turned back toward the prior and raised an eyebrow at him.

"That's right, child. Arthur was not the first to carry the sword. As long as men have tried to rule one another by might and not consent, as long as the strong have preyed upon the weak, Caliburn has waited for the man or woman with the strength, courage, and humility to carry it."

She could not stop herself from shaking her head slowly at the prior and William.

"That is not all." The prior glanced down and twisted his hands together, looking up at her with uncertainty. "Your father believed this, Gwendolyn. All of it."

Gwendolyn's expression shifted immediately, and she fixed the prior with a piercing gaze. "Leave my father out of this."

"I have proof," he said quickly.

"Show it to me. Now."

The prior hurried out a small side-door, leaving her to pace the length of the room, the leather soles of her boots grinding loudly against the stone floor. The prior returned and approached her a little timidly, holding out a rolled scroll of vellum that was tied with a faded green ribbon. She took the scroll into her hands, feeling the soft lambskin between her fingers.

"Gwyn asked me to scribe this for him when you were only a few months old. He was returning home from a campaign in Northumbria with the baron, and he stopped here. He was afraid that he wouldn't live to see you grown. He asked me to keep this for him, in case . . . ." The prior looked at her sympathetically and continued. "Gwyn visited our priory many times. He liked our Druid brothers. He said they reminded him of home, of his Welsh elders. When your mother became pregnant, Mogh came to us. He sent for Gwyn and told him his vision. Gwyn believed him."

Gwendolyn gently loosened the ribbon and unwound the scroll, holding it tilted toward William so that he could read it beside her:

My dearest daughter, fair Gwendolyn,

Mogh has told me that a king's sword awaits you, and I am afraid my time will have passed before you have grown to claim it. May these words give you comfort. May you hear my voice through Death's veil.

You are a warrior by birth. In our homeland all of the descendants of Arthur are known. There is no mystery in this. His offspring produced more kings across all of Wales than any other family of the Britons. But of these, Arthur was the greatest.

Mogh is neither magician nor priest. The brothers call him a seer, but this is also false. He has been my friend. Mogh feels the echoes of time, forces aligning to cause events, in the same way that you and I feel a shift in the weather. He reads the signs of what has been and what will come. He has warned me, and I will pass his warning to you. There is a terrible struggle coming to this land. It will last through your lifetime, and it brews now. It cannot be stopped, but its outcome will decide whether the future is ruled by reason and justice or by might and greed. This is the reason for Caliburn's return.

Caliburn is more than a sword, Gwendolyn. With Caliburn one wields the whole strength and will of the land in the blade. Nothing can repel the sword's cleaving edge, not even stone. This is your birthright, and at the time that you choose to claim it, others more powerful than you will seek the sword as well. Caliburn belongs to you alone. Never forget that.

I cannot tell you what you should do, but as in all things, follow your own heart. It will never fail you. Do not be afraid. Fight bravely, my daughter, and know that I wait to hold you in my arms again in the next world.

Gwendolyn rolled the scroll back up and tucked it inside her surcoat, her vision blurred with tears. The prior could offer no proof that her father had actually requested the letter, and yet the fact that her father had refrained from telling her what she should do or believe seemed to make the letter authentic. If the prior had meant to present her with a forged letter as a ploy to manipulate her, she reasoned, he would have been more forceful in his persuasion. She dried her cheeks with her sleeve self-consciously, moved by her father's words in spite of herself, and turned to the prior.

"Did this Mogh ever say where I'm supposed to find Caliburn?"

The prior pursed his lips and looked down.

"No, I didn't think so," she said quietly, then turned to William. "We'll leave for Launceston Castle in the morning to join Gerald and Simon and return to Penhallam."

She faced the prior one last time, her anger and frustration dissolved by her father's words.

"You are a Pendragon, my dear," the prior said softly.

Gwendolyn laughed under her breath and shook her head.

"No, that is the creation of Geoffrey of Monmouth, from a slight rearrangement of the Welsh words. The songs only record Arthur's mother, Igrayne. There's no mention of his father, which was too intolerable for the scholar from Monmouth. My father used to tell me the only thing the Normans hated more than a weak man was a strong woman.

"Thank you for this," she added, touching the place in her surcoat over the pocket that now held the scroll. "It is the only piece of him that I have. But it does not prove that I am, as you claim, Arthur's heir."

The prior's face dropped as she spoke the last words, and he realized he had failed to overcome her doubts. His shoulders slumped with resignation.

"If you will not believe your own father—" he began, but she stopped him with a warning look. He was not allowed to use her father's memory.

The prior nodded and said, "Very well. You are the priory's guests tonight. Follow me to your rooms."

The following morning, Gwendolyn and William waited in the yard outside the cloisters, both dressed in their full mail armor and the de Cardinham colors, with only their heads and hands exposed. The monks were already inclined to stare at the intimidating strangers, but when those who looked closely enough to see realized that one of the men was a woman, they gave a little frightful jump that reminded Gwendolyn of startled lambs. The chapel bell rang the hour of Terce, the third prayer of the day, and a line of monks filed quietly into the chapel to mark Pentecost, the hour that the Holy Spirit descended upon the Twelve Apostles. Taking care not to disturb the orderly procession, Prior Thomas emerged from the cloisters to accompany William and Gwendolyn to the stables. She noted the deferential greetings of the brothers as they passed by the prior, and heard him reply to each one by name. He was like a father to all of them, and it was easy to understand why men who had no intention of taking the Augustinian vows still found reason to visit the priory and its quiet simplicity.

A full bank of clouds blanketed the sky, leaving a bleak morning light. Gwendolyn fastened her saddle and her bundled belongings to Bedwyr in silence. She wore her sword and her belt, and her hands were clammy with sweat at the prospect of riding into a large town in full armor and weapons. She realized she was grateful for William's formidable presence beside her. Once they were rejoined with Simon and Gerald, they would return to Penhallam with all haste. She had already lost a day in figuring out how to stop Roslyn from obtaining a writ from some pliable official who would declare Robert dead solely on her sister-in-law's insistence.

They led their horses outside the monastery walls accompanied by the prior and swung up into their saddles to bid him farewell. Thomas gazed wistfully at Gwendolyn and silently reached for her hand, which she offered, thinking he only intended a parting clasp. She was taken aback as he solemnly pressed his lips to her fingers, in a gesture of homage, and her cheeks warmed with a fresh flush of blood. The prior stepped back and made room for her and William to turn their horses about and go on their way. At the edge of the meadow, before they entered the woods again, Gwendolyn looked back over her shoulder and saw the prior still standing where they had left him, watching them with a troubled expression.

5

GUESTS OF LAUNCESTON CASTLE

G wendolyn and William rode the path out of the woods and on toward Launceston in silence, their horses walking at a casual pace, side by side. Gwendolyn refused to discuss the bizarre claims of the prior; in fact, she had decided that she would instruct William never to raise the topic again. When they returned to Penhallam she would call for her lords to join her in a council, and she would tell them of Roslyn's threats. She was prepared to fight whatever forces came to Penhallam and her lords would stand with her, not only to protect themselves from Walter's tyranny, but also to stand on the side of Richard, their king.

Launceston was surrounded by a fortified stone wall, and when they arrived at the gatehouse, William announced to the guards who they were and what their business was at the tower. Gwendolyn paid the toll, ignoring the guards' suspicious glances at her sword, and they lowered their spears and moved apart to allow her and William passage.

Launceston was one of the three largest towns of Cornwall, along with Truro and Bodmin, and they jostled their way slowly through narrow lanes paved with stones, their progress slowed by carts and people and wandering livestock. When they finally reached the town center they found a cleared space crowded with merchants' stalls in a loose ring around a well. Gwendolyn finally had a clear view of the tower keep of the castle, high atop a hill overlooking the town. A stone curtain wall encircled the tower, and she could see watchmen walking the battlements high above them, keeping watch over not only the town, but also the surrounding countryside. Launceston had held a strategic position in Cornwall, commanding the Tamar River valley that separated Cornwall from the rest of England, from the time of King Alfred.

She was reminded again that England was in a state of war preparation because of Prince John, and she became uneasy, wondering whether the castellan at Launceston might have found reason to switch his loyalties to the prince. Although King Richard had generously given his younger brother title to Cornwall, the king had wisely kept its four strategic castles—Launceston, Tintagel, Restormel and Tremanton—for himself, held by families and magnates whose loyalty he trusted. Although now at least one of those castles would be in John's hands if Walter de Cardinham had returned to Cornwall, and she wondered how many other of Richard's castles might have turned during the king's prolonged absence.

"William!" she called out, and he turned around in his saddle. "Is it possible . . ." she began, unsure how to voice her concerns without revealing them to any prying ears in the throngs that surrounded them. She edged Bedwyr closer and leaned in toward him. "Could Launceston be in John's control now?" she asked quietly.

William shook his head without hesitation.

"Richard Reynell is the castellan here and at Exeter."

She recognized the name. Richard Reynell was a friend of Robert's. Although he was closer in age to Walter, he had found he shared neither Walter's taste for flamboyance nor his cruelty, or so he had told Robert. It was Richard who started Robert on the path to knighthood, and who had served as a mentor of sorts in place of Walter. Richard Reynell was as stout a supporter of the king as his own mother. He was only a knight, like William, and he was a man whose loyalty was not for sale. And yet, until she actually saw the castellan in person, alive and well, she could not be certain what awaited them.

William glanced down to her sword and tilted his head, signaling her to be ready to draw her weapon. She nodded back, and they turned resolutely toward the tower, directing their horses to climb the steep hill to the gatehouse.

At the top of the hill, the fortress walls loomed even more impressively, and Gwendolyn tried not to think about the size of the garrison that was likely stationed within them. The gatehouse was a large building, three stories high, flanked on either side by the adjoining curtain wall that surrounded the castle. They halted their horses inside the arched passageway, and guards moved into position on either end, their sharp spears blocking both the way in and any escape back out. William told them their names and that they had come to collect their men, who had brought a prisoner from Penhallam the night before.

"Richard Reynell knows me by name," William said patiently, holding a tight rein on his warhorse in the narrow enclosure.

"He's not here," the guard answered a little testily. "But your men are. Go find Barton. He will take you to your men."

The guards moved aside, permitting William and Gwendolyn to ride into the narrow castle yard. As she passed him, Gwendolyn asked the guard, "Who is Barton?"

"The jailor, my lady."

Gwendolyn blinked, then pulled up to a halt beside William as a stable boy ran out to hold their horses for them. She saw Penhallam's cart settled against the wall adjacent to the stables. The yard was a shambles, with scraps of food waste piled in the corners of the yard, picked over by rats, and a discarded shirt, broken wheel, bowls, and the shards of broken pots littering the ground. And although there were men walking the narrow battlements of the curtain walls above her, maybe a half dozen in all, the yard was completely deserted.

"That cart came from Penhallam last night," she said to the boy. "Please harness the horse and prepare it to leave. Tell the groom that I will settle our debt for the horse's lodging when I return. Keep these horses saddled. We won't be long."

The boy nodded shyly and took the reins of their horses, leading them away toward the stables, and she jogged lightly to catch up with William as he strode quickly to the tower and climbed the timber steps in two's to the hall above.

It took a moment for her eyes to adjust as she stepped into the dimly lit hall. The air was smoky from a poorly vented hearth that stood in the center of the room, and immediately her eyes and throat began to sting. She made out William's figure standing to the side of the hearth facing the dais, and she crossed the floor to stand beside him. Several of the garrison's men-at-arms filled the hall, in various states of dress, some eating, some sleeping noisily. A harried-looking young woman carrying a pitcher moved deftly between the men, filling the cups of those who were still awake without disturbing the slumbering forms underfoot. Contrary to outward appearances, in the castellan's absence the formidable stronghold had fallen into disarray, its men ill-prepared to defend any kind of attack. On the dais before them stood a carved, wooden chair, large enough for two men. The man in it almost filled it, and his overfed belly pushed his tunic out over his breeches, completely obscuring whatever belt he might have worn.

"William Rufus, I figured you were going to pay me a visit."

"Where are my men, Barton?"

"And you've brought a lady with you, I see." Barton looked her over slowly, his full lips forming a sneer as he took in her appearance. "Or maybe not," he added in a derisive voice.

"My men, Barton." William's mouth formed a thin line and he moved his hand to the hilt of his sword, but Barton was not to be intimidated so easily. The jailor stroked his beard, tracing the line of his jaw with a greasy finger, his eyes still on Gwendolyn. Following her constable's lead, she took a step closer and shifted her hand to her hilt. Barton's expression changed to a leer, and he said quietly, "How interesting."

"Where is your castellan?" she asked in a commanding tone that momentarily interrupted the jailor's toying glance.

"He has been called to Exeter."

"And this is the state you have allowed this proud tower to fall into in his absence," she chided him, jerking her chin toward the men sleeping and lying around them. At this the jailor straightened in his chair and adjusted whatever belt lay beneath the folds of his ample waist.

"You want to see your men? Follow me. You!" Barton shouted to the man-at-arms nearby who seemed the most sober and in a state of full dress. "Follow behind. If one of their hands reaches for a sword, cut it off."

Barton stood up and turned his broad backside to them, digging an iron ring of keys out of the filthy straw behind him. While his back was turned, William nodded to her with one eyebrow raised, and they followed the jailor down a narrow stairway to the ground level, then down another set of stairs to the dungeon below. A acrid smell filled her nostrils, the smell of human waste left to accumulate and of bodies left to rot. A single torch barely illuminated the large space, and she could see no guards anywhere. Manacles of heavy iron lined the walls and hung from the ceiling. Only a few of them did not hold a prisoner. Some of those unfortunate enough to have been brought to this place appeared to have died long ago.

At the far end of the room she made out the forms of Gerald and Simon, sitting on the floor, their arms in chains. She turned to Barton.

"Release my men." Her voice was barely audible, her jaw fixed.

"I'm afraid I can't do that," Barton answered, a satisfied smile creasing his cheeks. He was relishing the feeling of power over her, and she kept her expression bland. "Your men arrived with a prisoner that they had no authority to hold, who was guilty of no crime."

Gwendolyn opened her mouth to argue, then remembered what she had instructed her men to say, to save the captured mercenary from a summary execution.

"What did you do with the prisoner?"

Barton took a step forward, placing himself between Gwendolyn and William, and leaned forward until his face was only a hand-width away from her cheek.

"I released him, of course," he replied smugly. The jailor leaned back again and smiled at her, daring her to challenge him, and at that moment she heard a muffled thud as the hilt of William's sword struck the back of Barton's head. The jailor's eyes rolled up, his knees gave way, and he slumped into a pile at her feet. Before the man behind her realized what had happened she spun around and smashed her fist into his jaw, sending him over backwards. Both men lay still on the rank floor.

"We only have a moment," William warned, crossing the room to Gerald and Simon. She crouched down and pried the keys from Barton's hand and tossed them across to William, who was already beside Gerald, rousing him. William quickly freed him, and Gerald stood up unsteadily, rubbing his wrists and cursing while William helped Simon to his feet.

"Get moving," he instructed, gesturing toward the doorway and the bodies lying inert on the floor beside it. But then something caught William's eye, and he squinted in the gloomy light.

"It can't be," he said quietly.

He walked quickly up to one of the prisoners who stood in the middle of the floor, the full weight of his sagging body supported only by the hanging manacles, and looked closely at him. Suddenly he fumbled with the keys, unfastened the man's hands, and slapped his face to rouse him. The man was barely conscious, and William shifted his shoulder under the man's arm to bear the man's weight and help him step forward to join them. The man was taller than William, and he had a high, smooth forehead, gaunt cheeks that appeared on the verge of starvation, and pale hair that was long, dirty, and tangled. William moved quickly, half dragging the barely conscious man with him to join them. More slowly than she would have liked, they filed up the stairs to ground level. Gerald and Simon blinked in the daylight and supported the stranger between them as they climbed into the waiting cart, Simon shifting to the bench up front and taking the reins. Gwendolyn and William swung back up on their horses and turned to leave.

A man came running out from the stables shouting, but he stopped as Gwendolyn tossed him her small purse of coins. They crossed the yard and were through the gatehouse without incident. The guard eyed them, but, hearing no alarm, he allowed them passage. The plough horse took the hill down from the castle too fast, and the cart almost tipped all three men out when it leveled out into the square. Gwendolyn overtook William, cutting a path through the crowd. As they finally approached the town gate, Gwendolyn heard a commotion brewing behind her.

"You'd better go see about that," she said to the guards, nodding with her chin toward the growing shouts. As she had hoped, the guards mechanically grabbed their spears and ran toward the noise. She and William exited the gate out of the city as the portcullis dropped down behind them.

She pressed her knees against Bedwyr's sides and shifted forward in the saddle, urging the mare into a gentle lope, the fastest she dared go while being careful not to leave the cart behind. They continued at this pace for two miles, until they were certain that they had not been followed. From what she had seen in the hall, Gwendolyn doubted whether Barton or any of his men would be keen to give chase and leave the comfort of the tower keep.

They finally stopped at a stream to water the horses and tend to their passengers in the cart. Simon and Gerald had perked up considerably, but the third man looked weak and sickly, although he was awake and appeared to be aware of his surroundings. Gwendolyn dismounted and was nearly knocked over by an enthusiastic embrace from Gerald.

"Nicely done, my lady!" he exclaimed.

She pushed him away with a friendly shove, struggling not to make a face at the smell of his soiled clothing. "Knew I'd find you lying around enjoying the scenery," she said, handing him an oilskin filled with water. Gerald took a long draw from the oilskin and handed it to Simon. She glanced at their wrists, scraped and bleeding. "Put those in the cold water," she said, gesturing toward the stream. "It will help with the swelling and ease the pain."

William raised an eyebrow at her and she shrugged. "I listen to your father too," she said. She walked over to the cart to stand beside him, looking with concern at the man smiling weakly at her.

"This is Eric," William said. "We trained together."

Gwendolyn was certain there was more to the man's story than William was telling her, but she would wait for him to fill her in later. William had given the man his own oilskin, which he was carefully drawing from in small sips, although he appeared parched. He finally handed the water back to William, looked at Gwendolyn with lids half-closed, and smiled again.

"You are an angel," Eric said in a barely audible rasp.

William rolled his eyes. "He's going to be fine. In a few days you'll wish we'd left him at Launceston."

They arrived at Penhallam in the late afternoon, and the first thing Gwendolyn noticed was the quiet. She scanned the valley uneasily; men and women working the rows of fields nodded to them without smile or greeting as they rode past. Songbirds and farm animals filled the air with their familiar calls and bleats, but the village felt dreary somehow, even in the soft sunlight and long shadows. She twisted in her saddle to look back at William, and his face reflected her own apprehension. Turning forward again, she nudged Bedwyr to a trot. Out of habit she slowed to a walk as she entered the lanes between the shops and cottages and then realized there was no need. No children darted precariously around her and William's horses, chasing each other and playing games. The absence of their familiar shouts and laughter now registered with her, and her stomach fluttered inside her with panic. Pulling Bedwyr to a stop, she scanned the lanes and timber houses and yards. Shutters had been drawn and latched, doors were closed; no one milled about in the lanes who did not have a need to be there. She dismounted and handed Bedwyr's reins to William while she walked to the nearest cottage and knocked softly on the door.

Hawise, Martha's mother and Penhallam's midwife, opened the door a crack, recognized her, and smiled with relief.

"What's happened?" Gwendolyn asked. Hawise's children timidly peeked out from behind her skirts. Gwendolyn breathed her own sigh of relief at the sight of them.

"This morning, my lady, more of those men. They attacked Young Hugh while he walked the pigs beside the woods. Gamel is with him now."

Gwendolyn exhaled sharply and uttered a curse under her breath. Young Hugh was Anne's brother, a slight bundle of mischief named for his father. But if Gamel was with him, then the boy still lived.

"How many men?" She immediately thought of the prisoner Barton had released from Launceston.

"We chased four of them, but they all got away, back into the woods. And these men carried swords, my lady," she added. "No ordinary outlaws travel so well armed as these men."

Gwendolyn stared at Hawise for a moment, imagining the entire village, farm scythes, hoes, and clubs raised, charging with enough ferociousness to turn back four armed men. The rough and injured man William captured two days before was not part of this group. And if they carried swords, they could only have been more mercenaries. No knight or other household man-at-arms would attack a boy for his pigs.

She turned around in time to meet Simon as he drove the cart into the lane, Gerald sitting beside him on the bench and Eric asleep in the cart behind them.

"Take Eric to my father's house," William called to Simon, and then turned to Gwendolyn. "I'll get him settled there. Meet me in the hall."

She nodded and William led Bedwyr away as she continued on foot to Anne's house. Gamel stepped out of the cottage as she arrived, his brow deeply furrowed.

"You're back already? That's good. We need every man with a sword here now, it seems," he said, rubbing the lines in his forehead with a bony hand.

"Will Young Hugh be okay?"

Gamel looked at her gravely. "I don't know," he said, shaking his head. "He took a hard blow to the head. He has not yet woken up. I've stopped the bleeding, wrapped the wound; now it's between him and God. We'll know by morning."

Gwendolyn reached to put a hand on the old man's arm, but Gamel took her hand into his and studied it, gingerly turning it over in his hand. Only then did she register that her hand throbbed painfully.

"I believe this is broken, my lady."

She pulled her hand back, eyed the swollen knuckle, gave Gamel a half-smile.

"Not the first time. Won't be the last."

Gamel looked at her with softened eyes and shook his head. "You are your father's daughter. The bones must be bound to heal correctly."

Gwendolyn nodded. "Come find me in the hall when you're

ready. And I'll send Osbert to your house with bread and meat for your pottage." She waved away the old man's protests. "You have another patient waiting for you at home, a friend of William's. And from the look of him, I expect he's going to be eating a lot."

Gamel straightened himself up and shook his shoulders back. He bid her goodnight and walked with forced vigor back toward his own home to face his next patient.

When Gwendolyn entered Anne's family cottage, she paused first with the door slightly open and waited for permission to enter. Aveline motioned her into the room and turned back toward her son. Covered with a light blanket, Hugh lay on a straw pallet, looking small and helpless. His younger sister, Isolde, sat on her knees on the hard earth beside him, her small arm forming a protective arc in the straw around his bandaged head. She rested her head in the crook of her elbow, with her eyes closed. Anne stood at the hearth and nodded to Gwendolyn with dry eyes. Aveline's husband, Old Hugh, sat on a stool beside his son, while Aveline stood behind him with her hands on his shoulders.

Gwendolyn drew near to Aveline and stood quietly beside her, looking down at the figure of her son sleeping peacefully. She was at a loss for words in the midst of the family's vigil. Finally she placed her hand on top of Aveline's, small and fine like Anne's, and rested it there for a moment. There was nothing else to do and nothing to say. Gwendolyn took her leave from the family to join William in the manor house.

Inside the yard, Simon unharnessed the cart horse, lifting the heavy collar over its head while speaking in soft tones to soothe it. Her groom had not eaten in over a day and his breeches were soiled from his time in the dungeon, and still he tended to the horse first before seeing to his own needs. The horse stamped its feet impatiently and tugged at its lead, ready to be brought to the stables and fed.

"I've got this," she said to Simon.

"My lady," Simon said gratefully, and ducked toward the stables to find clean clothing for himself. Isabel stepped out from the stables, brushing straw from her tunic. She reached out and lifted the heavy harness from Simon's grasp and carried it back to its post to be hung and cleaned. She mumbled a polite greeting to Gwendolyn as she passed, which Gwendolyn returned, noting that Isabel plainly knew her way around horses and their keep. Even better, she seemed not to mind hard work. Gwendolyn stooped to check the horse's hooves and legs for soundness, and, with Isabel's assistance, settled both it and Bedwyr in the stables with a fragrant portion of hay. Gwendolyn went over to Bedwyr and checked her legs and hooves in the same fashion while the mare playfully nipped at her braid as it swung down in front of her. As Gwendolyn stooped over to pick up a hind hoof, a small bundle dropped into the straw before her, and she reached curiously for it. She recognized the small scroll from her father. The day's events had completely pushed the priory visit from her mind, and the letter felt foreign to her now, out of place here in her home at Penhallam. She tucked the scroll back into her surcoat, wondering how long her father had held the same scroll after the prior had finished writing it for him.

Gwendolyn entered the hall quietly, listening to the conversation underway between William and Tom, who were conferring at the trestle table.

"We need more men," Tom said forcefully to William as she approached.

"I've brought you more. As soon as he's on his feet, he'll be looking for a sword." William paused at her arrival. "If that's okay with you," he added, looking in her direction.

"If you vouch for him, he's welcome in the household."

"One man isn't enough, William! We need at least three." Tom slammed his hand on the table in front of him in exasperation and stood up.

"Eric Longbeard is worth three men."

Tom regarded William with his jaw thrust out, ready to protest. But William returned his gaze calmly, and Tom understood the conversation was ended.

"He'd better be on his feet within the week, William. We have no idea what's headed our way."

Gwendolyn silently watched Tom leave. The older knight acknowledged her with a simple "my lady," keeping his eyes directed forward as he passed. The attack on Young Hugh had happened on his watch. She knew Tom well enough to know that anything kind she might have said would have felt to him like pity. She waited several moments for him to be out of earshot before she spoke to William.

"Tom may still be right. People are scared. Bring in every man and woman with strength and size to train with the garrison. Their farm tools can be as deadly as battle-axes. Teach them to use them. And they need to learn to take a hit," she added, remembering the shock of the first blow to her jaw that had sent her onto her back, dazed and helpless. "Even if Eric is as you say, I doubt he would argue against any additional advantage we can muster."

William nodded and turned to leave when the pressure of her father's letter tucked into her surcoat reminded her of one more thing she wanted to settle between them.

"And William," she added, "I don't want a word repeated about what the prior had to say last night. Not to me or anyone else."

William turned and looked at her, folding his arms across his chest.

"You saved my life," she continued. "For that I owe you—"

"Nothing." William said firmly. "Whatever debt there may have been between us was settled long ago. You and Robert have given me a home, I have eaten at your table for years, and you have looked after my family like all other families at Penhallam."

Gwendolyn considered William's words for a moment. "And there will be no more mention of Arthur or Caliburn."

William looked disappointed, but he grudgingly agreed.

"Not a word."

Gamel entered the hall behind William, carrying strips of cloth and a wooden splint.

"If you're ready, my lady," Gamel said, standing beside William. William paused and she smiled and held up her injured hand, now an impressive black and purple around the middle knuckle.

William huffed lightly and turned to leave. "That should keep you out of trouble for a few days, anyway."

The next morning, Gwendolyn awoke before sunrise. Martha still slept peacefully across from her on the feather mattress that she usually shared with Anne. Gwendolyn quietly picked up her wooden shoes, draped her cloak across her shoulders, and awkwardly fished the scroll from her surcoat with her bound fingers. She pulled the heavy door to her room slowly open, only enough to allow her to squeeze through. None of the manor guard stirred as she padded on bare feet across the hall to the cold stone stairs and out into the star-studded darkness. Sliding her feet into her shoes, she walked out of the manor yard, over the moat bridge and toward the palisade across the stream. She walked with soft steps across the timber bridge toward Penhallam's outbuildings, but instead turned right to follow the banks of the stream, walking north until she reached the point behind the manor where the two streams that flanked it joined to form a slower, deeper stream that cut north to the sea.

She unbraided her hair, slipped out of her clothes, and walked into the dark, swirling water, feeling the current push against her as she gritted her teeth against the chill. The stars above reflected in the dancing water like a shimmering veil spread around her. Her skin stung with the cold, but she kept moving her body and forced herself to completely submerge her head and rinse the dirt of the road from her hair. She stood up again and vigorously rubbed her arms and neck, washing off a week's worth of dirt and sweat, then splashed the cool water into her face before carefully stepping back to the banks to dress again. Hanging wet, her hair reached past her hips, and she bent her head forward to comb the fingers of her left hand through the thick strands, trying to massage out some of the worst tangles. After a few failed attempts, she gave up and resorted to twisting her hair into a thick rope to wring out as much of the water as she could.

Sunrise had begun to fade out the stars in the east, and she climbed the stream bank and walked back toward the timber palisade, seating herself on the ground out of sight of the manor house with her back against the timbers. She drew her knees up to her chest, wrapped her arms around them, and created a warm tent with her cloak. Dawn had not yet broken, and she listened to the familiar sounds around her as the manor slowly roused to life. The problems she faced loomed large in her mind, and she was not entirely sure how to solve any of them. Follow your heart, her father had told her. But her heart could not tell her how to stop Roslyn from using her family's connections to force her from Penhallam. Even if the declaration of Robert's death were nullified later when Robert returned, the havoc that Roslyn and Walter could wreak upon Penhallam and its families in the intervening time would take years to recover from. And in the meantime, Prince John's mercenaries would continue passing through, more brazen with each encounter, picking off and stealing from the people she had promised to protect.

She reached into her cloak and pulled out the vellum scroll and began to absently stroke the ends of the ribbon between her fingers, considering her options. She could travel to Winchester to seek an audience with Walter de Coutances, the king's chief justiciar, but next to Roslyn she was no one. And without even a dress to wear, she would have to show up wearing a man's tunic and breeches, and the justiciar might arrest her for that just to make a point. She considered seeking out Hubert Walter, who was the king's favored counselor even if he was not yet officially Archbishop of Canterbury, but if he somehow learned a word about what the prior had told her, she would be locked up as a heretic.

And lying low in Penhallam doing nothing was not an option. Roslyn was desperate, and when she found out what Walter had been doing when he was supposed to have been in London, she would become even more so. Gwendolyn had to come up with a way to get in front of her sister-in-law's schemes, to protect Penhallam from John's rebellion and cut off Roslyn all at once.

She looked up and saw Anne in the distance, walking in the direction of the manor house, and hoped that this meant good news, that Young Hugh had woken up. Moving quickly, she joined Anne as she reached the bridge over the moat.

Anne's face was composed; she had always managed to bury well inside her whatever private burdens she carried.

"How is Young Hugh?" Gwendolyn asked her maid gently.

"He's awake and talking." Gwendolyn immediately smiled at this news. "But he sees nothing but a bit of light and shadow. Gamel says his sight may return with time, but..." She hesitated and cleared her throat. "He says to begin teaching him to find his way by touch and sound as soon as he's steady on his feet." She took a deep, slow breath and forced a little smile. "Izzy hasn't left his side in all this time."

Gwendolyn exhaled as if the air had been knocked out of her. Young Hugh was Aveline and Hugh's only son, and he had a knowing way with animals that had already caught the notice of Simon and Gerry, the overseer of the manor's herds of livestock. But blind, unable to find his charges or observe their ailments, his usefulness was diminished, perhaps beyond redemption.

"He can't be allowed to feel sorry for himself. That's why Gamel wants him up and moving as soon as he's able. To begin learning over again how to do the things he did before."

"Yes," Gwendolyn agreed, wondering how much that was really possible. "I'll have Simon ready for him as soon as Isolde can bring him to the stables."

"Thank you, my lady," she said, turning to look at Gwendolyn closely for the first time that morning. "My lady, you're a mess! Your hair!" She placed her fists on her hips and shook her head at her. "Why do you never let me draw a bath for you like any other fine lady?"

Gwendolyn smiled at the scolding, and for the brief time that Anne helped her to dress and comb her hair, she chatted lightly about William's plans to train the village men and women, and the fighting strength of the man they had brought back from Launceston. Not once did she allow the true extent of the troubles that weighed on her to surface. Anne's own troubles were more than enough.

Her first stop that morning was Gamel's cottage, to check on their guest. Despite what William had said, she knew there was a good chance she would find the man broken with fever, closer to death than the day before.

As soon as she had passed through the low doorway, however, she realized that she need not have worried. Eric was already awake, sitting upright on the pallet that he had slept on, his long legs swung over the side and feet planted squarely on the floor. His face was obscured by the large wooden bowl that he tipped to his mouth, draining the last of a broth. Alice, William's mother, stood beside him, waiting patiently for the empty bowl. A woman of few words, Alice nodded a greeting to Gwendolyn, grunted in reply to Eric's words of thanks, and disappeared into the kitchen at the back of the apothecary.

Eric smiled broadly at Gwendolyn, the ashen color on his cheeks from the previous day replaced already by a pale flush of pink, his eyes wide open and bright. With a little difficulty, he braced a hand against the pallet and pushed himself to standing. She could see that he had the looks and build of the people of the Danelaw, the northern region of England's Yorkshire coast where waves of Vikings had arrived in boats centuries ago to burn and plunder villages and carry the loot back to their homelands. After a time the flaxen-haired invaders had also discovered fertile farmland beneath their feet, and many stayed behind to begin a different life among the English. At his full height Eric would be taller than William, she realized, and he bowed his head slightly to avoid striking the thatched roof above him. Even in his emaciated state his frame was broad and solid. He took a step toward her slowly, his hand outstretched to her in greeting, and she fought the impulse to cover her nose at the smell that emanated from his clothing.

"I am in your debt, my lady," he said roughly, the rasp in his throat not yet healed. His hand was warm when she grasped it, and his grip was hard and strong.

"Then I hope you will stay to repay your debt once you have healed," she answered, and as Eric took his seat again on the pallet and listened quietly, she told him about the mercenaries and the threats facing Penhallam, including Roslyn. She noted that he made no remark about her masculine clothes or her sword and belt. The women of the Danelaw were known to be independent and fierce in a fight—qualities that were praised and admired in their songs and stories. When she finished talking he looked at her approvingly.

"You have accomplished all of this in your husband's absence?"

She nodded in reply and he shook his head, laughing softly.

"Well, I would have fought for you anyway, until my obligation was paid, but now I shall fight proudly. You have more sense in you than most of the men I've known."

"And you," she said, raising an eyebrow, "tell me how you came to be Barton's prisoner."

Eric smiled impishly. "I have a knack for pissing off the wrong man. Particularly husbands."

Gwendolyn felt her cheeks flush at the confession. She turned as William entered the doorway behind her, followed by his father.

"By the Devil's breath," William exclaimed, clearly pleased to see his friend recovering so quickly. "Look who's up!"

Eric raised himself to a standing position again, leaning against the pallet frame with a strained smile.

"The sooner you get those legs working again, the better," Gamel commented brusquely with his back turned. He emptied handfuls of fresh herbs from his mantle onto the table in the corner of the room and began to sort them into bundles for drying. William hung three rabbits, gathered that morning from the snares and freshly gutted, on a hook in the wall. The old man began to cough lightly, but the cough grew into a hollow rattle that was painful to hear. Gwendolyn watched concern shadow William's face, and he laid a hand on his father's arm. Gamel brushed his son's attention away with an irritated wave of his hand. Gwendolyn recalled something Hawise, the midwife, had said to her once about physicians being terrible patients.

"It's just a bit of dust," Gamel snapped. "I'm fine."

Alice walked in from the back of the cottage carrying a wooden cup that steamed with a concoction of dried herbs and flowers and handed it to Gamel. Her husband ignored her while he meticulously tied little knots of twine around the bundles of herbs.

"Make sure he drinks that," she called to William as she set the cup down loudly on the table in front of her husband. She leaned over close to Gamel's ear and added, "All of it." Gamel gave no acknowledgment, but Alice's hand lingered softly on her husband's arm for a moment as she turned to retrieve the rabbits and take them back to the kitchen in the rear room. "And for the love of the saints, William, get that man some clean clothes," she ordered before returning to the kitchen.

William looked doubtfully at Eric, who still leaned his tall frame against the pallet. "I don't think I have anything large enough to fit you."

"I do," Gwendolyn said. "When you are strong enough to walk to the manor and climb the stairs, I'm sure Anne can find clothes and boots in the de Cardinham chests that will serve. The baron was as tall as an alder, after all." She headed toward the door, but paused with one more thought. "William, take our guest to the armory and give him whatever he requires." She turned toward Eric. "I will pay the cost to arm you. I have a feeling you will repay the investment many times over."

While William and Tom patrolled the woods that morning, Gwendolyn joined the castle guard in training, pushing herself and the men to exhaustion. Her left arm tired and weakened too quickly, and when she and Gerald faced off against each other with staffs, the confrontation ended with a satisfying new cut above her brow. Later in the afternoon, she made rounds through the village, taking stock of who would work the long days of harvest, who would train with the guard to learn the ways of using a scythe as a weapon. She did not check on Young Hugh, wishing to leave the family in peace as they adjusted to their altered lives. But the next morning she carried bread and a cloth bundle of salted mutton to their house. Gwendolyn stood outside next to Aveline as she anxiously watched her son stumble in the lane and fall while Isolde stood several paces away, guiding him with her voice. Aveline held her hand over her mouth to muffle her concerned gasps, then finally turned away to go back into the house when she could take no more.

"It is a mother's most difficult work," she said as they entered the cottage together.

"What's that?" Gwendolyn asked, wondering if Aveline referred to the work of tending her children when they were ill.

"Allowing them the leave to make their own mistakes, even to fail. But it is the only way. I don't know how much he's capable of, and I would rob him of the chance to find out if I tried to shelter him from the pain of trying."

Gwendolyn paused for a moment to wonder at Aveline's wisdom. Anne's mother was right, and it explained her chambermaid's quiet self-confidence. Before she left, Gwendolyn had to insist forcefully to get Aveline to accept the meat; she only relented when Gwendolyn told her that Young Hugh could earn it back by returning to help Simon in the stables as soon as he was able.

Her morning errand done, Gwendolyn walked back toward the house, flexing her arms and shoulders to prepare herself for the morning's training in the manor yard. While she walked, she found herself reflecting on the work of motherhood—an undertaking with which she had no experience and little memory of her own days under its influence. Did all mothers wrestle with the same impulses as Aveline, knowing when to shelter and when to step away? Birds pushed their little ones to fly, sometimes even knocking them out of the nest. Gwendolyn had always found their actions cruel, but now, through Aveline's eyes, she saw such prodding toward independence in a new light. Something nagged at Gwendolyn's thoughts, like the answer to a riddle floating just beneath the surface. She stood still for a moment and paused her thoughts. She had learned that the best way to find an answer was to stop chasing it, and she turned her gaze down the valley, taking in the low ripples of green that stretched out to the horizon. A few moments later she broke into a run across the bridge toward the palisade and the buildings within.

"William!" she shouted, running toward the armory.

Her constable stepped out of the long, narrow building, the alarm on his face easing as he saw her elated expression.

"I know what to do," she said a little breathlessly, and paused to lean over for a moment with her hands on her knees. William regarded her with a quizzical look.

"I know how to deal with Roslyn and stop John's mercenaries, and maybe even John."

6

THE MERCENARY RETURNS

"It's too dangerous," William said after she had laid out her idea to him. "You are walking into a den of wolves if you go to London."

"Eleanor is a mother. She will listen."

"She is a queen first, and you'll pay with your life if you forget that."

"She doesn't want John to die, and if he keeps this up, that's exactly where he's headed." Gwendolyn stepped back and fixed her eyes on William, wondering if it was even possible for him to understand the visceral bond between mother and child. "She has buried three sons already. After Richard, only John is left. As both a queen and a mother, she needs John to live."

Gwendolyn stared at William and set her jaw. After so many years in her company, she expected he knew too well that her thoughts were as firmly locked as her expression.

"I will consult with my lords. I can't tell them everything, obviously. But if they agree to the idea, we will leave as soon as Eric has his strength back," she added. "And we will travel alone. I can't leave Tom shorthanded."

William hesitated for a moment and held her gaze. "Eric can do more than fight, Gwendolyn. He was a captain of his own mercenary company. He led them to Palestine with King Richard. With your permission I will leave him in charge of the garrison, over Tom."

"Do it, then, and there's no time to settle him in. We must get to London as quickly as possible. Roslyn may have decided to make a move and appeal to the Chancery herself to have Robert declared dead. There's no time to spare."

Gwendolyn walked quickly across to the manor house, thinking of all of the preparations she would have to make. Being away from Penhallam during the harvest was unappealing, but she knew she could rely on Osbert to oversee the hard work. At the moment her first concern was how quickly Eric could regain his strength, so she was pleased to find him seated on a stool in the hall when she entered from the stairwell.

"You are a welcome sight," she said, noticing his improved appearance even since the last morning. His hair hung in wet ropes past his shoulders, and the filth and dirt of the dungeon was gone from his skin and nails. He had also shaved off his beard, and his cheekbones and jawline were chiseled and strong. She realized now, looking at him, that he was quite handsome. He was shirtless, and she guessed he must have washed in the stream before coming up to the hall to dress in fresh clothes. "Stay there a moment while I rummage through the trunks for you," she said, turning toward her room. Just then, Anne stepped out from the passage to the private chamber, her arms stacked with shirts, padded linens to be worn under armor, and other assorted garments.

"Good morning, ma'am," she said efficiently, walking briskly past her. "Thought I'd go ahead and get this one sorted out." She placed the stack on the table in front of Eric, hardly looking at him. "Right, then, I'll leave you to it. Take whatever you like, leave the rest." She turned to face Gwendolyn. "Your armor, my lady?"

Eric's face had turned a vivid red behind them, and he kept his eyes cast downward to the table's surface. Gwendolyn had the distinct feeling of having intruded on something, and she carefully kept herself from smiling at the thought of what it might have been.

⁓

As Gwendolyn had hoped, Eric continued to regain his strength steadily. His weapon of choice, a large battle-axe that had been favored by the late baron, had been repaired and reinforced, and the blade honed to breathtaking sharpness. The axe's staff was as tall as a man, awkward and difficult to swing. But in Eric's hands the weapon parted the air like a falcon diving—precise, deadly and beautiful to watch. Eric's movements were graceful and confident, and his reach gave him even further advantage in combat.

He quickly earned the respect of the manor's men-at-arms with his instruction in fighting techniques brought back from Palestine. He spent hours in the yard with them to bring back his own strength—but also to learn each man's skill and character. He trained with each of them one-on-one and taught them how to better exploit their particular strengths and compensate for their weaknesses. When Gwendolyn took her turn against him, he had laughed with pleasure at the forcefulness of her attacks and her immunity to intimidation. The men responded to the attention, and Gwendolyn took note as the guard as a whole seemed to take on a new sense of brotherhood and pride. Eric was more relaxed with the men than William, making coarse jokes and teasing them good-naturedly. Within a short time the garrison transformed into a tightly disciplined unit. Where William had commanded the men, Eric was a natural leader, and he inspired the men to follow. His deference to Anne, however, was unmistakable. Although her maid's every outward sign showed indifference to the courtship, Gwendolyn had seen Anne rebuff suitors in no uncertain terms numerous times since coming into womanhood. This was the first time that she had permitted the attention to continue.

"We can leave tomorrow, my lady, if you are ready," William announced one night as they all quietly took their supper in the hall. Two weeks had passed since the day Gwendolyn had told William of her plan. In that time, all of the necessary preparations had been made. Osbert understood the work cycles and order of tasks for the harvest. Crude but effective arms had been distributed to the village and surrounding farmsteads. Isabel had awkwardly requested that she might stay at Penhallam through the winter, and her request had been gladly received by Simon and Osbert. The horses' hooves had been trimmed and freshly shod for the long journey. And when another small band of mercenaries, armed and on foot, had crossed Penhallam on their way to St. Michael's Mount, Tom and the manor guard had intercepted them with fatal results. Her injured hand had healed and the strength had returned to her grip. There was no reason to wait another day.

She looked around the hall at the faces of Penhallam's lords, knights, and squires, the families from the village that had joined them for the evening meal, Gamel, Anne, Young Hugh, and Eric. She and William had told her council of lords that they would travel to London to appeal for Robert's return and to petition the queen's intercession with Roslyn. The idea of Penhallam's case being raised in the royal court with the support of Eleanor had captured their imaginations and would elevate their small estate, they reckoned, to a status level with the great baronial manors of Cornwall, even that of Walter's Restormel.

"Yes," she answered as the room erupted into cheers. "We will leave in the morning."

"There's so much to see in London!" Martha said excitedly, still a little disappointed not to be joining her. "I can't imagine how elegant the ladies' dresses are there, and the fine ribbons and veils."

Gwendolyn huffed into her ale cup at the idea of wasting her coins on such baubles, causing a murmur of laughter to rumble across the hall.

"With luck, William and I will return before All Souls' Day. And the only ribbons we'll be carrying will be wrapped around a writ from Eleanor."

Gerald stood with his cup raised and swept his gaze around the room, his face already flushed from the ale.

"My lady," he began, bowing deeply, "I humbly request that you speak a toast in honor of your departure to go before the queen." He turned around to the room again with his arms stretched out from his sides, and calls of "A toast!" and "Baroness!" rippled the air around her.

She paused in her seat, waiting for the shouts to abate, and took a moment to consider her words. These opportunities were rare, and she liked to use them to point with laughter at the arbitrary customs that made skill with a sword, in a woman's hands, something to be ashamed of. When the hall had quieted down and all eyes were turned her way, she stood up and crossed the hall to the carved horn hanging on the wall beside the hearth. The horn had not been brought down from its hook since the night before Robert's departure, and it seemed fitting to bring it down on this night, to sanctify the journey ahead. Shouts of approval erupted again as she turned around, the horn held high in front of her. Tom rose and crossed to her with the jug of ale, filling the horn to the top and sloshing the overflow onto the straw below.

Gwendolyn smiled slyly and raised the horn over her head as the hall grew quiet again.

"Here's to our horses and here's to our men, and here's to the women who ride them both!" It was an old Breton toast, a favorite of Robert's father, but she had reversed the sexes from the traditional verse, giving the women the upper hand. The hall erupted into hoots and laughter, and Gwendolyn felt her chest tighten with affection for each person around her and in all of Penhallam, and she sent a silent prayer to whoever might be listening that this was not the last time they would stand together in this hall.

William was up before dawn packing their provisions, filling oilskins with water, and giving Eric last details about the layout of the land and the vulnerable places where the guard's watch should be doubled. He had watched with disappointment the night before when Gwendolyn had crossed the hall to take down the horn for the toast. She was unaccustomed to so much ale, and last night's drink had been for celebration—rich and strong. The headache he expected her to have this morning would slow them down and leave her more obstinate than usual.

When Gwendolyn joined him shortly after sunrise, she went about her business wordlessly, her mouth a grim line. She wore a fresh tunic, leggings, and her leather boots. Anne had combed her hair and plaited it into the usual braid. Her cloak was thrown back over her shoulders, and he saw that her sword and dagger both hung from their sheaths on her belt. However she might be feeling, he realized, she had not let it compromise her preparations to leave. Anne told him that she had also packed Gwendolyn's surcoat bearing the de Cardinham colors into a satchel that included a second tunic and leggings, and secured the bag to Gwendolyn's saddle. William waited patiently while the squire tied the bundle of her hauberk behind the satchel and she took one last draw of water from the oilskin Simon offered her. Finally, with just one acknowledging glance in William's direction, she firmly placed her foot in the stirrup, took hold of the saddle with both hands, and lifted herself up and astride her mare.

They rode through the day in near silence, speaking only a

few words when they stopped to eat or give the horses a rest. They followed the same road to the southeast toward Launceston, but before they got too close to the town, William led them on a detour to skirt around to the east in case Barton or his men might still bear a grudge. After they passed Launceston they turned east and crossed the Tamar River by ferry. The river valley lay shrouded in thick mist, and the horses stamped their hooves nervously during the crossing. The hair on William's arms prickled as they set foot on Devonshire soil, and he took notice as a shiver ran up his spine. He knew there was good reason for the feeling of foreboding that even the horses had seemed to sense.

The entire county of Devon had been set aside as a royal forest, governed by the king's forest law. Hunting was forbidden, except for the lesser birds and rodents, and poachers could be hung by the neck or worse. No trees could be felled, and the only farming and grazing allowed was what had already been in place when the Normans had first arrived more than five generations back. The towns of Devonshire had grown in the last hundred years, and the enforced preservation of lumber and fields had become a problem for laity and clergy alike.

Because of the forest law restrictions, Devon also had preserved within its borders the structures and marks of those ancient peoples, pagans and spellworkers, who had lived there in ages gone by. The remains of their long houses, fortresses, and pasture walls—many of them still in use where possible—stood as visible reminders of days long past and now forgotten. For William, other reminders also remained, undisturbed and timeless. The traces of old spells and rituals lay across the land like a web of invisible pathways, connecting wells to sacred tors and their places of worship in between them. Here in the wilderness, magic was still a living thing, as potent as the day it was first cast.

"We should make camp soon, my lady," William shouted over his shoulder to Gwendolyn. She looked so miserable and tired that he laughed quietly to himself when she answered him with a mute nod. Gwendolyn had pulled her cloak up around her shoulders and she sat hunched in the saddle against the chilling wind. There was good grazing here for the horses, and he recalled the stiffness that set into the bones when the body was unaccustomed to long hours of riding. A little farther on they reached a small, shallow stream where they dismounted to water the horses and fill their oilskins.

"We'll stay here tonight," William said, scanning the area with his eyes narrowed. The banks of the stream were thick with brushes and hedges that would conceal their camp, and the surrounding grass was thick and green. Once they had settled in with the horses grazing contentedly nearby, they spread their blankets on the ground and arranged their saddles to support their heads. Gwendolyn handed William a large share of the smoked fish that she had bought from a stall beside the ferry crossing at the Tamar. William was relieved to see her appetite returned, and she fell asleep within minutes of finishing her small meal and stretching herself out on her blankets.

He watched her soberly, wondering what dangers he led her toward. When they entered towns, they could expect the usual jeers and challenges thrown at her by strangers who took offense at her attire and the weapons she carried. As long as he stayed nearby, these were only slightly concerning. But John and his desire for Caliburn was another thing, and Gwendolyn refused to exercise caution against a threat that she did not believe existed. Worse still, once they reached London and the royal court, he would be powerless to protect her. The proposition she intended to make to Eleanor, if she could even gain an audience with the dowager queen, was far-fetched at best. And Eleanor could find other uses for her. It was not unheard of for a marriage to be annulled to allow a baron or other magnate to take for a wife whichever woman the man's fancy had chosen, regardless of her husband's protests.

Gwendolyn stirred in her sleep across the fire from him, pulling her cloak up to her ears. Quietly, he approached and crouched down to touch her cheek. Her skin and fingers were chilled, and a wet mist began to fall as darkness settled around them. William hesitated for a moment, then retrieved his own blanket and returned to lay himself down cautiously beside her, watching her closely for any sign of waking. Making camp out in the open, he knew he would not sleep unless he could be certain he would awaken instantly if she moved. He eased his cloak over both of them and hesitated, but she remained fast asleep. He dropped his arm across her waist and fell quickly into a deep and dreamless sleep.

Gwendolyn awoke in the morning to find William bundled close behind her, and as she blinked in the morning light, she realized that she had not slept alone. She sat up and turned around to look at him. The only man that she had ever slept so closely beside was her husband.

"You were cold, my lady," he said simply.

If it had been anyone else, she would have considered the move presumptuous to the point of insult. But this was William. She had no doubts about his intentions, and however competent she was in defending herself, the fact was that while they travelled alone, she was safer sleeping in her constable's grasp than not.

William stood up and began gathering their belongings, avoiding her eyes. He handed her a bread roll for breakfast and walked away to collect the horses. Thankfully the fog and nausea from the previous day had passed, and she felt her appetite return with a vengeance.

They rode through a fine drizzle that morning that soaked through their clothing and dripped into their eyes. The dampness had turned the cobbled roads slippery, slowing their progress. As they carefully picked their way over the slick stones, Gwendolyn found her thoughts wandering. Waking next to William that morning had taken her back to the brief time she and Robert had spent together as husband and wife before he left to join the king's crusade.

She had never been sure of Robert's affection toward her, even after their marriage. During the summer of her fifteenth year, despite the extensive education she had given herself in Restormel's library, the baron had found a young man of acceptable parentage who would have her. The third son of a scholar from Exeter, he had a brutish disposition and claimed her education was only a sham, given the feeble nature of the feminine mind. Robert happened to have been home on a visit when the young man and his parents came to meet Gwendolyn and make their decision. Gwendolyn recalled how Robert had sat quietly at the table during the evening meal, watching the young man closely and listening to every word from the parents, particularly the would-be groom's snobbish mother. On the next day, Robert had found her in her sitting place at the top of Restormel's tower, joking with the castle's day watchman about the snooty habits of their visitors. Robert had asked her to walk with him, and she had hopped down and taken his hand, the same as she had done since their childhood days together. Except this time he had taken her on a path across the fields and to an ancient tor that overlooked all of Bodardel, and here he had asked her to consider him as an alternative to the scholar's son. She remembered the shock that had hit her then, never having imagined that she herself would become a member of the de Cardinham family. But the shock had only lasted for a moment. She had folded her arms and regarded him with a raised eyebrow. She was certain that her expression had been full of mocking—in the way only achievable by teenaged girls.

"Robert, there are many ladies far better suited for you. Why would you throw away the opportunity to make a strong match for yourself to marry a girl with no name, no status, and no wealth? Unless you've fallen in love with me, that is." Even then, she would not have teased him so mercilessly if she had had any suspicion that he bore an actual affection for her.

"You're right, I'm not in love with you," he had answered off-handedly, then lightly placed his fist against her shoulder; that one gesture was the only leftover between them from their rough-and-tumble childhood games. She had stood quietly while he explained to her at length his plan for acquiring a title and building Penhallam into an estate that would rival his older brother's holdings at Restormel. It turned out that growing up as Walter's younger brother had only been a little less tortuous than growing up as the baron's ward. Robert had already seen the signs of waste and neglect taking hold of Restormel. He planned to take up the cross and join their new king on crusade; he would prove himself in battle and earn the king's favor, which would eventually be rewarded with land and a title—such dispensations possible only from the throne itself.

"And you," he had added at last, "must hold Penhallam and see to its defense and survival in my absence. There is no other woman so qualified to do this as you."

Her thoughts had already raced of ahead of him, and she had seen clearly what purpose he set forth for her and what it would require. The thought made her smile, and she had leaned back, thinking of the vow she had made to herself just a few years ago when she had first read Plato's words. She had straightened up and become deadly serious.

"I want a sword."

"And you shall have one."

She had turned sixteen shortly after their wedding, and although her body bore all the signs of womanhood and she bled regularly with the moon's cycles, Robert did not touch her as a husband. She knew that men and women coupled their bodies, as she had discreetly spied in Restormel's hall on those nights when she awoke to the sounds of moans and grunts in the darkness. She also knew that the coupling led to children in the belly, and for this reason alone she was grateful that Robert did not press himself upon her. And yet, when they were lying on their backs in bed one night, she had finally asked him why he did not make a husband's use of her. He had winced at the words as if she had slapped him.

"You are not to be used, Gwendolyn. Your body is your own."

She had lain beside him, speechless in the darkness, and realized that she had underestimated him, and that her loyalty to Robert would be as great, if not greater, than any wife had ever felt for her husband. Robert had given her this opportunity to be who she was, and he had thrown respect and kindness into the bargain as well. Her deep sense of obligation to Penhallam, to its people and its fields, to its wealth and defense, became her marital vow. It was the only thing he had asked of her, and she had gladly, eagerly risen to the task.

By the end of the day, they had passed through the town of Lydford, crossed the river Lyd and reached the western edge of Dartmoor. The moors would be rocky and windy, and Gwendolyn was relieved when they stopped to make camp to allow the horses the better grazing for the night.

"It's about nine miles across to the next town," William said, raising his hand to his brow to scan to the east in the fading light. "If we move fast and find safe crossing for all of the rivers, we can be across the moor by midday tomorrow and spend the night in Chagford," he continued, turning to face her. "Then on to Exeter."

"Maybe we can skirt that town, as well?" she asked hopefully, remembering the spurned scholar's son.

"That would probably be a good idea," William agreed.

They unfastened the blankets and saddles from the horses, William laying his far from her as he had when they had first settled the night before. Gwendolyn watched him lay out his blanket and prepare his bed across from her. When he was done she stood up, walked over, picked up his belongings, and set them down next to hers. If they were going to travel through the wilderness together, a small bit of his propriety around her would have to give. He could not protect her from a distance.

"Stop treating me like such a woman," she said, and she left to go relieve herself before settling in for the night.

After another restful night, she woke to find William lying on his side, propped up on an elbow beside her and staring at the last of the stars in the pale sky. He had a distant and troubled expression, as if he were lost in thought. She left him to whatever gloomy omens he thought he saw in the morning mists and turned her back to him, her face toward the dawn. Despite the rush they were in, she had started to enjoy these mornings, waking up slowly to the added warmth of a near body and the casual peacefulness of the country.

"We must travel across Dartmoor as quickly as we can without risking the horses," he said after a long pause.

Gwendolyn sat up and brushed her hair from her face, narrowing her eyes.

"What are you saying? Is it overrun with highwaymen? Has John placed his men there? What?"

"No, it's not that, Gwendolyn. It's what you cannot see. God does not rule Dartmoor, and the things that do don't believe in Him."

Gwendolyn stared at him, feeling her contented mood slip away.

"Don't talk to me about witchcraft, William. Or God, for that matter. Both would have me fall to my knees in fear and trembling, helplessly awaiting the fate they have chosen for me. You believe what you want. We will cross Dartmoor as quickly as you like, but only because I'm in as much of a hurry as you are." She strode across the grass toward Bedwyr, but suddenly felt the need to settle the conversation for good and spun to face him again. "I fear no man's god nor any devil, William. The only thing I fear is Evil, and I've seen plenty of that to know that it usually walks on two legs and fears dying as much as anyone else."

William stood up and began gathering his belongings. Although her constable's dire warnings were easy to dismiss as nonsense, she found herself unfastening her armor from her saddle and putting on her hauberk. Instead of her cloak she wore her surcoat and wrapped her weapon belt tightly around it, across her hips. She was resolved not to allow Robert's faith in her to be proven unwarranted. Whatever lay ahead of them, she would face it as herself, not concealing her sword or her pride in carrying it.

They broke their fast wordlessly with a piece of bread and hard cheese, packed up, and set off due east across the moor. A thin fog had settled across the low swells of green and rock with the morning, but the ancient stone tors could still be seen standing tall atop the hillcrests, watching over them like sentinels from another time. William took the lead, following the Lydford Way, a well-worn road traveled by the Romans, their stone markers still visible at the crossroads. They rode at a gentle canter, taking care to avoid the ruts and large rocks that would have been treacherous to the horses' legs.

Gwendolyn was surprised by how few people they passed on the road. Devonshire seemed to be raw country, largely uninhabited except for the scattered farms and tinners and a small handful of towns in the vast expanse. A little farther along, they approached a small stream with a thrown-together timber bridge stretched haphazardly across it. Tinners had diverted the water downstream from the bridge, using the currents to sweep away the sandy banks and reveal the layer of dark ore beneath. William should stop, she thought, watching him approach the bridge without slowing. Even if he was familiar enough with the road to know that the bridge was sound the last time he had passed through here, these aged structures were known to be fickle; she had heard tales of a sudden collapse from Tom, Penhallam's old knight. William continued straight over the bridge without breaking stride, his warhorse's hooves echoing solidly on the planks. Gwendolyn held her breath and followed over the bridge behind him.

William picked up speed ahead of her, still less than a full gallop but true to his comment that morning that they would cross Dartmoor as quickly as possible. They came to two more streams, these without bridges, and William led them splashing through the frigid, shallow waters. The cold wind across her face made her cheeks and lips numb and drove tears from her eyes back across her temples and into her hair. They pushed on, William holding the pace just to the safe side of recklessness. After a while, Gwendolyn's mare was breathing hard, but she still had plenty of run left in her. William's warhorse, however, appeared to be starting to falter. She could see that the stallion was tired, his powerful neck drooping and his stride becoming shorter and choppy. William sensed his horse's fatigue too. He straightened up in his saddle and called back to her, leaning gently back on the reins and slowing his warhorse to an easy lope. He guided his horse beside her and pointed to the horizon as she and Bedwyr came level with him.

"We're almost across," he yelled over the horses' hoofbeats. She steadied herself to look into the distance and saw dark green vales and swells of forest ahead of them, maybe a little more than a mile away. The mist from the morning had cleared, and the day's sunlight warmed the top of her head and shoulders. As their horses settled in side-by-side, blowing hard from the long run across the moor, he held her gaze for a moment, and then their luck abruptly came to an end.

William's horse let out a terrible squeal and dropped forward, its right foreleg splayed sideways by a large, dome-shaped stone in the roadway that had been concealed by tall grass. The sudden jolt threw William up into the air, safely clear of his horse, but he slammed hard on his back onto the road. Thankfully his horse fell and rolled onto its side, saving its knees and recovering quickly to stand trembling beside Bedwyr. After a moment struggling to catch his breath again, William pushed himself up to sit in the road and get his bearings again. Gwendolyn stood by with the horses as he rose uneasily to his feet, looking a little dazed.

"I'm okay," he said, his voice guttural as he gingerly brushed dirt and grass from his clothing.

She gave him a moment to walk around and shake his arms out and then passed his reins across when he reached for them. He took in a shaky, shallow breath and turned to his horse, closely inspecting its legs one after the other for cuts. Finding none, he tugged on the reins and led the stallion forward a few steps to observe whether it favored any of its legs. Finally satisfied, he lifted himself stiffly back into the saddle and exhaled slowly.

"You should know that the people who live here still worship their own gods when they are outside of church. As far as they're concerned, they're not taking any chances on who's right about Heaven and the afterlife. Just be aware that witchcraft and magic are an accepted part of life when we get to Chagford."

"To each his own," Gwendolyn replied; she would not argue the point with him anymore. She steered Bedwyr to fall into step behind William as they walked the last bit of distance to the edge of Dartmoor.

Gwendolyn gazed down upon the small village of Chagford for the first time as they crested a wide, green hill and began a slow descent to the broad valley cut by the river Teign. Robert had tried once to describe the beauty and wildness of Devon to her, but had finally shrugged and given up. She understood now as her gaze swept the wide swells of green hills, sweet meadows still blooming with late wildflowers and clover. The village nestled in the bottom of the valley, gray thatch rooftops of cottages and town buildings peeking out from the surrounding trees. All around the village, pastures lined the sloping sides of the valley, their ancient stone walls creating a boxy pattern like patches in fabric. The forests in the distance, away from the river, had begun to change for autumn, their swaths of green leaves giving way to pale gold that would soon burnish to copper and deep scarlet. She inhaled deeply and wondered how William could bear such deep apprehension in the midst of such beauty and calm.

By the time they arrived in town the sun was still high in the sky and business was in full swing. Tinners were hauling their smelted tin to town in small two-wheeled carts that they pulled themselves or, if they had been successful enough, hitched to a horse. They brought their ingots to the tin dealers for assaying and payment, if any payment was still owed to them after deducting advances. From the looks of the storefronts, the tin dealers seemed to be enjoying a comfortable living in Chagford, and the varieties of wares for sale meant the town's prosperity had caught the attention of the guilds and trades. The different occupations that came with the wool trade—sorting the fibers from soft to coarse, fulling, dyeing, and weaving—lined the lanes also. Despite crippling taxes, the last of which had gone toward the king's ransom, Chagford's prosperity was obvious.

Unlike Launceston, the streets of Chagford were broad and smooth, and she rode comfortably beside William. She noticed a few disapproving looks cast in her direction, but she ignored them. If she was going to travel outside of Penhallam, she would have to develop a thick skin against those who would judge her simply for the peculiarity of her appearance.

They approached Chagford's only inn, at the far end of the village, and dismounted at the doorway. The thought of shelter, warm food, and grain for the horses was welcome after three days of hard travel. Gwendolyn handed William the purse of coins from her belt and stood outside with the horses while William, still looking a little foggy from his brush with disaster, entered the timber building to find the innkeeper.

Outside, Gwendolyn turned her back to the road while she studied the construction of the inn. Its freshly hewn wood beams were visible where they protruded from the plaster walls, and she was wondering how many officials had been paid to turn a blind eye to the harvest of the timber when she became aware of a growing murmur behind her. She turned around and found a handful of men gathered around her and the horses.

One of the men stared at her belligerently. He wore a fine shirt of green and golden weave and a long, black cloak held at the shoulder by a jeweled pin. In the moment that it had taken her to notice the gathering and register the hostility, three more men had joined. She was now facing a small mob, she realized. She blinked and looked at the well-dressed man who seemed to be the instigator, her expression openly innocent and puzzled.

"You may not stay here, witch," he said in a growling voice. "Get back out to the moors where you belong. You'll bring none of your dark magic to these godly people."

Gwendolyn blinked again, realized what charges the man laid upon her, and began to laugh. If only he knew how firmly she refused to believe in any of the foolishness he spoke of.

Predictably, the man took her laughter for defiance, and this direct insult to his authority was an offense even worse than her alleged companionship with the devil. She realized too late that she had inadvertently made the confrontation personal. His countenance became hateful, and he and the crowd tightened their circle around her. She quickly dropped the horses' reins and drew her sword. A small gasp passed over the crowd as she brandished her weapon. The air became charged with the promise of violence.

"William!" she shouted loudly, wondering what kept her constable.

The crowd had stepped back at the sight of her flashing weapon, clearing an arc out of her range, but the tide of aggression was beginning to shift again as they calculated their numbers against her.

"William!" she called again, a note of urgency in her voice.

The door of the inn opened and William stepped out, unaware of the danger, his sword still sheathed. In a blur one of the men lunged from the crowd to William's side, pulled his sword from its scabbard in a single stroke, and took a defensive position beside Gwendolyn, threatening the crowd with William's sword. She could not turn to see the man's face and risk taking her eyes off of the remaining men arrayed before her, but she was grateful for the stranger's assistance and said so. The crowd stepped back again as Gwendolyn and the man stood back-to-back, their swords defining a half-moon that none of the mob dared breach.

"Nigel," the well-dressed man said, addressing her defender, "Step aside."

"Lay one hand on this woman and you will taste my metal when I shove it down your bloody throat."

The man's eyes narrowed and his jaw worked with fury as he stared at the man beside her.

"You will leave this town with the witch and her consort, and you may never return."

"Gladly," Nigel replied, "But you owe me for my work."

"I owe you nothing. Consider it your fine for drawing a sword on me and defending a witch."

Gwendolyn heard the man beside her mumble a curse and spit.

There was something familiar about him that she could not place.

"Your debt will be paid one way or another." Nigel tilted his head toward Gwendolyn. "Now would be a good time to get back on your horses, my lady."

Gwendolyn risked a sideways look at the man beside her, and she recognized the mercenary William had captured at Penhallam and that Barton had freed at Launceston.

"Allow us safe passage and we will leave peacefully," Gwendolyn announced evenly.

The well-dressed man grudgingly nodded and spread his arms wide against the crowd, stepping back and creating an opening for them. William and Gwendolyn mounted their horses while Nigel stood guard with William's sword, and then William reached down to help Nigel up behind him. William and Gwendolyn held their swords drawn as they walked out of Chagford and across the bridge over the river Theign, the crowd sullenly watching them leave.

After they had traveled about another mile beyond the town, William abruptly pulled the reins back and jerked his warhorse sideways, dumping Nigel onto the ground.

Nigel managed to land on his feet with his fists raised, but William had drawn his sword and held it level with Nigel's head.

"That's for taking my sword."

"You idiot," Nigel said contemptuously, lowering his arms. "You had no idea what was going on out there. If they had gotten the jump on you—and they would have if I hadn't been there—you'd be dead now and she'd be in the back of a cart being hauled back up the Lydford Way to the gaol."

"Lay off, William," Gwendolyn ordered. "He's right." She dismounted beside them. "We might as well camp here tonight. The horses are tired, and we've got to pick up the pace. We should be well past Exeter by tomorrow evening."

"And you're travelling on foot," William added angrily to Nigel.

"No, we're buying a horse for him tomorrow. Nigel may travel with us as long as he pleases."

She turned her back to the men while she unfastened the cinch and removed the saddle and blanket from Bedwyr. As she turned around, she caught the last glint of the triumphant smile Nigel had flashed at William, and she dropped the saddle and smacked the back of his head hard.

"Don't make me change my mind," she said roughly, and he grumbled a contrite apology. "Tell me your story. Why did you join John's men?"

"You think I went with that ogre of my own free will?" he asked, staring at her with eyebrows raised in an incredulous look. "What a life you have enjoyed, my lady!"

She whirled around to face him. "You know nothing of my life and are in no position to judge me. Are you not a free man?"

"I wasn't, until you killed the last man who paid for me. Now I suppose I am."

7

THE FACE OF EVIL

Around the fire that night Nigel told them his story, and as he spoke, Gwendolyn realized how little she really knew about the circumstances of people's lives and the depths of cruelty men were capable of. She had always considered Walter de Cardinham an aberration, but as Nigel's tale unfolded, she started to believe that the kindness of spirit she was so well accustomed to at Penhallam was the real exception.

Nigel was the unacknowledged son of an ambitious man who had eventually secured for himself the title of Bishop. The man had never accepted Nigel, although it was known that he had had an affair with Nigel's mother. Instead, the man had publicly called his mother a whore who sought to take advantage of his meager means to secure a stable income for herself and her bastard child. Nigel was the spitting image of his father, a circumstance the bishop and all other men of consequence in London conveniently ignored. Fathering children outside of marriage was commonplace; holding one man accountable, particularly a man whose contributions to the city were so undeniable, would have been, in their eyes, a senseless exercise in hypocrisy.

When his mother had died, the man who owned the room where they had lived put Nigel to work to pay off her debt of rent. When Nigel had proved too difficult to manage, the man had sold him to a mercenary captain who took him to France. Nigel grew up in the company of the soldiers, fetching water, polishing weapons, and ducking fists, and yet by a mixture of cunning and luck he survived to reach adulthood and join the company. After years of service the captain was killed in a siege at Rouen. Nigel only had enough coins to travel back to England.

He had gone to London to find his father, but instead he found a young woman and discovered, for the first time in his life, tenderness. They had a daughter and Nigel indebted himself again to provide her with a home, clothes, and food. His wife died of a fever in the spring, and their landlord, a merchant and a supporter of John, had sold him to the man Gwendolyn had killed. The merchant, Master de Lacy, had kept Nigel's daughter as insurance for Nigel's loyalty to the mercenary. Nigel was on his way back to London now to retrieve his daughter and travel north, where a man's freedom was not so easily traded.

"How old is your daughter?" Gwendolyn was thinking of her own years without her parents, remembering the isolation and despair.

Nigel's face softened for the first time since she had known him. "She's seven years old, with the good sense of her mother, thank all the saints."

Gwendolyn sat quietly and looked at William's face across from her, illuminated in the firelight, trying to discern his expression, but he was staring into the fire, lost in thought. Nigel had risked his life to save hers, and at personal cost to himself when he clearly had nothing to spare. Everything inside her told her she could trust this man, that his code of honor was the only thing he had that no one could take from him.

"When we arrive in London, we will go with you to find this merchant, your Master de Lacy. I have my own business with the dowager queen, but I owe you for your protection today. Before I go to the White Tower to seek an audience with Eleanor, we will first see your daughter safely returned to her father."

William looked up at her with his eyebrows raised, and Nigel stared at her in amazement.

"You have an invitation to the Tower of London? To go before the queen?"

Gwendolyn cleared her throat.

"No, but I will gain admittance to an audience with her." She offered no further explanation and Nigel glanced between the two of them, reading the silent exchange on their faces. He shifted a little uncomfortably, unaccustomed to finding himself on the receiving end of an offer of help—and from two people whose rank clearly out-distanced his own by a large measure.

"Suit yourself," he finally said a little awkwardly, then frowned and shook his head in silent reproach. He stared into the fire a moment, then quietly said, "Thank you," as if the words were a foreign language in his mouth. He turned and looked her in the eyes and said the words again, slowly and clearly. "Thank you, Lady Gwendolyn."

They had eight days of solid riding ahead of them to get to London. They rode slowly the first day, the two men doubled up on William's horse until they arrived near Exeter. The town had swollen beyond the city walls in a sprawl of quickly built, ramshackle houses and merchant stalls. Among them they found a stable that made all of its business off the large number of visitors—merchants, clerics, and scholars—travelling to and from the great city. William bought a sturdy horse, and Gwendolyn said they would make up for the expense by sleeping in the open every night. Although none of them discussed it, they were all relieved to avoid the chance of a repeat of the events in Chagford.

East of Exeter they picked up a broad, flat road, paved with gravel and flanked on either side by shallow ditches. They followed this road east to Dorchester, then turned northeast, riding past Old Sarum, Silchester, Runnymede, and finally arriving in the late afternoon at the farming settlements that spread over the fertile floodplains west of the London walls. Gwendolyn had made inquiries from the travelers that they met at the Winchester crossroads to confirm that the dowager queen remained in London. Queen Eleanor was occupied with overseeing the accumulation of wealth and coin to be paid to the holy emperor for Richard's ransom. Not only was the queen in residence, but the town also hosted the emperor's treasury agents—four portly men who had acquired a reputation for their appreciation of strong drink and stronger women. Apparently London had something for everyone.

They entered the city through the arches of Newgate at considerable cost in tolls. As they approached the gatehouse, Gwendolyn looked up and shuddered at the sight of several spiked heads of executed criminals jutting out on their pikes from the top of the gatehouse. Inside the walls, she felt assaulted by the sheer numbers of sounds and sights that surrounded her. She held back tightly on Bedwyr's reins to pause for a moment and take it all in. The air was thick with rich smells, some the familiar odors of human excrement and rotting waste, some the vastly more pleasant aromas of baking bread and roasting meat. Shouts, calls, and conversations competed for her attention on all sides, through the lanes and from the windows and rooftops above her. To her right, she could see the skeletal spires of St. Paul's Cathedral, an edifice to the glory of God more than one hundred years in the making, reaching over the rooftops as if to brush Heaven itself. Even from where she stood beyond the city gate, the ringing collision of hammers on stone could be heard over the din that filled the streets around her. London had been flattened by fire as recently as the reign of King Stephen, and yet no trace of the damage remained visible, so quickly had the city recovered and rebuilt—wisely, with stone and tile wherever such expense could be afforded. Sewers and conduits carried the filth of waste from the streets to the Thames, creating a famously noxious brew during the seasonal floods. William and Nigel drew up alongside her and motioned that they needed to move on. Their horses were in need of rest and grain, and their first business was to settle their mounts at a stable.

London seemed to be full of every kind of amusement and

diversion. Gwendolyn was pleasantly surprised to also discover that her dress and appearance seemed to cause not the least stir or notice among the throngs in the streets or looking down from the buildings and houses that crowded around them. Nigel led them into the heart of the city, past the meat market and the grain market, then turned south to the one bridge across the Thames that would lead them to Southwark. He stopped in front of the bridge and turned to them, looking a little apologetic.

"There's a stable for your horses and suitable lodging here. Southwark's a little more colorful than London, but you'll pay a dear penny for lodging in the city."

Gwendolyn nodded, and the three of them carefully threaded their way across the tightly packed span of famous timber whose construction, maintenance, and commerce was overseen by a monastic guild created by King Henry II solely for that purpose, the Brethren of the Bridge. Market stalls and houses and a variety of chapels to one saint or another lined the bridge and drew the large number of visitors, creating an impressive congestion of traffic and drawing from widely diverse walks of life. Beside this bridge, a new stone bridge was under construction, its stone footings rising like pillars in the swirling river. Gwendolyn's stomach grumbled with hunger as they picked a route past the stands selling dried fruits, roasted meats and other treats, but there was no time yet to pause to eat. Ahead in the shadows, Gwendolyn spied an attractive woman standing beneath the sagging eaves of a tavern. The woman leaned casually against the whitewashed wall, watching the crowds ebb and jostle in front of her with a keen eye. Her thick, dark hair hung loosely over one shoulder to her waist.

She wore only a tunic cinched by a wide belt over bare thighs, and she gestured with her hand to catch William's attention. As he turned to look, she lowered her shirt and exposed a full, rosy breast to him, offering it with her hand and nodding toward the tavern door. Gwendolyn nearly laughed out loud and wondered if William would come back later to the tavern to take the woman up on her offer. From her position behind him she was unable to see his face or whether he had acknowledged the woman, but she could see his ears turn a vivid shade of red.

When they reached the south bank of the river, Gwendolyn turned in her saddle to follow William's gaze back the way they had come, and she took in her first view of the White Tower, east of the city on the north bank of the Thames. The building stood tall, imposing, and impenetrable, overlooking the river. Her mouth became dry as she realized how close she was to the seat of power in England. Her stomach churned anew, this time with doubt and uncertainty. Perhaps William was right and she had been a fool to think she could be welcome inside this fortress, much less into the presence of the king's mother. She turned away and reminded herself of the child whose safety she had promised to secure first.

Nigel turned right into a narrow lane lined with taverns. At the far end of the lane, there was a low, long building with a wide door to accommodate the passage of livestock. They rode to this doorway and dismounted, and a large, muscular man stepped out into the daylight, blinking and frowning. When the man's eyes fell on Nigel, he immediately scowled.

"Don't think you're lodging your stolen horse here, cur," he said, folding his arms and blocking the doorway.

"Get off it, the horse is paid for, you unfortunate spawn of a three-legged dog," Nigel retorted, jutting his chin toward Gwendolyn and William.

The man looked Gwendolyn and William over carefully, his hand stroking his broad jaw.

"You're with him?" he asked skeptically, his scowl still in place.

Gwendolyn nodded, hoping that the trade of insults had been in jest.

The man turned back to Nigel and relaxed, then cuffed Nigel hard on the shoulder with a hand the span of a man's head.

"Maybe fortune's wheel is finally turning for you," he said, smiling. "I don't know how you're back, and on a horse, no less. Master de Lacy has gone to Lincoln—he said he was going to find you and Ella and bring you back."

Nigel shook his head gravely and handed the man the reins to his horse. "He's lying. He sold me off to a mercenary for Prince John. And that man is dead now, thanks to her," he added, gesturing with a thumb toward Gwendolyn. The man took a closer look at Gwendolyn, then smiled slightly. "This is Gwendolyn de Cardinham, of Cornwall, and her constable, William Rufus."

The man nodded respectfully to both of them, noting the colors on their surcoats, their fine horses and sword belts.

"It is an honor, my lady. Peter Marshal, at your service."

"I haven't been in Lincoln," Nigel continued, "and may God have mercy on Master de Lacy if Ella is not safe in his shop right now."

"We're going with you," Gwendolyn said to Nigel, turning to retrieve her cloak from the bundle secured to her saddle. "I am not known here. Surely for a reasonable number of coins Master de Lacy's wife will be happy to be free of the care of your child."

Peter huffed at her comment. "She is . . ." he stammered, searching for a less coarse description, ". . . . an unpleasant woman. And if she's been lying all this time about Ella, then you'd better hurry."

Nigel nodded, and Gwendolyn could see anxiety rising behind his determined gaze.

After quickly settling their horses in with Peter, the three of them crossed the bridge again on foot, pausing only for a moment to purchase a handful of rolls and move on. With her cloak concealing her surcoat and weapon and her hair and nails dirty from the days of travel, Gwendolyn realized she was a pale comparison to the finely dressed women they passed, tastefully coiffed in veils that even Roslyn would have envied, their hems and mantles adorned with seams of fine pearls and ribbons. She walked between William and Nigel, practically at a jog to keep up, and the crowds instinctively parted for them, sensing the presence of a man-at-arms before they even saw William's sword. For his part, the years growing up in a company of mercenaries had imbued Nigel with an aura of lethal purpose that remained palpable even though he was completely unarmed.

They proceeded quickly up Watling Street to the grain market, then north until they were close to the Guild Hall. Here, the merchants' homes and shops crowded together in narrow store fronts that concealed long dwellings inside.

"Master de Lacy's house is just this way," Nigel said, a little out of breath. "His wife will be minding the shop now."

They made another turn onto a narrow lane, and at one of the shops Nigel stopped, took a deep breath, and stepped up through the doorway. Gwendolyn followed him, and William stayed outside, keeping an eye on the street and blocking the shop entrance.

Stacks of finely embroidered linens were set out on a table, the tiny stitches of the needlework impressive in their detail and craftsmanship.

A woman stepped into the shop from a doorway that led to the back room. She walked toward them with a bland smile on her face, eyebrows raised in feigned subservience that Gwendolyn guessed was the woman's customary greeting. As she came near them, the woman stopped and squinted, her expression frozen, as she appeared to recognize Nigel.

"What are you doing here?" she asked, casting a sideways glance at Gwendolyn as she addressed Nigel.

"I've come for Ella. Send her out and I'll leave."

The woman paused, staring closely at Gwendolyn, and Gwendolyn realized Mistress de Lacy was sizing her up, trying to piece together whether Gwendolyn was a woman who could create trouble for her or not. Although the length of Gwendolyn's cloak suggested she came from money, no self-respecting woman of title would have stepped out in such a poor state of grooming and complete absence of adornment. Gwendolyn smiled, hoping she had the woman thoroughly confused. The woman seemed to make up her mind and cleared her throat.

"I'm sorry, but she's not here. She ran away a week ago. I've asked all over the city, but no one's seen her. You have no idea the trouble I've gone to trying to find her, walking the streets every morning."

Nigel started to protest, his face immediately red, but Gwendolyn placed a restraining hand on his arm. She picked up one of the embroidered cloths beside her and looked at the woman.

"This is very fine needlework," Gwendolyn said, raising her eyes toward the merchant's wife. "I've never seen such fine detail in the pattern, and with such small stitches."

"Thank you, I have more in the trunks if you'd like to see them," the woman offered, her demeanor shifting slightly. Gwendolyn was appalled as she realized that the woman had taken her observations for flattery and was trying to make a sale to her. She watched as the woman moved toward the trunks that lined one side of the shop.

"Actually, I was wondering how they're made," Gwendolyn said.

"Oh! Well, my mother taught me. I've been sewing since I was a girl."

Nigel was becoming agitated beside Gwendolyn, and she tightened her grip on his arm.

"Well, then, you have quite a skill. Perhaps you could open one of the trunks for me?"

The woman smiled with her lips only, her eyes darting uneasily to Nigel and back to Gwendolyn. As she turned her back on them to fumble with the latch that closed one of the trunks, squinting and leaning in to better see the lever and hook, Gwendolyn noticed the enlarged knuckles of the woman's fingers. It was true that the woman had spent a lifetime sewing, but her days of stitching the fine patterns seen in her shop now were far behind her.

"Bring Ella out now." Gwendolyn allowed her rage to be heard in her voice. "You didn't sew these. You can hardly see the latch to open the trunk. Only a child's fingers could produce stitches like these."

The truth started to dawn on Nigel, beside her. He had been gone for three months, and the shop was filled with stacks of the same extraordinary needlework. He pushed past Gwendolyn and charged to the back of the shop.

"Ella!"

The woman turned to scream, but Gwendolyn had drawn her sword.

"Don't," Gwendolyn said softly. "Please, don't. Let this be the end of it."

Nigel's heavy steps could be heard charging up the stairs in the back of the shop. Gwendolyn and the woman faced each other silently, Gwendolyn with her sword drawn, the woman glaring.

"That girl belongs to me!" the woman said venomously.

"Not anymore."

"When my husband returns—" she threatened, but her words were interrupted by Nigel entering the room again from the back, carrying a small girl in his arms. Gwendolyn's heart sank at the girl's emaciated appearance, the sunken eyes and hollow cheeks. Her fingertips were swollen and raw from hours of handling needles and thread. Nigel's face was purple with rage, his cheeks damp with tears.

"Go!" Gwendolyn yelled at him. "Take her before you do something you'll regret that will take you from her forever. Go!"

She turned back to the woman, who began protesting immediately. "I fed that girl! I gave her clothes, a bed, and a skill she can use to support herself for the rest of her life! I've done nothing wrong!"

Gwendolyn backed away slowly, her eyes brimming with tears, aware that she was looking at the real face of evil, this unholy marriage of greed and indifference to suffering. Nothing that the prior or William could tell her about demons, ghosts, or the Devil himself could surpass the level of cruelty inflicted by living people with hearts of stone.

"When your husband returns, you may tell him that Nigel and his daughter are in the household of Robert de Cardinham. I am on my way tonight to the Tower for an audience with the dowager queen. You'd best start packing now for a long journey outside of London," Gwendolyn ground the words out through clenched teeth. "Know that I will inform the queen of your treasonous support of John's rebellion by supplying mercenaries and money for the cause."

The woman stared at Gwendolyn furiously.

"And why would anyone believe a girl who dresses and acts as a man over a respected member of the guild?"

Gwendolyn met the woman's eyes, remorseless and full of righteous indignation, one last time before she turned without answering the woman's question to step out into the street.

Outside, William stood beside Nigel, both men's faces hard with outrage. Ella had curled up against Nigel's chest and closed her eyes, her straw-colored hair spread across his arms. Whatever ill feelings William bore toward Nigel, for now they appeared to have been forgotten.

"I hope you left her choking on her own blood."

"Not quite, but I don't think she or her husband will bother you any more just the same."

"How can you be sure?"

"Because I'm going to inform Eleanor and the regents of Master de Lacy's support of John."

Nigel grunted. "I'd like to be there for that."

"I'll need your witness, so you're coming along whether you want to or not."

Gwendolyn turned toward the Tower, but Nigel reached for her arm.

"The queen will be dressing now, preparing for the evening. She takes a late supper with the court and then retires to receive visitors in her chamber before closing the doors to confer with the regents. She stays up well into the night. You would be wasting your time to go to the Tower any earlier than midnight."

Gwendolyn stared more closely at Nigel. "How do you know the queen's habits so well?"

"I've watched Master de Lacy when he's had to bring matters before the regents or the justiciar. It took him weeks sometimes to gain an audience."

"Well, we don't have weeks to spare. But Ella . . ." she said, looking with concern at the small girl still quietly snuggled against Nigel's chest.

"She'll be okay. We'll take her to her aunt."

The three of them walked back the way they had come, across the bridge into Southwark and back up the street where the horses were stabled. She guessed that they had walked a little more than a mile, and the entire way Nigel did not once shift Ella in his arms, even though Gwendolyn was certain his muscles must have been aching. Nigel turned into one of the taverns, a long, narrow room lit by candles and oil lamps. The earthen floor was covered with fresh straw, and a woman moved between the two rows of tables removing cups and plates and collecting coins that she tucked into a pouch in her apron. She turned around as they took their seats and when she recognized Nigel, she smiled with clear, soft eyes and came over to them.

"Master de Lacy said he'd sent you and Ella to Lincoln in his place! It's been nearly two months! I was worried about you two," she said as she bent over to Ella. She reached her hand out to move a strand of hair from the sleeping child's face, but as she neared the girl and saw the sunken cheeks, the frail arms and raw fingers, her expression changed to shock.

"What's happened to the girl, Nigel? Where have you been?"

Nigel looked up at her wearily and said only, "It's a long story, Mae."

Mae looked at William and Gwendolyn and nodded a mute greeting, then turned her attention back to Nigel and Ella, her eyes full of questions.

"We can talk while we eat," Gwendolyn said, and Mae recovered herself and nodded. She returned from the kitchen quickly with a plate piled high with bits of roasted meat, greens, sliced onions, and bread, and a pitcher of watered ale. Nigel roused Ella in his lap, and she smiled at the food spread before her. She shifted around and began delicately picking at a small, roasted bird while stealing shy glances at William, seated beside them.

Ignoring her customers, Mae sat through Nigel's recounting of the merchant's betrayal, how he had sold him off to the mercenary to support John, promising to use the payment to keep Ella clothed and fed and housed for so long as Nigel continued to serve the captain. He described Gwendolyn's interception of their group in the woods, and her quick reflexes that had saved her and her maids' lives. He also described Gwendolyn's refusal to see him hanged as a traitor, the confrontation with the mob in Chagford, and the race to London. Mae took in the story with wide eyes, and regarded Gwendolyn with a sort of fearful respect that Gwendolyn pretended not to notice as she ate slowly, fortifying herself for what she was afraid was going to be a long night.

When Nigel told Mae of their visit to the de Lacys' shop, Mae sat up with her eyes shining.

"Those horrible, horrible people! I was there just a week ago to see the embroidery for myself! It's all the women of London are talking about! Mistress de Lacy practically threw me out of the store when she saw me, said her fine things weren't for tavern maids like me. If I had only known . . ." Mae looked again at Ella, who sat in Nigel's lap playing a game with some of the bones of the roasted birds, lining them back up into the semblance of a much larger bird with fearsome, grasping claws. Mae stretched her arms out to Ella, and the girl hesitated for a moment and then climbed down from Nigel's lap, ducked under the table, and climbed into Mae's embrace. Mae cradled her against her bosom, murmured to her softly, and began rocking her, and Ella's eyes immediately drooped again.

"She's the image of Aliene," Mae said quietly, planting a kiss on the girl's forehead. Gwendolyn noted the resemblance between Mae and Ella and realized the girl's mother had been Mae's sister.

Nigel's eyes softened at Mae's words.

"Can she stay with you?" Nigel asked. "It could be a few days."

"Of course," Mae responded, her attention completely focused on Ella.

William and Gwendolyn looked up as the tavern door swung open. The light from outside was blocked momentarily by the frame of Peter, the stablehand they had given their horses to that afternoon. He walked into the tavern, followed by two boys only a little more than half his height. When his eyes found Mae and their group, he moved quickly toward them, his expression changing to relief at the sight of Ella asleep in Mae's arms.

"She was at the shop?" Peter asked as the boys reached for the generous leftovers on the plates while Mae shooed their hands away and admonished them to remember their manners.

Nigel nodded and Gwendolyn pushed the plates toward the boys, who thanked her and sat down and began to eat.

"She's staying with us," Mae said, rising slowly and shifting Ella to Peter's extended arms. "Go settle her in the back on our bed, love, and I'll make up a plate for you." Mae left them to tend to her customers, and Gwendolyn watched her as she made her rounds in the tavern, addressing each person by name.

They waited in the tavern until dinner had passed and Mae closed the kitchen. Gwendolyn's head ached with fatigue, but she put her discomfort out of her mind, rallying herself for the several hours still ahead of her. Up until that moment she had put the visit to the Tower out of her thoughts, focusing instead on Ella and conversation with Mae and Peter. But now that the time had come, she felt her stomach twist with nerves. Mae had provided a bowl of water for her to clean herself up a bit and had rebraided her hair, fastening the end with a small ribbon that she wound around snugly several times.

William noticed the change that came over her and nodded. "It's time."

8

GUESTS
OF THE TOWER

B y night, London transformed into a different city. Packs of feral dogs roamed the streets, hunting rats and scavenging behind the taverns and through the empty stalls of the meat market. Houses and shops were closed and boarded up, their windows tightly shuttered. Only the occasional torch brought any light into the lanes. Nigel quickly led them through Southwark, past the taverns and houses of prostitution, both now quiet for the night. They strode silently across the bridge and over to the nearby docks. The White Tower had been recently fortified with a moat, and they would enter the stronghold by ferryboat. When they arrived at Billingsgate, they picked their way through the few gathered merchants and seamen who were busy negotiating passage and overseeing the loading of supplies and goods for shipment. The pace of trade out of London had become fierce; ships that were ready to sail at first light would get the advantage at the markets of Gascony, Poitevin, Breton, and Flamand.

Nigel waved them over when he found what he was looking for: a flat, small skiff apparently abandoned and unoccupied. He found the skiff's owners, thick-armed ferrymen sleeping beside their oars in a nearby corner, and roused them awake. A few coins from Gwendolyn helped to get the men to their feet, and Nigel quickly arranged their passage.

William took his seat on a narrow bench beside Gwendolyn in the back of the boat, and Nigel sat down facing them, his back to the Tower as they approached it. Gwendolyn watched the ferrymen's oars glide through the dark currents of the Thames as they navigated the river to bring the little boat around toward a darkened archway. The looming fortress brought the reality of everything she was about to put at risk home to her. Beside her, she sensed William's tension in the rigid line of his profile and the bared knuckles of his clenched grip on the edge of the bench. Her palms began to sweat, and her heart thrummed in her chest.

"You don't have to do this," William said quietly.

"And that is why this has even a chance of working," she whispered back to him.

The ferrymen maneuvered the boat under the archway and alongside another dock on the small island now defined by the moat. New construction had been raised around the southwest portion of the Tower grounds, defining what she guessed would eventually be a protective outer shell of walls, towers and outbuildings to house and guard the growing royal offices of exchequer, the curia regis, the justiciars and chamberlain. There would also be comfortable apartments to house those unwed heiresses whose properties had escheated to the crown, so that women and property both could be doled out strategically to accomplish the kingdom's requirements of securing peace at the borders, acquiring property, and rewarding loyalty and service.

Six guards stepped forward to meet the boat, their lances raised, steel tips flashing in the torchlight. Another man threw a loop of rope around the point of wood at the prow of the boat while his partner reached for the iron ring at the stern and ran a thick rope through it. They were captured, she realized, but not permitted to disembark. The ferrymen sat still in their positions at the oar locks, their staffs laid across their knees. Both men stared blankly ahead, impassive to whatever fate might befall their passengers. An older man, stout and tall with closely cropped white hair, stepped out from the standing guard and approached, the polished links of his mail armor glinting while he looked them over with an affronted expression.

"What's your business here?" He spoke to William in Norman French, the language of the crown and all those who circled around it.

Gwendolyn stood up and steadied herself with her hand on William's shoulder.

"I come to see the queen, on a matter for her ears alone." Her Norman French was as flawless as the guard's.

One corner of the man's mouth drew back in amusement as he took in her armor and attire.

"Do you now? And might you carry a summons from the queen requesting your presence?"

"I have nothing but my name. I am Gwendolyn de Cardinham, wife of Robert de Cardinham. Tell your lady who I am and
she will permit me to come before her."

"I personally know every soul who my mistress will permit in
her presence, and you are not among them. Go now, before I add
your heads to the spits lining the riverbank."

Gwendolyn's chest was so tight she could barely breathe, but
she held herself and her voice steady as she spoke.

"It will be your head that gazes into eternity across this river
if you fail to advise the queen of my arrival."

The man chuckled and considered her quietly for a moment
and then turned his gaze to William and Nigel. Both men returned
the unshaken gaze of soldiers. His expression seemed to sober a bit,
and he turned and gestured to one of the guards to run to the Tower
with the message of Gwendolyn's arrival. When he looked back to
Gwendolyn, his eyes were still hard, but she detected a little amusement in the corners of his mouth. While they waited, Gwendolyn
took note of the high quality of the weapons and armor worn by
the men, the stone-like stillness with which the guards held their
position. If the guard returned from the Tower with bad news, she
doubted that she and William would be able to draw their swords
to cut the ropes and break free before the guards were upon them.
She realized her life, as well as William's and Nigel's, were all in the
balance before she had even stepped foot on the Tower's soil. She
remained standing, fighting the impulse to place her hand on the
hilt of her sword and brace for combat.

After several moments, distant footsteps were heard returning at a run. Darkness shrouded the guard's features until he was

only a few paces away. He stopped abruptly in front of his captain and nodded. The man turned to Gwendolyn, his eyebrows raised.

"Well, I suppose there's a first time for everything, my lady," he said, extending his hand to help her step from the boat.

"Thank you," she replied graciously, taking his hand and stepping aside for William and Nigel. "You serve the queen well."

The man nodded to her and sent two guards to walk with them to the Tower. "You may keep your swords, but if you draw them, you will die where you stand."

None of them needed this bit of instruction; the show of force just to gain entrance had provided them all the guidance they needed to understand what sort of decorum would be expected of them in the Tower. As they crossed the yard, Gwendolyn noticed that construction on the new buildings was in full swing despite the hour, and the chinking and grinding clamor of tools, the shouts of men working, and the bustling of carts of stone and earth caught her attention. Their escort followed her gaze.

"Her ladyship sleeps during much of the daylight and the construction disturbs her. So they work at night." Gwendolyn nodded, wondering what the other residents of the Tower thought of being forced to follow the queen's schedule. But then she guessed no one cared to ask them, either.

The guard led them up a set of wooden stairs that led to the first floor above the ground level. The relatively flimsy stairway had a defensive purpose: it could be easily disposed of in times of siege. At the top of the stairs they entered into a small stone antechamber that had been added by Eleanor's late husband, where they encountered four more guards. The men stepped aside as their escort continued forward, and they entered a large hall that stretched before them the entire length of the Tower's western wall. They followed the guard through a side door into the adjoining room and to the corner of the building, where a spiral staircase led them to the rooms above—the queen's anteroom and the larger hall where she received guests and heard and decided upon all matters brought before her.

Gwendolyn paused for a moment at the top of the stairs, taking in the crowded room. The high walls were covered with long tapestries, depicting hunts, courtly romance, and one of a king standing at a large round table surrounded by knights, undoubtedly King Arthur from the descriptions of Chretien de Troyes. Eleanor was known for her taste for the wine of her homeland, and the cups that were passed here were not the wooden cups of watered ale that Gwendolyn was familiar with, but rather pewter and glass goblets, again characteristic of the queen's preference for beauty and elegance. The room hummed with low conversations from huddled groups, and there was a momentary pause as Gwendolyn stood in the doorway while those assembled took in this new stranger and her companions. Beside her, William pointed out in a low voice those members of the royal court who were almost as famous as King Richard and his family: William Marshal, the model of chivalry who had risen from a humble birth to the post of regent; Aubrey de Vere, the eldest son and heir of the Earl of Oxford; and Gerald de Barri, the royal clerk and chronicler. He recognized others, but as they entered the room their escort caught the attention of William Marshal with a subtle gesture and then left them without a word to return to his post.

Gwendolyn took a step back involuntarily as William Marshal strode up to them.

"You are Robert de Cardinham's wife," he said, bowing slightly to Gwendolyn. "You know, I think Robert blames himself for Richard's kidnapping. Apparently he was the one who threw Duke Leopold's banner from the wall at Acre." William Marshal also spoke to her in the tongue of the ruling class.

She looked at him questioningly, and the man gave a sonorous, full-chested laugh that went all the way up to his eyes and seemed to make the room somehow more welcoming.

"I am William Marshal, although you may call me 'the Marshal' as everyone else here does, and I have not met your husband, but Richard seems to like him quite a lot." The Marshal looked to Nigel and William, who both stepped forward and introduced themselves.

"What matter have you come to bring before the queen? Because if you are petitioning for Robert's return, I can advise you now that you are wasting your time."

The Marshal's voice had changed to the serious tone of a court official, and Gwendolyn squared her shoulders and shook her head.

"What I have to say is for the queen alone."

The Marshal exhaled and raised a warning eyebrow at her.

"My lady, you and your men gained access to the Tower over a quick death at the dock on the honor of your husband's name. And with the same currency you may yet gain an audience with the queen this night. But no one comes before the queen without first advising me or her justiciar, Walter de Coutances, of the nature of your business."

The Marshal stared at her and maintained his position, and Gwendolyn realized she would have to disclose her intentions.

"I have come to offer my queen a means to persuade John to abandon his rebellion."

William Marshal said nothing, but his mouth opened slightly. Gwendolyn guessed that the man was not accustomed to being taken by surprise, and he drew his brows together and squared his jaw.

"Do not play me for a fool, Lady de Cardinham. You may have made certain…compen-sations for the extended absence of your husband," the Marshal said, nodding toward her sword, "but you have thrust yourself into a different world here. The fates of entire nations are decided in that chamber," he said, wagging a thick finger toward the heavy carved door across the room from them.

"This is no ruse," William said beside her. "Bring Gerald de Barri with us when we go before the queen so that she may consult him. He is descended from one of the princely families of Wales on his mother's side. He will vouch for the truth of my lady's words."

The Marshal eyed her severely again.

"If this is true, then there's no time to waste. Stay here."

William Marshal crossed the room quickly and pulled the heavy doors open enough to allow himself passage inside. After a few moments, a stream of finely dressed courtiers and petitioners began to file out of the doors in a noisy commotion, some complaining and others searching for a familiar face in the crowd to continue passing the evening in pleasant conversation.

Gwendolyn heard a familiar voice rise above the clatter, complaining loudly.

"But we have been here waiting to be heard for five nights! Who could possibly be so important that isn't here already?" Gwendolyn whipped her head around in time to make eye contact with Roslyn de Cardinham.

"You!" her sister-in-law screamed across the room. "You don't belong here! What lies have you told to get this close to the queen?"

The room had grown so quiet that Roslyn's last words echoed in Gwendolyn's ears and she felt her face grow hot as Roslyn crossed the room to confront her. But with her back turned and in the midst of her rage, Roslyn did not see the Marshal exit the queen's chamber behind her, nor did she hear his footsteps as he covered the distance to her in three strides. He grabbed Roslyn by the elbow and she turned around with a gasp of indignation.

"Step aside, Lady Roslyn." His voice was polite and even, the genteel tone of a practiced courtier.

Roslyn stammered and took a few steps backward, making way for Gwendolyn, William, and Nigel to follow the Marshal. William Marshal called out to Gerald de Barri, and then ushered them all behind the great wooden door that separated the hall from the queen's private chamber.

~·¦·~

As in the hall, the queen's chamber for receiving guests was lined with tapestries and fine furnishings; however the room was not as well lit, and the softer lighting bathed its occupants in a golden glow that Gwendolyn realized would be more flattering for a woman advancing in years. The queen herself sat in the center of the room in a cushioned, carved chair that was elevated on a wooden dais. She held out her hand as they entered, and a silver-haired, well-built man stepped forward from the side of the room to take it, steadying her rise, although she hardly seemed to be in need of the assistance. At more than seventy years old, Eleanor of Aquitaine had kept the shape of a much younger woman, and her eyes were as lively and bright as Gwendolyn suspected they must have been in her youth. Her dress, a deep blue silk, fit snugly across her waist and hips, and the bosom was adorned with small beads of black glass that glinted like flame in the light of the candelabra that stood nearby. As Eleanor stood up, William and Nigel bowed deeply and took positions on one knee on either side of Gwendolyn.

"I understand you have something rather interesting you would like to discuss with me," Eleanor said directly.

Gwendolyn hesitated with a momentary confusion and then recovered her senses and joined William and Nigel on one knee before the queen. She had known that Eleanor would be an impressive woman, unlike any other she had met before, and yet she was entirely unprepared for the effect Eleanor's presence had on her. She understood why men were rumored to have fallen in love with the queen on sight. She could not imagine how powerful the queen's charisma must have been in the vigor of her youth.

The queen turned to the man beside her who had taken her hand. "Walter, I don't believe any other woman has ever knelt before me as a knight."

The man nodded in agreement. "A first, madame."

Gwendolyn thought she might have heard in the man's voice the lilted tones shared by the people of Cornwall. She realized she was staring at Walter de Coutances himself, the king's justiciar and the most powerful man in England while Richard was away.

"My son has written to me of your husband, Lady de Cardinham. It appears he has the capacity both for brash action and discretion, a rare balance for a man-at-arms."

"There are few men like Robert," Gwendolyn said quietly.

"And few husbands, I suppose," the queen continued, gesturing toward Gwendolyn's armor and weapons.

Gwendolyn blushed under the queen's examination, holding her tongue and allowing the queen to lead the conversation.

"I wore a sword once myself, when I was not much older than you, child. It ended disastrously. Tell me, what means do you offer that has not already been tried to persuade my youngest son to cease his attempts at stealing the throne from my older son? I admit I find your boldness in presuming to counsel my counselors bordering on offense."

"Yes, madame," Gwendolyn replied, lifting her eyes to meet Eleanor's.

Gwendolyn's heart pounded in her chest, but the moment had come. She took a deep breath and plunged forward.

"You and your family, my lady, have made the tales of King Arthur famous. As Chretien de Troyes's patron, your own daughter has brought the legends to life from across the centuries to our own time."

"He was the first and perhaps the greatest of the English kings," Eleanor replied, somewhat pointedly.

"But that's just it, my lady. The Welsh claim him as their own. They have their own tales of Arthur; many claim them as prophecies, still alive on the tongues of their bards today. These prophecies claim that Arthur will return, and that Caliburn, his sword, will find him. Your son John believes the prophecies, and he has been searching the countryside for the sword. John believes that he will be unstoppable against any army if he possesses Caliburn. Even against Richard himself."

Eleanor's eyes flashed darkly, and Gwendolyn knew she had entered treacherous ground.

"I will not speak ill of my son or his folly in front of you, and I advise you not to do so, either," she warned coldly.

"I do not, madame. I offer you an opportunity to bargain with the prince for that which he seeks."

Eleanor's hard stare remained fixed on Gwendolyn, but her expression softened slightly and she gave Walter de Coutances her hand as she stepped back and settled into her chair again.

"You have my attention. Continue."

"I have been told that I am a descendant of Arthur, and that Caliburn comes for me."

Despite the many thick tapestries lining the room, Eleanor's laughter echoed around them in cascades of mirth. Gwendolyn waited patiently, her cheeks burning with humiliation. Even the Marshal chuckled to himself behind her. Eleanor took a deep breath and sighed, composing herself and returning her gaze to Gwendolyn, all trace of malice erased.

"Thank you for that bit of entertainment. Court business is usually so dreary, but this has been positively refreshing."

Gwendolyn looked down for a moment and licked her dry lips.

"The descendants of Arthur are known in Wales, and my father claimed their legacy. My father was a Welsh warrior, a prisoner who escaped from your husband's war camp at the Battle of Crogen in the Ceiriog Valley."

Eleanor tilted her chin askew slightly at this revelation.

"Henry never forgot that," she said quietly. "He would not have punished the remaining prisoners so severely had one not escaped in the night."

Silence dropped over the room with the gravity of Eleanor's comment. Henry's barbaric treatment of his prisoners had sealed the Welsh hatred of the Norman "foreigners" for generations. And yet, if her husband's father, the Baron Fitz William, had not rescued Gwyn in the night, Gwyn would not have met her mother, and she would not be alive to offer herself—and Caliburn—to the disposal of an English queen.

"You must know then," Eleanor said, "how your father managed to escape?"

"The Baron Fitz William, Robert de Cardinham's father, took him and fled. My father saved the baron's life in an act of chivalry in battle. The baron knew Henry too well. He couldn't leave my father to whatever fate the king had in store for him."

Eleanor stared into the distance beyond them, as if she searched back through time to private moments with her late husband. Gwendolyn watched the queen's eyes grow misty, and the queen shook her head, clearing away the images. "These tapestries are nothing next to the great weaving we all play our parts in, willingly or not." She seemed to be speaking to no one in particular, or perhaps to her late husband.

"Madame, if I may?" William asked softly, his blue eyes clear and unblinking.

"And you are?"

"William Rufus, Constable of Penhallam, madame."

Eleanor nodded, as if she recognized the name. "You may speak."

"Like you, my lady does not believe any of these prophecies. But she sees in them an opportunity. Your clerk, Gerald de Barri, can attest to the truth that Arthur's descendants still fight for Wales today. And my lady carries proof that her father claimed their kinship."

"That would be interesting to see," Eleanor said, returning her gaze to Gwendolyn and presenting an outstretched hand. Gwendolyn reached into her surcoat and pulled out the rolled letter from her father. She hesitated before passing the letter to Eleanor.

"It is all I have of him, my lady. My father and mother died when I was a child."

Eleanor nodded slightly without emotion, and Gwendolyn passed her father's letter into the queen's hand.

Eleanor gently opened the vellum scroll and sat quietly as her eyes traced back and forth across the lines of script. When she was done, she handed the letter to Walter de Coutances to inspect and turned her gaze to her clerk.

"Gerald, what say you to all of this?"

Gerald de Barri was a wiry man of medium height with a shock of ginger and gray hair standing mostly upright over a high, smooth forehead. He had stood by quietly for the entire conversation, intelligent eyes twinkling.

"This presents a most intriguing possibility, madame," he answered.

"You traveled with John in Ireland. Will he believe this?"

"Well, I can vouch for the present existence of the descendants of Arthur in Wales. And the Welsh prophecies are well known. Geoffrey of Monmouth made careful alterations to them in his Prophecies of Merlin, so that the tales favor a Plantagenet legacy. But John of Cornwall, whom I have discredited in my own writings, correctly claims that the prophecies predict the expulsion of the Normans by the Welsh, who regard themselves as the last of the original Britons. It is the reason we have worked so hard to adopt the legend of Arthur as our own and thus rob the Welsh of their greatest hero."

"Indeed," Eleanor agreed. Gwendolyn's eyes grew wide and she glanced sideways at William to try to read his reaction. The Plantagenets had been using the lore of Arthur for their own ends already.

"The only missing piece," Gerald continued, "is whether this . . . unusual woman is indeed the heir of Caliburn from the prophecies."

"Of course she isn't," the queen responded. "But if we can persuade John that she is, what difference does it make?"

"Exactly," Gerald agreed.

"Who else has been told that you are Caliburn's heir?"

Gwendolyn paused to think, grateful for the distraction from her aching knees. She realized that she had found the proposition so absurd that she had kept it entirely to herself.

"Yourselves, madame," she answered confidently. "And the prior of Launceston, and a wandering soothsayer."

At the mention of Launceston Priory in Cornwall, Walter de

Coutances's cheeks rose in a faint smile.

"Your friend, Walter?" the queen asked.

"Thomas, madame. A friend from my childhood."

The queen appeared satisfied and folded her hands into her lap comfortably.

"Stand up," she directed Gwendolyn, William, and Nigel, and waited patiently while they repositioned their coats and weapons back into place. Although she remained seated, Eleanor's chair on the elevated dais kept her above eye level with Gwendolyn and her men. She raised an eyebrow and gave them her decision quickly.

"You have indeed presented a most ingenious means of bargaining with my youngest son. You are now the guests of the Tower. You may not leave until I have given my permission, and then you will go where I tell you to go, and you will say what I tell you to say. You have offered a great service today, and I will reward you when this matter involving my sons has been resolved."

Gwendolyn stood blinking for a moment, grasping what the queen had said, aware of Nigel beside her stifling a protest in his throat.

"But, madame, this man," Gwendolyn began.

"Whatever it is, it will wait."

"One of the merchants in London, a dealer in linens, is a traitor, a supporter of John's rebellion. This man is a witness."

"You mean de Lacy?" William Marshal spoke up from behind her and Gwendolyn and Nigel turned to face him. "We've known about him for weeks. He's run off to Lincoln with his tail between his legs, waiting to see which way the tide turns."

"Master de Lacy held this man's daughter," Gwendolyn continued, nodding toward Nigel. "De Lacy forced her to stitch the embroideries he sells. She's only just been reunited with her father."

Eleanor looked closely at Nigel for the first time and narrowed her eyes.

"You were the man sold to the mercenary captain? Where is he now?"

"Dead, my lady. She discovered us in the forest outside Penhallam," he said, gesturing toward Gwendolyn.

"Really?" Eleanor said with disbelief. "This isn't all for show?" she asked, sweeping her hand to indicate Gwendolyn's appearance.

"I have trained with Penhallam's guard, madame."

Eleanor leaned back in her chair, her eyes moving from Gwendolyn to William to Nigel. "Fascinating," she murmured softly. "Why didn't you kill him, too?" She indicated toward Nigel.

"There were four of them, madame. I could only get the two of them before the other two ran off."

"But you're helping him now."

"Nigel saved my life in Chagford. There was a crowd. Men don't always like to see a woman carrying a sword."

"No, I suppose they do not," she replied slowly. The queen continued to regard them all closely, and Gwendolyn was certain that the queen was calculating and weighing all of the options and possible scenarios behind her gaze. Finally Eleanor's eyes landed sharply on Nigel.

"Are you John's man or not?"

Nigel shuffled uncomfortably beside Gwendolyn. She held her breath, wondering how he could answer the queen without slighting her foolish son who might legitimately be his king one day.

"I am whoever's man you tell me I am, my lady."

Gwendolyn exhaled and Eleanor's eyes warmed with approval at his answer.

"You look very familiar," she said. "Why?"

Nigel returned her gaze and replied without a hint of guile, "I've just got one of those faces, my lady."

"Nonsense," she retorted. "But I respect discretion. Where is your daughter now?"

"With her aunt, in Southwark."

"I'm sure her aunt will take excellent care of her. I'll have food and clothing delivered tomorrow."

Nigel flushed beside her, and again said the words so unfamiliar to him. "Thank you, madame."

"Now go and rest. Prepare to travel tomorrow."

"But my father's letter . . ." Gwendolyn's voice trailed off. She knew what the answer would be before it was spoken.

"That bit of proof must stay in my keeping," Eleanor said without apology. "I'm sure you understand why."

"Yes, madame." Gwendolyn fixed her jaw and forbade tears to rise. Instead, she turned on her heel and followed her men out of the room.

The queen's antechamber hushed immediately as the Marshal, Gwendolyn, and her men stepped back into the brightly lit hall.

"Wait here a moment," William Marshal said to them, then crossed the room and had a word with one of the men standing in a small circle. The man nodded and left the room through a side passage while the Marshal signaled to two other men to join him in returning to the queen's audience behind the heavy doors. As he swept past them again, the Marshal said simply, "Someone will come to show you to your quarters," and then he disappeared again into the queen's chamber.

Gwendolyn turned to William and Nigel as a low hum of conversation resumed around them. Nigel avoided her eyes, his jaw set.

"Nigel, I'm sorry," Gwendolyn began, but he cut her off with a wave of his hand.

"Ella will be fine. Mae won't let her out of her sight, and the extra food will be more than that family has on their table in a whole month." Nigel nodded to himself, squaring his shoulders. "And whoever would have thought a bastard like me would end up in the queen's service?" He allowed himself a small smile. "I may get something out of this if I live to see the end of it. Enough for Ella and me to make a fresh start."

William nudged Gwendolyn and she turned around to see Roslyn approaching her again, calmly this time. She leaned in closely and whispered into Gwendolyn's ear.

"You may have beaten me to the queen, but it won't do you any good. My family is thick with bishops and barons," she said quietly. "I will have you out of Penhallam by midwinter."

Gwendolyn took a step back and regarded Roslyn with an amused expression.

"The queen has invited us to stay in the Tower as her guests, Roslyn." Roslyn's face blanched at this news. "And in fact, your name didn't even come up just now. Did it, William?"

William made a show of stroking his beard, looking upward as if searching his memory.

"No. No, it didn't. Well, there was that bit about a Flemish donkey."

Roslyn's jaw set again. She turned back to Gwendolyn, her expression dark with spite.

"Do you know why no one here approaches you? Why every member of the court stays to the far side of the room from you? It's because of the smell, Gwendolyn. You stink of filth and dirt, like an animal. Very fitting."

Roslyn turned around, her elegant dress sweeping the floor, and returned to her companions with gliding steps, her chin held high. Gwendolyn watched her, noting the gulf between a woman like Roslyn, who went to such effort to create the appearance of power and authority, and a woman like Eleanor, who exercised both so easily.

9

A LAMB
FOR THE PRINCE

Despite the unfamiliar surroundings, Gwendolyn slept soundly that night, not waking up until a chambermaid arrived for her. Gwendolyn had been provided a private room in the line of stone buildings that flanked the western end of the Tower yard. The mattress she had slept on, though narrow and too short for her, was stuffed with goose down and covered in soft, fresh linens scented with lavender. William and Nigel, on the other hand, had been shown to straw pallets in the passageway outside her door. As her constable, William had relocated his pallet to lie across the threshold, blocking the doorway to her room. To have slept anywhere else would have been considered an abandonment of duty.

Early the next morning, Gwendolyn found herself gently woken up by a shy maid with a stack of sweet rolls and fresh linens. Gwendolyn took a moment to see that the maid had given food to her men also and then listened while the maid explained that a bath had been drawn for her and her men, and that Gwendolyn would be the first to bathe. Clothes would also be provided, and if Gwendolyn would allow her and her men's swords and armor to be taken to the armory, the Tower's craftsmen would mend and polish their equipment. Gwendolyn agreed to everything, aware that there would be no point in arguing with any of it anyway. She stepped outside to greet William and Nigel and tell them what was in store for them. Ignoring their grumblings, Gwendolyn followed the maid downstairs to a room adjacent to the kitchen, where a large, wooden tub had been filled with steaming water strewn with rose petals.

But this was to be no relaxing, peaceful bath. Two broad-girthed women followed her in, and as soon as she had dunked herself naked into the tub, they proceeded to scrub her from head to toe until she thought her raw skin would bleed. When they were finished with her, the quiet maid returned with pale linen and rich green fabric draped over her arm.

"You will wear these," she said simply, setting the clothes down on a chair and leaving again. Gwendolyn stepped out of the tub and the burly women dried her with equal indifference and then dropped a clean linen chemise down over her head. The scratchy fabric had never been worn before, and Gwendolyn wondered if the gown had been made that morning by the Tower's seamstresses. She fit her arms through the sleeves and was surprised to find that it fit perfectly, even with her long arms and height. The women next reached for the green gown and paused, waiting. Gwendolyn looked at them questioningly.

"Lift up your arms," one of them sighed impatiently.

Gwendolyn did as she was told, then had to bend over so the women could reach her wrists to settle the fitted sleeves of the gown over her arms and down to her shoulders. They tugged her long hair out from the back of the dress and pulled the gown snugly over her waist, then dropped the full skirts to the floor. Able to see again, Gwendolyn realized that the gown had an open seam on each side that ran from the armpit to her waist. A leather tie laced up the seams, holding the fitted dress close to her body while allowing her arms full range of movement.

"Oh," she said aloud, realizing the dress had been modified to account for the peculiar needs of a woman who carried a sword. New stitches at the wrists revealed where the long drape of fabric, so popular among women of wealth to better emphasize their willowy figures as well as their ability to afford such extravagance of fabric, had been removed and the sleeve repaired. "This will do nicely," she said quietly to herself.

"Thank the queen," one of the women said matter-of-factly and gestured for her to step outside, where yet another maid waited for Gwendolyn, holding a pair of embroidered boots and a comb of whalebone.

Gwendolyn's hair was combed out, but it was not braided, as she preferred, nor was it pinned up in coils, as was the custom for married women. As her hair dried with the rough combing, the curls became ragged and disorderly. Before long, Gwendo-lyn realized that her hair was taking on the appearance of a wild mane. The young woman holding the comb sighed, stood up, and fetched a jar from one of the shelves lining the walls of the massive kitchen. Working from one side around to the other, the maid rubbed scented oil into the long strands of Gwendolyn's hair, smoothing the bristling curls into soft waves that finally tumbled gracefully around her waist.

"Come on, then. I'll take you to the armory."

Gwendolyn followed the maid and found herself out in the sunshine as they crossed the Tower yard to a stone building whose anvils and forges were shared by the blacksmiths and the armorers. Many of the laborers in the yard paused to look at her respectfully as she passed, and she wondered who they thought she might be—a marriageable heiress under the wardship of the crown, perhaps, or maybe the widow of a well-situated baron, coming to plead for her future position. Whatever they were thinking, she was confident that "descendant of King Arthur" was nowhere in their musings. William and Nigel were already inside, dressed in their new shirts and leggings, with oiled leather boots that reached to their knees. Nigel's astounded expression at the coif, hauberk and leggings that were being fitted to him brought a smile to her lips. William was occupied inspecting the new rivets in his mail tunic approvingly, as the man beside him pointed out other repairs and improvements made to his armor. William was the first to notice her arrival, and his mouth froze in mid-sentence as he recognized her.

"By the blood of—" he began under his breath.

"Shut up," she said quietly as she walked past him and turned again to watch Nigel. The armor that Eleanor was giving him cost more than every penny he could have earned in three years as a mercenary. It meant much more than protection in battle. This armor elevated him to a different circle. It visually identified him as a man of means and property. When he was presented with a new surcoat bearing the de Cardinham colors, he looked up and saw her watching him. She nodded back to him and nudged William beside her.

"He's your man now, William."

William regarded Nigel with unmasked reservation. "If you say so."

They were brought back before Eleanor not long after midday. This time, they were brought into a separate room behind the receiving room where she had held her audience the night before. Here, Eleanor sat up in a large, beautifully carved bed, supported by a pile of cushions behind her. A tray of cheeses and dried fruits lay on top of the blankets beside her, and not a strand of hair or article of clothing was out of place. Her eyes followed them attentively as they entered, and Gwendolyn had the feeling of being appraised like sheep at the wool market.

Sunlight streamed in through glass-paned windows, giving the room a sense of grandeur not unlike the newer cathedrals with their high, arched windows. Walter de Coutances was in the room again, seated on a stool beside the hearth and looking tired. A second man who Gwendolyn did not recognize stood near the door that they had entered, and William Marshal entered the room behind them, looking not much better than de Coutances, but, with his quick step and lively eyes, apparently better able to tolerate his fatigue.

"This is much better," Eleanor said, casually reaching for a piece of fruit before continuing. "John was my husband's favorite son, and John thanked him for it by betraying Henry on his deathbed. Richard had already won, Henry was dying, and John, for reasons known only to him, delivered the mortal blow with his disloyalty. Whatever faults John was born with, Henry's indulgence only made them worse. And John is unfit to rule at present because of it. For the Plantagenet legacy, and for stability and peace on this island, Richard must live long enough that John, if he also survives, will have endured enough of Life's instruction to overcome his flaws and grow into a fit and able leader of men.

"Lady de Cardinham, I have considered your proposition, and I have discussed the matter with my counselors, but there is one thing I must know first. You have put yourself into personal danger by coming here. Why? What do you hope to gain for yourself?"

The queen waited patiently for Gwendolyn to answer. Gwendolyn took several moments to consider her words, having learned that the larger portion of the victories in negotiations could be credited merely to knowing when to hold one's tongue, and being comfortable with the silence that followed. However, the queen's face remained impassive and unreadable while she waited for Gwendolyn to respond, and Gwendolyn realized that the queen would have learned the same tactic long ago.

"The mercenaries that I intercepted were only the first. Brutal men loyal to John continue to cross Penhallam on their way to St. Michael's Mount. They have attacked our farms and my tenants, and they have stolen our livestock. I realized the rumors of who I am could put an end to it if I came to you so that you could use me to bargain with John."

"You want nothing else, then? No purse of silver or perhaps

additional lands for your husband?"

Gwendolyn looked Eleanor in the eyes. She realized that Ros-lyn had had her audience with the queen. "I had hoped not to lose the lands we already have to my husband's brother and his wife."

"Ah. There it is," Eleanor said lightly. "One dispute between brothers could be settled by solving another dispute between the royal brothers?"

Gwendolyn stood silently, unsure what to say. Revealing Wal-ter's support for John could end badly for the entire de Cardin-ham family, not just Roslyn.

"I was already aware of Walterus de Cardinham's support for John." The queen used Walter's given name from his father, a relic of pre-Norman England that Walter had dropped when he came of age. "It is a strange position for a mother to be in. I cannot fault a man for being loyal to my sons—either of them. But John is wrong, and some of his supporters fan the flames of his disil-lusionment, playing the boy right into the hands of the King of France. Phillip would love to have an excuse to bring his armies to our shores. I am afraid Walterus de Cardinham is one of these."

Gwendolyn's stomach felt light inside her. Eleanor had as much as declared Walter a traitor to the crown. For once, she felt a bit of sympathy for Roslyn.

"And you, child," continued Eleanor, "are still a virgin."

Gwendolyn gasped as the air seemed suddenly to be sucked out of the room. A quiet rustling filled the room as all of the men, even de Coutances, turned their eyes onto her. She had closed her eyes with the shock, and when she opened them again the first face she saw was that of her furious constable standing beside her. He had warned her that Eleanor could decide to use her as a reward for some baron needing compensation, and she had withheld from him the truth of her unconsummated marriage and how easily assailable her position as Robert's wife actually was.

Gwendolyn exhaled slowly. "How did you know?"

"Lady Roslyn suspected it, but now you have confirmed the truth."

The small trace of sympathy Gwendolyn had felt for Roslyn vanished. Suddenly Gwendolyn felt ridiculous in her new dress, with her scented hair draped down her back in full, red waves. Eleanor had been preparing her, as a present that she could give away.

"Lady de Cardinham," Eleanor said softly. "I have no intention of taking you from Robert. Unless that is what you wish," she added, probing whether Gwendolyn's affection might have already diminished during Robert's long absence.

Gwendolyn shook her head.

"Then I will take no action in regard to the unconsummated state of your marriage. But be warned," Eleanor said sharply, tapping her finger against the bed, "do not persuade me to change my mind in this by failing to do as I instruct you in a moment. Do we understand each other?"

"Very well, madame."

Eleanor took a deep breath and sighed, shaking her head in admonishment at Gwendolyn.

"Lady, you are in a precarious position, the dangers of which I am certain you do not fully appreciate, but your man here surely does," Eleanor said, indicating with a nod toward William. "If I could send you directly to Robert now to consummate your marriage, I would. I am your ally, but circumstances require that I make use of you now. I cannot place your life above those duties that only I can fulfill. My life was never my own. Be glad that yours will be again, when this is over."

"Yes, madame."

"All right, then." Eleanor straightened up in her bedclothes and stretched, leaning back against the cushions. "As it turns out, a few days ago one of our spies brought news that John has found an ally in a sorcerer, a powerful wizard. Or so he believes." The queen rolled her eyes and shook her head. "The charlatan apparently has advised John that, according to the stars and other portents, Arthur's heir walks now upon English soil, and the sword's return is imminent. If John were to locate and capture Arthur's heir, then Caliburn would also be his. Of course, both the sorcerer and John have assumed that the heir of Caliburn is a man." Eleanor pursed her lips and gave a small laugh.

"All three of you are to travel south to Arundel. I sent a messenger ahead of you last night. The castle there is well fortified, close enough to reach in a few days, but far enough from John and his supporters for your protection. I will send word to John that the heir of Caliburn has been found, that you are loyal to Richard, and that he must cease his rebellion.

"You are the lamb, Gwendolyn, staked in the meadow to draw the wolf out of the woods. If I can delay John at all with this distraction, even for a few months, it will be enough time to get the ransom to Germany and free Richard. In the meantime, you must stay alive and safe. If you are kidnapped or killed, you are of no use to me. John's belief that he has a real sorcerer guiding him has made him bold and foolish. I cannot predict what he might try in order to get to you.

"You are to travel with reasonable haste, and you will sleep under tents that I provide to you. I am sending a dozen men-at-arms, under your constable's command, to guard you. You shall wear your de Cardinham colors and full armor when you travel, even though it will slow you down. You cannot take any chances. And that means you cannot tell anyone else what you have shared with me of your ancestry and these prophecies. I cannot guarantee that there are not others out there who also believe these legends to be true, and who would capture you for their own use."

Eleanor popped a dried apricot into her mouth and chewed it thoughtfully. "When you reach Arundel, you will stay there to await my further instruction. Walter de Coutances will accompany you to ensure my wishes are received in Arundel. William d'Aubigni, the earl of Arundel, is his friend and a steadfast supporter of Richard. You can trust him absolutely. D'Aubigni will do whatever de Coutances says he must, no questions asked."

Walter de Coutances stiffly stood up and ran a hand through his hair, looking noticeably less composed than he had the previous evening. He crossed the room to them in long strides and offered his hand to Gwendolyn.

"My lady," he greeted her and then turned toward William. "Your horses have been brought up from Southwark. I will take you now to the garrison to select the men who will accompany you." William nodded and turned on his heel to follow de Coutances out of the room, then paused and looked back at Nigel, still waiting beside Gwendolyn.

"Soldier! To attention!"

Nigel snapped out of his reverie and dashed to follow William, moving awkwardly under the unfamiliar weight of a full mail tunic.

Shadows cast by the newly constructed curtain walls angled across the Tower yard in the afternoon sun by the time their group was ready to depart. In the end, over thirty travelled in all: de Coutances and his clerk; one of the Tower's junior chaplains; William, Nigel, and the twelve men from the Tower garrison; five squires; Gwendolyn and the maid who had first woken her that morning; and lastly, a handful of staff to set up camps, prepare meals, dig latrines, and other work to make their travel more comfortable. In addition to their own provisions, they brought three carts laden with grain, meat, supplies, and equipment to be delivered to Arundel. All of the Tower guard wore surcoats emblazoned with the golden lions against a blood-red sky that was the herald of the Plantagenet family. William rode up and down the lines as they prepared to leave, calling orders to a handful of the men to take positions around Gwendolyn first in the event of an ambush. So far, Eleanor had managed to stay one step ahead of John's plans, but where Eleanor easily dismissed John's sorcerer as simple fraud, Gwendolyn knew that William would have allowed for at least a possibility of truth in the rumor.

Gwendolyn sat astride Bedwyr in full armor, the de Cardinham colors of points of gold arrayed in battle formation against a background of black vivid on her new surcoat. As much as Eleanor had said to her during their meeting, there was still much that the queen had left unsaid, and it was those open questions that weighed on Gwendolyn now. What would William d'Aubigni, Earl of Arundel, have to say about the queen's decision that he should house and keep the queen's "lamb," all but painting a target on Arundel Castle for John and his men? William had told her as they had gathered in the yard that William d'Aubigni was highly respected among the queen's magnates, and that he was no fool for John. Arundel was situated near the coast, and when one of John's boats of Flemish mercenaries had tried to make landfall at a sheltered cove nearby, their boat had been spotted by d'Aubigni's men. All of the mercenaries but one were killed, the last one spared only to be transported to the Tower to give information and suffer execution. Now, as the seasons changed, the time for launching elaborate military campaigns was drawing to a close. But the rebellion would continue, played out as games of intrigue, politics, and shifting alliances—the surreptitious sort of battle that was John's special, if singular, talent.

The sound of a trumpet blowing echoed through the yard and she watched curiously as everyone who was not on a horse knelt down and bowed their heads and an expectant hush fell over them. Finally, she saw a group emerge from the Tower and walk across the green toward them, the queen walking in the center of the configuration, surrounded on all sides by guards and her advisors. When they approached, Walter de Coutances stepped to Gwendolyn's side and nodded pointedly to her that she was to dismount. She quickly shifted to the ground and knelt beside the justiciar to receive the queen.

Eleanor stood before Gwendolyn in an emerald gown lined with beads of dark gray pearl, unlike any Gwendolyn had seen before.

"Your service begins now, my dear," Eleanor said with a polite smile. The dowager queen put her hands out, and one of her attendants stepped forward with bowed head and placed a small vellum scroll onto her palms, then retreated back again.

"Orders to William d'Aubigni to keep you safe," she said, extending the scroll toward de Coutances.

"Yes, madame," the justiciar replied as he took the scroll and tucked it into his surcoat.

"And as for your father's letter," she said, turning to Gwendolyn, "I will keep it safe, child. You have my word that I will return it to you when this is over."

Gwendolyn marveled that the queen would have guessed the one worry among all others that had weighed most heavily on her thoughts. She bowed her head slowly in a show of well-earned respect.

"Thank you, madame."

Eleanor nodded her regal chin slightly. "May merciful Christ protect you and keep you safe."

On his cue, the bishop of London, resplendent in a silk tunic and woolen robe stitched with adornment as fine as the queen's, stepped forward from the entourage and began to chant prayers and benedictions over the party. He walked slowly down the line of gleaming armed men, horses, and carts, gesturing the sign of the cross over them as he went. As the bishop passed down the line of men, Gwendolyn saw the queen's expression register shock for a brief moment and then compose again into her usual, impassive visage. The bishop's head remained bowed in prayer as he slowly walked to the end of the line and then returned to the group surrounding the queen. Eleanor watched his movements with hardened, disdainful eyes, then swept around on her heel, silk gown rustling, and strode back toward the Tower. The tight configuration of men and attendants kept lockstep with her until they disappeared as one body back into the stone walls of the keep.

Gwendolyn and de Coutances rose to their feet and Gwendolyn walked over to William, but he avoided her glance and conferred solely with de Coutances. The gesture was petty, but she realized she had underestimated either the risk she had ventured by presenting herself to Eleanor in her barely married state or how badly her omission had scared him. Either way, he was obviously still angry with her. There would be words between them about it later. She turned to walk back up the line to where a squire stood holding Bedwyr's reins, and she spat into the dirt with irritation that, on top of everything else, she should also have to contend with the threat of being traded off to a man as property simply because she was a woman and a virgin.

The party mounted up onto their horses and carts, and the Tower's guard formed two orderly columns as directed by William, one on either side of the line of travelers. William took the lead, and he sent Nigel to ride in back, guarding the rear. Gwendolyn rode in the middle of the line, a guard on either side of her, their wooden shields hooked to their saddles and lances' ends resting in leather cups attached to their stirrups. As they moved forward in formation, they were an impressive display of discipline, strength, and intimidation.

The herald's trumpet blew again as their procession exited the Tower grounds through a gate under construction to the west of the Tower yard and over a timber bridge that spanned the new moat. They crossed westward through London, back the way Gwendolyn, William, and Nigel had entered the day before. Gwendolyn watched the stares created by their procession, and found it amusing to exit London in such a spectacle after their anonymous and ragged arrival. They passed out of the gates and onto the open road again, where they turned southwest onto another wide road that had been excavated centuries ago by the Romans. This road would take them most of the way to Arundel, and Gwendolyn settled in for what she hoped would be an easier and more comfortable ride than the travel to London had been.

10

HOUNDS OF HELL

William rode up and down the line, checking in with each of the men, learning their names and observing their demeanor with one another. Their new captain's casual conversation would have a relaxing effect on the men, but Gwendolyn knew, as she watched William, that his chatting had a purpose and that he was discovering more about the new men in his command than they were telling him. He had taught her that the strength of any fighting unit lay in the cohesiveness between its members; hidden rivalries, old wounds, and personal scores to settle were as life-threatening as a faulty shield strap. As she followed his movements while he reviewed the ranks of the Tower guard, she realized that she had learned more in William's company than the mere wielding of weapons.

Behind her, Nigel settled into his new charge as second in

command, given to him by William as they had loaded up to leave. Nigel had taken stock of all the weapons and given orders to the squires and pages for their duties during the stops they would make to water the horses and to give the armed riders an opportunity to dismount and ease the stiffness from their limbs. No one spoke to her, which suited her for the moment. With time, the Tower guard would come to see her as one of them, as her own men at Penhallam had. She smiled to herself, imagining the first opportunity to train together in the morning and the fun of taking advantage of the errors these new men would make in underestimating her.

They had traveled maybe a half-dozen miles when it was time to stop and take shelter, before nightfall overtook them. William picked a flat meadow alongside a stream, and as soon as they stopped, all of the travelers hopped down from their carts or dismounted from their horses and went to work. Fires were lit, wood gathered, water carried. Gwendolyn walked through the bustling camp, leading Bedwyr to water at the stream, and listened to the light-hearted remarks and raillery exchanged by the men of the Tower guard as they efficiently built a pen for the horses, dug a latrine, and staked tents. She had a moment of nostalgia for Penhallam and the fellowship of the manor garrison, but she walked on, tending to her own duties. By the time Gwendolyn had watered Bedwyr, removed the saddle, and checked the mare's hooves, her private tent was already erected and outfitted with a soft pallet to sleep on, a basin and jug of fresh water on a small trestle table, and a brazier ready to receive coals from the fire that was now burning at the center of their encampment. Tall, iron stakes in the ground held up tallow candles that gave the inside of the tent a soft, inviting glow. Her maid, Sybil, followed her into her tent and made to reach for her armor and then paused, her eyes smiling. Gwendolyn realized Sybil would have no idea what to unbuckle first or how many layers she would find beneath.

"You'd better call for one of the squires," Gwendolyn suggested, and Sybil curtsied and wordlessly darted from the tent. Gwendolyn unfastened her cloak and began to unbuckle her sword belt when the tent flap moved again and she turned around to see William ducking his head to step in.

He paused just inside the opening, stooping slightly so as not to brush his head on the canvas above, and took in the comforts provided by Eleanor with raised eyebrows. But then he turned to face her, and his surly scowl dropped back into place.

"You might have told me," he said curtly.

"It was none of your business," she replied, matching his tone.

"Your safety is my business."

She looked him in the eye; she could not fault him for his loyalty. But there were some things that were hers, that were private, and always would be. "You choose to take folklore as truth, that you are the prophesied guardian of the heir of Caliburn. That is your prerogative, but don't—"

"I made a promise to Robert. I gave him my word, if it ever came to it. My life for yours."

Gwendolyn stopped where she stood, her mouth frozen in mid-argument. A moment of astonishment blocked all other thought.

"He had no right to ask that of you."

William held her gaze, unflinching, unmoved. "He didn't ask. I offered. He accepted."

Gwendolyn felt her chest rise and she took a long breath and let it out slowly.

"I didn't risk my life to save you when I was not yet a man so that I could stand by the next time you were in peril," he continued.

Gwendolyn backed up a few steps and settled herself down onto the pallet behind her. She leaned forward and rested her forehead against her palms. "Save you," had been his words, and she felt rebellion against them welling up inside her, solid and undeniable. She had been a girl then, a child. But not now. She was not his to save. The easy banter of the camp carried on outside her tent, but she paid no attention to it. There was a slight rustling at the tent flap, and one of the squires leaned in, smiling, but when he saw their faces, felt the tension between them, he mumbled an apology and withdrew. Gwendolyn sat upright and faced William again.

"I am no man's to save. Not yours. Not Robert's." William began to protest, but she silenced him with a flick of her hand. "And if I had told you, it wouldn't have changed a thing. We would still be exactly where we are now." Her voice was reasonable, calm. "Anyway, you've kept your own secret—you and Robert. This deal that you made without my consent or knowledge."

"You knew I was responsible for protecting you."

"Not like this," she argued back to him, her voice low. "This is different. You believe this pact you have made gives you authority to know and direct every part of my life." William looked down to his feet and she knew she had struck on the truth. "Admit it.

This has been the one, the constant point of contention between us, William." She held him with her gaze. "Understand this now. Your sacrifice does not give you control over me."

"Gwendolyn. I . . ." William paused, calmer now, and she saw him struggle for words. "I should have been prepared for the risk you took. I should have known."

"It was private," she said, an angry edge rising again in her voice.

William opened his mouth to say something more, paused, and then turned his back to her, pacing the few steps that the tent allowed.

"Why . . . why did you and Robert never . . ."

She watched his back as he crossed his arms. He already knew the most personal part of it. He might as well know the rest.

"Because I never wanted to."

William turned and lifted his face to her, his eyes softening as his brow relaxed. He did not know Robert well, and he had assumed that her husband would have the character of any other son of a wealthy baron—spoiled, entitled, not the sort to set aside his husband's right and body's desire over the reluctance of a young wife.

"And Robert accepted that?"

"Robert de Cardinham is the best man I have ever known."

William stood quietly, patiently, while Gwendolyn explained the circumstances of her marriage, the bargain that she and Robert had made with each other: that he would leave her in charge of Penhallam, with her oath to protect its people and see the land and the estate to greater prosperity, while he won the king's favor and reward in service in Outremer. Gwendolyn did not share with William whether any real affection existed between herself and Robert, because the fact was that she was unsure herself. And after having been apart for so many years and the gulf she had crossed from that time to become the woman she was now, she was not sure that she was even capable of that kind of affection. Her woman's life thus far had been full of hard work and struggle and not much else. There was no time or even a desire for any sort of companionship other than that of Penhallam's household. The romantic songs of the troubadours held no interest for her, and she had never felt the longing or desire that they sang about. For his part, she had no idea how the years of war, the cruelty and predation of repeated siege and battle, might have changed Robert. She stood up and shook the tension out of her arms. None of this would interest her constable, in any case.

"When he returns—" William began, but then stopped and looked away.

"When he returns, I don't know what will happen," she admitted.

William paused to look at her, as if he had not really seen her until that moment. She was not, by any measure, the same woman Robert had left years ago. He turned to face her squarely and took a step closer so that he stood before her, almost eye-to-eye. She stood her ground, unsure what to expect, and saw the flinty expression he gave to his men-at-arms when they lined up in full armor for his inspection. She braced herself in case she was about to receive the stiff shoulder slap William usually reserved for Penhallam's men-at-arms.

"I'll see you at training tomorrow," he said, then shook his head and sighed before turning to step outside of her tent.

The following morning, Gwendolyn awoke to moonless star-light and roused Sybil, asleep on the straw across from her. She could hear the Tower guard outside stirring and she was eager to dress and join them for their morning exercises before camp broke to resume the journey to Arundel. When Sybil held up the new green dress to her to put on, Gwendolyn told her to put the garment away. She needed no reminder of her sex and the loss of freedom that had almost come with it.

She emerged from her tent comfortable in leggings and a belted tunic borrowed from the squires, her hair pulled back again into a single braid. The stars had disappeared and the liquid glow of pale dawn began to spill across the sky from the east. They would have friendly weather that day for their travels. She sucked in a deep breath of fresh air, happy to be out of the noise and clutter and stench of London. Her hands had begun to grow soft from lack of training, hard calluses had sloughed away, and she followed the sounds of William's and Nigel's voices to where the Tower men were assembled, her spirits high with the prospect of rough exertion and physical challenge against new opponents.

When she arrived, the men of the Tower guard had already faced off against one another in pairs. With the addition of Nigel they were an odd number, and as soon as he saw her William called to her to take position against the odd one out. She scanned over the heads of the sparring men and spotted one who was stand-ing to the side, waiting his turn to practice with the others. She picked her way carefully through the men until she stood before him, a slender young knight by the name of Tristan. Tristan cast an uncertain glance in William's direction as Gwendolyn took a wooden staff from one of the squires. She was about his height and build, slightly more lithe, a good match for training. She assumed a combat posture, and Nigel tossed Tristan a wooden sword.

"She'll take your head off, soldier, if you keep standing around like an idiot."

William called out for the paired fighters to shift positions and start again, and Gwendolyn's staff struck out and smacked her opponent on the side of the leg, dropping him onto one knee before he realized what had happened. She quickly completed the well-known series of moves in her attack: staff against collarbone, tip thrust under jaw. She had held back from actually inflicting injury with the last two blows, but it was clear enough that he would have been instantly killed had the battle been real. And although her assault had been utterly predictable, the young knight had hardly moved his sword, which in this setting was the same as an insult. Gwendolyn withdrew her weapon and extended a hand to help the man up, which he refused. Looking around her, she realized the other men had stopped their combat practices and were staring at her and her opponent. Their hardened faces reminded her that these were some of England's best fighting men, part of a company of men hand-selected by William Marshal himself to guard the very blood that ruled England. Not only was she a newcomer from the relative backwater of Cornwall, she was a woman, and she had strolled into the middle of their training and dropped one of them without receiving so much as a scratch. Not that Tristan had made much of an effort to defend himself.

Tristan hesitated, his boyish blue eyes prematurely aged by a deep scar that crossed from his brow to his cheek. He had probably been quite handsome, she thought to herself, and wondered if he resented the loss of his looks to his vocation. Perhaps she reminded him of a love who had abandoned him after the injury. Then again, perhaps he was glad to be free of such fickle affections. As all of these thoughts crossed her mind, he still would not raise his sword against her. This would not do. But there were other ways she could get him to fight her. As the clatter and grunts of men fighting with wooden weapons rose around them again, she tried to rouse him to anger to encourage him to fight her.

"I met your sister yesterday," she said evenly, holding his blue-eyed gaze coolly. "I was given a tour of the Tower stables. She said she likes her oats very much."

Like her attack with the staff, the taunt was unoriginal and well known, but it succeeded anyway. Tristan snarled, raised his weapon, and lunged. She deflected the clumsy attack with her staff and spun to face him again as he stumbled past her. He lunged at her again, swinging his weapon downward in rapid hacking attacks. She watched his eyes and anticipated every movement, blocked them all smoothly, and when he hesitated to catch his breath she smacked the staff hard against his ribs.

William, who had been walking among the men to observe their skill and technique, stepped in behind her opponent and tapped him on the shoulder.

"Stings, doesn't it?" he asked Tristan.

"My side is fine, sir," he replied sourly.

"Not your ribs. Your pride." William approached the knight,

and Tristan stood up straight at attention and glared past Gwendolyn into the distance. William leaned in close to speak into his ear in a low voice.

"If you think you are looking at a woman," he said and paused, gesturing toward Gwendolyn, "you are wrong. You are looking at a killer, and that is all that matters."

Gwendolyn felt herself blanch at the words, but they were true. She held her ground as Tristan regarded her with narrowed eyes as he weighed William's description of her as a "killer." William took off his shirt and took the man's wooden sword from him. He signaled to the attending squire, who dashed over with a similar wooden sword for Gwendolyn and took her staff from her. The other men stopped their exercises and gathered into a loose circle around them, watching with curious anticipation. Another squire handed William and Gwendolyn each a round wooden shield.

William turned to face her again, grinning, fully transformed from the man she was coming to know as her fussing guardian into the lethal warrior she had first met at Penhallam shortly after her wedding. The effect was almost feral as he circled her with predatory grace. He stopped and moved his sword arm in a smooth arc, weapon extended, defining the space around him.

"This is where I can kill you."

She and William had not faced off against each other in years, William preferring to observe and comment as she fought with Gerald or Tom rather than engage her directly himself. She stepped toward him to the tip of the wooden blade and measured the distance. When she knew his reach, she looked up again and nodded.

He crouched low to the ground, spreading his stance, a smirk inviting her to advance. The wooden sword in her hand was clumsier than her weapon, and poorly balanced. But the point of the exercise was timing, judgment, movement, tactic. She stepped in, swinging low, causing him to lower his shield to block her, and she used her weapon alternately as a club and a spear, beating and jabbing, and blocking his return blows with her own shield. But then William unleashed himself. He rained down his blows with such force that splinters flew from the shield and he pushed her back. She stumbled and fell over flat onto her back, limbs and thoughts disorganized in the confusion of finding herself lying on the ground. The point of his sword immediately went for her neck before she could roll or raise her shield to protect herself.

"Like that," he said to Tristan, as she raised herself back up to standing again. Tristan nodded and stepped forward, but she was enjoying herself too much. William's war experience made him the best opponent she had ever faced off against. She shifted back to battle stance, shook a lock of hair out of her eyes.

"One more time, William," she said with a toying grin. "See if you can do that again."

In spite of the chill his battle-ready leer sent through her, Gwendolyn took position facing him again. All eyes of the Tower guard were fixed on them now. She realized with unexpected pride that William was truly a master of combat, of his sword, and of himself. For a moment it was easy to imagine how terrifying he could be in the pitch of battle, streaked with blood, roaring with his weapon high.

As she approached to his right, swinging and hacking with

more force than she realized she had in her, he shifted his rear foot half a step backward, expanding his reach and increasing his stability. But he had also exposed his forward leg just enough, and she adjusted the swing of her blade to strike the target he offered. Too late she realized that he had anticipated her movement; he had simply baited her. His foot went out and she was sent sprawling into the dirt, to the laughter and amusement of the surrounding men. She hit the ground hard, opening a cut in her chin and knocking the air from her lungs. Slowly, she rolled over, pushing dirt and gravel from her lips with her tongue and spitting it out onto the ground beside her.

He was not holding back, and she understood immediately. He was giving her the chance to prove herself to the Tower guard, to earn their respect by refusing to give up or walk away from a fight.

Gwendolyn stood up and brushed the dirt from around her face and clothes and found her footing again, her cheeks flushed. Without a thought, her far hand formed a fist and flew out to slam squarely into William's jaw. She noted with satisfaction how quickly she had recovered—quickly enough for her fist to catch him by surprise. She shook the sting from her hand, hoping the crunch she had heard was only the knuckles and not her recently mended bones cracking. William steadied himself and turned to face her, a pleased smile spreading across his face.

"That's more like it, my lady." He worked his jaw side to side, made a show of massaging it to the amusement of the Tower guard, although she knew his jaw, more granite than bone, was perfectly fine.

She stepped back, stopped tending her stinging hand.

"In Cornwall, that would pass for courtship. Next time don't go so easy on me."

The Tower men broke into laughter, and William stepped back and bowed graciously toward her. He turned and walked outside the training ring, stretched his arms up to put his shirt back on, and resumed giving orders and directions to the men. They dispersed into pairs again, and she found herself faced off against a different man this time, a stout, ruddy-faced man who had watched the encounter with William closely and appeared eager to test her mettle himself. After all, the novel opportunity to match his brawn against a woman so obviously skilled and relentless might never present itself again. They fought with staffs, and he came at her with a force and talent for killing that took her breath away. This was nothing like training with the guard at Penhallam. These men of the Tower had spent years in France at the tournaments and in siege, spending every waking minute preparing for, fighting, and recovering from battle. William called out to the men to switch, and after a brief shuffling of opponents Tristan stood across from her again, the gleam in his eye warning her that he had learned his lesson. This training was more real, more thrilling, than any of the mock battles she had fought at Penhallam, and she was discovering an appetite for it, for the sheer purity of the blows, the simple elegance of strategy and elemental match of wits and strength, guts and nerve. She advanced and attacked over and over, and each time Tristan easily deflected her, sometimes smacking her unprotected hands roughly with the staff, sometimes sending her slamming to the ground on her backside. Every time, he patiently pointed out to her the error she had made, how she had left her body exposed and vulnerable. Her arms and shoulders burned with exhaustion. She noticed her hunger and dismissed it; the gnawing inside would pass.

While they trained, squires and staff broke camp, packed and stowed belongings and equipment, and prepared a small morning meal. The priest called for morning prayer, and as she walked with the other men back toward the rest of their group, she realized from their coarse jokes and casual manner that she was one of them already. Walter de Coutances blinked in shock at her bloodied appearance when she arrived to break her fast with the others, and she grinned irreverently back.

When she passed William again on her way to find Bedwyr and mount up, she leaned toward him and said quietly so that only he could hear, "Thank you."

⁓

They traveled at an easy pace again for most of the day, and the miles comfortably dropped behind them. Sybil had come to accept that her new mistress was unlike any she had served before and that her work was limited to the simple tasks of tidying her things and helping Gwendolyn to dress. There were no fresh flowers to gather, no elaborate hair styles to weave, no ribbons or wimples or elegant dresses to look after except the one, which Gwendolyn refused to wear anyway. Instead, Gwendolyn had suggested that she acquaint herself with the different types of armor she wore and their proper care and use—an obviously preposterous idea. However, Gwendolyn had deliberately provided Sybil with an excuse for lingering in the company of the squires, and the young maid took full advantage of the opportunity that day.

As they rode, Walter de Coutances took position alongside Gwendolyn and introduced himself to her. Together, they reminisced about Cornwall, their shared homeland, sometimes falling into the Cornish language that few in this part of England spoke.

"Is it true," Gwendolyn asked him, after they had been talking for a while, "that your family are descendants of Trojan fighters who escaped before the city burned?"

De Coutances's mouth pursed with a suppressed laugh.

"That would be the full and complete invention of my friend Gerald de Barri, my dear."

She raised her eyebrows in amusement. "He is quite a master with words, isn't he?" she mused. "Perhaps one day he will tell my story, if I am fortunate."

De Coutances laughed again. "Be careful what you wish for, as they say in the East. De Barri won't consult with you before spinning his tales."

Gwendolyn sat back in her gently rocking saddle, thoughtful, and ventured another question.

"Why don't you claim the title of Justiciar openly? Both Richard and the queen acknowledge your appointment, and your authority is unquestioned."

"Exactly," he answered, cocking an eyebrow at her. "There is no need for me to do so. And integrity prohibits it. I will serve in whatever capacity my sovereign requests of me. But I took a stand at the synod of bishops called in the first year of Richard's reign that clergy shall be prohibited from holding secular offices of the court. I cannot help that Richard has appointed me to the role of

Justiciar, and I have given him my oath to serve him, but as I am also Archbishop of Rouen, I cannot at the same time and in good conscience flaunt the title of Justiciar."

"If there is a prohibition against clergy holding secular offices, it doesn't seem to be very widely known," she said with a little sarcasm.

"You have struck on the principle weakness of the law—of any law. Once legislated, although it may be entirely right and good and full of wisdom, no law is worth the paper it is written on if it is not taught and enforced." De Coutances stared ahead as he spoke, effortlessly reciting the principle of laws that she had already found and admired in the late baron's library.

"You have read Plato," she observed quietly, and de Coutances turned to her with the pleasure of finding a kindred soul writ across his face. They continued talking well into the afternoon, passing away the hours, oblivious to the mission they were in the midst of until de Coutances reminded her with a question.

"So you are descended from Arthur?" He asked the question in a low voice, just above a whisper.

"So I'm told," she answered quietly, her jaw fixed in a derisive grimace.

"You don't believe it?"

She scoffed haughtily at his question for reply. "Do you?"

De Coutances looked into the distance. "No, if I am honest, I do not."

At that moment William galloped up beside them from the front of the line.

"The weather is changing. We must make camp quickly."

Gwendolyn noticed then that the wind had picked up, and she pulled back on Bedwyr's reins and scanned the skies around them. Bedwyr tossed her head in agitation and pranced sideways beneath her, sensing the coming storm. Ahead, coal-dark clouds came rolling toward them over the rise, and the bleating of sheep seeking shelter in their nearby pastures could be heard over the branches rustling from a nearby thicket of trees. Gwendolyn urged Bedwyr to a gallop and caught up to William at the front of the line.

When she reached him, he raised his arm and abruptly pulled to a stop, signaling the column to halt. Nigel had urged the stragglers from behind, and the travelers pulled up into a tight formation.

"We make camp here!" he hollered over the wind, pointing to a small circle of trees no more than a hundred paces from the road. "Hurry!"

William sent half of the guard to the small circle of trees to begin preparing the ground for camp. He knew there would be no time to scout for water; fortunately they had filled all of their oilskins and watered the horses at the last stream. He ordered the remaining guard, under Nigel's direction, to escort the rest of the travelers to the campground. William watched the men and Gwendolyn reorganize for camp as he kept a wary eye on the surrounding ridges and valley. Although he doubted that Eleanor could have already sent word to John that Caliburn's heir had been found, and thus expose Gwendolyn to the risk of kidnapping or worse, he knew from experience that a small group setting up a hasty camp was distracted—and therefore vulnerable.

A nagging sense of unease, inexplicable in the gentle autumn morning, had plagued him since they had broken camp after training. It was the sort of vague dread that he knew better than to try to shrug off. As a precaution when they had set out that morning, he had sent two men from the Tower guard to ride out as scouts: one leading in front by half a mile to see that the way was clear, and one trailing behind to ensure that no one followed. The campfire being lit now would signal them to return with haste, and he waited anxiously for the sound of a charging rider on the road. Before the full camp was pitched both men had returned; all was clear.

Darkness fell quickly, aided by the blanket of clouds that seemed to roll over on top of them. With their axes and hammers, the knights and squires had sunk iron stakes into trees and ground, lashed down tent flaps, and overturned carts to shelter supplies. The horses were gathered in a makeshift pen among the trees, already turning their tails into the wind and dropping their heads to eat from the small troughs of grain that had been set out for them.

Nigel stood near the opening to the camp enclosure, watching the skies, when William approached from behind and stood quietly beside him, scanning the last shadow of horizon.

"You've done quite a job training her. I never would have believed a woman could hold her own against fighting men like that if I hadn't seen it myself." Nigel seemed to be inspecting the sky as he spoke, and William smiled lightly as he recognized a compliment. But in many ways, Nigel's sentiments were misplaced.

William wondered how he could have failed to notice the transformation in her, so stark and obvious in front of his eyes all this time. The answer, he was afraid to admit, was simply that he had chosen not to notice. The truth was that he preferred the younger Gwendolyn, uncertain of her own strength and dependent on him for protection and instruction. But that Gwendolyn was gone, and this unyielding woman stood in her place.

"She did it all herself. She's never quit, and she's never given up on anyone, especially not herself."

Nigel nodded, shuffled a toe into the ground self-consciously.

"She could've given up on me from the first time she met me. I don't know why she didn't," he said quietly, shaking his head.

William sighed with fatigue and turned to Nigel. "It's who she is. If she sees any value in you, you'll spend the rest of your life trying to live up to it."

He turned to walk back into the camp, leaving Nigel alone to puzzle over his words.

Large, heavy raindrops began to fall as William ducked his head into the one tent where all of the travelers huddled together. Only two candles illuminated the interior, and loaves of bread, chunks of dried meat, and water pouches were being passed about in the dim light. Even with the storm upon them and everyone safely accounted for, the tense feeling that an attack was about to be sprung was still tight in his gut. He selected four of the nearest men from the guard and sent them out on the first shift to keep watch, then went to Gwendolyn where she sat with Sybil, allowing the maid to run a comb through her tangled hair.

"She said it would settle her nerves," Gwendolyn said softly, her expression warm. She eyed him closely and sat upright on her stool.

"What's wrong?"

William shook his head.

"It's probably nothing. I've had this feeling ever since we headed out this morning. Something's...not right."

"Maybe it was just the storm," she offered. "Even the animals can sense these things."

"You're probably right," he said, ignoring how unconvincing he had sounded.

"Anyway, the scouts found nothing, and the watch will warn us if anyone approaches," she said gently. "We've all got our armor on and our weapons at hand. Whatever comes, we'll be ready for it."

Nigel entered the tent and his gaze landed on Gwendolyn in time to see her place her hand reassuringly on William's arm.

William pulled back uncomfortably, feeling color rising in his cheeks, and stood up. "Keep your sword nearby tonight."

The storm raged with impressive fury, even pulling a large branch down into the horses' pen and causing a momentary panic until the horses were settled again out of harm's way. But well into the night the gale winds relented, the rain softened to a steady thrum on the tent canvas, and the squires were able to cease their constant vigil of emptying the pools that gathered in the sagging fabric over their heads. Everyone breathed more easily, and blankets were unrolled and bundles set up as pillows as, one after the other, the travelers settled in to sleep for what remained of the night.

William switched out the guard for fresh men, pleased to find that the second shift had managed to find a corner of the tent in which to catch a little sleep before he came to rouse them to relieve the soaked men outside. He was still on edge, but with the worst of the storm having passed, along with most of the night, he started to relax a little. For a moment he might be able to lie down and sleep before sunrise. He found Gwendolyn toward the rear of the tent, somehow sleeping on her own, neither in the company of Sybil and the other young women, nor among the Tower guard. He eased himself down onto the edge of the blanket that she had been given for a bed and lay down beside her on his back. He was fast asleep within moments.

Deep and guttural sounds of snarling and the higher pitched cries of shouting men in the distance roused Gwendolyn beside him, and he felt her sit bolt upright as she woke. She grabbed her sword and dashed for the tent opening before he could stop her, followed closely by Nigel and the guard. William scrambled to clear his head and swore as he dug under the blanket to find his sword.

He could hear mayhem breaking out in the darkness outside. Gwendolyn shouted for a torch, but by the time he stepped out of the tent she was gone. He struggled to see in the blackness, to make out the churning forms of bulk and shadow while the nearby watchmen's shouts turned into screams of pain and terror. He drove forward into the black night, toward the shouting that was closest to him, and what he saw stopped him in his tracks.

Three huge wolves alternately circled and leapt at the man who had taken the east watch. The man used both shield and sword to defend himself, but he was stumbling and weakened. The wolves were circling for the kill. And though he had seen wolves plenty of times stalking in the fields and woods, he had never seen the likes of these massive, shaggy creatures that turned and paced before him now. In the darkness, their eyes flashed with a crimson light that caused him to stop and shudder, as if foul death itself had taken shape in the night. He charged forward again, then stopped at the sound of Gwendolyn's shouts. She had flanked to the far side of the wolves and he could make out the silver glint of her sword as she waived it, trying to draw the beasts from the wounded watchman. But the wolves ignored her, and he watched in horror as one leapt, swiping a massive paw at the guard and making contact with his neck.

He and Gwendolyn both screamed and charged forward from opposite sides, swords drawn. The wolves withdrew a few steps, scattering apart as they retreated, but the distraction would only be momentary. Gwendolyn took position in front of the wounded guard who stood motionless, slumped over his shield. William caught sight of the dagger clenched in her other hand and realized that she held no shield to protect herself. He could not risk pursuing one of the beasts and giving the others the opportunity to attack, so instead he took a defensive position in front of her.

She kept her gaze focused on the stand of shrubs beside her, and without turning her head she yelled, "Circling to the right!"

Around them other battles were underway, and from the pitched growls and shouts he feared they might be outnumbered. The wolf nearest to them turned its eyes upon him, and William froze. The wolf growled, deep and low, and took a step toward him. William stared into the wolf's eyes, and recognized the beast from his childhood dreams of long ago. He heard the other two growling nearer to Gwendolyn. Without another thought he charged the animal in front of him. The wolf reared up on its hind legs and swung its head, snapping its jaws and pawing at the air, but William held tight to his blade and thrust it deep into the beast's neck. A feeling of fire spread across his back, but he did not let go of his weapon. The wolf staggered back and warm blood spilled over his hands as the animal fell with a whine at his feet.

Behind him Gwendolyn shouted, waiving her sword at the two wolves that remained. They padded back and forth before her, ready to spring at any moment. William saw the larger of the two crouch slightly, and he flung himself into the air in front of her, meeting the beast in mid-leap. The wolf clamped its jaws on his forearm as they both fell down to the ground in a tangled pile. He was aware of the sound of his own screams, the feeling of his arm being crushed, and he waited for the beast to shake him like a child's doll, snapping his neck. But Gwendolyn had also lunged forward and she thrust her sword through the wolf's neck and into its skull. The animal lay still where it fell beneath him. Gwendolyn freed her sword and spun around, but there were no more growls or movements around them. The third wolf had fled back into the night.

The confrontation had passed in a matter of moments, and over the screams and snarls that continued in the distance, yelps could also be heard. Squires finally emerged with lit torches, and the last of the surviving beasts were run off. William turned to the man propped against the shield, but the body toppled over as soon as he touched it, the open eyes staring blankly. One of the squires arrived bearing a torch, and only then did they see the tear in the man's throat. The squire crossed himself, and Gwendolyn turned her head.

They carried the dead man to a circle outside the tent where the other members of the guard had gathered along with Nigel and Walter de Coutances.

"Christ on the cross," Nigel muttered, breathing heavily from his own fight. The dead were laid out in the grass, side by side. Four men were lost—three guards and one squire. Each of them bore ghastly wounds that ripped through hauberk and flesh alike. It was the worst Gwendolyn had seen, but even William and the seasoned soldiers recoiled at the leg connected only by sinew, the nearly severed spine. As the torch passed over the men's faces, Gwendolyn sucked in a quick breath. Tristan lay among the dead.

De Coutances looked the corpses over as his clerk hovered at his shoulder with a torch that trembled in his grip. The archbishop looked up at William across the bodies.

"What did this?" he demanded, his eyes wide.

William hesitated, swallowed the truth, and said, "Wolves, Your Grace."

"It was the Hounds of Hell!" one of the Tower men shouted, and a gasp and muffled screams were heard across the way from the others still huddled in the tent. "Just look! It's lying right over there!"

"Shut up," Gwendolyn ordered through a clenched jaw. "They were only wolves." She looked up severely at the men around her, daring them to contradict her, but each held his tongue.

De Coutances motioned to his clerk and they walked to the trampled area where one of the beasts lay. After a few moments he returned.

"William Rufus is right. These were wolves." There were no more protests after the archbishop's pronouncement. "These men fought bravely. Wrap their bodies and lay them in my cart. I will see to their burial in Arundel." He turned to William and Gwendolyn and said quietly, "See that we arrive there tonight."

While the squires gathered the scattered horses, banging on the grain buckets and calling out into the night, William oversaw the bundling of the bodies into tent canvases that would not be needed again. Wounds were dressed and wrapped with clean bandages, and William allowed Gwendolyn to cleanse the cuts in his back. The wolf's claws had raked across the back of his left shoulder, but the angle of the strike had been indirect and his mail, now damaged, had protected him from a deeper wound. His left forearm was bruised and painful, but the bones were still in place and intact. Gwendolyn only carried a new gash across her right cheek, below the eye. It would leave an attractive scar, he told her.

~·'·~

With yelling and sharp orders, Gwendolyn pushed the camp to be back on the road and moving before sunup. She would not afford the rest of the travelers any chance to catch a glimpse of the remains of the fallen beasts. She was certain that these were real animals and no hounds called out against them by the Devil, but she could not risk a panic among the travelers. William said nothing to her as they quickly packed and mounted up, but she knew he was thinking of the sorcerer the queen had mentioned, and she wished the queen had kept that piece of information to herself. She looked up and saw De Coutances dressing hurriedly beside his cart, one of the squires assisting him with his full armor and sword belt. From their conversation she was well aware that the archbishop had not dressed for combat in years except as may have been required to participate in ceremony. But now as she watched him, he donned the fine gauntlets and coif of the Tower armorers without hesitation.

They proceeded slowly, the carts and horses struggling through the deep mud that sucked and clung to their hooves and the cart wheels. More than once, de Coutances's cart, burdened with the fallen men's bodies, became so mired that several of the riders had to dismount to lift the wheels free of the muck so they could move on. Every one of them was exhausted and scared; many were wounded. But they worked hard to cover the ground as quickly as they could. Passing one more night outside of the protective walls of Arundel was not an option any of them was willing to consider.

Gwendolyn rode immediately behind William, at his direction. He had sent a forward scout to ride out ahead and kept the rest of the men in tight formation together with the group. She huddled inside her cloak against the autumn chill, feeling plain outrage simmer inside her. She had seen the beasts, had killed one of them herself, and she was certain that they were no ordinary wolves of the forest, nor were they the product of witchcraft or sorcery. And the fact that they had left the horses unmolested had not escaped her notice. Whatever those animals were, they were bred to be kill- ers of men and nothing else. Someone, she clearly understood, was too cowardly to face them in a fight and had sent dumb animals to do their bidding. Raising a pack of beasts like those would have required a significant amount of wealth and resources. And when it came to cowards with wealth at their disposal, she knew whom to place the blame upon. Somehow, Prince John had found her.

II

THE WALLS OF ARUNDEL

As they crossed into the county of Sussex, they were greeted by a mounted guard of five men bearing the colors of the Rape of Arundel and holding their lances at the ready. Walter de Coutances, astride his warhorse, rode to the front to join William and Gwendolyn. She watched the captain of the Arundel guard eye William without expression and then appear to recognize King Richard's justiciar. The captain lowered his weapon while his men arrayed themselves behind him with their lances held level, their attention turned both to the road and to the woods behind them.

"Your Excellency," the man greeted de Coutances. "Welcome back to Arundel."

Walter de Coutances thanked the man, looked over the small band that he led.

"Where is your sheriff?" William asked from beside her, and

the men looked at one another uneasily.

"He's gone to Marlborough, sir."

"William Marshal's brother, John, is Sheriff of Arundel," de Coutances said to William. "But he also holds Marlborough Castle for Prince John and remains loyal to his lord. John's rebellion may be the man's ruin before it's all over."

The Arundel guard looked over the exhausted travelers and their disheveled carts, noting the fresh bandages on the Tower knights.

"Our camp was attacked by wolves," Gwendolyn said, and the leader of the Arundel men turned his horse in her direction and looked her over closely, taking in her surcoat and weapons and the cut below her eye.

"We met the queen's messenger from the Tower two days ago, and your scout this morning. We've been expecting you." The man eyed Gwendolyn skeptically. "A pack of wolves caused all of this?"

"And killed four of our men," de Coutances replied.

The man continued looking them over and walked his horse in a circle around the group, but finally nodded to de Coutances and spurred his horse back to join the rest of his men.

"We are under orders to patrol the roads, so we cannot escort you to the castle. But we will travel with you as far as we can."

"Thank you," de Coutances answered graciously. "Is d'Aubigni in residence at the castle?"

"Just returned from Norfolk last month, sir. The queen has ordered him and all of the lords of Sussex to prepare their men and defenses across the coast."

"In case the King of France makes good on his promise to support John with an invasion," de Coutances added. "Well then,

the earl should be in high spirits. The only thing William d'Aubigni enjoys more than preparing for a war is fighting one."

The guards rode with the group for close to a mile, gathering the news from London from the travelers, some asking after
their family members that still lived there. Their captain finally
signaled to his men, and as they gathered to return to the edge of
the Rape he called out to de Coutances.

"The storm has swollen the Arun, but the bridge on the
Chichester road is sound. Tell the guard at the bridge what you
have told me. They will see Richard's herald on your shields; they
know to watch for you." De Coutances thanked the men again,
and the guard reined their horses about and charged back up the
road the way they had come, leaving the forlorn and weary group
to continue on their own.

The sky remained bleak and gray for the rest of the day. A
steady misting rain had soaked through everything, and those
who could huddled together in carts and under blankets to stay
warm. The travelers crossed the Arun without incident and
entered a wood as the day began to slip away. Gwendolyn could
see her breath in the chill air, and she loosely held Bedwyr's reins
with exposed fingers numb with cold. She imagined a spacious
hall with a warm fire and full cups of ale to put the ache in her
bones out of her mind. They had barely eaten all day, only partially
due to their rush. The shock of the night's events and the loss of
the men weighed on them all. These men had lived, fought, and
survived together, side by side, for years. They were like brothers
to each other, and each carried stories of the fallen men. Even
Gwendolyn carried a small part of Tristan's story, and she passed

the time in the saddle reviewing what she had learned from him a day ago in training.

They emerged from the woods into pastureland, and a small road, wide enough for a single cart and recently paved, branched off to their left, heading south. Their progress was easier on the large stones, despite the horses' hooves occasionally slipping on the smooth surface. As darkness fell, the keep of Arundel Castle came into view, aglow with torch light and borne up into the sky atop a high hill like a Norman trophy. Their own group carried torches, and soon a call rang out from the castle guard that kept watch from atop the battlements. A trumpet blast from a distant ram's horn sounded, and a dispatch of Arundel's guard streamed down in an orderly line to meet them. Arundel's men were accompanied by the forward scout that William had sent ahead of them that morning, and the man glowed contentedly with the intake of liquid mirth from the castle hall. Finding their man safe and a little drunk put the rest of the group at ease. Their journey had ended, and they were now a few paces from a hearth and the full hospitality of a castle well provisioned to outlast a siege.

With Arundel's guard leading the way, the procession wove along the southern flank of the broad hill that supported the motte and grounds of the castle. The hill would have a commanding view over the Arun River valley, and the longer they rode, the more Gwendolyn felt herself awed by the sheer scale of the fortress they had come to. The round keep would have been imposing enough atop the hill, but the conquering Norman armies had elevated it further with an earthwork motte. Passing beneath it, she could see the curtain walls extending out from either side of the keep, angling down the motte. There were no windows, not even the narrow slits used by archers, in the walls of the keep. The gatehouse that now loomed in front of her was to the right of the motte and at a lower elevation. If she could gain access to the battlements atop the walls, she could get a better view of the extent of the castle grounds and their fortifications. Tomorrow, she told herself. For now, she needed to finally remove her armor and tend to her parched throat.

They approached the castle gatehouse, the only way in or out of the walls that encircled the castle grounds. Three stories high and built entirely of stone, the gatehouse promised a well-equipped garrison. They entered through an arched enclosure protected by a portcullis not unlike the gatehouse at Launceston. But the scale of this castle was much larger, on a par with the castle at Windsor. Such were the heavily fortified defenses to be found surrounding the site of the Norman armies' entry into England more than a century earlier. The barrel-vaulted passage through the gatehouse led out into a large, oblong yard that stretched out to her right, bounded in by the protective walls. The yard was filled with the cottages and fires, tents, and equipment that supported a military stronghold under orders for war readiness. At the far end of the yard, she could make out the outline of a well, and, behind that, several stone buildings that backed up to the curtain wall, adding to its defensive strength and providing accommodation fitted with the luxuries suited to a king's tastes. Half a century ago, Arundel Castle had become famous for hosting Empress Matilda and withstanding a half-hearted siege by her rival, her cousin King Stephen. Later, Matilda's son, King Henry II, was rumored to have spent a small portion of the royal treasury to add a comfortable apartment and chapel to the castle's accommodations and to finish out the stone walls and connecting towers that now encircled its grounds. Expenditures had also included improvements to the rooms within the keep, even adding a privy with a latrine chute to the motte hillside to satisfy the modesty of the occasional mistress who might have accompanied him on his hunting trips to Arundel.

Grooms, attendants, and men-at-arms met them in the yard beyond the gatehouse, instructing them to dismount from their carts and horses. Walter de Coutances was immediately ushered back into the gatehouse and up to the battlements atop the wall, to walk up to the keep to meet with the earl. Tents had been erected already to house the new arrivals, their white canvas glowing with the oil lamps lit within them, and the members of their party were directed to one or the other tent for rest or food or tending of their wounds as needed. The yard buzzed with organized commotion, and Gwendolyn felt her fatigue finally settle in with thoughts of a soft pallet to sleep on. No bloodthirsty hounds would breach these fortifications. She slowly eased herself down from the saddle, gently shifting her weight onto her chilled and aching legs, and rubbed the top of Bedwyr's head under the bridle straps as the mare turned her head toward her. After a few moments, grooms came for their horses, but before Gwendolyn could unfasten her oilskin for a drink of water one of the garrison knights approached her and William and told them they were to join the earl in the hall. She suppressed her disappointment, rallied herself, and followed William and the knight back into the gatehouse and up narrow steps to the top of the wall.

The castle keep, four floors high, stood directly ahead of her. She filed up the steep path that Walter de Coutances had taken moments before toward a shabby network of wooden scaffolding that climbed up the face of the keep. Construction of a large gatehouse that would extend out onto the battlements and guard a new entry into the keep was underway. Additional fortifications were also being added to protect a second well that served the keep. The current doorway into the keep, arched and surrounded by elaborately carved stone molding, was offset from the battlements, so that the doorway opening hung in the side of the wall like a large window. Access was gained only by crossing over from the battlements on a precarious bridge of timber planks that clung to the side of the keep. In the absence of a gatehouse, the timber walkway and offset entry were another means of defending the keep, since the timber planks could be easily cast down or burned in a time of siege. She took a deep breath, looked straight ahead, crossed over, and turned into the doorway, William right behind her.

They passed up a few stone steps and turned abruptly right into the castle's great hall. All of the buildings inside the keep were constructed of timber and plaster, using the circular shell wall as their outer wall. She and William stepped up into a long, curved hall that took up at least one quarter of the length of the inside of the keep. Hearths, each of them fitted with an iron spit large enough to roast a hart, had been built into the shell wall on the right side of the room. Vents moved smoke from the fires out of the hall but kept their warmth and light inside for the guests. As below in the yard, the hall was filled with guests, those up above dressed in the fine fabrics and gleaming adornment of well-heeled merchants and barons. As part of its role in a time of war preparation, Arundel Castle had opened its gates to its lords, tenants, and vassals—and all of their knights and men-at-arms. She spotted Nigel standing to the side with a group of the Arundel garrison. He was in the middle of an animated conversation, gesturing largely with his hands. She guessed from the men's rapt expressions that he was telling them about the beasts that had attacked them in the night.

Someone thrust a pewter cup into her hand, and she gratefully drank, feeling the warmth of rich, unwatered ale spread through her. A moment later Gwendolyn realized the room had grown still. She looked around her, puzzled, and surveyed the room for the cause of the sudden quiet, but all eyes had turned toward her. With her cloak thrown back over her shoulders and her mail armor and weapons flashing in the firelight, she had forgotten that she was among strangers. She felt William step in behind her protectively, heard the rustle of his armor as his hand shifted to cover the hilt of his sword. A cough and a cleared throat echoed against the walls in the tense silence.

"God's bones! Can I finish my story or do you people need to gawk a little longer?" The men beside Nigel chuckled, giving the rest of those gathered permission to exhale and laugh with them. She felt William's breath against her neck as he breathed again, and she felt her shoulders relax as the thrum of conversation resumed.

Gwendolyn's gaze fell on another woman, dressed elegantly but without adornment, who stepped toward her, her chin graciously raised and her gaze appearing to look out over all of their heads and into the distance. People wordlessly parted before her as she walked, opening a path. She had a faint smile on her face, and seemed to be listening intently to the small movements around her. This would be the lady of the castle, Gwendolyn surmised as the woman walked toward her. Suddenly, one of the women who had been handing out cups of ale set her tray down and dashed forward to take the lady's hand.

"It's a full house tonight, my lady," the woman said softly, guiding her mistress safely toward Gwendolyn and William.

"Yes, Agnes, thank you," she replied warmly, then turned her gaze forward, extending both of her hands to Gwendolyn and William. Her dark brown hair, laced through with gray, was swept away from her face in loose waves down her back, and her eyes were misted over with silver clouds that blocked her vision. Her gaze, directed toward them but not at anything in particular, remained warm and welcoming despite the fact that she could not see the faces of those she greeted.

"We weren't expecting you so soon, but welcome to Arundel," she said to them in smooth English. While Norman French was the language of the royal court, away from the king and his family his subjects reverted to the language of their land. William reached forward and took her hand lightly and introduced himself and Gwendolyn. Matilda d'Aubigni tilted her head and felt William's hand inside hers. She smiled softly.

"A lifetime in battle and a soul as soft as rain," she murmured quietly, then released his hand and turned to Gwendolyn. She extended her hand and stood patiently while Gwendolyn paused and looked at William, noting the deep crimson that had spread up his neck to his cheeks.

"It's all right, my dear, I don't tell fortunes. But not being able to see people's faces has loosened my tongue. I have a habit of saying the first thing that comes to mind."

Gwendolyn reached forward and took Lady d'Aubigni's hand into her own, and Matilda startled and looked confused for a moment.

"Oh!" Matilda reached forward with her other hand and touched Gwendolyn's cheek gently with her fingertips, then relaxed again.

"And here's the one with the soul tough as iron, inside the shell of a woman," she said lightly and laughed. "I would guess from your grip that you've a sword nearby that you call your own."

"Yes, madame," Gwendolyn answered, slightly abashed.

"Fascinating," Matilda murmured again, then swept about to lead them through the hall and called out behind her, "Follow me!"

Gwendolyn strode swiftly behind Matilda, struggling to keep up. For a woman without sight, Matilda moved around her home with grace and speed that was hard to match. Gwendolyn ignored the muffled comments and stares from the arrayed lords and ladies and men-at-arms as they took in her appearance, dressed and outfitted as well as any knight. The novelty of her presence among them would wear off soon enough. In a few days they would forget to notice her at all.

Matilda led them to a trestle table set up on a raised dais, where they found Walter de Coutances and William d'Aubigni deep in conversation near the hearth. William d'Aubigni's back was to her, but she could see de Coutances's grave expression clearly by the glow of the firelight. William nudged her elbow, and she joined him in taking a seat at the table beside the earl.

William d'Aubigni turned around and started when he saw her, then flashed a half-smile that seemed entirely lacking in humor.

"So it's true! A woman carrying a sword who fancies herself the descendant of King Arthur himself!"

Gwendolyn did not return the smile. She noted the insult behind the earl's words, and her fatigue had left her long past any attempt at courtly pretense. She responded curtly, "The first bit's true. The rest is rubbish, except that it may be useful to stop John."

She set her cup down in front of her and stretched her neck and arms, ignoring the earl's frozen expression and narrowed eyes. De Coutances continued the conversation before the earl could respond.

"I've filled the earl in on the queen's request that he guard you while she negotiates with John. As you've seen, the castle is already in a state of war readiness. Our arrival doesn't change anything d'Aubigni wasn't doing already."

Gwendolyn turned to the earl and nodded.

"I am indebted to you. Thank you."

Matilda d'Aubigni had seated herself beside Walter de Coutances, and her husband noisily shifted a plate of nuts across the table in front of her so that she would hear their location and could help herself to them. Gwendolyn noticed the gesture; despite his rough manners she realized that she liked the earl.

"I would like to train with your men while I'm here, if that's acceptable to you," she said.

The earl turned his face to her in shock.

"Don't be absurd. You'll be killed."

William laughed from the other side of her, and the earl frowned and leaned forward to peer around Gwendolyn at him.

"You're her constable?" She thought that his question held a hint of accusation in it, and she wondered if William was about to pick an argument with the earl on their first meeting. De Coutances seemed to be growing increasingly flustered across from her.

"I am, my lord." William stared forward into his cup, but the corner of his mouth was pulled back in a faint smile.

"And you think it funny that she proposes risking life and limb just for show?"

"It's no show," he replied soberly.

The earl stared a moment longer at William, then sat back again, shaking his head.

"Take her hand, my love," Matilda urged gently.

Gwendolyn offered her near hand—her sword hand—to the earl, and he took it into both of his, which were warm and strong. Both her palm and her fingers were larger than the earl's. Years of hard work had swollen her knuckles, and callouses from hours spent in training lined her grip and the heel of her palm. These were not the hands of a pampered lady. They bore all the marks of a seasoned man-at-arms.

"I don't understand," he said quietly, letting go of her hand.

"There's nothing to understand," William said, turning to the earl. "She is what she is. I trained her myself."

The earl hesitated, looking between Gwendolyn and de Coutances for some sort of explanation, and finally shook his head in surrender.

"I'll be damned. Never thought I'd see the likes."

"She killed one of those beasts last night," de Coutances added. She felt the earl's gaze survey her closely.

"And what do you think they were?" he asked her. "The devil's own mongrels? Or just wolves, as Walter here insists?"

"Neither," she answered, turning to look at the earl. She was taller than him and his white hair had thinned on top of his head, but his eyes, small and bright, pinned her with his question. She thought of Tristan, of the good men who had lost their lives already to Prince John's obsession and cowardice, and felt her hands tighten into fists in her lap. She spoke freely, her voice bitter. "I believe it was a new kind of dog, bred solely to hunt and kill men."

She watched the earl lean back thoughtfully and ponder her explanation as his mind ran through the implications.

"There are few who would have the means for such an undertaking," he said, stroking the bristle on his chin.

"Exactly," she replied, and raised an eyebrow at him suggestively.

"What? You believe Prince John is behind this?" The earl's eyes were wide.

"Until I hear a better explanation."

D'Aubigni looked to the other men at the table who had also witnessed the beasts, neither of whom appeared persuaded by Gwendolyn's suggestion.

"William, you were there. What is your opinion? Has John found another means of waging battle without risking his own neck?"

Gwendolyn scoffed under her breath at the question; the earl had lit upon the other reason she found it likely that the beasts were the work of Prince John. Breeding dogs to do his fighting for him was exactly the sort of craven behavior she would expect from a man with John's reputation.

William exhaled and turned his gaze toward de Coutances.

"The queen mentioned a sorcerer..." he said in a low voice.

At the mention of the queen's rumor Matilda gasped and the archbishop slammed his cup down onto the table, causing the contents to spill and those nearby to startle at the outburst.

"She said John *believed* he had found a sorcerer," de Coutances growled. "For that belief alone he could be excommunicated for heresy. For the love of the saints, William, I'm surprised at you."

Gwendolyn watched William purse his lips together and nod, staring down at his cup again. He would say nothing more of it.

D'Aubigni turned back to de Coutances and thrust his chin at him. "Then what say you, Walter?"

"As I've said, wolves. Nothing more than that."

"They ignored the horses and came only for the men," Gwendolyn said quietly.

D'Aubigni scanned their faces, but no one appeared interested in carrying the conversation any further.

"Well. All that really matters is that they can be killed," he finally said.

"And by a woman." The remark came from over her shoulder, and everyone at the table looked up to the dark-haired young man standing behind her.

"Edmund, my boy! Join us!" The earl stood up with a broad grin and slapped the youth on the back as he moved around the table to take his seat next to his mother, Matilda d'Aubigni.

"Thank you," Gwendolyn answered, emptying her cup.

Edmund pushed a dark lock of hair out of his eyes and settled into his seat. "I meant they can't be that ferocious, if a woman could kill one of them."

There was an awkward pause at the table, but Gwendolyn laughed aloud. The youth sitting across from her was her age and wore a knight's belt as she did, but his belt carried adornments of pressed silver and his hands seemed as battle-hardened as his mother's. He was a young trifle, testing with hard words to provoke a challenge that she felt confident he could not meet.

"Well said, young Edmund," she said lightly and turned to her hosts. "And, if it's all right, I'd like to head back out to the grounds below to my tent. I would guess the guard gets an early start in the morning." She had felt the telltale twisting in her lower belly and knew she would want to be close to her small stash of rags in the morning.

"You're staying up here in the keep. After last night's attack, I'm not taking any chances with you," D'Aubigni said, and Walter de Coutances nodded in agreement from across the table.

She opened her mouth to protest, but William spoke up ahead of her.

"I agree. I'll stay up here as well."

"The men have already carried your things up, and your maid has arranged your room," Matilda added.

Gwendolyn sighed. There was no point in arguing. As Eleanor had said, for now her life was not her own.

"Very well," she said, pretending at least to herself that her assent in the matter had been necessary. As she rose, William stood beside her.

The earl waved to the woman who had assisted Matilda earlier and signaled to her to come join them.

"Agnes will show you to your room. And William," he added, "there's a boar that's been terrorizing travelers, charging out of nowhere like a mountain with knives. My warden has found his tracks, so we're heading out after him tomorrow. You and Walter will join us."

William smiled and thanked the earl, although Gwendolyn was certain that the distraction and pageantry of a boar hunt held no interest for him. But it was an honor to have been invited; his new position as the captain of the Tower guard required that he participate in such formalities. They both made their farewells and followed Agnes out into the center of the keep, in the open air. Gwendolyn noticed as they left that her time at the earl's table seemed to have already improved her standing among the men and women of Arundel, as no nods or whispers accompanied her exiting passage back through the hall.

"There's the privy," Agnes said as they passed a small hut against the wall to their right, "and that's your room, there," she added, pointing across to a row of guestrooms on the first floor that jutted out over the ground-level storage area where grain and supplies for a siege had been neatly stacked and counted. The room at the end of the row had one window with its shutters open, and the soft glow of a tallow candle faintly illuminated the inside of the room. Gwendolyn excused herself to the privy then rejoined William to climb the smooth timber stairs. As they entered the doorway they found themselves in a welcoming, if sparse, room.

Fresh herbs of lavender and horsemint had been scattered across the floor planks, and a tin brazier stood on its iron pedestal in the middle of the room, giving off a comfortable warmth. Gwendolyn's fatigue returned to her quickly, and there was hardly time to sit on the edge of her wood-framed pallet before she felt her eyelids droop. A small trestle table stood in one corner with a jug on it, and a trunk in the opposite corner held her belongings. Sybil was nowhere to be seen.

She bent over and began to fiddle with her boots, realized it was hopeless, and instead stood up to remove her cloak and weapons belt.

"I don't suppose there's any chance of us getting squires to help with the armor," she said, only half seriously. The group from the tower would be down in the yard, making use of the ale and song to push away the terror and deaths of the previous night. She and William were left to their own devices.

William stood behind her, took her weapons belt from her as she removed it, and laid it against the wall.

"Face me."

She did as she was told. He had a strange look on his face, and she remembered his unflappable propriety toward her. He leaned in and unfastened the coif from around her neck, tossed it beside the belt, then waited for her to lift up her arms and bend toward him so that he could lift the heavy hauberk off of her. There was no place to hang it, and he let it pile onto the floor as well, wincing visibly as the rings grated against each other. With any luck, she thought, the earl would have an armorer on a par with the man in the Tower.

She helped him with his own armor, and held his gaze briefly before pulling his hauberk up and over his head and outstretched arms. There was nothing to it, and yet she felt her cheeks warm as she dropped the mail tunic beside her own. She still wore the quilted layers of padding and linen that cushioned the hauberk against her when she dropped herself onto the pallet and wordlessly rolled to face the wall. She fell asleep within moments.

The following morning arrived gray and misty, with a salty breeze blowing in over the marshes from the south coast. Gwendolyn wrinkled her nose at the moist air and found herself longing for the sharp winds of autumn at Penhallam. The harvest would have been gathered by now; celebrations and feasts would be underway. She wondered whether Anne and Eric were still falling in love, or whether their affections might have ebbed with increased familiarity, as happened so often for the young. William was gone, which was expected. A boar hunt would need to be already in the vicinity of its prey by dawn. The men and their hounds would have departed out of the castle grounds before the parish church rang Matins.

Gwendolyn entered the great hall in time to grab a scrap of bread to break her fast. Matilda d'Aubigni looked up at the sound of her footsteps and smiled, as if she had been waiting for her. She rose and approached, stepping nimbly over the thick layer of rushes on the floor. The earl's wife was dressed simply in a woolen gown dyed the color of autumn wheat. The golden hue warmed Matilda's complexion and complimented the nutmeg strands of her hair. She took

Gwendolyn's rough hands into her own, which were small and soft.

"How did you know it was me?" Gwendolyn asked, hoping that her question was not rude.

Matilda laughed. "Agnes advised me, my dear. Unfortunately, when I lost my sight, there was no gift of second sight to replace it."

Matilda led Gwendolyn toward the dais where a platter of dried fruits had been set down. The young mothers who had babes at the breast were sitting together in a small group to the side, and Gwendolyn noticed one of the mothers with tears rolling down her cheeks, struggling to help her tiny, fussing baby take the breast. Matilda paused and approached the group, leaning down and placing a hand softly on the woman's shoulder.

"May I?" she asked, her hand outstretched toward the baby. The mother said yes, and Matilda settled onto her heels behind the young mother and felt her way gently around to the baby's head. The mother held the baby in the crook of her left elbow with the baby's head tucked in toward the breast, and Matilda shifted the baby slightly to the mother's right, toward the center of her body so that the baby had to tip her head back a bit to get to the breast again. Suddenly the baby opened her tiny mouth wide and the entire pink of the breast disappeared as Matilda deftly guided. For a moment the hall seemed to breathe a full sigh of relief with mother and baby as the milk flowed at last into the hungry little mouth.

Matilda stood up again and straightened her skirts. "I will have a bath drawn for you in the kitchen," she continued, returning her attention easily back to Gwendolyn and reaching to hold her hands again. "Your room cannot have been comfortable. I always feel like I've gone to the wilderness every time we come down from Norfolk."

"A bath?"

Gwendolyn felt her chest flutter at the prospect of stripping down in front of even Matilda and her maids. Only some of her belongings had made it to the trunk, and she could feel the first seeping warmth between her legs as her bowels twisted again with a fierce cramp. Now was not the time for a bath, and she needed to find rags quickly.

"I promise, you will be quite on your own," Matilda assured her.

Gwendolyn hesitated, a flush rising to her cheeks. Matilda still held her hands, and Gwendolyn watched the older woman's expression transform to one of recognition.

"Oh, my dear," Matilda said, "I'll send Agnes for some tea. How terrible to be travelling with all of these men at the time of your flow."

Matilda called to Agnes to follow after them and led Gwendolyn into the room directly beyond the hall. The d'Aubigni's private room was as large as the hall, but a clutter of crates and bundles made the space feel tighter, more intimate. Matilda knew the exact location of every object and moved through the room with ease. Agnes caught up with them, and Matilda gave the girl a quick instruction. She turned her attention to Gwendolyn as Agnes left again with a quick curtsy.

"Sit here, please." Matilda gestured to a large chair, lined with tapestries and felted wool. Gwendolyn sat down, awkwardly noticing how dirty her shirt appeared next to the fine fabric. Matilda perched herself lightly on a stool in front of her, both hands resting open in her lap, palms up, looking expectantly at Gwendolyn.

"Your feet."

Gwendolyn hesitated, shifting in her chair, not sure if she had heard the earl's wife correctly.

"Give me your feet," she repeated, as if her request was entirely obvious and Gwendolyn was being a bit daft.

Gwendolyn frowned and lifted a foot tentatively toward Matilda. The older woman took the foot firmly in both of her hands and brought it to her lap, expertly pulling the leather boot off and pushing the hem of Gwendolyn's breeches up her calf.

"And the other." Matilda said a little impatiently, and waved her hand in the air at Gwendolyn's other leg. Gwendolyn obediently proffered the other foot and Matilda stripped it down like the first.

Her head bowed, Matilda began to massage the tender part of Gwendolyn's heel around the tendon and anklebones, gently at first, then more firmly. No one had ever touched her feet before, and Gwendolyn sat rigid in the great, soft chair.

"Breathe," Matilda said softly, then turned her face up to Gwendolyn. "This works better if you will relax."

Gwendolyn settled back into the soft fabrics, closed her eyes, and took a deep breath. After some time she heard Agnes's light footfalls enter the room, then a wooden cup being set on the table beside her and the trailing steps quietly closing the heavy door again. Gwendolyn's heels were surprisingly tender, and relaxing was difficult when her insides between her hips felt like they were twisting into a knot of angry serpents. Matilda switched to the other foot, and Gwendolyn took another deep breath. Her lower back ached, but as Matilda began working on her other heel, it was as if the clamp that had taken up residence in her lower belly slowly loosened its grip. Her insides even tingled a bit, a welcome change, and she sighed. She noticed how comfortable the chair was, smelled the anise herbs of the tea steaming beside her.

"How did you learn to do this? You must teach me. The women at Penhallam must know about this."

"This causes the womb to soften, to release your flow and relax. You must not do this for a woman who is with child until it is time for the child to be born," she admonished her sternly, and then softened her expression. "I was fortunate to have a midwife, a woman of the marshes near my home in Norfolk. She did this for me, during those brief spells in between children, to heal the womb. And when it was time for the baby to come, her hands on my feet encouraged the child to birth. But that was more than forty years ago, during the reign of Stephen of Blois."

Gwendolyn frowned, puzzled. "You and the earl have kept your youth well, for having lived so many years."

The older woman shook her head and smiled softly. "The earl is not my first husband."

Matilda was quiet for a moment, and Gwendolyn settled back comfortably into her chair as the older woman collected her thoughts.

"I was first the wife of Roger de Clare. He was many years older than me, and the year that he became an earl, he chose me as his wife. He was kind enough to ask me himself, and I saw in him fairness and justice." She took in a deep breath. "And the man was handsome," she added, smiling. "The only times that I wasn't pregnant were when he was away. By the time I was thirty-six, I had given birth to eleven children. Seven still live today."

Roger de Clare, Earl of Hertford, was known throughout England as "the good earl" for his treatment of his lords and tenants across his vast lands. She had overheard the Baron Fitz William tell stories of the man to his sons, as instruction in the proper management of their own lands. It had never occurred to her that such a man would have also had a rich personal life, apparently full of the blessings of a happy marriage. She exhaled and sat up.

"How old were the children when your husband died?"

"The twins were only a year old; John was three. But Richard, my oldest, was twenty. He succeeded his father and became the third Earl of Hertford."

"Richard de Clare? The Earl of Hertford and Gloucester is your son?"

Matilda smiled, and Gwendolyn realized she was looking at one of the Eve's of English nobility, a woman who had birthed and raised a generation of men and women who would each play their parts to plot and steer the course of the country. And that was only with her first husband.

"Roger went to Oxfordshire for a while to settle some of his transactions for the coming year with the tradesmen there. But then he became excited about something else happening in the county. All of the foreign scholars had been expelled from Paris, and the returning English academics had taken up residence in Oxfordshire, of all places. Apparently the merchants and tradesmen and their lords thought England needed its own universite to rival any other, and so the scholars simply started to teach. There was no organization, they had no buildings of their own, but they began instructing whoever came to learn, for whatever they could pay—oftentimes in the fresh air. You see, there was no limit on what they could teach, and the freedom...well, he said it was intoxicating.

"But he died there, away from us." Matilda sighed again. "I thought I would crumple at first. I was so young when I married, I was an heiress in my own right and the only life I had known since childhood was my home with Roger. Richard looked after us, of course. He had just married Amice Fitz William, another heiress, but only twelve years old. I raised the girl myself along with the rest of my brood. It was seven more years until Richard finally slowed down and took any notice of her. And by then a certain strong-willed man, younger than me by eight years, gave me the chance to start over again. William d'Aubigni was an earl's son. He could have picked a much younger bride with many more childbearing years ahead of her, but over his father's protests he married me. I promptly produced an heir, and Stronghand d'Aubigni, as my father-in-law liked to be called, died smiling, knowing that his title would be carried on. After little William there were four more, Edmund being our last." Matilda d'Aubigni smiled and shrugged. "As I see it, I've lived two full women's' lives. And I am grateful to have lived every moment of each."

Gwendolyn looked at the slight, silver-eyed woman in front of her and shook her head. Men valued strength and size and waged wars over territory and title. Meanwhile, the future of the country was actually the prerogative of the women whose soft, yielding bodies bore and fed the next generation. Matilda had stopped massaging her ankles and Gwendolyn sat up, smiling, then admonished herself and reached out to touch Matilda's hand.

"Thank you," she said sincerely.

Matilda smiled serenely, her high cheekbones and smooth forehead now seeming regal to Gwendolyn.

"Agnes has left a stack of clean rags in your room. Let me know if there is anything else you need."

Gwendolyn stood up and finished the tea that had cooled beside her while she and Matilda had talked.

"You've treated me like a daughter. It's not something I'm accustomed to," Gwendolyn admitted.

Matilda's expression shifted with a shadow of sadness.

"Yes, I heard about that," she said. "My husband had a lot of questions for Walter de Coutances about you after you left last night. He really has no idea what to make of you."

"You don't seem to mind how I am," Gwendolyn observed dryly. Matilda stood thoughtfully for a moment.

"Why should I mind whether a person fits my notion of who they're supposed to be? You would be the best authority on that, I believe. Any argument I might make otherwise would be arrogance in the extreme." She smiled at Gwendolyn, her clouded eyes shining. "He'll come around. He is a just man at heart."

12

HUNTER
AND HUNTED

A hunting party of eleven men headed out of the gatehouse in the starry darkness before dawn. The earl's hunting dogs barked excitedly as they bounded ahead searching for the boar's scent, followed by the trackers and huntsmen whose job it was to handle the hounds and tend the fallen boar. The earl and two other lords that he had also invited rode fine coursers bred to stand their ground against a charging beast, and all three men carried the long spears specially designed for hunting boar. Edmund was not among them; the earl's youngest son had left the hall during the night for the town of Arundel, and his father had waited for a long while before finally sounding the hunter's horn and departing without him.

The party passed westward below the castle grounds and then picked up the main road heading north. After a short while they cut to the west to take the high road to Chichester, traveled a few more miles, and then turned north into the woodlands of a low-lying valley. Here, the thick canopy of trees would produce acorns and chestnuts and other fruits of the forest that were the boar's favored autumn treat. The men slowed their horses, listening to the renewed baying of the hounds in the distance as they scoured the forest floor for any trace of the boar's scent. The huntsmen ran ahead on foot, ready to blow the horn once the trail was found. The riders proceeded forward cautiously, listening carefully to the clamor of barks and voices ahead of them. Once the trail was found, the dogs would pursue first to flush the prey out into the open. The huntsmen, who would have to be swift runners to keep up with the dogs, would join the pack while they held the boar at bay.

A wild boar was a dangerous quarry, known to use its tusks to slash the bellies of horses and men alike. The hunters carried boar spears that were sturdy and long, but more importantly, that held a cross-bar at the base of the blade that prevented a charging boar from advancing up the shaft and goring the hunter's horse with its knifelike tusks. William knew that a man like the earl would have hunted boar every year since his boyhood, and he hoped that d'Aubigni would not charge ahead impulsively at the call of the huntsmen on this first hunt of the season. William had been with the late Baron Fitz William when the baron's impatience had cost him his favorite horse. It was a brutal lesson that he would not forget.

William and de Coutances hung to the back of the group. Others could have the glory today; they had only come along because of the earl's invitation. William's injured forearm ached and sported deep purple and blue bruises that encircled it completely, and he said nothing to de Coutances, who was preoccupied with composing something appropriate to say at the burial of the men who had died a day ago. The dead knights from the Tower were the best of the best, the sons and nephews of magnates and barons. Their remains would be buried at the Arundel parish church, but de Coutances had promised to record their deaths at Westminster when he returned to London.

For a while the hunting party saw no game at all. The earl told them as they rode out that he had sent out his tracker every day of the last seven to locate their quarry, and the man had at last reported that a small herd of red deer gathered in a clearing nearby, north of the road by a few miles. The man had also reported that he had found the telltale scrapes of a boar sharpening its tusks along the trunks of the forest trees. The scrapes were higher and deeper than any he had observed before, and he had suggested enthusiastically that a beast of significant proportion had moved into the area. This accorded with the accounts of nearly trampled pilgrims and merchants who had had the misfortune of drawing the boar out as they had passed through its territory. Despite the ongoing work to be done at Arundel, the earl could not resist going after the boar while the trail was fresh. And, he boasted, he could claim that the hunt was a service to protect those passing on this well-traveled market route.

Suddenly the hounds bayed urgently in the distance, and the men came to attention in their saddles and urged their horses forward to follow, abandoning the road that cut through the wood to race through the underbrush and hanging limbs. William followed in the rear of the group, ducking the lashes of the branches that snapped back toward him as the riders in front passed through.

Rain began to fall, the large drops noisily colliding with the leafy canopy above them and passing through onto the hunters below. The falling rain muffled the sound of the baying, and the men urged their horses to pick up speed before they lost the call of the pack altogether. They were moving quickly through high grass and brush, a risky exercise given the uneven ground and stones that lay hidden beneath. Their horses slipped and stumbled, but still the group urged their mounts faster toward a large clearing.

Watching from several paces behind, William saw d'Aubigni's horse suddenly stumble and fall forward to one knee, then quickly right itself and continue onward at a choppy trot. The earl was an able rider, and he remained firmly in the saddle as his horse regained its stride. Holding onto his horse's mane tightly with one hand, the earl leaned far out of his seat and forward, feet completely out of the stirrups. He stretched down with his other hand to try to check the horse's forelegs for any cut or wound from the fall. The earl was still in this precarious position when the horse suddenly reared up on its hind legs and lurched sideways in fright. The earl was thrown badly off balance, and he clung on with one hand in the horse's mane while he struggled to right himself again. Terrified, the horse squealed and bolted ahead through the woods, and this time the sudden lurch dumped the earl onto his back among the high, wet grasses.

Over the sound of the falling rain the men heard a guttural squeal from a large clump of brush, and a massive blur of brown and black fur charged out at them, scattering the men and their horses. The earl had rolled and pressed his body low to the ground where his horse had dropped him, staying hidden in the tall grass. William spurred his warhorse ahead to join the others in the clearing. The boar had stopped and swung around to face the group again, its nostrils flared red as it tossed its head menacingly. The boar warily regarded the dispersed group with its eyes rolling, swinging its head from side to side to look at each of them before it pawed the ground, preparing to charge again. Its tusks jutted up and out from its lower jaw, as sharp as blades, and the angry beast tossed its head at them with a series of low grunts. The earl's spear was still attached to his saddle and had been carried too far away by his spooked horse to be of any use. Of the two other men who had brought spears, only one was willing to get close enough to the boar to try to use it, while the other had positioned his horse to put a solid tree trunk between himself and the boar and now carefully steadied his horse to maintain their position.

The man with the spear lifted it gingerly in his right hand, attempting to control his terrified horse with the other. The earl shifted slightly where he lay in the grass. The boar immediately whipped its head around in the direction of the movement.

"Stay down!" William yelled loudly over the rain, which had begun to pour down heavily. He quickly took in the scene around him and weighed the options. If the boar charged the earl, it would swing its head low to attack with its tusks and then trample the man beneath its hooves. William's sword would be useless against the boar while he remained on his horse; by the time he was close enough to use it, his horse would be mortally wounded. Without the assistance of the baying dogs it was unlikely that the man beside William holding his spear aloft would succeed in landing a killing blow. The crest of the boar's thick shoulders stood as high as a man's chest; it would be able to charge and attack again even after it had been speared through if the strike failed to kill. One of the men beside William found his horn and sounded a loud call to the huntsmen to bring the dogs quickly. William held his horse steady and tried to position himself between the earl and the boar. But seeing its forward path beginning to close, the boar lowered its head and charged toward the opening back in the direction from which it had come, directly toward the earl where he still lay in the grass.

The man with the spear hurled it awkwardly at the boar, and the blade bounced off the tough hide as if he had thrown a stick. For William, everything moved slowly now, as on the battlefield. He drew his knife from his belt and leaned forward in the saddle, urging his horse at a gallop toward the boar. In a heartbeat his horse was charging alongside the animal, tusks pointed safely away from the horse's flank. William freed his feet from the stirrups and threw himself over the boar's heaving shoulders. His face burrowed into its stinking fur, but he had thrown his left arm over the neck and his fist closed around the rough bristles to cling on. He hung from the right side of the animal and drove his dagger up into the boar's throat behind the jawbone with all of his strength and then jerked the blade sideways. The beast stumbled and rolled, its speed and size carrying it in a deadly tumble along the slick ground, finally coming to rest within a few paces of the earl with William firmly pinned beneath it.

William lay still under the motionless body. A sticky warmth spread across his chest as the boar's blood seeped through to the ground. The boar had dragged him over rocks and wood, and he gingerly tried to move his arms or legs, but the weight of the boar was too great. The huntsmen were immediately at his side, and together they lifted the boar clear of him. He lay motionless for a moment, filling his lungs with fresh air and trying to put out of his mind the thought of how close he had just come to death himself. Slowly, he rolled to his side and pushed himself up with one hand to sit in the mud with his legs drawn up toward his chest. The rain continued to pelt the men as they set about preparing to carry the animal back to the castle. William found himself joined where he sat in the mud by the earl, who, with an ashen face and shaking hands, wordlessly sank down beside him and pulled out an oilskin of ale from beneath his cloak. He took a long drink and then passed it to William, along with his dagger that he had retrieved from the steaming carcass. William took a long drink and turned his face upward toward the rain to wash the mud from his nose and eyes.

Finally, the earl staggered to his feet and extended a hand to William to steady him as he rose to his feet in the slick mess. Calling to the hounds, the earl plunged his knife into the boar's belly and pulled out a large, steaming chunk of liver, pulling pieces apart with the knife and throwing them to the dogs. The earl's huntsmen had already chopped down two young saplings by the time William was ready to mount his horse again. They quickly trussed and hung the carcass from the rails to be carried between two of the horses back to the castle, while their riders walked beside them. The rain stopped as they carefully picked their way back to the road, and William rode quietly beside Walter de Coutances, feeling the light breeze drying his clothes.

"That was close," de Coutances observed, staring ahead.

William exhaled and nodded at the archbishop's understatement.

"I thought I was going to have one more man to bury tonight," he added.

"Don't worry on my account," William said. "Today wasn't my day."

The archbishop looked at him sideways with a furrowed brow. "Our times are in God's hands, William. Only He knows the day and hour of our death."

William stared straight ahead, his face inscrutable.

"You are a more learned man than I, Your Excellency."

William suspected that Walter de Coutances was aware that he was being humored, and that William held onto the old ways of Cornwall and the legends of Arthur and the prophecies.

"William," he said sharply, "I am here on the dowager queen's order, but I am a man of God first. If you believe the prophecies about Arthur and Caliburn that the Welsh and their Druid friends have been carrying all these many years—"

At the mention of the Druids William suddenly pulled his warhorse to a halt and faced the archbishop.

"Yes, I grew up in Cornwall, remember?" De Coutances continued, his features suddenly sharp like a hawk's. "There was a spring on our estate, an ancient place of witchcraft still visited by the Druids. I have met them. And whatever good intentions they may carry in their hearts, the things that they believe are heresies, and their sin makes them easy tools for the Devil's use. I have sworn to keep Gwendolyn safe while the queen has need of her, but that's as far as my duties reach. I cannot protect you or her from charges of sorcery or witchcraft, if it comes to that."

William looked closely at the archbishop, his expression sober.

"I understand," he said, and urged his warhorse forward again. Neither man shared another word with the other for the rest of the return to Arundel.

Gwendolyn was not at the castle when the hunting party returned. After she left Matilda, she had walked the walls of Arundel, marveling at the towers that guarded the grounds and provided a commanding view over the Arun River valley to the east and south. The king's apartments at the eastern end of the lower bailey would enjoy a beautiful view out over the valley at sunrise, while also allowing the king to keep his own watch down the river toward the sea—the route of entry for any invading army.

From the battlements over the king's apartments she scanned the town below. No protective wall encircled the buildings or fields, which explained the large numbers of families that had moved themselves, their belongings, and their livestock up into the castle's lower bailey during the threat of siege. Across the river from the town, a wide, elevated causeway had been built to carry travelers safely eastward across the marshes. Flat boats full of supplies and various goods—textiles, ore, lumber, grain, and animals, moved up and down the river, and a small ferry carried passengers back and forth between the banks. Merchant stalls, some no more than makeshift tents open to the weather, stood along the main road through town. Beyond those, a few buildings—the houses of lords, taverns, and the parish church—occupied the slightly higher ground at the foot of the rise upon which the castle grounds stood. Only the church and a few other buildings were built of stone; the rest were built of timber and plaster, their walls gleaming and pale. The lanes between the buildings lay crooked and winding, mimicking the bend of the river that justified the town's existence.

She found Nigel with the garrison's captain in the room above the gatehouse, acquainting himself with the castle's extensive armory. All around her laid the evidence of the preparations for siege and the threat of war from Prince John, and yet her step was light. Her time with Matilda had lifter her cares from her shoulders, reminding her that even while kings rose and fell, life would go on. A few men from the Tower guard passed through and acknowledged her as one of their own with a joke and a slap on the shoulder, causing the captain of Arundel's guard to raise an eyebrow. None of the other men batted an eye as Gwendolyn lifted and held a sword, admiring its craftsmanship and moving it slowly through the air to test its balance in her grip. The man finally smiled faintly, shrugged his shoulders, and returned his full attention to the conversation he was having with Nigel.

After a while, Gwendolyn tapped Nigel on the shoulder and told him she was heading into town. None of the exhausted Tower guard would be training that day, and she was feeling restless. He hardly looked up as he grunted at her, "Take your sword."

"Always," she answered, and she swept back up the battlements to her room in the keep to don her cloak and sword belt.

As an afterthought she tied her purse of coins to her waist and then headed back down the battlements to the lower bailey and out the gatehouse toward town.

She wandered down the main street, which ran straight through town to the ferry landing. As she had hoped, the stalls she had seen from the castle walls sold not only the expected trinkets and shiny baubles, but also freshly baked treats of a tantalizing variety. She followed her nose to one of the awnings, taking the jostling crowd of men and women below it as a good sign.

Two women stood behind a table under the awning, one with muscular arms and shoulders pounding and kneading a large mound of dough while the other tended the fire of the makeshift oven they had built with a stack of stones and mud. Gwendolyn noticed a long strip of cloth tied around one of the table legs; the other end of the strip securely held onto a baby that crawled beneath the table, playing with a small bundle of wool and sticks. The baby turned and played with one of the women's toes while Gwendolyn watched, and giggled with delight when she wiggled them back at him. Gwendolyn could see from the stacked sacks next to the oven that they used ground almonds and dried apricots in the dough. When her turn came, Gwendolyn stepped forward and bought a roll for herself, flaky and rich with butter, and a few more to carry back for the women with babes in the hall. She realized she had nothing to carry the rolls in, and she folded her cloak up into her arms to wrap the bundle snugly. She handed the woman a little more than she had asked for, but not so much as to insult, and turned to head back to the castle.

With her arms full of her awkward load, she scanned the

town and decided she would come back the next day for more exploring. But as she skimmed her gaze over the tops of the heads around her, she caught sight of Edmund d'Aubigni moving quickly away from her through the lanes. He was alone and walking with a little difficulty, as if he were carrying a load on one side. She craned her head around and struggled not to lose sight of him. No one greeted Edmund as he moved; in fact, they seemed to grimly clear to the side before him, their eyes cast down. Edmund had reached one of the stone buildings, and he stepped swiftly up an alley and then turned left into a narrow passage that ran between two houses. She kept her eyes focused on the place where he had disappeared and reached it as quickly as she could, but he was already gone again. She dashed down the narrow passage, dropping the rolls as she ran. When she emerged again she swept her gaze left and right and caught a glimpse of Edmund slipping into the low doorway of a tavern. She turned and made her way around the people and carts that blocked her and darted down the alley, breathless when she finally ducked into the doorway after him.

Men and women in various states of undress and drunkenness sat about the tavern's tables and in the straw on the floor. Off to one side along the wall, linen screens were hung to create some semblance of privacy for those seeking the women's services, but one of the couples apparently preferred the convenience of the wall. Edmund stood across the tavern with his back turned to her, enjoying the laughter of the onlookers as he held a boy aloft, pinned with one hand against the wall in front of him, dangling by his shirt. The boy was maybe half Edmund's age. The earl's son held his dagger at the boy's crotch, and the boy gasped pitifully for air in choked sobs, paralyzed with fear. A dark stain suddenly emerged down his pant leg, and Gwendolyn breathed a sigh of relief when she realized that the pants were only wet with urine and not blood.

"What do you think you're doing with my page?" Gwendolyn demanded in a loud, level voice.

The laughter subsided and Edmund twisted his head around from his sport to see who dared to challenge him. When he saw Gwendolyn his grin stretched broader and he flashed his teeth at her, his lips curled like a wolf sizing up its next meal. Edmund carelessly dropped the boy to the ground like a plaything that he had grown bored with, and the boy quickly dashed out the door.

"There goes your page," Edmund jeered with laughter. "That dog's good for nothing but a good beating now and then."

"You're disgusting," she said, barely audible over the laughter that resumed around her. She swept her gaze around the room again and recognized some of the men from Arundel's garrison. As her eyes registered their faces they cast sideways glances at each other.

"You shouldn't talk to me like that." Edmund advanced toward her, the knife still in his hand. No one in the room moved to restrain him. Gwendolyn drew her sword smoothly and held it in front of her, waiting, her eyes intent on Edmund. She ignored the shuffles and scrapes around her as the men in the room suddenly took notice that a blade had been drawn among them. The men of the garrison drew their weapons and Edmund held them off with a gesture of his hand in a show of chivalry, but Gwendolyn was not fooled. She fully expected Edmund would not hesitate to order his men to cut her to ribbons if he felt he could do it without making himself look like a coward. She watched his hand flicker indecisively near the hilt of his weapon, which hung from his waist in an elaborately carved scabbard.

"You've never actually used that thing, have you?" she asked, flicking the tip of her sword toward his, but immediately the bawdy room took her gesture to be indicating the young man's manhood, which hung in the same approximate area as his weapon, and new laughter erupted. Edmund's face flushed scarlet, and his brow dropped into a dark ledge under the shadow of his hair.

"Shut up!" he yelled to the room, but the laughter only increased.

"You bring this humiliation upon yourself," she said just loudly enough for Edmund to hear. She turned on her heel and swept back out of the tavern, leaving the d'Aubigni's youngest son seething behind her.

Out in the lane, she looked around for the boy Edmund had terrorized. She knew the child would be hiding, and she began to look for the places she would have sought out herself when she was younger. A cart leaned against the wall a couple of buildings down and she slowly walked toward it, looking beneath its wheels, but there was nothing there. She straightened up, searched the lanes again with her gaze, and spotted a stand of tall oaken barrels at the end of an alley.

As she approached the barrels, she heard a child sobbing. She leaned over the barrels, saw the tawny shock of hair in the shadows beneath her. The boy gasped for air as he sobbed, and his shoulders shook beneath a threadbare shirt. She hoisted herself up to sit on top of one of the barrels with her back toward him, staring across cultivated fields to the river.

"You're safe now," she said.

She could tell as the boy struggled to gulp down his sobs that he had heard her. She felt the urge to put her hand on top of his head or his shoulder, but she did not know what she would do after that. She had never been the one to comfort a child before. His breath shuddered inside him as he worked to cease his crying, and it sounded as if he might be able to speak.

"Where are your parents?"

The boy cleared his throat and answered her.

"Dead."

Gwendolyn sighed. Of course, she thought; Edmund would have chosen a victim with no defenders who might come back later to settle the score. The boy looked up at her. His features were swollen and blurred with tears, but he recognized her as the woman who had challenged Edmund, and a glimmer of relief flashed in his eyes. She remembered herself from so many years ago in that glimmer. The parish church rang the hour of Sext, midday, and Gwendolyn's stomach grumbled.

"Can you walk?"

"No, mum," he hesitated, then mumbled with shame, "my pants."

She remembered that he had wet himself in the tavern.

"You know," she said matter of factly, "there's something that the men in armor, with their swords of steel, never talk about. But they all know about it."

She paused while he looked up at her, his miserable expression registering a little curiosity.

"Often times, when they're facing down their enemy in battle, or even just before a charge, they do exactly what you just did. There's no shame in it. There's nothing they can do about it. It just happens. And sometimes," she added, leaning in closer to whisper and raising an eyebrow for effect, "they even shit themselves."

The distraction worked, and for a moment the boy's shock helped him to forget his own predicament. His jaw hung slightly open, and she nodded at him.

"It's true. I've seen it myself."

The boy stood up, but she shook her head.

"Stay hidden; I need to go get something." she said. "Promise to wait for me?"

The boy looked at her and nodded.

"I'll be right back. I promise."

She hopped down and ran back to the stall where she had bought the rolls. She paid for a few more, and then held up five more coins in her hand to the woman behind the little table.

"I'd like to buy your apron," she said.

The woman paused her work and looked at Gwendolyn with confusion. "But that's more than ten times its worth. And I need my apron, mum."

"So do I. Please, take it."

The woman eyed her a little uncertainly, but she took the coins from Gwendolyn's palm, put them into the pocket of her full skirt, and untied the apron from around her waist, shaking her head. Gwendolyn thanked the woman, took her purchases, and hurried back toward the barrels, saying a prayer that the boy would still be there when she returned.

The boy looked up from his hiding spot when he heard her footsteps, and the relief in his eyes this time was plain. She held up a roll and the apron.

"I thought you could use these."

Scanning all around him again, the boy stood up. Fumbling with the strings, he tied the apron around his waist and then looked down to see that the cloth hid his front past his knees. Satisfied, he let her help him out from his hiding place, over the barrels and onto the ground in front of her. He was sturdily built, standing as high as her chest, but he could not have weighed more than her cloak. His eyes were brown with a golden hue even under the gray sky. She looked over the light threads he wore and wondered how he kept from shivering against the damp cold.

She handed him one of the rolls, and he took it a little tentatively, but then a third of the roll disappeared in a single bite. His body relaxed as he chewed.

"Thank you," he mumbled sheepishly around the mouthful.

"What is your name?"

"Michael," he answered, taking a smaller bite.

She watched him eat, mulling over her options. Surely the boy could be put to better purpose than suffering for Edmund's ill-begotten amusement.

"Michael, I would guess you to be about ten years old," she said, taking his measure with a quick glance. "I arrived yesterday at Arundel, and I am a long way from my home. I have no need of chambermaids; what I need is someone to tend my weapons and armor while I remain here for the next few weeks. I need a page. Do you think you would be interested in this work?" Michael's eyes grew large and he noticed the sword that hung in its scabbard at her hip.

He quickly recovered his voice. "Oh, yes, mum. I would be the best page ever!"

"All right then, follow me. We're going to the castle."

"Up there? That's where he lives."

She saw the fear return to his eyes, his body tensing again. Looking up from this vantage point, she had to admit that the castle walls seemed more threatening than protective. "Yes, well, so do I. For now. He won't be able to hurt you there. I'll make sure of it."

Michael looked up into her eyes and held her gaze for a moment, then made his decision and began walking toward the main road, not looking back as she turned to join him.

After they had climbed out of the town and taken the road that would lead them to the gatehouse, she was aware of Michael stealing a few sideways glances at her.

"I'm taking you to a man, a mercenary raised by mercenaries, who will be in charge of your instruction. His name is Nigel Fitz Richard, and you must do whatever he asks of you."

"Yes, mum," Michael replied solemnly. "What should I call you?"

"Lady Gwendolyn will do for now," she replied.

13

THE SECRET REVEALED

Gwendolyn looked up in time to see the hunting party winding on the road from the west up toward the gatehouse, still far ahead of her. Except for the earl, de Coutances, and William, the men all walked on foot. Two riderless horses walked side by side, held on tight leads by the men who walked beside them. The hunt had been successful, she realized, but she was too far away yet to make out what sort of quarry had been killed. She quickened her step, and Michael jogged beside her to keep up.

By the time they arrived, there was a commotion in the yard in front of them that had nothing to do with the slain boar. The massive beast already hung by its hind legs on a rack and had been set upon by men with knives to be gutted and prepared for roasting. A small crowd had gathered round the earl, and Edmund's voice, dramatic with concern and protest, could be heard above the others. He must have come straight back to the castle, she realized. And the only reason he would have been in such a hurry to get back would have been to make sure his father heard his own version of the events from town first. Just like Walter de Cardinham, she thought, and spat onto the ground to clear the foul taste of her memories.

"You! Take his spear! Bring my father some water!" She could see the earl waving his son away half-heartedly.

"I'm fine, Edmund, I'm fine. William took the worst of it. He saved my life."

Edmund's lips pursed together and he cast a suspicious glance at William.

"Did he? Thank you, then," he said tersely, and William nodded without looking at the petulant son, easing himself stiffly from his horse. While Edmund remained distracted with his fawning over his father, Gwendolyn paused and turned to Michael.

"Take these up there," she said, handing him the extra rolls that she carried and gesturing with her chin toward the keep. "And be careful crossing over to the doorway into the keep. Keep your eyes about you. Tell anyone who asks that you are my page, and bring these to the women sitting with the infants in the hall."

Michael nodded and set off, readily distancing himself from Edmund. She watched until he had begun the ascent up the stone walkway atop the curtain wall and then turned her attention toward William. The man was streaked with mud and blood from head to toe, and he moved gingerly as he lifted his oilskin for a drink of water.

"What happened?"

William handed his horse's reins to the groom who came to assist him and turned to her, his eyes flashing.

"Where were you?" he countered. "I saw you coming up the hill toward us. And who was the boy walking with you?"

"I went to town."

"Alone?"

She set her jaw and stared back at him. Walter de Coutances walked past them on his way to the gatehouse and she reached out to put a hand lightly on the archbishop's arm.

"Your Excellency," she said politely, "what happened?"

De Coutances stopped and shook his head, running a hand through his silver hair.

"The earl was thrown from his horse just as the boar showed. D'Aubigni would have been trampled if William hadn't hopped on top of the boar in mid-charge to bring it down."

Gwendolyn turned back to William and crossed her arms. "And you quarrel with me for taking a walk in plain sight of the castle."

"Yours was an unnecessary risk," he replied sharply.

"Say that again after I tell you what I've discovered."

William had his back turned to her, loosening the straps on his saddle and retrieving his scabbard, but when he turned around to face her she saw the scrapes and mud again.

"But it can wait," she continued. "I'll have new clothes sent to you, and warm towels in the kitchen so you can clean up. Are you injured?"

She watched him make a show of rolling his shoulders and tilting his head left and right, working out the kinks. "Everything seems to be working."

She shook her head and sighed. "The boy's name is Michael. He's an orphan. And he's my page."

＊＊＊

She was sitting on the edge of the wooden pallet she slept on, waiting for him when he returned from washing up in the kitchen. He stood framed by the doorway, dripping wet and dressed only in his leggings, while steam rose from his body in the crisp autumn air. Looking at him, she could not imagine why he had not yet taken a wife. It was not unusual for men to wait until they had achieved a certain station in life, acquired a certain amount of wealth, so that they were in a position to bargain for an even greater gain in wealth and title from the match. Women, on the other hand, had no such prospect of increasing their wealth prior to marriage; their value lie in their ability to supply heirs. The arrangement resulted in many poor matches between older men and much younger girls. Thus the courtly joke that "love and marriage do not mix." But William was in his prime; Robert had already granted him land at Penhallam's northern border, and, short of a title, William's thrift and position had made him one of the more well-off men in the area. But then another thought occurred to her.

"Have you refrained from marrying because of me?"

William paused in the doorway, startled, then narrowed his eyes. "Don't flatter yourself."

Gwendolyn smiled at the retort, and William entered and crossed to the stack of clean clothes that Agnes had left for him. He picked them up and gave her a sarcastic look. Gwendolyn took the hint and retreated across the room to face the wall while he dressed.

"I meant, is it because you believe in the prophecy, that you're supposed to be my guardian, that you haven't married yet?" This was not what she had planned to discuss, but considering how much time they had spent together lately, the question had begun to stand out in her thoughts. In any normal circumstance, William's duties to Penhallam would leave him constantly in the company of men. But while he believed in and fulfilled his supposed duty under the prophecy of Caliburn's return, he would be constantly in the company of a woman—not an easy thing to explain to a wife.

"I don't see where that's any of your business," he said flatly behind her, grunting as he pulled on his shirt.

"It's not my business, William," she replied, a little exasperated. "But am I not allowed to be concerned for your wellbeing? As a friend?"

She heard William's movements pause behind her, and a long silence passed between them while he finished dressing.

"You can turn around now."

When she faced him again, he had seated himself on the bed to pull on his boots and he had on a pair of new leggings, expertly stitched.

"I have no desire to marry. It has nothing to do with the prophecy."

They had always been direct with each other; she would not begin second-guessing him now. She decided the question was answered and moved on to the topic of actual interest for the moment.

"There's something you need to know about Edmund. All that carrying on when you returned from the hunt wasn't just the concern of an overly protective son. It was an act."

She described for William the scene that she had walked into in the tavern, including the fact that Edmund apparently had his own gang of men from the garrison, no doubt enjoying the benefits of his purse while puffing him up with false flattery and thoughts of standing up to his father to demand an even larger purse. William's jaw tensed when she told him about Edmund's torment of Michael, but he breathed more easily and the corners of his mouth lifted when she told him about finding the boy and bringing him up to the castle.

"Well, we shouldn't be here for much longer. Eleanor will have spoken with John by now, by messenger if not in person. This plan of yours will come to its end, John will agree to stand down, or he won't—either way Eleanor won't need you here any longer, and we can return to Penhallam. And then maybe you'll reconsider the prophecy, and might search in earnest for the sword. Tintagel is hardly a day's ride from Penhallam."

She raised an eyebrow at him. "Don't hold your breath."

Nigel stepped into the doorway behind her with his hand firmly on Michael's shoulder beside him.

"This fellow says he's your page?"

Gwendolyn's expression softened at the sight of the boy, clearly distressed that Nigel was about to toss him back out onto the streets.

"He speaks the truth. He's with me."

Michael heaved a sigh, looked up defiantly at Nigel, and

stepped out from under his grip. Nigel scoffed lightly at the boy's cheekiness.

"The procession to bury the four who died at the camp is forming in the yard. We should all be there."

Gwendolyn nodded. "Stay here," she instructed Michael. "We won't be long. Bar the door behind us," she added, noting the carpentry that had been added to the door during the morning, no doubt at William's insistence.

Michael did as he was told, and Gwendolyn, William, and Nigel stepped out of the keep across the rickety planks to the battlements atop the curtain walls, and walked down the steep hill to the gatehouse and out into the yard.

The men who died would have come from noble families of the court, families with their own burial plots or crypts at their parish churches in their home counties. It would have been understood when the men joined the Tower guard that their remains would be buried where they fell if they died in service. Nevertheless, they would receive a Christian burial, with their bodies intact, close to the holy altar of the Arundel parish church. Their souls would be sent out on their journey to Heaven's gates by none other than the Archbishop of Rouen.

The mourners, mostly the village poor who were paid with food and drink to walk beside the dead and chant prayers, stood beside the cart that carried the enshrouded bodies. The mourners held candles, heads bowed in prayer beneath their borrowed mourning cloaks. Gwendolyn, Nigel, and William joined the group, standing behind the others who had come from London with them. A biting wind had picked up from the northeast, and the mourners carefully shielded the flames of their candles to keep them lit, gritting their teeth against the stings of hot beeswax that blew against them.

De Coutances raised his voice above the others, his chants ringing off the surrounding walls with a clarity and purity that Gwendolyn had not expected. Together with the gray shadows overhead and gusts of wind, de Coutances's haunting voice brought a sense of bleak inevitability to the moment, a reminder that death eventually came for everyone. The mourners formed into a loose procession, and the men tasked with hauling the cart lifted up the wooden arms and leaned forward, starting the group on its own journey down to the village.

Nigel and William stepped slowly on either side of Gwendolyn, and before long they found themselves bringing up the rear of the procession on their own.

"People are still saying this was the Devil's work," Nigel said under his breath as they walked. "The ones who saw the wolves, or whatever those beasts were. I've been with them most of the day, checking on the wounded, getting the others back to arms and their armor repaired. They've been telling the Arundel guard that they were set upon by demons, called out by the Devil's servant, and they're looking for someone to blame."

The three of them kept walking, each with their own thoughts, and Nigel interrupted again. "And by Christ's blood, William, what happened on the hunt today?" he hissed. "The boar is practically the Devil's hearth hound. And now, the day after we arrive, one nearly tramples the earl?"

"Boars are known to charge; it's why men like the earl love to hunt them," he answered in a harsh whisper.

"That may be true, but most of the people here who carry weapons are as tense as a bowstring right now. They're already ordered to war readiness, the king's been gone for years, his brother's running around saying he's dead anyway, and now they have a company from the Tower joining them with four dead and twice as many wounded and no good explanation for what attacked them. And last night the earl's son started in about John having a sorcerer." Nigel stopped and faced them. They were standing alone far below the castle walls. "We are surrounded by fighting men, just arrived from across the county, itching to draw their weapons, and the earl is off hunting boar instead of drilling some discipline into them like he should be." Nigel paused and shifted his weight, eyeing them both soberly. "I've seen this before. I don't know how safe we are here."

William and Gwendolyn hesitated and looked at each other. They each had their own news to share with Nigel. As they resumed walking, now far behind the burial procession, William recounted for them the lecture and warning de Coutances had given him on their way back from the hunt.

"He's an archbishop," Gwendolyn said, somewhat nonplussed. "What else would you expect from him? Why were you compelled to mention sorcery in front of him last night?"

"These things are real," William argued, and she sighed beside him.

"It's one thing for you to say that to a barely married, minor landowner from Cornwall; it's quite another to say it to the Archbishop of Rouen and King's Justiciar."

William shook his head. "We have no idea how John is going

to react when Eleanor tells him she's secretly holding the heir of Caliburn for him. William d'Aubigni is helping gather Richard's ransom with collections across Sussex, and Walter de Coutances is her right-hand man. Arundel is one of her most important strongholds. If John finds out de Coutances has been sent here, it won't be difficult for him to figure out you might be here as well. And right by the coast, an easy distance for any mercenaries or French armies and their ships."

"There won't be any French armies," Nigel said confidently.

"You can't be sure of that," William retorted.

"Philip's too busy scooping up every territory he can closer to home right now. He wants all of his armies in France, to bring more lands back to his command while Richard is indisposed. If John were worth anything, he'd be over there protecting his legacy instead of looking for favors in overthrowing his brother. Every person in contact with the prince is playing him for a fool."

William folded his arms while they walked, thinking through what Nigel had said. It occurred to Gwendolyn that the two men were having a civil discussion, sharing information and each weighing the other's opinions. The rancor of their earlier days seemed to have disappeared entirely. "John could still send mercenaries to kidnap her for himself, but d'Aubigni's men can handle them. Which leaves a sorcerer, if John has one."

"Which leaves nothing," Gwendolyn interrupted. "I'm safe here. Now about Edmund."

She told Nigel about finding Edmund in the tavern, entertaining himself and some of the drunken garrison by tormenting a boy. Nigel listened to the story wordlessly until she was done.

"One of the Lusignan brothers did nearly the same to me when I was a boy," he finally said.

"Seems we've both been the sport of spoiled sons."

Nigel fiddled absently with the clasp of his scabbard as they walked, and he questioned her for more detailed descriptions of the men from the garrison that she had seen in the tavern with Edmund. They had entered the muddy lanes of the village and were within a few blocks of the parish church.

"The Arundel garrison may be divided," she warned. "From the way he greeted Edmund last night and his preference for the distractions of hunting boar, the earl is either unaware of the faction forming against him in his own garrison, or he's unconcerned. Either way, he's made himself, and us by extension, vulnerable and exposed."

Nigel nodded. "I'll keep an eye on it. The garrison captain's a good man. Even if the earl's unaware, the captain will keep his men in line or he'll make an example of the troublemakers."

She stopped and turned to face them.

"I won't leave Michael here when we leave. Edmund will kill him."

"Agreed," William replied, and Nigel nodded.

By the time they joined the others again in the churchyard, the shrouded bodies had been laid in a pit dug for those who were not wealthy enough to have bought a final resting place inside the church. Gwendolyn shook her head picturing it, the generations of families plundering the country, carrying out bloody sieges in service to some would-be sovereign, burning villages and fields and bringing famine and destruction in their wake, all to gain the favorable reward of a duke or king. Then these same families used a portion of the plunder, filthy with the blood of their victims, to establish churches, abbeys, and priories and continue the cycle of plunder and bloodshed all over again. In return the Church treated them as venerated saints when they died, their bodies laid out beneath the stones and their souls prayed over daily. It was a routine that the Church benefitted from, thrived upon, and elevated with all of the trappings of Christian glory. These men going into the pit now deserved better for their sacrifice. She grunted and turned on her heel to return to the castle and Michael.

For the rest of the afternoon, Gwendolyn walked Michael around the castle grounds, making sure that he was widely seen in her company. She had given him one of her own shirts, which he wore belted with a rope, and she had cleaned his face and hands with well water. With a little polish he had turned into a respectable looking boy, and as they made their rounds the older women patted him on the head sweetly and some of the men patted him on the shoulder or gently teased him for his oversized shirt, telling him they had worn the same when they were boys. Michael had brightened up, and when they got to the gatehouse to meet with Nigel, he even flashed a brief smile.

"Show him how to polish the rust off the weapons, starting with the axe," she told Nigel. Michael's eye's widened as Nigel reached for a battle-axe that hung on the wall. The weapon's staff was nearly twice Michael's height.

"You can start with this," he said, showing Michael how to position himself safely in a seated position with the blade lying across his lap and handing him a soft, worn stone and a rag.

"Nigel will be within earshot of you at all times. Not that I'd expect Edmund to ever set foot inside an armory," she added with a crooked smirk.

By the time she arrived back up in the castle keep, Arundel's kitchen staff had set out stacks of bread trenchers and two large pots of stew in the hall for the evening dinner. The boar had been put on a spit over an open fire down in the lower yard in the midst of the tents and campfires. Music and singing could be heard through the two windows that looked out over the grounds below. Many of those who had been in the hall the night before were now down around the fires, enjoying the crisp autumn evening. The clouds had finally moved past, revealing a glittering, moonless sky.

"Thank you for saving my life today, William," d'Aubigni said casually as he approached with a cup of ale. Edmund still shadowed his father, and he glanced at William with a sour expression.

"I was simply in the right place at the right time, my lord." Gwendolyn walked up to William's side, nodded curtly to Edmund, and greeted the earl. Edmund hardly looked at her.

D'Aubigni smiled graciously. "I've always considered false modesty a sign of a duplicitous nature. But on you, William, I think it's genuine. You don't seem the sort to take praise easily."

"It's hard to imagine it's ever really warranted."

The earl nodded. "Spoken like a true man of combat. You know as well as I do that today could as easily have ended with two men dead. Except that it didn't," he added, gesturing toward William with a piece of bread in his other hand. "And you risked your life for mine," he said. "For that, you do have my deep gratitude."

William held the earl's gaze momentarily when Edmund spoke up and put his hand on his father's elbow, as if his assistance was needed for the earl to continue to stand.

"The boar has the reputation of being the Devil's own beast, familiar with the demons and the realms of Hell."

The earl laughed out loud and pulled his arm from his son's grasp.

"Yes, it does have that reputation," William agreed. "If this is the worst the Devil's got, I'll sleep easily tonight."

"But there's more, isn't there?" Edmund persisted. As he spoke, Walter de Coutances approached their little group. "Last night you mentioned that Prince John has found himself a sorcerer."

"And the archbishop rightly corrected my misstatement," William quickly replied, indicating to Walter de Coutances. "John only believes he has a sorcerer in his service. It's not the same as actually having one."

"Our instruction is very clear on this," de Coutances added, "The faithful are to shun the sorcerer and the witch. The practices are unnatural and against God's holy order. He alone provides for our needs; He alone holds past, present, and future in His almighty hands."

"And anyway, we have Caliburn's heir among us," the earl joked to his son. William and de Coutances immediately jerked their heads up at the remark, which the earl had said loudly enough to be heard by those nearby.

"Your ruse is safe here," d'Aubigni assured them, and put an arm around Edmund's shoulders. "There is not a person in Arundel who is either a supporter of John's rebellion or a believer in the prophecy of Caliburn's return."

Edmund pulled back from his father and pushed his hair out of his eyes.

"Really?" he asked, his gaze falling on William with a look of amusement that seemed to Gwendolyn to carry more than a hint of real excitement. She realized Edmund had assumed that William was the rumored heir of Caliburn.

"Over here," Gwendolyn said with a smile, daring Edmund to disparage her again in front of his father. She watched the young man's features shift in disbelief as he realized that Gwendolyn, and not William, was the fabled heir of the prophecy.

A momentary hush fell over the hall, and Gwendolyn and William followed the shift of attention to the doorway, where a tall, hooded figure had appeared. He arrived unescorted by any of the Arundel guard, which meant that he was both familiar and trusted. The man pulled his hood back, revealing a mantle of snow-white hair that hung past his shoulders and disappeared into the folds of his pale cloak. His face bore the wear of years spent out of doors, and his features appeared polished and worn, as if they had been carved in wood. The man's face was kind, but it seemed there was more etched within its lines than could be drawn from a single lifetime. The earl crossed the room to the man and greeted him warmly with his arms extended.

"Mogh, old friend, welcome! I didn't expect your visit so soon this year. I apologize that I have not yet send a messenger for you, but we're fully occupied here, as I'm sure you know." The earl reached out and offered his hand to the visitor as he approached, and then looked puzzled again. "But—you've come alone? Surely you haven't traveled to Arundel alone?"

At the mention of the visitor's name, Gwendolyn immediately stiffened and stared more closely at the stranger. Both the prior and her father, in his letter, had mentioned a seer named Mogh. How many men could walk this island with his name? She realized she was staring at the very source that had connected her personally with the Welsh prophecies so many years ago. He had known both her mother and father, and he had been with William when he had lived at the priory. She held her breath waiting to hear what business brought him to Arundel. She also realized from Walter de Coutances's shocked stare that the archbishop knew Mogh as well. De Coutances had told William as much after the hunt, as William had described his conversation with the archbishop to her and Nigel that afternoon.

"Nay, my lord, the others remain on the far side of the river. We've only just arrived to our wintering camp last night," the man replied softly, scanning the room with pale blue eyes that reminded Gwendolyn of William's and seemed to miss nothing. "I have come to speak with an old friend."

ACROSS THE BRIDGE

"That one," Mogh said, raising his long arm with a bony finger extended, pointing to William. "I would request his company, if you can spare him, until the morrow."

The earl turned to William as he stepped to the earl's side.

"You know this man?" the earl asked.

"From many years ago. Arundel is armed to the teeth and well-guarded. I can join Mogh at his fire for one night. We will stay nearby."

Walter de Coutances and Gwendolyn had approached, and the archbishop spoke first.

"Why do you have need of this man?" he asked with the sharpness of an interrogator, but Mogh's expression remained calm and warm.

"Archbishop," he said respectfully. Mogh's eyes seemed to

twinkle, and Gwendolyn wondered whether he had known de Coutances as a boy.

"I find I am surrounded by old friends," Mogh observed. "And of course you are Gwendolyn," he continued as his eyes fell on her. "Your beauty matches your fierce heart. I am honored to meet you," he said, and bowed his head. Gwendolyn found she had taken a step back, equal parts mesmerized and repelled by the magical aura that surrounded the man.

"Yours was not the only estate in Cornwall that I visited, Your Excellency," Mogh finally answered de Coutances. "I met William as a novice at Launceston Priory, along with your friend Prior Thomas. And the earl here has been kind enough to allow my band of wanderers to camp nearby in the weeks prior to midwinter, when we must be off again."

"I hope you have abandoned your heretical beliefs, Mogh," the archbishop said bluntly. "I will pray for your soul."

"I thank you for the kindness," Mogh replied in a soothing voice.

De Coutances, somewhat deflated, added, "It's good to see you again. I had heard you had stopped coming to the spring at Easter."

"We do not get around as we used to," Mogh replied with a shrug. "We are all older than we can count."

The earl put a hand on Mogh's shoulder.

"You and I both, my friend. As ever, you and your camp are welcome in Arundel. Just be careful. It wouldn't hurt to have someone on watch during the night. Our towers will signal if we see anything, but where you are, you're vulnerable to the east."

Mogh thanked the earl, and William turned to Gwendolyn.

"Sleep here among the Tower guard tonight. And don't do

anything foolish while I'm gone." The hint of a smile pulled the corners of his mouth, but she stared back at him stone-faced. Since the first mercenaries had crossed Penhallam, William had barely left her side, and he had scolded her just that morning for stepping out to town without him. He would not be leaving her now if he did not consider it essential, and she realized he had shown no surprise at the old man's sudden appearance. Suddenly Gwendolyn stepped forward and put her hand on William's arm.

"Wait," she said a little breathlessly, looking at Mogh. This all started with you, she wanted to protest, but Mogh stared placidly back at her.

"I am not the source of these events," he said kindly. She stood frozen, her jaw fixed in mid-question, as he and William stepped out of the hall and into the night. She felt a pull to go with them, but something stronger held her back, rooted where she stood. She discovered that she did not want to venture too deeply into William's world, even when presented with the opportunity. The singing and laughter from the castle yard drifted up to her again, and she watched their backs, side by side, as the men descended along the battlements down to the gatehouse.

The d'Aubigni's had returned to their seats on the raised dais at the far end of the hall. Edmund had characteristically excused himself to go to town, and a group of barons moved in to fill the void around the earl that Edmund's departure opened up. Walter de Coutances stood behind the earl, leaning over and whispering into his ear. The earl's expression was grim, and he nodded to whatever de Coutances was telling him. A sense of unease came over Gwendolyn, some sort of foreboding, and she retreated to an empty spot along the wall with her thoughts. The evening passed slowly, and she felt awkward and alone. In Penhallam she craved solitude, but here among strangers, the absence of companionship felt isolating. And yet she had no desire to approach any of the barons or even kind Matilda d'Aubigni to struggle through the niceties of light conversation. She was exhausted in body and mind, and the only fellowship she could tolerate was the sort that could be still with her in companionable silence.

As the candles burned down, families and men-at-arms began to settle in for the night. Some of the men keeping watch along the towers returned and others left to take their place. After the younger guests had fallen asleep, curled beside the hounds or bundled into their mothers' skirts, one of the women began to sing in low, haunting notes a familiar song of love lost to the grave. Conversations paused and all but a few of the remaining candles were extinguished. Gwendolyn recalled the song from her days at Restormel, and she closed her eyes to follow the familiar verses.

Hath any loved you well, down there,
Summer or winter through?
Down there, have you found any fair
Laid in the grave with you?
's death's long kiss a richer kiss
Than mine was wont to be–
Or have you gone to some far bliss
And quite forgotten me?
What soft enamoring of sleep

Hath you in some soft way?
What charmed death holdeth you with deep
Strange lure by night and day?
A little space below the grass,
Out of the sun and shade;
But worlds away from me, alas,
Down there where you are laid.

The song ended in the silent hall with its last notes lingering in the air. Gwendolyn looked around her and saw tears brimming even in the eyes of the battle-hardened knights. The darkened hall remained hushed, and when Michael and Nigel appeared in the doorway, she raised her arm to catch their attention. She had already settled herself into the straw, using her cloak for a blanket. The parish church had rung the hour for Compline prayers long ago. Michael found space in the empty straw beside her, and Nigel left wordlessly to return to the garrison at the gatehouse.

The boy settled himself down on his side facing her, his features delicately outlined by the faint glow of nearby hearth embers. He stared at her solemnly for a moment and then reached up with both of his hands to place them on her cheeks, framing her face. He silently mouthed the words, thank you, held her gaze a moment longer, then withdrew his hands and turned over to face the wall. Gwendolyn smiled to herself, knowing that Michael slept that night warm, safe, and fed—possibly for the first time in years.

William stared across the campfire at Mogh, his old teacher. A gourd was being passed around the circle, and the woman to his left, a slight form almost concealed in the pile of blankets that she had draped about herself, took a long draw. Without looking she passed the gourd to her right and William raised it tentatively to his nose. A familiar, bitter smell made him pinch his eyes closed and wince.

"You'll not be sleeping tonight, William Rufus," Mogh said gently from across the fire. "It's time to open you up."

At Mogh's words, the hairs stood up on William's arms despite the heat of the nearby flames. William took a deep breath and held it, to keep from smelling the brew, then raised the gourd to his lips and quickly swallowed several large gulps. The liquid landed in his stomach like a fire, and immediately his insides clenched in protest. William knew this rite. Prior Thomas called it "the bridge." The liquid in the gourd was a remedy, when taken in small sips, to ease pains. In larger amounts it caused waking dreams, sometimes nightmares. But its chief effect was to blend all of the sensations—taste, sound, image, scent, touch—into a singular experience. Sounds acquired shape and color, which in turn gave off a smell that could be felt with one's skin and tasted on the tongue. Prior Thomas had not crossed the bridge himself, but he was there once when Mogh did. He had told William that Mogh's breath became so faint, his heartbeat so slow, that the prior had thought his friend had died. The prior had sat beside him through the night praying, only to have Mogh awaken at sunrise so serene and composed that he had spent the next several days in complete contentment. Even a sharp kick from the priory's mule had left him laughing and applauding the mule for its spirit and precise aim.

The woman to William's left began to sway side to side, chanting some forgotten verse in a low voice, barely audible. To his right, an older man who looked to be about the same age as Mogh sat still as stone. William turned his gaze back to the fire and waited. The cramping in his guts had ceased, replaced by an unsettling numbness that seemed to be spreading throughout his body. As the numbness crept up his chest, he had the sensation of being unable to catch his breath. He felt an impulse to panic, and Mogh's voice reached him, from across the fire or someplace farther way.

"Have faith, William. You are safe. Nothing that you will see tonight can hurt you, but it is all real. More real than the life you imagine yourself to be living."

William lifted his head to gaze across the fire at Mogh, but when he did, in Mogh's place he saw a young man with a wide smile and shining teeth. An aroma of nutmeg filled his head, and he looked up and saw a dense flock of birds flying overhead. He vaguely recalled that it should have been nighttime, with darkened skies, but the radiant blue that spread overhead was more beautiful than any sky he had yet seen, and he found he did not mind the sudden switch to daylight.

"Are you ready?" The young version of Mogh stood beside him, and William began to lift himself to standing but found his body fixed to the ground. He looked down and found that his chest and legs had become the gray, gnarled trunk and roots of a hazel tree. He started to scream, but Mogh's hand on his shoulder calmed him.

"You are safe. This is your soul revealing itself to you. Your body is not hurt." Mogh laughed softly. "The hazel tree is an apt manifestation for you. The tree is known for its gifts of wisdom and foresight. And here you were, thinking you were just a fighting man at heart."

Mogh pulled on William's arm, and he found his legs restored beneath him. The sky still glowed a vivid cerulean that sounded like birdsong pulsing through his veins. He stood and faced Mogh.

"Turn around, William."

William turned his head around to peer behind himself but could see nothing. Mogh nudged his elbow and he took a few steps, turning his back to the young man. In the distance, the ground in front of him became disturbed, as if something tunneled under it at a great speed. He narrowed his eyes, tried to squint to see into the distance. As the movement came closer, he realized the ground was in fact falling away, disappearing into an abyss. He turned to run, but before he could cover more than a few steps the crumbling earth fell away beneath him and he found himself clawing through the air, surrounded by clods of earth and turf.

"Remember, William, you are safe. Always safe."

Mogh's voice sounded ancient again, and so far away. William surrendered to the fall, his nostrils filled with the rich, pungent scent of the dirt that surrounded him. His vision was completely blocked, but he could breathe. Wind rushed past him, and he noticed the air around him beginning to clear. He felt as if he was falling into a hidden underworld that lie beneath the one he had spent his life upon until that moment. He landed with an easy splash into a cool lake. He gulped in mouthfuls of the water to wash the dirt from his mouth, and the water tasted fresher than any spring he had ever drunk from on the earth above. He swam easily to a sandy bank and climbed out onto verdant grasses. Everything felt brand new, as if he were the first person to see these colors, to lie upon these blades of grass. He took a deep breath and closed his eyes, stretching his arms out to the sides. If this was the bridge that Prior Thomas feared, it was not all that bad.

"William!" The urgent whisper came from beside him; the voice was Gwendolyn's.

He opened his eyes, and a man in full armor and helmet, already bloodied from his past battles, stood over him with his sword in both hands, poised to plunge the blade down into William's chest. William yelled and rolled to his side, and the blade struck into the earth beside him. The man reached for the blade to pull it from the earth, but the blade stuck. It would not budge again. William watched curiously as the man struggled, bracing against the ground and gripping the hilt with both hands, until the scene became comical for him and he laughed out loud. The man stopped his efforts, stepped back, and reached up to remove his helmet. William gasped as he recognized Prince John before him, aged at least twenty years older than the young man who caused so much chaos now. John had passed through Cornwall two years ago, an unpleasant experience for all who had been forced to provide him and his entourage lodging and quarter. But this older version of the prince was haggard and dark shadows lay beneath his hollow gaze. William realized that he was looking upon a king and not a prince. John glared at him for a moment, then replaced his helmet and turned again toward the sword. But the sword had changed. It had begun to glow with an unearthly light. John stepped back and raised his hands to shield himself, but William discovered that the glare did not hurt his eyes. He watched the sword's illumination grow until he lost sight of everything else. At last the light blinded him, surrounded him with the singing of distant voices. Everything was washed away in that moment—all of his foreboding and dread, the terrible things his sight had shown him since he was a boy. In a way Gwendolyn was right; they weren't real, because they could not last. He realized, deep in his bones, that in the great length of time, there would be this peace that had engulfed him, that had always been and always would be. It could not be touched or destroyed. It simply was, and all else was not.

A gentle flutter of movement brushed past him, and a woman glided ahead of where he stood. She wore a white gown, and he could not see her face, but long red hair draped down her back past her waist. She walked straight to the sword, lifted it out of the ground with one hand, turned and swung the blade through the middle of King John's body. The figure that had been John became a tower of crows that scattered noisily and flew away. The woman turned to face him, the glowing sword still raised in her hand. With a rushing noise, the blade seemed to swallow back up the brilliant light that had shone from it, and for a moment the metal flashed with a dazzling gleam of silver, then became an ordinary sword again. Gwendolyn smiled softly, returned the sword to the earth. She turned her green eyes to him for a moment, then faded from sight until only a single white dove flapped its wings in mid-air where she had been and flew away.

William awoke the next morning lying on his side in the same location near the fire where he had sat the night before. A leaden sky hung close overhead, and he shivered inside his cloak. The fire burned low before him, but its embers still gave off a soothing heat, and he sat up slowly and shifted himself closer to the circle of stones that served as a hearth. Neither of the others that had sat beside him the night before could be seen anywhere. In fact, he realized as he scanned around himself, he was quite alone.

The Arun River flowed by gently in the distance, and the walls of Arundel could be seen beyond that, rising above the river valley. He sat still for a long moment while his mind recalled every detail of his vision from the night before. The memories were vivid and sharp, and the sense of serenity that had concluded his dream still hung about him like a song that had stopped in mid-verse, its notes still shimmering in the air.

The images had seemed so real that he could not stop himself from brushing away the grasses and leaves on the ground around him to see if there would be a mark where John had thrust the sword. But he found the ground undisturbed except for the impression left behind by his own slumbering body.

Movement behind him caught his attention and he turned around. Mogh approached him, a slight smile showing white teeth, and handed him a heavy oilskin.

"For the thirst," he said, and William became suddenly aware of his parched throat. He loosened the top of the skin and carefully poured the cooling liquid into his mouth, savoring its freshness that reminded him of the water from his dream.

"Where were you?" he asked the old man, wiping his chin with his arm and handing the oilskin back to Mogh. "Where has everyone gone?"

Mogh looked at him closely, his eyes twinkling, and began to laugh. Confused, William chuckled lightly with Mogh, but an uncomfortable feeling crept into his gut. Mogh's laughter grew quiet and then changed into a dry cackle. Warmth seeped into William's mouth from the back of his throat, and he became aware of the unmistakable metallic taste of blood. He felt light-headed and staggered a step forward. Mogh became quiet and William staggered back a step and lifted his fingers to the warmth that trickled from his nose. When he pulled them back, his fingertips shined red and wet with his blood. His vision began to blur, and the figure that was no longer Mogh stepped aside. Behind him lay the body of Gwendolyn, twisted on her side, pinned to the earth by her own sword. William tried to scream, but only a strangled gurgle came forth as he fell to his knees beside her. He could feel his life slipping away from him, and he was too weak to hold off the darkness.

The first sound he registered was his own screaming, then Mogh's soothing voice beside him. The others came too, and gentle hands pulled him upright to a seated position.

"You're okay, William. It was only a dream. You're awake now."

William jumped to his feet and looked wildly about himself, then buckled over again to vomit onto the ground. His body heaved violently and repeatedly, emptying itself completely. When the spasms finally stopped, he slowly raised himself to standing and wiped his mouth with his arm. He brushed away the gourd of fresh water that one of the women offered.

"I'll get my own, thanks," he said roughly.

His head throbbed and the forceful retching left him trembling, but he felt strong—and very alive. The sky overhead gleamed sparkling and clear, as if it had been washed clean.

Mogh stood beside him and William turned to face him. The fire had been built up again and the smell of baking bread and stew wafted across to him.

"The sorcerer is real," he said, adjusting his cloak around his shoulders.

Mogh nodded. "Yes." The old man looked William over carefully and tilted his head to the side for a moment.

"You need to give yourself time for your blood to thicken again," he told him. "You need food."

"I can't stay here," William answered, his throat chafing. He ran his hands quickly over his belt and beneath his cloak to ensure that he had all of his belongings with him. "He means to kill her."

Mogh reached out and gripped his forearm. "The sorcerer is not coming for you, William. You and Gwendolyn will go to him of your own volition. It is already written. He will lure you both to him, using your best qualities to bait you. And this sorcerer is a master in the ways of death in the same way that your father uses his herbs and powders for healing. But he is more powerful. His dark magic has disturbed the very song of time."

William placed a hand on top of Mogh's, and for a moment the two men held each other's eyes in silence, both aware that this could be the last time they would stand in each other's company. Mogh released William's arm, and William took off at a run for the river and the ferry across. He did not pause or look back.

15

THEATER
IN THE HALL

Gwendolyn paced the floor of her small room, fuming. Since the morning that William had returned from Mogh, almost a week ago, she had agreed not to step from the castle's protective walls until he was certain the danger had passed. She had complained bitterly when he asked her to forego joining the Arundel guard in training, but she had heard the mix of urgency and genuine fear in his voice. William had slept each night lying across the threshold of her door, and he practically stood outside the privy whenever she went to relieve herself. He followed her when she walked the battlements, and his glowering presence had effectively ended any conversation she might have had with Arundel's residents. Even Matilda, who generally preferred the company of women, only made light small talk with her now. She found his constant lurking irritating and unnecessary, but his loyalty to her was indisputable. She trusted him and believed he would not ask her to endure such confinement without cause. Knowing this, however, did not ease her temper.

Edmund had spent most of his time in town for the last several days, which was fortunate for all of them. When Edmund was at Arundel, the earl's son kept close to his group of men-at-arms from the tavern and cast furtive glances toward William and Gwendolyn. She found the treatment preferable to the snide remarks and leers from their encounter in town, but his demeanor was starting to affect the other residents of Arundel, who did not want to be seen as favoring these outsiders that the earl's son obviously disliked. A polite coolness had settled over their expressions and curt comments, and both William and Nigel were on edge because of it. Gwendolyn, however, felt certain Edmund's behavior was simple retribution for his humiliation by her hand at the tavern, and she ignored it.

St. Crispin's Day approached, reminding her of how many days had passed since she had left London. It seemed that she should have heard some sort of direction from the Tower by now. Walter de Coutances walked the battlements daily, partly to ease his own growing frustration, partly to consult with the earl over the siege preparations. De Coutances had directed the assault against the castle at Windsor last summer that had eventually driven Prince John's rebels out and returned the fortress to Eleanor's control. The similarities between Windsor and Arundel in the design and arrangement of their fortifications made his continued lingering in Arundel at least not entirely without purpose. A moat had been quickly excavated and filled by the marsh water that bubbled up around the front of the gatehouse to prevent tunneling beneath the walls, and carpenters were busy chopping trees and shaping the trunks into pikes to fill the ditch at the foot of the motte. All of the towers along the curtain wall had been well stocked with wood, for use in heating cauldrons of oil that could be poured onto wooden ladders and siege machines and the men with them, then lit.

In the midst of this activity, Gwendolyn felt useless. She had followed de Coutances when he permitted it, listening closely to absorb the man's experience and knowledge as he went about advising the earl. But the idleness of the last week had left her with raw nerves and a foul temper. She was reaching her limit, and with the close of each uneventful day, her willingness to continue to give weight to William's fears waned a bit more. She told him so, followed by a long list of the fortifications and military precautions that surrounded her and ensured her safety. He had listened, unmoved, even though he could see for himself how nearly intolerable the confinement had become for her. He shook his head at her.

"There is no sorcerer," she growled at him. She wheeled around and punched him hard in the shoulder, watched with satisfaction as his anger flared.

"I saw you dead," he repeated, glaring at her and rubbing the smarting muscle. "I will not see it again in the flesh."

"What did Mogh say about your vision? What if it was only your own fears that fueled your imagination?"

William grunted and turned away from her. The constant time in each other's presence had stoked the sparks of their usual conflicts to a steady blaze.

"It wasn't. You cannot leave the castle."

She narrowed her eyes, watched him pace the floor near the door.

Some sort of commotion stirring in the grounds below the keep caught their attention. Men shouted near the gatehouse, and William and Gwendolyn both grabbed their swords and charged down the timber steps and across the courtyard to the arched passage that led to the doorway out of the keep. They found the passage already blocked by the foot soldiers from the hall who had rushed out ahead of them. They paused and waited while the Arundel guard carefully navigated the planks to the battlements in single-file.

"Prince John Plantagenet!"

The call came from the guard below, at the gatehouse, announcing the arrival of the king's brother. Everyone froze where they stood and looked below to the yard.

The gatehouse guard stood at attention, spears raised, but at a respectful distance, while attendants ran to assist the prince and his men. There was a moment of confusion as Arundel's guard and the grooms, pages and steward paused and looked at each other. There was no precedent for a moment like this. Eleanor had resisted the regents and refused to issue orders for her younger son's arrest. One day it was possible that he would wear the crown legitimately, and Gwendolyn understood that his mother would not undermine his reign before it began by permitting him to be treated by his future subjects as a common criminal. But this was also the man leading an active rebellion against their king, threatening their coasts with Flemish mercenaries—a known threat to the crown.

John himself solved the moment by unfastening his weapons belt and leaning over to hand his sheathed sword and dagger to the gatehouse guard. At his example, the rest of his men did the same. Their weapons secured, a palpable breath of relief passed across the yard and the attendants smiled and approached the visitors.

John had arrived with only a few men. He was obviously confident of his safety among men like Walter de Coutances and William d'Aubigni. And he was travelling light. Not everyone knew what their king's younger brother looked like. Travelling with a small entourage and no fanfare or display of colors enabled him to travel quickly, as any other well-off free man going about his business.

William and Gwendolyn watched John and his men dismount below and allow their horses to be taken to the stables by Arundel's grooms. One of the men who accompanied John pushed his hair out of his eyes in a familiar gesture, and Gwendolyn recognized Edmund. They must have crossed paths in town, she realized. Of course Edmund would have leapt at the opportunity to ingratiate himself to the king's brother. John swept his gaze around those assembled in the castle yard, took in the preparations for war—the tents, rows of bows and spears and other pole weapons leaning against the wall where the castle armorers had been mending them, tightening strings, sharpening blades. He nodded with smug approval and turned his gaze up toward the keep.

"William!" he shouted, and William gave a start beside her.

John raised his hands to form a cup around his mouth and shouted again. "William d'Aubigni! Second Earl of Arundel!"

William exhaled, then stepped back, away from the doorway. Walter de Coutances and d'Aubigni approached behind him, and the rest of the guard cleared the way to the doorway to the keep. The two men stepped forward into the opening.

"Walter! Mother said I would find you here. You've been busy." John called out the last words in a singsong voice, like a parent scolding a misbehaving child.

"Do we have business to discuss?" de Coutances called back, suppressing his agitation.

"Yes, we do," John answered. "May I come up for a bit? I'm sure you'll understand that I'd like to keep my men with me." John had extended his arms, palms up, in supplication, the image of innocence.

De Coutances leaned toward d'Aubigni and the two men conferred in hushed voices. Finally, d'Aubigni answered the prince.

"You are welcome at Arundel, John, as were your father and grandmother before you. Your men are welcome, too. I'm sure you understand that it is no insult that Arundel's men will hold on to their swords."

"I would expect nothing less from my family's constant champion," John said with a magnanimous sweep of his arm. From the clear space behind de Coutances and d'Aubigni Gwendolyn could see the whole display. She rolled her eyes and turned away, William close on her heels behind her.

"Oh, for the love of the saints, William!" she complained. "It wasn't John that killed me, was it?"

She looked up and saw that Matilda d'Aubigni, Lady of Arundel, had issued fast orders as soon as the prince's arrival was announced. Two men carried a wooden chair, large and elaborately carved, out to the dais and set it alongside the chairs of Matilda and William d'Aubigni. Gwendolyn recognized the chair that she had sat in the morning that Matilda d'Aubigni had massaged her heels and cured her of her pains. Two women were making fast work of the fouled rushes on the floor, sweeping and bundling them out as quickly as two more women arrived with arms overflowing with fresh straw and herbs. Buckets of water were splashed over the trestle tables to clear crumbs and dry wood was thrown onto the fires. In a matter of minutes their efficient work transformed the hall into a well-tended, hospitable setting for the king's last surviving brother.

Arundel's guests and guard filed back into the hall, finding places on either side along the walls to make way for the prince and his men. Some of the barons whispered among themselves uneasily, but the fact that the prince had arrived so unceremoniously with only a few men was taken to be a good sign, perhaps an indication that John was ready to admit the folly of his actions and step back into line as his brother's supporter. De Coutances and the earl had stepped out onto the battlements to symbolically meet the prince halfway, and they walked back up the steep aisle to the keep with him. Their voices could be heard approaching, and an expectant hush fell over the hall.

William d'Aubigni and Walter de Coutances entered the hall first, followed by Prince John, then Edmund, then John's men. A stream of onlookers from the castle grounds filed in last, and many of Arundel's guard, including those loyal to Edmund, abandoned their posts for the opportunity to be close to their sovereign's infamous brother. Nigel and Michael came in and took their places along the wall beside Gwendolyn and William. She protectively pulled Michael in front of her, her hands resting on his shoulders.

Gwendolyn's gaze followed John closely, sizing the man up. He was shorter than she had expected, with a smooth brow and thick, dark hair that framed his face in waves. Large brown eyes conveyed a warmth that seemed in conflict with his reputation for cunning and ambition. What hatred he must have borne for his father to have forsaken the man upon his deathbed, she thought, recalling the account she had heard from the earl. John was undeniably handsome, with balanced, elegant features, and he carried himself with catlike grace. She decided, watching him, that she had underestimated him. This enigmatic man may not have the qualities of a warrior, but he was nonetheless a formidable opponent. And yet, something about his expression, the way that he seemed to take in the room like a jackal surveying a pasture of lambs, caused her to shudder inside. This man might also have a capacity for savagery that left honor and decency far behind.

Edmund took his seat on the dais at his mother's feet, looking pleased with himself. Matilda, staring contentedly into the distance, reached her hand out and touched his head affectionately. Prince John's dark eyes flashed around the room as he took in the assembled crowd, a mixture of armed men, barons, and lords, wealthy merchants and their families. His lip seemed to curl a bit with pleasure.

De Coutances stepped forward with an extended arm.

"My lord, perhaps you and I can retire to private quarters to discuss our business," he offered in diplomatic tones.

John smiled, flashing his teeth in a predacious grin.

"That's hardly necessary," he chided the justiciar. "I have nothing to hide from the good people of Arundel."

This is a performance, Gwendolyn immediately realized, and she braced herself for whatever scheme the prince was about to unleash on them.

"You follow my mother's orders, Walter, and I can't fault you for that. But when I received her note that the Welsh prophecies were true, that she had in her custody the actual heir of Caliburn, I could hardly believe my eyes." He paused, gave his audience a moment to get in on the joke. "Really, did you think I could believe that she," he said, indicating toward Gwendolyn and raising his voice, "a woman, could be a Pendragon, Arthur returned, the heir of Caliburn?" He scoffed under his breath, and Gwendolyn took in the muffled exclamations and gasps of laughter that passed around the room. This was John's show entirely, and these people, whose lives had been so uprooted and cast into uncertainty by the prince's attempts to seize the throne, were enthralled by it. "Who could believe such ridiculous heresy?"

De Coutances stared, and Gwendolyn saw with disappointment that the justiciar had been taken by surprise. John had turned their ploy against them, held it up for ridicule and made them look like fools.

"You, obviously, John," William d'Aubigni answered loudly, ignoring the rhetorical nature of John's question. "There are too many witnesses to count who are familiar with your obsession with the stories of Arthur Pendragon and Merlin. It's no secret that your brother, King Richard, announced that his nephew Arthur would succeed him to the throne specifically to taunt you, because he knows your greatest fear is that all of those prophecies will indeed come to pass."

The hall was quiet again, and Gwendolyn smiled a little as John struggled to maintain his composure.

"A boy's passing fantasy was all that it was. I've grown up now, d'Aubigni, enough to know that that woman's only value is between her legs. And that ground remains unplowed, as of yet," he added, turning to Gwendolyn as another wave gasps and whispers rolled around her. "You may as well return to my mother at the Tower, Lady de Cardinham, because you serve no purpose here. Unless you would like to suggest another means of distracting me," he said slyly.

Gwendolyn felt the muscles in her arms tense at John's reference to her unconsummated marriage. Nigel grunted beside her, ready to spring upon the prince at the first excuse. John had been thinking ahead when he offered his sword belt in the yard below; no honorable man would raise his weapon against one unarmed. She felt William's movement beside her as his hand tightened around the hilt of his sword. She had no idea how the information had found its way to the prince, but she would not play into his attempt to unsettle her. "I am certain my husband would want to answer your claims personally, if he weren't delayed in service to King Richard in his captivity." John's lips pursed into a smirk at her remark.

"Your husband is no longer delayed, Lady de Cardinham," he said, holding her carefully indifferent gaze. "Robert de Cardinham has been released from service. Did Mother not send a messenger to inform you? Ah, well, she is advanced in years."

"She is the dowager queen, and I'll believe it when I hear it from her," Gwendolyn replied evenly.

John nodded slightly to her. "Your fidelity to my mother is commendable, if misplaced. But then, there are always those trying to use my mother to obtain some reward, through trickery or worse. Rumor has it that a sorcerer plagues my family now."

A low murmur passed around the hall and one of the men from the Tower guard muttered, "The beasts!" Walter de Coutances finally found his voice and stepped forward.

"The only rumor of a sorcerer that I am aware of, John, involves you and your obsession with Caliburn. If you have spoken truthfully tonight, and have repented of these preoccupations of yours, then I am glad to hear it."

Prince John hesitated, and Gwendolyn watched him considering his next move with the same precision as a player in a game of chess. Perhaps she could unsettle him with her own revelation.

"You sent your men, Walter de Cardinham among them, to attack the abbey at Glastonbury and search the crypt. You were searching for Caliburn."

John turned his gaze to her, his mouth drawn to a fine line.

"Your brother-in-law told you this himself?" Gwendolyn knew John was too smart to ask a question that he did not already know the answer to, and she replied truthfully.

"Walter de Cardinham has not been seen or heard from since Glastonbury. Like most of your supporters, he has been forced into hiding."

"I was there!" Nigel yelled angrily beside her.

John tilted his chin slightly and turned his gaze to Nigel,

slowly sweeping an appraising eye over him.

"My goodness, and this is the best that my substantial treasury can muster for me, is it?"

Some of the barons in the crowd laughed at the prince's remark, and Gwendolyn knew better than to call the prince out as a liar. Nigel stared straight ahead defiantly but said nothing more, and John turned toward the justiciar with a triumphant sneer.

"This woman is of no interest to me, Walter. Mother's attempt to control me has failed. Again."

De Coutances exhaled a heavy sigh.

"I will convey your message to her. In the meantime, I cannot allow you to leave Arundel."

For a moment Gwendolyn saw rage flash into the young prince's eyes, then just as quickly he set it aside and forced his mouth into a thin smile.

"And yet you have no authority to hold me here, either," he countered. "Even as justiciar, you would not defy my mother's wishes."

De Coutances hesitated, and Gwendolyn knew in that pause that John smelled victory.

"Will you give me your word," de Coutances said slowly, "as a Christian and a Plantagenet, that this is done, that you renounce your rebellion against your brother?"

John turned away from de Coutances and looked down, and Gwendolyn watched his shoulders slump beneath the fine cloak. With his question, de Coutances had brought an end to the prince's posturing. All of John's military efforts had failed. His mercenary boats had failed to find any unwatched little slip of coast where they could land. Only a few barons and a smattering of castles had taken up his cause. His last effort, an attempt to bribe the Holy Roman Emperor with help from the coffers of Philip of France, had resulted only in the depletion of his treasury.

John turned back to face de Coutances. "You have my word."

A stunned moment passed over the hall, followed by an eruption of cheers. John stood in the middle of the room, his features drawn down and the flashing grin from just moments ago replaced by a grimace.

William d'Aubigni stood up from his seat at the dais and the hall became quiet again. "Forget all of this tonight, John, and take your rest here. Your father's apartments are very comfortable, and I'm sure a man such as yourself will find his bed furnished with fair companionship." William d'Aubigni did not smile as he spoke.

John turned to face the dais and extended a hand graciously to the d'Aubigni's son. "Edmund, perhaps you would accompany me to the king's apartments below. I would like to take their measure, for my future visits to Arundel as your sovereign. My tastes differ somewhat from my father's, as you know." Although he spoke to Edmund, John fixed his gaze on the earl as he said the words.

Edmund stood up, grinning like he had won a tournament ribbon, and joined the prince in the middle of the hall.

"I won't stay long," John continued to the earl, "My men and I will be gone by morning. You can tell my mother that I am retreating north, to my castle at Nottingham, if she would like a word with me."

D'Aubigni nodded, "As you wish." He turned back toward the dais and muttered under his breath, "Somehow I will recover from my disappointment," drawing muffled laughter from his nearby men. The brief flash of rage rose again in John's eyes, and again he suppressed it. He laid a possessive arm across Edmund's shoulders and swept out of the hall with the earl's son at his side, his men close behind.

Gwendolyn took in a deep breath, as if John's exit allowed fresh air into the hall again, and then crossed the room directly to Walter de Coutances and the earl.

·ᴗᴗ·

"He's lying," she said firmly, and the earl looked up at her with a gleam in his eye.

"Of course he is," he replied lightly. "He is John Plantagenet."

16

ACCUSED

"The trick now," William d'Aubigni continued, "is to discover his true course before he's got anything underway. Cut him off at the knees before he gets started."

Walter de Coutances huddled in a tight conversation in a corner of the hall with his secretary, the man who had traveled with him since the Tower. He talked directly into the man's ear, and his secretary nodded, his lips moving as he memorized the justiciar's orders. Within moments the man pulled his cloak about his shoulders, raised his hood to cover his head, and swept through the hall and down the steps to exit the keep.

"Leofwin will leave now and travel without stop to the Tower, changing to fresh horses along the way. That will bring him to the Tower by midday tomorrow. With John here under our watch, the prince can't send anyone out to intercept him. Eleanor will know tomorrow everything that John has said here today. She will send her orders for you—and for us—after that."

Gwendolyn smiled at the justiciar, and the realization started to settle in that perhaps this really was over, and she and William could return safely to Penhallam again, maybe in a matter of days. She turned around to face William.

"What do you think?"

William cocked an eyebrow and shrugged. "We'll see. John is up to something. He's not done, not just like that."

"True. But whatever it is, apparently it will have nothing to do with me or Caliburn."

William gave her a warning look.

"Don't be so sure."

The mood in the hall had turned almost festive, with laughter and broad smiles glowing in the warm light from the hearths. No one spoke to her or even acknowledged with a look that she was there. The reason for her stay at Arundel had been revealed, with all of its far-fetched absurdity, and allegations had been made against her marriage. She felt invisible, like a phantom in the midst of their jubilation, and she found she was grateful for it. The sun had begun its descent, and the call to Vespers rang from the parish church in the village beyond the walls. Many of the revelers, Matilda d'Aubigni among them, filed out of the hall to cross the courtyard and climb the steps to a small chapel above for prayers, leaving a handful of the fighting men, women with children, and a few others behind in the hall. Michael waited for Gwendolyn, standing out of the way near the wall with Nigel. The boy had an anxious expression, and she extended her hands to him again.

"De Coutances has sent a messenger to Eleanor," she told Nigel, and the mercenary nodded, his distaste for the prince and his words still evident in his eyes. She sighed and placed a hand on his arm, and Nigel's attention snapped to her gaze.

"Thank you, Nigel Fitz Richard."

Nigel blushed, cleared his throat.

"We may be free to leave Arundel soon. Where will you and Ella go?"

Nigel narrowed his eyes and looked past her, over her shoulder. "I don't know. The only family she's got is in London, but I can't provide any kind of life for her there."

"That's not her only family."

Nigel turned his eyes back to Gwendolyn with his brow drawn down as he puzzled over her words. She reached out to Michael and drew him near again as William stepped to her side.

"Perhaps the five of us can return to Penhallam together," she casually suggested.

Michael's face broke out into a grin and he looked up at Gwendolyn, William and Nigel. Nigel finally understood her remark about family, and he stood up a little straighter.

"We always need more good men," she continued. "And if Robert's on his way back, and Walter on the run, we may find ourselves spread thin if we need to send men to guard Restormel until Walter can pay his way back into good standing with the crown."

"If I can be of service," Nigel said, looking to William a little uneasily.

"We'll have to return to London first anyway, to retrieve my father's letter and find out if Robert really has returned, as John said."

Heads turned as Edmund re-entered the hall, his black cloak flowing behind him. He crossed to the dais and stood expectantly before his father.

"The prince has decided not to stay after all, Father," he announced loudly with a confident smile.

Walter de Coutances looked up suddenly from behind Edmund, and d'Aubigni rose from his seat, his face purple with rage.

"Where has he gone?" D'Aubigni shouted at Edmund. "Edmund! What have you done?"

"I have saved you from a judgment of treason, Father," Edmund said slowly, appearing to enjoy the effect his words had on the earl. D'Aubigni fixed his glare upon Edmund, but Gwendolyn could see a small question of uncertainty cloud his eyes.

"Go on," he said, his voice laced with threat.

Edmund turned on his heel, looking around the room. He had been a fast student of John's, Gwendolyn realized. She felt William tense beside her, heard the rustle of his cloak as he pushed it away from his left shoulder, clearing the way for his sword.

"John did not make an empty accusation when he claimed that a sorcerer had turned his unholy attention toward his family."

Again Edmund paused, allowed his words to register. He slowly reached inside his cloak.

"John has trusted me with the proof."

Edmund pulled out Gwendolyn's letter from her father.

The letter was rolled, still tied by its ribbon, but she recognized it immediately: the thickness, the shade of the vellum, the smudge of mud when she had unrolled it after swimming in the river.

"What is that?" the earl snapped, irritated at having to entertain his son's theatrics any further.

"A bewitched letter," Edmund said darkly, unrolling it and revealing the familiar script. "Given to Eleanor to cast a spell upon her—by that woman and her wizard!" Edmund spun around and pointed his hand, which still held the letter, at Gwendolyn and William. Gwendolyn's heart raced, and without thinking she reached for the letter in his hand.

"Do you see, Father? She reaches for it! She knows she is discovered!" Edmund crossed to the hearth and cast the letter into the flames. "Here's what we do with witchcraft at Arundel, Lady!"

"No!" Gwendolyn cried out and lunged toward the hearth, but too late. As the vellum caught flame, the edges curled and a thick green and black smoke poured from it as it burned.

"See for yourself! See the smoke of Hell come forth from her charm as it burns!" A noxious fume filled the hall, and Gwendolyn and the others began to cough and cover their mouths.

Walter de Coutances held the edge of his cloak up against his mouth and nose, but he stared with wide eyes at Gwendolyn and then William.

Edmund coughed loudly and continued. "They sought to exploit the queen and her concern for her sons by tricking her into an absurd plan, all to gain their reward: title to the lands of John's faithful servant, Walterus de Cardinham." Edmund stood triumphantly in front of her and William. Gwendolyn realized that the four men of the Arundel guard that had stayed behind from Vespers were the men loyal to Edmund.

"You did something to the letter," Gwendolyn gasped. "She promised . . ."

The earl stood up from the dais and crossed the hall to his son, his fists shaking with rage.

"And this man—" Edmund began, pointing at William.

"That's enough," the earl said, cutting him off. His tone was deadly, and for a moment Edmund seemed to lose his resolve, but he looked around the hall, saw his men nearby, and pressed on in a lowered voice.

"This man just spent an evening in the company of a known, self-proclaimed augur. You give shelter to the very sorcerer that has plagued the Plantagenets, Father. The Devil's own servant."

As he spoke, Edmund's men had approached and stood silently behind the earl and Edmund. D'Aubigni was completely unaware of their presence, Gwendolyn realized. William seemed to recognize the danger as well, and he stepped toward the earl to offer protection if needed.

"I will remind you that William saved my life," the earl warned his son.

The next few moments unfolded before Gwendolyn like something unreal and distant, a terrible dream.

Edmund drew his dagger, holding it high over his head, and lunged at William. The earl's son had never actually shed blood or put himself in the way of danger, and his inexperience caused him to hesitate a fraction of a moment, long enough for the earl to grab his left arm and throw him off balance. Edmund's men grabbed the earl, and Edmund lurched at William as the earl lost his grip. William had pulled his sword, but Edmund fell into him, his dagger piercing William in his side at an odd angle beneath his armpit. William staggered back from Edmund, his sword lowered, and he felt a warm flow seep down his side as Edmund withdrew, with the dagger still in his hand. Nigel and Gwendolyn drew their swords and advanced on Edmund's men, just as Edmund recovered himself, brandished the weapon high over his head in both hands, and turned back to William, who was leaning against the wall. William pushed himself up to standing as Edmund lunged at him again, but this time the earl flung himself between them. Edmund's blade, intended for William, disappeared deep into his father's chest instead.

Edmund stumbled back from his father, his hands raised as if he could repudiate his own dagger. He stared with wild eyes at the ornamented hilt that protruded from the earl's chest. Blood poured from the wound and his father dropped to his knees before him, open mouthed and staring, then onto his side. William d'Aubigni made no further sound except for the release of his last breath.

"Oh, Father," Edmund murmured, tears spilling onto his cheeks.

Edmund looked around himself with darting eyes. His men had formed a circle around him, swords raised, held in check by Nigel and Gwendolyn. The women and children who had stayed behind from Vespers cowered in a corner near the dais, and Michael pressed himself against the wall nearby, behind Gwendolyn and Nigel. William leaned against the wall, breathing in small sips, but he held himself erect, sword ready. Walter de Coutances stepped forward and reached down to pull the earl's sword free from his belt. The old archbishop drew the blade in a fluid movement and turned to join Gwendolyn and Nigel, facing Edmund and his men, the aged warrior's eyes sharp and dark.

Edmund's men had their mail tunics on, but no coifs or helmets. Gwendolyn was aware of her lack of armor and shield, but only to register that her blows must be precise. There was the briefest pause as the two bands of fighters faced off.

"Your father's death was an accident," de Coutances said evenly. "The dagger was not meant for him. I saw it myself. You have been infected by John's ambition. You can still stop this, Edmund."

Tears streamed down Edmund's cheeks and he shook his head. "It is done," he said faintly. Gwendolyn saw no hesitation in the eyes of the men that surrounded Edmund. They had cast their lots with the earl's son long ago; they were ready to follow through with whatever consequences might come of it. They were paid fighters, nothing more.

"She will come with me," he whispered hoarsely, looking past his men to Gwendolyn.

"You would need an army," she replied, standing firmly beside Nigel.

"No," he said, then raised his eyebrows and shrugged. "You care too much. You will follow of your own accord. It is just as he said."

With Edmund's men holding them at bay, Edmund strode swiftly to Michael, grabbed him by the shoulder with one hand, and punched him cruelly in the face with the other with such force that the boy was stunned. He turned on his heel for the doorway, dragging the bleeding boy on stumbling legs with him.

"Give me time to get away!" Edmund shouted behind him as he ran out.

And then the melee broke out. Edmund's men advanced on Gwendolyn, Nigel, and the archbishop. The man in front of her doubled over as the point of her sword pierced straight into his stomach, her powerful forward thrust puncturing through the mail armor. William had stepped in from behind, and the three remaining guards were immediately occupied defending their own lives. One of the women who had not gone to the chapel for Vespers, the wife of a baron, started to scream. Edmund was right; Gwendolyn would follow him of her own accord, and when she caught up with him, she would make sure he would never lay a hand on Michael again. She saw her way clear to the doorway. The others who had left for Vespers would hear the screams and come running at any moment. Before her way out could be blocked, Gwendolyn darted out of the hall, down the steps, and out of the keep.

She was out of sight before William could stop her. She ran toward a trap, and he was certain she realized it and chose to go anyway. He was also certain that the trap had been laid by John's sorcerer and not by the prince himself.

The man before him lunged and missed, but William's blade found his thigh, high up beside his groin. Blood poured from the wound and the man staggered unsteadily, tried to raise his sword once more and then fell to the straw face-down. Walter de Coutances had backed into the dais and was falling backward defending himself as Nigel pulled his blade from the chest of the man in front of him. De Coutances froze, gauged his opponent's movements, and rolled to his side at the last moment as the man's blade missed its mark and splintered the wood beside him. The man raised his sword again but then arched forward, his eyes wide open in shock as Nigel's sword ran through him from behind. Nigel pulled his sword free, helped de Coutances to his feet, and turned to William.

"She's gone after him," William said loudly as the others entered the passageway outside the hall. "Stay and defend Arundel. This may only be John's distraction to take the castle. Gwendolyn and I can handle Edmund."

"Go," Nigel said and abruptly turned to join de Coutances. Members of the garrison had arrived from the gatehouse and began filing into the hall. De Coutances took charge and began issuing orders to the men to take up arms and post a watch in each of the towers along the curtain walls.

William pushed his way through and out the doorway of the keep, across the timber planks, and onto the battlements. He walked quickly down toward the gatehouse, aware of the surging warmth down his side. Over the clamor in the keep behind him he heard Matilda's voice rise up.

"It isn't true! You're wrong! Edmund!" She shouted her son's name, and a long silence followed. As he rushed forward, William could not help imagining the grim scene inside the hall, de Coutances comforting Lady d'Aubigni as she came to grasp the extent of the horror that had so suddenly come to pass in her home. He reached the gatehouse, stepped out into the yard, and shouted for his horse and his hauberk.

From the keep above, a man's voice suddenly yelled out, "Stop her!"

William looked up and saw Matilda d'Aubigni step to the doorway and out to the narrow footbridge without pausing.

She dropped straight off its edge without a sound, her green dress billowing around her. It happened so fast he doubted for a moment that he had actually seen it. More screams sounded from above, and the doorway to the keep was filled with the d'Aubigni's guests, looking down in horror. Screams and wails carried across the grounds from the keep, and de Coutances appeared in the doorway. William watched the archbishop step forward, gaze downward for a moment, and then turn away. More of the garrison charged up the battlements to the keep. It could have been an accident, and William expected de Coutances to report the death as exactly that so that Matilda could be buried in her church beside the earl. But William knew from his vantage point that Matilda's steps had been deliberate. She had gone to join her husband. He turned away sadly. The earl and Matilda were beyond his help now.

With a few hasty questions from the small unit of men left at the gatehouse, William learned that Edmund had said the boy had fallen and that he was taking him to his family. The boy was bleeding and confused, and they had rushed to get him on his way. Gwendolyn had ridden off on Bedwyr moments after Edmund; she had not paused in the gatehouse long enough even to don her mail tunic. But William knew there would be no armed men waiting for Gwendolyn. Even John would be elsewhere, unwilling to associate himself with whatever trap she rushed toward. Edmund's trick with the letter from her father had been effective, but it was only a trick. Somewhere, John had the real thing.

The guard had seen Gwendolyn take the road back to the west and north—the only way out of Arundel other than by ferry across the Arun. She would be counting on Edmund's horse, with its heavier load and stockier build, tiring faster than Bedwyr. By the time William was in the saddle and charging up the road in the falling darkness, he guessed she might be a mile ahead of him.

The pain in his side burned like a hot coal. He held the reins in one hand and pressed his left arm tightly to his side to stanch the steady seep of blood. The image of Gwendolyn's galloping mare swam before him, and he leaned forward over his warhorse and closed his eyes. It was becoming harder to breathe, and he coughed fresh, red blood onto his horse's neck. The wound had punctured his lung, he realized, and he bled on the inside, as well. If the bleeding did not stop, his lungs would fill. His racing heart would pump the blood more quickly to drown him.

William sat up and shook his head. He reined his warhorse to a stop, turning slowly in the darkness to scan for any sign or sound of Gwendolyn. His horse pranced beneath him, causing his saddle and armor to creak and rustle noisily, but he finally settled the stallion with a hand to its neck and a few low, soothing words. A road branched to his left, following the base of a low hill, and he turned his head that way, listening intently for a moment, then swung his horse about and charged down it, still pressing his arm tightly against his side.

Scant moonlight filtered down through the clouds that gathered overhead, but it was enough to follow the pale, chalky road. He slowed his warhorse to a walk, looking intently down at the trail. He finally saw something that caught his interest and he pulled his horse to a stop and carefully dismounted. A small spot of blackness, like a dropped circle of cloth, stood out against the pale road. William crouched, brushed the darkness with his fingertips and raised them to his nose. He faintly detected the metallic scent of blood, probably Michael's. An owl silently glided past him from a nearby stand of trees along the hillside, and William realized he could hear no galloping beats in the distance.

A sharp chill passed through him, like a jab. The sorcerer was near. He led his warhorse forward a few steps and stopped again, looking at the hillside. William closed his eyes and focused on his breath, struggling to keep pushing air evenly into his lungs. He heard a small rustling in the field beside him and turned around. Squinting in the darkness, he realized he was looking at Bedwyr, lazily grazing in the small clearing. He recognized the rhythmic sound of her contented munching on the thick grasses. But where was her rider? A darker shape farther off in the distance he recognized as Edmund's mount.

Every moment that passed mattered now. He scanned the hillside again, eyed the small cluster of shrubby trees and rocks that stood nearby, and stepped toward them cautiously. He felt a small breeze, cold, brush across his face. The hills in this part of England were rumored to be tunneled through with caves used by smugglers, bandits, and even furtive lovers. He reached up with his arm to push the branches out of the way, feeling a new stream of warm blood flow down his side from the exertion. A wall of cold air pushed into him, and he turned back and led his horse across to the meadow and dropped the reins, then returned to enter the cave.

He stepped into blackness and immediately stumbled on the rocks that littered the narrow passageway. With arms extended to the walls on either side to support himself, he felt his way forward, testing each step before trusting his full weight on his footing. The pathway descended sharply, and the further he went, the colder the air became. The passageway grew so narrow that he was forced to turn sideways and inch forward in the blackness. William swallowed, fought the impulse to turn back. The sound of wind blowing through tunnels reached him from ahead, and he pressed forward and found himself in the middle of an opening with level ground. A slight breeze came from the right, and a faint glow could be seen in the far distance. His confidence returned, William strode toward it.

He approached the opening and saw the scuffs and blood left behind by Edmund and Michael as they had passed through. As he turned the last corner, his stomach clenched and he stopped in his tracks. A putrid stench of decay and bile caused him to gag, bringing spasms of pain from his wound. A faint orange glow lit the gloom ahead of him, and he realized that the passageway opened up onto a large chamber. He could hear small, rustling noises ahead of him, but then something reached out from beside him and grabbed his arm. William spun around to see Gwendolyn, waiting there in the opening, a finger raised to her lips.

She had paused here, he realized, to scout out the chamber from the safety of her hiding place before charging in. She held up two fingers in the air, and William nodded. Two men were inside: Edmund and the sorcerer. He pressed himself against the wall and leaned in more closely, straining to hear. There was a faint whimpering that he took to be Michael, and a steady, low murmur of words that he could not make out. Suddenly the chanting stopped.

"Well, all of our guests have arrived. Let's invite them in, shall we?"
Michael screamed a blood-chilling, high shriek.

Gwendolyn dashed into the chamber with William right behind her.

Walterus de Cardinham stood behind a large, stone table, and he turned and smiled graciously to them, as if he stood in the hall of Restormel and had invited them for one of the great feasting days. William heard Gwendolyn grunt with disgust as she recognized the face of her childhood tormenter.

"William! Gwendolyn!" Walter said cheerfully. "So glad you could join us!"

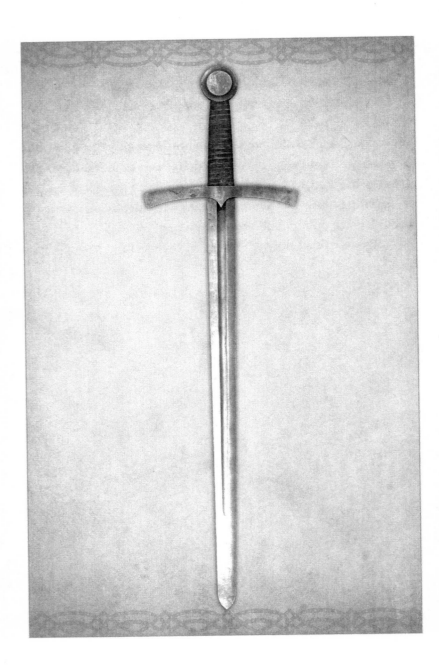

17

THE SWORD BREAKS

Even in the dim light, Gwendolyn could see the ashen, slick skin of William's forehead and cheeks. Her constable had lost blood, perhaps too much already. She had known he would follow her, that his loyalty permitted no other choice. She turned her attention to Walter and drew her sword; she would finish this herself, now.

She had stepped into a dimly lit chamber larger than the hall at Arundel. Walter stood at a wide, stone table immediately in front of her, his lips moving softly as he resumed his chant and focused his attention on pulling the skin off of a writhing serpent that he held up in his hand. On the opposite wall a hearth large enough to walk into held a low fire with a cauldron bubbling over it. Animal pelts covered the ground in front of the hearth, and one of the beasts from the attack on the camp lay comfortably upon them, its massive chin resting on crossed paws. Its red, unblinking eyes followed her movements. Two heavy, carved wooden chairs sat at the far end of the chamber. Edmund sat in one of these, looking small and defeated, elbows on his knees and head hung down. Michael sat in the other, dried blood on his face, clutching his left hand to his chest. Bright, red blood ran down his shirtfront. She realized Edmund held a knife, and dark blood stained his hands.

"Don't worry, I started with the little finger," Walter began and looked up with apparent amusement as Gwendolyn charged him, sword raised, teeth clenched. He wore no armor, stood too far from the pole weapons leaning against the back wall to defend himself. He made no attempt to defend himself and calmly resumed his chanting. She raised her sword, swung with her full strength to sever his neck.

The ringing clash of her sword against stone echoed around them in the halls. Her blade, made of brittle English steel, broke in half. The greater part of her blade clattered to the floor somewhere beyond in the darkness.

She stumbled backward, bewildered, not comprehending the lightness of the stubby hilt she held in her hand. Her ears rang with the explosive impact.

"What . . ."

Walter regarded her with a bored, contemptuous glance and paused his chanting again.

"You've lost a lot of blood, William," he commented without emotion as he stepped out from behind the table.

William stepped toward him, sword raised.

"That won't work here," Walter said evenly. "At least, not on me. You're welcome to use it on him, if you like." He indicated with his chin toward the slumping form of Edmund. "His purpose has been filled. I'm done with him."

Edmund jerked his head up.

"No! You said you would teach me! You promised!"

"Why would I waste my talent and energies on a fool like you?" Walter snapped loudly, turning on the stricken younger man. For a moment Gwendolyn felt a pang of pity for Edmund; John had used him badly. "The fact that you believed me only proves the point."

Walter turned his eyes to the beast lying on the pelts, uttered a command in unintelligible words, and the animal stood up and turned to face Edmund, its massive hindquarters tensing to spring. Gwendolyn backed up in horror, afraid of what she knew would come next. Edmund shrieked and darted toward the opening behind them, but the beast leapt and landed with its paws on top of him. Before Edmund could scream again the beast scooped his body up into its great jaws and shook him violently. When it stopped, Edmund's body hung silent and limp. The beast dropped the corpse to the floor, casually turned around and returned to its place by the hearth.

Walter turned back to them, his eyebrows raised. Even with the orange glow of the fire reflected on him, his skin looked rough and gray, like marble, and Gwendolyn could see fine webbed lines like veins around his eyes and hands.

"You really should have listened to William, dear sister," he said sardonically. "His loyalty alone should have tipped you off. Such steadfast devotion can't be inspired by myths or the troubadour's empty songs."

Gwendolyn looked back over her shoulder, gauged the distance back to the narrow passageway where she and William might have a chance of escaping.

"You won't make it," Walter said, growing annoyed. "My dog will catch you in three paces. And anyway, you won't abandon the boy. Really, Gwendolyn, it's over. You've lost."

He was right that she would not leave Michael. Walter had been there for her childhood, he had been the worst part of it, and she realized that he had known exactly how to manipulate her, to bring her to this point. But Walter never thought things through; he used things up—Restormel, his father's love, and now apparently his own body.

"What are you?" she asked with unmasked disgust, playing on Walter's pride to buy herself some time and maybe an idea.

"I am impenetrable to any weapon, unfortunately for you and William. I have made myself like stone, you could say." The conceit in his voice for his monstrous deformation turned her stomach. "The weak, human flesh rots and dies under my spell to be replaced by something harder, everlasting." He smiled in a thin smirk at her. "Now all I need is a sword."

"I don't have Caliburn. Surely you know that."

Walter sighed. "Gwendolyn, you are truly the most simple-minded woman. Caliburn will come to you. Through William."

"Go to Hell!" William spat at Walter, then wheezed and staggered forward a step from the effort. He coughed, and she turned to see his lips bright red with blood. "I see you," he snarled. "Your soul has become as vile as your body. You will never carry Caliburn."

"Actually, I rather think my body is finally catching up to my soul in degrees of vileness—wouldn't you agree, Gwendolyn?"

Gwendolyn made no response, but continued searching the chamber for another way out, some other way of defeating Walter without the beast getting to her first.

"Caliburn tried to come to you once already, but William was too far from you when he went for it, and it stayed behind, locked in the other world." Walter walked past her to William, and William stepped back from the powerful stench.

Walter leaned in, locked his eyes on William's. "Dream the sword again," he whispered, and as Walter's enchantment took hold, William's head drooped, his knees buckled, and he dropped to the ground.

Gwendolyn stood breathlessly, looking at the inert form of William on the ground. She placed the remains of her broken sword back into its scabbard, realizing that there was nothing for her to do with it. It suddenly struck her as funny, given the prior's and William's insistence that she would wield Caliburn, that she was now going to die with just a stub of sword to her name. She took comfort in knowing that, if Caliburn were indeed real, at least her failure in obtaining it meant Walter would not have it either. And maybe she could still save Michael.

"Let the boy go. He doesn't understand what he's seeing. He is an innocent. Spare one life today."

Walter's face softened as he turned to face her again. "I pity you," he said. "I did my best to teach you, to show you the power of cruelty. John understands this. He has been a truly excellent student." Walter flicked his gaze back toward Michael momentarily. "I require a witness, someone credible to vouch for what has happened here today, that the sword is indeed Caliburn. Michael is here to be that witness. He will live while I have need of him."

Walter looked down at the slumbering shape of William and bit his lip distractedly, narrowing his eyes.

"A little encouragement, perhaps," he mused, then turned on his heel and struck Gwendolyn across the face with his fist. It was like being struck with a club, and she heard the bones in her cheek crack. She fell over backwards and struck the back of her head on the stone floor as she went down. She breathed in gasps, struggling against the blackness that seemed to want to swallow her, feeling her face explode with pain. From far away she heard Michael screaming again.

Walter paced the floor between her and William, his agitation growing.

"I don't understand! Why isn't it working?" He walked back over to her and kicked her hard in the ribs, but this time she reacted. She grabbed his boot in both hands to anchor herself and swung both her legs around hard to Walter's knee, tumbling him off his feet and onto his back.

William's eyes flashed open across from her.

"Your sword!" he rasped weakly.

She sprung to her feet, drew the blade from its scabbard, completely restored, and plunged it down through Walter's chest and into the stone floor beneath him.

For a moment Walter looked at the protruding end of the sword with a funny, puzzled expression, and then she saw understanding form in his eyes. Her brother-in-law smiled at her with something like relief.

"You did it," he said gently and closed his eyes. Before her, his body recovered the ruddy tones of ordinary flesh as the spell was broken, and Walterus de Cardinham died as peacefully as if he had gone in his sleep.

She pulled the sword free, and the sound of Caliburn dropping to the floor rang through the chamber as she fell to her knees by William's side and cradled his head in her lap. His body rocked with his shallow, panting breaths, and he tried to calm her tears with soothing words. Michael arrived by her side, his own tears flowing.

"Hush, Gwendolyn. I've had worse," William lied softly.

She growled through her tears at him and turned to Michael. "Can you make it back to Arundel?"

Michael nodded bravely. She tore a strip of fabric from the hem of her tunic, wrapped his hand tightly to slow the bleeding.

"Ride Edmund's horse, it knows the way. Send Nigel. Go!"

Michael jumped up, took one last, worried look, and sprinted down the passageway into the darkness.

A movement near the hearth reminded her of the beast, and she gasped, fetched her sword and spun around, the blade raised high and ready.

A smallish hound, black with a funny-looking gray, whiskery muzzle, stood looking at her with shining brown eyes and wagged its tail expectantly. She burst into a fresh sob mixed with laughter and sheathed her sword. Taking her response as encouragement, the dog came up to her and stopped beside William, then began licking his face. Gwendolyn knelt beside him again and nudged the dog aside. The hound walked around to the other side of William, sat down, and watched them with ears pricked forward.

"Tell me how to fix you," she said stubbornly.

William opened his eyes and struggled for breath.

"You did it. It's up to you now," he whispered. She watched him close his eyes and try to relax his gasping breaths.

It became immediately clear to her that William was preparing himself to die, here in this cave. He was giving up.

"No!" she roared defiantly, and the dog scampered a few paces away, then turned to watch again from a safe distance.

She gathered a fistful of his shirtfront and pulled him upright to a sitting position, pulled his arm across her shoulders and reached with her near arm around his back. She jammed her shoulder into his armpit and pushed up with her legs, grunting loudly under the strain.

William cried out with pain—a good sign, she hoped. The pain would keep him awake. Bearing his weight and yelling at him to move his legs, she got the both of them down the passageway to the opening that led to the narrow tunnel. She paused for a moment to lean him up against the opening. She would have to go first and drag him through behind her, using her legs to pull. She could only see out of her right eye; the left had swollen shut and throbbed sharply. The dog ran ahead of them, then stopped and looked back over its shoulder and barked at her as if it scolded her for dallying. She wedged herself into the passage, then reached back and took hold of William by the arm and another fistful of his mail tunic and pulled him in after her.

"Come on!" she yelled, both at herself and William. His eyes flickered open for a moment, then rolled closed again. She took another small sidestep, then dug in her heels and pulled with all her strength. She was breathing hard from the struggle, but she kept working them slowly down the passage. She had been careful to turn William's wounded side away from her so that she did not cause him to lose more blood with her rough tugs on his arm and shoulder as she dragged them both along. Step by step, foot by foot, she worked in the confined blackness. Step, shift, dig in, pull. She was out of breath and her lungs and arms burned, but she could not stop to rest. Something inside her, bewildered by what she had witnessed, knew she would be lost without William, that she fought for both their lives and for something more than that, something she could not begin to know or understand yet.

She heard the dog run off and disappear ahead of her, then a bark and footsteps approaching at a run.

"Hello? Gwendolyn?" a confused but familiar voice called out. She had brought them more than halfway down the length of the passage, and she looked up to see an orange glow at the end of the narrow corridor. Nigel appeared carrying a torch, his face pinched against the stench as he peered into the darkness. The dog stood at his feet.

"Nigel! William's dying!"

Nigel's eyes flashed wide as he registered the situation. He laid the torch down where he stood and propelled himself into the opening, reaching her almost instantly. He blinked when he saw the disfigurement of her face, then took her by the hand and hauled her bodily down the corridor. She stood at the narrow opening and held the torch aloft, shining the light for him as he dived back in to get William. Moments later he emerged again, blowing hard, with William at his side, leaning against him. He crouched down, bent William's body across his thick shoulders, and stood back up. She carefully led the way up the rocky steps back to the cave opening, moving as quickly as she dared while the dog ran ahead of them barking. Outside, the three guards from the Tower waited for them, holding their horses. Using their shirts, the guards improvised a bandage for the wound in William's side. They all knew that William's chances of arriving at Arundel still alive were slim, and that sliver of possibility made them work all the faster. By her own orders, Gwendolyn sat behind William on his warhorse, holding him up in the saddle with one arm pressing his body against hers, holding the horse's reins with the other. One of the men led Bedwyr. None argued her authority, and they galloped back to Arundel, horses' hooves flying, as the coming dawn lit the horizon like polished steel ahead of them.

Arundel's guards cleared the way for them as they raced through the gatehouse into the castle yard. Gwendolyn steered William's horse straight for the surgeon's tent, where the surgeon himself and Arundel's men-at-arms met her to receive William into their arms and carry him inside. The surgeon found a pulse, faint but beating. William still lived.

Steam rose from the trembling and exhausted warhorse, and Gwendolyn felt herself almost swoon from the pain of her cracked and broken bones as she lowered herself to the ground while one of the grooms held the reins. The pain of the jarring ride back had taken her beyond any limit she might have thought herself capable of enduring. She felt her legs tremble beneath her, and one of the squires ran over and tried to lead her to one of the other tents to await the surgeon. She grunted angrily and pulled her arm out of his grasp.

"Water," she rasped, searching with her good eye for the surgeon's tent again and heading back that way.

Walter de Coutances ran down from the keep, his long cloak flowing behind him. The archbishop arrived flustered and out of breath, and he cringed at her misshapen face when she turned toward him.

"William?"

"He is alive, barely. The surgeon is doing what he can." She stared straight ahead, focused on the pain in her skull, the fire in her side where Walter had kicked her, to quench the emotion that she felt well inside.

"John will be held accountable for this. His ambition and empty promises have brought undeserved ruin to this family."

"This was Walter de Cardinham's doing," she said coldly. "He offered himself as a sorcerer to John, caused everything you see here."

De Coutances considered her words and shook his head in bewilderment.

"I've met Walter de Cardinham. He was a courtier and flatterer and a fool for John, but I never would have guessed him a charlatan for the black arts."

"He was no charlatan," she replied in a low voice, staring ahead.

De Coutances turned to regard her with a mixture of shock and disbelief, and she returned his gaze without waver or apology. A sword that should not have existed hung from her scabbard, warm against her body. The sword had come to her invisibly, impossibly. And whatever purpose the sword had chosen her for, she suddenly understood that her survival until its fulfillment depended on her staying hidden with it, concealing the truth of its origin. She realized that she must keep its secret, deny that it even existed. And to do so, she must also allow the darkness that Walter had found and spent his entire life nurturing to disappear with him. Walter de Coutances did not want to believe that these things existed and neither did she. But she no longer had the comfort of ignorance. She cleared her throat and spoke again, giving the archbishop the rational explanation he wanted.

"Walter de Cardinham was not a charlatan," she repeated. "He was a murderer, cold-blooded and ambitious. His body will be set out in the wilderness, food for the animals, and he will be forgotten." De Coutances's face shifted with an upwelling of pity at her words, and she knew that he would dig no further, lest he uncover a truth that he would rather have left unknown. She turned away, lifted the tentflap, and entered the surgeon's tent to begin her vigil beside her faithful constable.

A short time later a feisty, little black hound ran directly into the gatehouse passage and barked at the guards to gain entry, snapping at their ankles and spears until she came running and ordered them to allow it to pass. The mutt ran straight to the surgeon's tent and lay down beside the tentflap opening, where it stayed for the next several days. Later that afternoon, Walter de Coutances sent Nigel and the guards back to the cave to retrieve the bodies of Walter and Edmund, and, on Gwendolyn's insistence, to then pile up and set fire to everything inside. A group of masons would follow in the morning to seal off the entrance with rock and mortar.

All of Arundel was in a state of mourning. Long bolts of black cloth hung from the towers and the battlements. Meals were taken silently, without song or verse. Walter de Coutances sent another messenger, a young member of the Arundel guard, on a swift horse to the d'Aubigni's estate at Wymondham, Norfolk, to retrieve the eldest son of the late earl and Matilda. But de Coutances sent no word to the Tower. Arundel castle had been a favorite of Henry's, and de Coutances had seen enough grief wrought upon this honorable family by Plantagenet schemes and greed. He would not risk some opportunistic transfer of the privilege of Arundel while the third earl was in transit.

Gwendolyn sat inside the surgeon's tent beside the pallet where William lay, only getting up to relieve herself or fetch a bite of bread. She tilted William's head and lifted the surgeon's strong tea to his lips, giving him small sips. He had not awoken, but he reflexively swallowed the pungent liquid. Michael had come in to sit with her, but she could see how anxious he became staring at the motionless warrior lying before him. The surgeon had had to cut away the stump of finger bone left behind by Edmund's cruel torture in the cave, and Michael had fixed his jaw and not cried out, even though tears streamed from his eyes. Gwendolyn had never seen such bravery in a child, and she wondered at the man that would grow from such an unflinching, resolute boy. She laid a hand on top of his head and promised to come get him when William stirred. Nigel stepped inside briefly, and Gwendolyn sent Michael with him. William dozed through the night and into the next morning, but as the sun approached its highest point a fever set in, and he sweated and moaned in the bed. She wiped the sweat from his brow with clean, damp rags, and when the surgeon's apprentice came to change the bandages around William's chest, she helped the man shift and roll William's body.

When they were alone, she allowed herself to draw the sword from her scabbard and inspect it closely. Slowly, she turned the shining blade over in her hands. In every respect the sword was identical to her own, down to the worn leather strap that wrapped the hilt. But the blade was something else entirely. It was forged of steel unlike any she had ever seen. The blade had a grain to it, in even, regular ripples more tightly formed and perfectly aligned than any swordsmith in England could produce. The pointed tip and edges of the blade were dangerously sharp, as she discovered the first time she touched it. But the most breathtaking discovery happened when she first swung the blade and the tip caught in the thick timber pole that stood in the center of the surgeon's tent.

The tip dug in and grabbed, but the blade curved gracefully into an arc and neither crimped nor snapped. When she pulled it free again, there was no bend or crease to the steel. The steel flexed back, like a willow, as true and straight as it had been forged. She stared at the blade, dumbfounded. Testing it again, she pressed the tip into the timber pole and then leaned her full weight against it. Again, the blade bowed and pushed back against her, then recovered its original, undistorted lines when she released it.

She sucked in a shivering breath and stepped back. Tales of swords like these, rare and made from foreign steel, had come back with the crusaders a generation ago. But no one knew the secret of their making. She stared, her one eye unblinking, at the weapon in her hands, and felt a chill run over her skin. Indestructible, she thought, like truth. And in truth was there redemption?

Was it the sword itself that undid Edmund's spells and freed him in his last moment, just before death? William moaned and shifted beside her, his fever strong. She returned the weapon to its sheath, picked up the rag again and soaked up fresh water from the bowl beside her and resumed the slow ritual of mopping his head, chest and arms.

By the morning of the fourth day, the fever broke and William woke up. He tried to speak, but Gwendolyn held the tea for him and told him to drink. He looked at her closely for a moment, as if he was unsure whether he was dead or dreaming, and then closed his eyes with a heavy sigh. She ran to find the surgeon, and within two more days, William had recovered enough of his strength to climb the battlements to the keep and the hall.

De Coutances's secretary returned that night from the Tower with word from Eleanor. From Arundel, John had fled to King Philip's court in Paris and abandoned his supporters in England. With winter almost upon them, the Flemish mercenaries had given up their attempts to cross the channel to invade the English coasts. Only a handful of castles had held out for John. Eleanor had sent men to Tickhill and Marlborough, and those castles were again secure. William Marshal's brother, John, had forfeited his life at Marlborough rather than renounce his loyalty to his lord, Prince John. Only the stronghold of Nottingham remained in John's control. Eleanor would not order a siege during the winter months, but would allow the keeper of that castle the hard season of snow and darkness to come to his senses. She prepared to leave for Germany to personally escort the treasure of her son's ransom, and she ordered Walter de Coutances back to the Tower within ten days, along with William d'Aubigni, to travel with her. Hubert Walter, she announced, was to replace Walter de Coutances as Justiciar, effective upon their departure on Christmas Day.

"Another archbishop at the head of Richard's government," de Coutances muttered to himself in disappointment after he finished reading the letter.

They stood in the hall with only a handful of the lords of Arundel, barons from the nearby estates. The threat having passed, most families had returned to their manors, taking their empty stomachs and requirements of comfort with them. The castle clerk and chamberlain, stewards and kitcheners all moved a little more slowly, breathed a little more easily. No funeral mass was held for the earl or his family. Those ceremonies would be carried out at Wymondham Abbey, where no one would be the wiser as to how so many in one family had come to meet their untimely ends on the same day. Walter de Coutances planned to record their deaths on the last day of his office as Justiciar, December twenty-fourth, 1193, allowing plenty of time for the cart carrying their remains to arrive safely at their final resting place to the north.

Arundel's guard kept a regular watch at the towers along the curtain wall, and everyone in the hall snapped to attention as the guard sounded the call of approaching men, armed and on horseback. The call for the portcullis gate rang out, and the creaking of heavy wood and metal slamming into place rose to the keep.

The bones below Gwendolyn's eye had healed enough that the swelling had receded, and she joined the men in drawing their swords and marching out onto the battlements. But when they peered over the wall to the road below, by the gatehouse torchlight they saw eight men on horseback waiting calmly for admittance. The man in the lead, riding a heavy, black courser, removed his helmet and pulled off his coif. He sat on his horse easily, almost gracefully despite the bulk and weight of his armor, and thick locks of black hair flowed to his shoulders. He turned his gaze up toward them and nodded, a subtle salute. His countenance carried a grave somberness, the weight of grief mixed with duty, beyond his years.

"We will leave for London the day after tomorrow," de Coutances said quietly beside her. "William d'Aubigni, Third Earl of Arundel, has arrived from Norfolk."

18

A GAMBLE WON

Mae's tavern bustled with the usual evening mix of sailors and merchants, young lords and travelling families, when Nigel, William, Michael, and Gwendolyn arrived. They had parted ways with de Coutances, d'Aubigni, and the returning Tower guard at the bridge across the Thames to Southwark, but Gwendolyn and her men were due at the Tower later that night to present themselves before the dowager queen. They had already left their horses with Peter, and Gwendolyn had smiled this time as Nigel and the larger, broadly muscled man ritually exchanged their usual insults and barbs. Mae's face lit up when she turned and saw them, and she dashed away from a customer in mid-sentence to greet them.

"Stay right here, don't move!" she said breathlessly and then disappeared into the kitchen. A moment later Gwendolyn spied a small girl in a cream linen dress, slight with rosy cheeks and shining eyes, who ran out into the tavern. She hardly recognized Ella as Mae followed behind the little girl, then crouched down beside her and pointed through the dim light toward them where they still stood near the door. The girl stood on wobbling tiptoes, craned her neck, and squinted her eyes. She suddenly squealed gleefully and ran across the tavern and up into Nigel's waiting arms.

"Papa! You're back! You came back! I knew you wouldn't leave me! I knew you would come back! Mae told me every day that you loved me more than anything! More than the sun! More than jewels! She told me you would tear down a castle wall with your bare hands to come back to me! Oh, Papa!"

Ella tightly wrapped her little arms around Nigel's neck and pressed her face against his cheek while he choked back a sob and blinked to clear the tears brimming in his eyes.

"Oh! And Papa!" she said, leaning back in his arms, her nose level with his. "I have a grandpa! Did you know that? He's a very important man," she said, gravely serious. "He's a bishop."

Nigel's jaw dropped, and he stared at Mae as he gently lowered Ella back to the ground. Gwendolyn looked down as Michael peered shyly around William at the little creature, so bubbling with life, and Ella reached for his hand.

"Your father has acknowledged you as his son and Ella as his granddaughter," Mae said matter-of-factly. "The dress she's wearing is his gift, and he has taken her out publicly, let it be known that she is the Bishop of London's granddaughter. He boasted that his long-lost son was discovered, serving the queen herself."

Nigel's eyes flashed with hatred.

"Lying cur," he said quietly. "Why now?"

"The Marshal told me the dowager queen saw it," Mae said, a little apologetically. "She accused him, threatened him, and he confessed."

Nigel clenched his jaw. "He had no right. He is a weak man with not even the shred of decency to have provided for the mother of his offspring or his own child, not even in secret in all these years. And now he tries to weasel himself into the high regard of his granddaughter only because the Queen of England ordered it."

Gwendolyn placed a hand on his arm, bringing him back to the present moment, to the warmth of the tavern and the friends that surrounded him. He took a deep breath.

"You are no longer penniless or homeless," she reminded him.

Suddenly Ella giggled with delight.

"What a funny little dog! Is he yours?"

William's hound had followed them from Arundel, a tireless companion, sleeping beside William every night and annoying his warhorse with nips and barks every day. The dog sat on its haunches in the straw facing Ella, pricked its ears forward and tilted its head, and she squealed again and laughed.

"Go find yourselves a place to sit," Mae said, smiling again and ushering them into the tavern. "I'll be back in a bit."

They found an uncrowded end of one of the long tables where they could talk in private, although none of them seemed to feel much like talking. The memory of Gwendolyn's letter from her father and Eleanor's betrayal in losing it still gnawed at Gwendolyn, and the secret of Caliburn weighed heavily between her and William. A maid circulated among the tables with a pitcher of ale, and they sipped from their full cups in silence. Ella sat beside them in the straw playing with the hound, lifting its front paws and placing bits of straw on its nose while the dog played along patiently, occasionally licking her cheeks and nose, to her utter delight.

Mae returned with a platter of bread and roasted scraps and cups of weaker table ale for Michael and Ella. Ella seemed to notice Michael again, and she inspected him closely as he leaned in shyly toward William.

"What happened to your hand?" she asked innocently.

Michael's left hand was still in bandages, but the tips of his thumb and remaining fingers could be seen. He held it up, and she gasped as she realized that the last finger was missing. She sat, rapt, while Michael told her the story of what had happened, as he remembered it. By the time he finished his tale, complete with embellishments that elicited startled gasps and squirms from Ella, their meal was nearly finished. Ella turned her face up to Nigel with large, sorrowful eyes.

"Is it true, Papa?" she asked.

Nigel regarded her with a father's protective affection and tossed a scrap of roast to the hound waiting patiently at their feet.

"Yes. Every bit."

"Oh!" she exclaimed and turned back to Michael with a mixture of reverence and awe evident in her little features. Gwendolyn took note of the way Michael seemed to sit a little taller on his bench, puffed his chest out a bit, and she smiled inwardly.

"But there's one thing, one mystery, that cannot be explained," Nigel continued. "You see, Gwendolyn's sword broke when she tried to slay the sorcerer the first time."

Gwendolyn and William froze in their seats and stopped chewing, their eyes connecting silently, waiting to see where Nigel was going with this tale of his.

"So the question is, how was she able to slay the sorcerer later, when he fell?"

Nigel allowed the question to hang out there, and Gwendolyn watched Michael frown and realize the problem, the inconsistency in the story.

"William still had his sword," Gwendolyn answered. "I grabbed it."

Nigel wordlessly looked from her to William and back again. Michael and Ella were satisfied with the explanation, though; both were apparently unaware that unanswered questions still remained. Nigel had made one thing clear to Gwendolyn and William without coming out and saying it: he knew that Gwendolyn carried Caliburn. And he knew that the sword's existence must be kept secret.

They finished their meal at a leisurely pace and settled Michael and Ella for the night in the back of the tavern, behind the kitchen where Mae's family lived and slept. The hound lay down between the two children and settled its whiskered chin down onto its paws in the same way it had done in the cave, when it was still a beast. Only this time its brown eyes followed them with the protective, unblinking attention of a guard dog. Before they left for the Tower, Nigel paused and turned to Gwendolyn, reaching inside his cloak.

"I believe this belongs to you," he said, handing her a bundle of rough linen with something solid wrapped within its folds. She took the bundle and casually unwrapped the cloth.

The broken end of her sword lay across her hands.

"I found it in the cave and hid it in my cloak. No one else saw it. No one else knows."

A shiver prickled across her skin and she felt her mouth go dry. She showed the shard of her old blade to William, and he gingerly picked it up as if he handled a holy relic. To anyone else this bit of metal would have been just the broken bit of a mediocre weapon, not uncommon to find in any field or stream. But to them this was proof of the inexplicable mystery of the sword that had come to Gwendolyn, thrust through from another world to theirs, though by whom and for what purpose they still did not know.

"Thank you," Gwendolyn said quietly. She held out the linen for William to place the shard back in, wrapped it back up, and looked back at Nigel.

"Would you carry it for me?" she asked, handling the bundle back to him.

Nigel's eyes warmed with pride.

"Yes, my lady."

~۱۱~

When their ferry arrived at the Tower gatehouse later that night, the same silver-haired captain of the guard was there to greet them, along with the same impeccably armed and disciplined men-at-arms. Only this time the captain was expecting them.

"You're late," he accused her as soon as they drew near.

She could not help smiling at the curt greeting.

"God's bones! And what a smell you lot carry!" he exclaimed

and stepped forward to take Gwendolyn's hand.

Nigel glowered darkly in the torchlight as he rose to step out onto the stone embankment.

"I'm sure three days on the road leave you as fresh as a baby's butt," he muttered.

"Baby donkey, maybe," William added behind him.

The captain shook his head.

"I can't imagine what business the queen would have with you blackguards. Try not to touch anything while you're in there. And don't think you'll be staying for the night this time, either."

Gwendolyn nodded graciously. "Thank you. It's nice to see that the queen's invitation doesn't make you any more pleasant."

The captain raised his eyebrows at her. "If you didn't look tougher than your own men, here, I'd think you were flirting." By his standards she knew he had just given her a significant compliment, and the corners of her mouth lifted slightly.

They followed their escort into the Tower and up the stairs to the hall outside the queen's rooms. William Marshal greeted them again, looking more haggard and worn down than she had seen him a handful of weeks earlier.

"I'm sorry for your brother," she said when he turned to her.

The Marshal nodded wordlessly and cleared his throat.

"You're going in next," he told them. "She's cross tonight. She hasn't got the full ransom, which she never expected to have, but it's still much less than she thought she'd have by now. She's got a hell of a negotiation ahead of her in Germany. Young William d'Aubigni's doing very well, though. Without meaning to, he's charmed her entirely," he said with a little wonder.

The Marshal looked at Gwendolyn more closely for a moment and narrowed his eyes. She watched his courtly smile fade as he took in the fresh scars on her face, the misshapen bone of her left cheek. She had lost weight, and it seemed that the way the Marshal looked at her now was not that different from the way the people of Penhallam had looked at Eric when he had first arrived from Launceston's dungeon. She held his gaze with a hardened, inscrutable expression, vaguely realizing the extent to which the last few weeks had changed her.

Moments later, the heavy wooden doors swung open wide enough for Walter de Coutances to step out, find them in the room, and motion for them to come inside.

Familiar with the drill this time, Gwendolyn walked in and knelt, head bowed, before Eleanor. William and Nigel joined Gwendolyn on one knee to either side of her.

"Turn your faces to me," Eleanor snapped impatiently.

Gwendolyn lifted her eyes and quickly took in the room around her. Walter de Coutances stood near the window, his expression dark and sulking. She recognized the energetic, short man standing beside the queen as Hubert Walter, the new Archbishop of Canterbury and Richard's appointment in absentia to the office of the justiciar. Young William d'Aubigni stood at her other side, dressed coarsely for an earl, and yet he seemed to be the most polished and consequential man in the room.

"You! Nigel Fitz Richard!" she began. "Why did you not tell me that Richard Fitz Neal, Bishop of London, was your father?"

Nigel hesitated to answer, and Gwendolyn wondered if he would be able to come up with words to address the topic of his father that were polite enough to be spoken in the queen's presence.

"He sired me on my mother, madame, but he was never my father."

Eleanor cocked an eyebrow at him and sat up a little straighter.

"Well spoken," she remarked, sounding a little surprised. "The past is done, and I cannot correct the loss of your mother or your wife or any other suffering that was visited upon you in his absence. But he appears to be sincerely repentant. Do you wish to know him, to welcome him into your and Ella's lives now?"

Gwendolyn stole a glance at Nigel, and he looked as if he were struck dumb, astonished that Eleanor should take an interest in his private life.

Eleanor had apparently read his expression too, and she continued. "It is my pleasure, as a woman, to exercise my station to hold men accountable for their private wrongs when they would not hold themselves accountable. Do you wish to know Richard Fitz Neal?"

Nigel shook his head. "No, madame, I do not."

"Very well, then. I shall order him not to interfere in your life or Ella's except as you may see fit to request of him at some future date, if ever."

Nigel bowed his head. "Thank you, madame."

"And you, my dear."

The queen held out her hand, and William Marshal approached and laid a scroll, bound with a ribbon, in her palm, which Eleanor then extended toward Gwendolyn. When she recognized the scroll, Gwendolyn felt her breath rush out of her.

"Rise, my dear. This is yours. Thank you for your trust in lending it to me."

Gwendolyn felt tears rise, and she frowned and blinked against them.

"But I saw it burn."

"No, child, you saw a copy burn. And a very good one, from the sound of it. Walter told me. The fact that you still came here to complete our bargain when you believed I had broken my word to you speaks highly of your character and loyalty. And now," the queen said, standing up from her seat. "Hand me your sword and kneel again before me."

Gwendolyn hesitated with a moment of confusion and scanned the faces of the men around her. Nigel grinned at her; the Marshal nodded and gestured with his chin for her to do as she was bidden. But William watched her with raised eyebrows and a hint of alarm in his eyes, reflecting her own thoughts. Not a word had passed between them about the sword or the horrors of the cave. And yet they seemed more of a single mind since that day, their few conversations merely incidental.

She tucked her father's letter into her cloak, pulled her sword, handed the hilt to the queen, and knelt before her.

Eleanor fixed her haughty gaze upon her. The queen seemed to enjoy the weight of the sword in her hand. She held the hilt up to examine it more closely, noting the ordinary crossguard, the leather wrapping. Her eyes traveled to the blade itself and the queen paused, a strange expression of disbelief coming over her face, but only for a moment. She turned to Gwendolyn.

"There is no precedent for what I am about to do, Lady de Cardinham. I have consulted the archbishops and justiciars, present and future, and they advise me that you cannot rely upon this act to confer any legal right or title upon you. But you carry a sword and you appear to be of a mind and talent to use it. More importantly, you inspire others to follow you. I have come to the conclusion that I would fail my duty to my son if I allowed you to leave the Tower without securing your oath of homage to Richard as your liege lord, above all others. And I will confer upon you the customary title of Sir Knight, and by the force of your will and character may you succeed in exercising the rights thus afforded to you."

Gwendolyn considered the queen's words, understood their implication. In short, she had shown herself to hold enough martial ability to pose a threat to the crown. The knight's oath was used to ensure that the warrior's weapons and violence were only put to his lord's protection, against his lord's enemies and never against his lord's own home. In exchange for the oath, the knight could acquire title to his own lands and the rents and fees that he could collect from them. But in her case, the return for her oath was an empty gesture. Among women, only a widow with children held title to lands in her own right, and then only until her eldest son reached majority and assumed his inheritance. She was being asked to perform homage, to give her oath, in exchange for...nothing. Her eyes strayed again to Walter de Coutances, and he looked away.

"You have my oath," Gwendolyn replied evenly, her green eyes reflecting her clear understanding of the meaning of this unorthodox ceremony.

Eleanor raised Gwendolyn's sword in her right hand and laid the flat of the blade against her right shoulder, then the left. It seemed to Gwendolyn that she felt the sword's blade tremble in the queen's hand, and Gwendolyn's thoughts raced like Bedwyr running with the bit in her teeth, but she reined them in immediately. It was ridiculous, she told herself, to suppose that the queen somehow could have recognized the sword.

"I dub thee Sir Knight."

Gwendolyn bowed her head again, wondered what, if anything, useful could come out of such a charade of a ceremony.

"And now, hasten yourself to Penhallam, Sir Gwendolyn." Eleanor passed her sword back to her. "Rise, all of you," she added sharply, turning her back to them to step back up into her chair. "Robert de Cardinham is returned," she continued, staring at them keenly as she settled back into the elaborately carved chair. "That was the only thing that John related to you that was true. And by the accounts of my spies, John actually believed Walterus de Cardinham a wizard, his own Merlin, who would deliver Caliburn to him and then kill you. I understand his plot involved an attack on your constable here, and kidnapping and torturing a child to bring you to Walterus."

"Yes, madame," Gwendolyn replied coolly.

Eleanor grimaced, plainly disgusted with the actions of her youngest son although she still refused to condemn him publicly.

"Now that he has lost his wizard and given up the idea of obtaining Caliburn, he has abandoned his rebellion here in England. Penhallam is safe. Your gamble has been won."

Gwendolyn stepped back between Nigel and William, suddenly wishing she could be far from the Tower, the Plantagenets, and everything to do with the court, schemes of war, control over men and their swords. She found herself grateful that Cornwall's lands stretched so far to the west and were so infrequently visited by the court or its representatives.

Eleanor nodded to Hubert Walter, and he stepped forward and handed each of them a small purse of soft kid leather.

"This is a small amount in return for the sacrifices you have risked, but I'm sure you are aware that every penny is needed to purchase Richard's return. Robert shall succeed to the title of Baron that was held by his father, and to the privilege of Restormel on behalf of Richard, King of England, in place of his brother, Walterus de Cardinham." Eleanor held out her hand again and Walter de Coutances stepped forward, handing another scroll to the queen. "This is my writ, sealed by my own hand. As for Roslyn de Cardinham, her fate lies in the hands of Robert, her new lord. You should find her attitude toward you much improved upon your return."

Gwendolyn nodded again, the news falling flat on her ears. Even personal victory over her sister-in-law felt petty next to the responsibility of the sword that she now carried. She took the scroll from Eleanor and added it to the one she carried already in her cloak.

Eleanor looked them over again with one last, aloof glance and announced curtly, "You have my leave."

～ﬗ～

On a crisp November morning three days later, four horses carrying three unremarkable men-at-arms and two children passed through Newgate, heading west on the Watling Road out of London. They carried light provisions, the standard rough weapons of landless fighting men, and their horses, while well-fed and prancing lightly in the cool air, did not mark them as men of rank or exceptional wealth. A nondescript hound, black with flecks of gray around its muzzle, loped easily ahead of the group, a self-appointed leader. Upon closer look one might have found the red-headed rider, whose thick waves of hair stopped in a sharp edge just below his chin, more handsome than the others despite his deep auburn locks and the raffish scar across his cheek.

Gwendolyn looked to Michael, riding beside her on a stout pony, and smiled. He had nearly cried in her arms when he had first seen her in Mae's tavern after she had shorn her long braid. But she would take no chances on her return trip to Penhallam. The sword was too precious. She could travel more easily and without threat of harassment if she took on the appearance of a man. And so she had handed her knife to Mae and asked her to do the honors. The effect had been immediate, and William had nodded with approval when he saw it. She had no idea what Robert would make of it when he saw her, but her first concern was safe passage to Penhallam. Her changed hair was only one of the reasons that she put Robert out of her mind for now. Her husband, gone for so long, waited for her now at Penhallam, as she had waited for him, and she could only assume that the years would have changed him as much as they had her. She wished that she looked forward to seeing him again, but she carried the news of Walter's death, by her hand. She shuddered with a deep breath that failed to relax her thoughts; at least Walter's treachery to the king had been well known.

Ella rode with Nigel on his horse, sitting in front of him in the saddle, and she kept up a steady stream of chatter and songs through most of the morning, frequently reaching her hands up to play with Nigel's face or to make braids in his horse's thick mane.

William pulled his warhorse alongside Gwendolyn and Bedwyr, looking straight ahead into the long shadows cast by the autumn morning sun.

"What will you do when we get back to Penhallam?" he asked.

She raised her eyebrows and sighed.

"I don't know," she finally answered, completely honest. "It's a blank slate, now. The sword..." Her words trailed off.

William nodded, continued staring ahead.

"There was no good time to bring this up before," he began, and she turned to regard him with a curious expression.

William cleared his throat and continued. "When I nearly died, while I slept in the surgeon's tent, I dreamed." He turned to face her and held her gaze.

She nodded slowly and turned from him, narrowing her eyes to look far out to the horizon, as if she could see into the future.

⁓⁓

A little more than one hundred and fifty miles west and north of Gwendolyn and William, at the foot of a wide mountain in the kingdom of Deheubarth in South Wales, a woman pulled a heavy mantle about her shoulders and grunted at the bitterly cold wind that swept in from the north. White hair spilled over her shoulders like spun silk, and her eyes, sharp and lively, scanned the clouds above. A listless drizzle misted her cheeks like morning dew, and she smiled softly. She closed her eyes for a moment and stood still, face upturned, perfectly content. Slowly she opened her eyes, blinked the moisture from her lashes, and turned around to step inside the small hovel that she lived in, modest but well provisioned. A dung fire burned in the hearth, and the light and warmth were welcome to her old bones and failing eyes.

"Well, Mogh," she said to no one in particular, in the ancient tongue of the people of Powys, "you were right after all. Looks like I'm going to have visitors."

HISTORICAL NOTES

The story weaves through the events, people and places of southern England, autumn of 1193. The following characters in the story are based on actual individuals, and incorporate, to the extent reasonably confirmed, details of their lives (where they lived, who they married, how many children they had, where their loyalties laid, when they died). Where historical detail is not available; where events are known to have occurred but not how or why; where plausible details could be suggested that would have, for obvious reasons, been omitted from the historical record–into those gaps I have written my story. Characters that are not listed below are entirely the product of my imagination.

Baron Robert Fitz William

Robert de Cardinham

Walterus de Cardinham

Richard Fitz Neal

Geoffrey of Monmouth

John of Cornwall

William Marshal

John Marshal

Henry de la Pomerai

Henry II, King of England

Eleanor of Aquitaine

Prince John Plantagenet

Richard I, King of England

Walter de Coutances

Hubert Walter

Gerald of Wales

Richard Reynell

William d'Aubigni, Second Earl of Arundel

Matilda St. Hilary de Harcouet

William d'Aubigni, Third Earl of Arundel

History nerds such as myself may enjoy looking up these individuals to find dates and life events that are included in the story. For example, the Second Earl of Arundel, William d'Aubigni, and his wife, Matilda, are both recorded as having died on December 24, 1193. I found the date an intriguing coincidence—particularly given that it also happened to be the last day that Walter de Coutances held the office of Justiciar, as he was replaced by Hubert Walter on Christmas Day, 1193. The how and why of their deaths and the delay in recording them, as presented in the story, is entirely fictional. You will also note that there is no Edmund d'Aubigni listed above; the treacherous son is likewise my own creation. Nor is there any evidence that Walterus de Cardinham took the side of Prince John in his rebellion of 1193. And while Richard Fitz Neal was indeed Bishop of London in 1193, Nigel, his bastard son, is also purely fictional.

The foundations of Penhallam are still visible in Cornwall and can be visited by the public. Through the wonders of Google maps I was able to locate and view them remotely. I relied heavily on Guy Beresford's impeccably descriptive account of the excavation of Penhallam in the latter half of the last century, The Medieval Manor of Penhallam, Jacobstow, Cornwall. Mr. Beresford states in his introduction that the excavation finds have been presented to the Royal Institution of Cornwall at Truro. Perhaps one of the time-ravaged artifacts housed there was an everyday object of Robert de Cardinham himself.

Arundel Castle still stands and can also be visited by the public. The Earldom of Arundel is the oldest continuing earldom in English peerage, followed closely by the Earldom of Essex. The original Norman doorway to the keep is partially visible, offset from the battlements as described in the story. The historical reason for the offset design is unknown and thus open to speculation. This is one of the "gaps" that I have employed as a significant detail in the story.

The Battle of Crogen, where Gwendolyn's father meets the Baron Fitz William in battle, is an historical event, as was the horrific treatment of the twenty-two prisoners captured by the defeated and humiliated King Henry II. I have suggested that her father was an intended twenty-third prisoner, and that his escape left only twenty-two prisoners for the historical record that we have today.

The song sung in the lonely night in the hall of Arundel is "Song from Chartivel," by Marie de France (1155 – 1189), described by one source as the most popular female poet of the Middle Ages.

It is important to know that this period in English history saw a surge in scholarly achievement, an expansion and normalization of jurisprudence and governmental administration, a burst of artistic expression in verse, song and music to such a degree that several historians refer to the time as a sort of mini-Renaissance (for example, see *A History of England*, Edited by Felipe Fernandez-Armesto, Vol. 2, Early Medieval England, by M.T. Clanchy). The writings of Plato and Aristotle were newly re-discovered, and translations of these pagan, pre-Christian meditations on the nature and purpose of knowledge and wisdom, war and government, found their way to the academies and private libraries of the time. The church initially welcomed, then ultimately condemned, the ideas on the supremacy of reason put forth in these writings, and so began a battle for the intellects of men and women that continues to be waged by some of the religious leadership today. In any case, a series of catastrophes would fall upon the English (and Western Europe) in the coming centuries that would decimate the populace and set back by hundreds of years the social, economic, and political advancement that had shone with such bright promise during this time.

As a final note, it is true that there was, at this time, a popular Welsh nationalist legend prophesying the return of Arthur to rout out all non-Britons (and there were many by this time, and setting aside historical evidence that the Normans themselves were descended from clans of Britons that had fled to northern Gaul centuries back). There was also a deliberate campaign of propaganda by the Plantagenets to counter the prophecy, highlighted most notably by Richard the Lionheart's sanctioning of Glastonbury Abbey's claim to have discovered the tomb of Arthur and Guinevere upon the abbey's grounds (which of course bore no relation to the abbey's desperate need to raise funds to rebuild after a devastating fire). The Plantagenets found further assistance in the writings of Gerald of Wales and Geoffrey of Monmouth, to co-opt the legend and make Arthur their own.

I am embarrassed to admit that none of this was known to me at the time that I initially conjured my tale of a woman heir to King Arthur, living in England during the turmoil of Richard I's reign, defending the land and its people from the gaping maws of a self-interested court and its never-ending wars. Happy coincidence followed happy coincidence as I began my research.

And yet, the story that you have just read is actually the second iteration of this tale. The first, I confess, took more license than the genre will support with the historical facts of the time. Fans of this period would have spotted the inconsistencies immediately. So I dug quite a bit deeper into my research, and while I preserved the essential arc of the characters and the plot, in all other respects the story was completely rewritten. The geography of the tale was flipped, the politics of the time were brought into sharp relief, and fictional characters and locations were replaced by actual as much as possible. This is, I believe, a reverse engineering of the "proper" way to write historical fiction.

The legend of King Arthur, Merlin, Excalibur, and all of the many facets and tales that have grown up around it over the centuries presented a unique challenge in identifying the state of the legend as of late 1193. The legend has its birth in Welsh folklore and oral tradition, the original date of which is impossible to identify. From there, a handful of textual retellings, including Gildas and Bede, commit the tale to the historical record, in each case with additions to the legend. In the time period of our story, Geoffrey of Monmouth's widely read *Historia Regnum Britanniae* includes an account of Arthur's life, followed by his *Vita Merlini*. By 1190, Chretien de Troyes had written the first Arthurian romances, including mention of the Round Table, the quest for the grail, and Lancelot's forbidden love for Guinevere. Although I mention de Troyes in the story, I treat his additions to the tale as purely fictional from the perspective of Gwendolyn and her contemporaries. It cannot be ignored that de Troyes's chief patron was Eleanor of Aquitaine's daughter, Marie of France, Countess of

Champagne, and that his works must thus be considered part of the overall campaign to civilize and trivialize the tale of Arthur to mere courtly entertainment and romance. I have relied upon the excellent *Cambridge Companion to the Arthurian Legend* to provide a snapshot of the state of the tale of Arthur in 1193, and as a base from which to draw "known" events from the legend, and to foreshadow, through Gwendolyn's adventures, additions to the tale that would come in future versions, as if she were the forgotten historical basis for those new details. I also found *Pendragon*, by Steve Blake and Scott Lloyd, of invaluable assistance in illuminating the Welsh origins of the original Arthurian legend, including the absence of mention in the ancient texts of Uthyr as Arthur's father.

And while Gwendolyn is the hero of our tale, the main character, ultimately, is Caliburn (only later known as Excalibur). My own addition to the legend is the following proposition: that Caliburn does indeed return to us, through the ages, to the hands of those humble, true, and courageous enough to wield it. And that it is the trials, tragedies, and victories of each episode that cause this legend to remain so compelling, over the passing of at least 1500 years of human history, and that continually provide new and relevant material for its retelling.

E. A. Haltom
Austin, Texas
Autumn, 2013

ABOUT
E. A. HALTOM

E. A. Haltom lives in Austin, Texas, with her husband and children, and (at last count) one dog, four cats, and six chickens. She has enjoyed careers as a criminal prosecutor, a grocery clerk, a massage therapist, a technology lawyer, a mother, and most recently, a novelist. She has lived in, worked in, studied in, and/or traveled in Ireland, England, Scotland, France, Italy, Germany, Mexico, Kenya, Nepal, India, and Tibet, although it is the adventures of the heart that she has taken with her family that have brought her the highest joys—and the deepest sorrows. In her spare time she enjoys gardening and planning excursions with her family.